# THEIR FROZEN GRAVES

BOOKS BY RUHI CHOUDHARY

*Our Daughter's Bones*

# THEIR FROZEN GRAVES

Ruhi
Choudhary

bookouture

Published by Bookouture in 2021

An imprint of Storyfire Ltd.
Carmelite House
50 Victoria Embankment
London EC4Y 0DZ

www.bookouture.com



ISBN: 978-1-80019-247-8
eBook ISBN: 978-1-80019-246-1

*To my parents*

# PROLOGUE

*Lakemore, WA*

*October 22, 2018*

The bell rang.

Mackenzie checked the time. It was nine in the evening. There was no car outside. Expecting to find her stout neighbor wanting to borrow something, she opened the door.

What she saw made her legs buckle. A violent tremble raked through her insides, her brain rejecting the alarming sight.

*No.*

Her father stood in front of her. The hair on his head and jaw was thin and white. His skin had sagged and wrinkled with time. But it was the same face—the face that was burned into her memory. The same man Mackenzie and her mother, Melody, had buried in the woods by Hidden Lake, twenty years ago.

*You have to help me bury him.*

"Micky?"

Mackenzie felt like she was resurfacing from a dream. She waited for her vision to swim or crack or even sway a little. But the sight of her aged and very much alive father, standing at her doorstep, was unbending and solid.

"Micky? Are you okay?"

Mackenzie strained to listen to the little sounds around her, to ground herself. Leaves rustling, car engines, Vera Lynn's voice drifting from her speakers… *anything.*

Suddenly, a car driving past her house let out a brief honk.

She snapped out of her daze and moved on autopilot. Her hand slid to the hall table, where she opened the drawer and pulled out her Glock.

She aimed the gun at him. Pointing at his head.

"Mick—"

*You have to help me bury him.*

"Hands out of your pockets."

*You have to help me bury him.*

"But—"

*You have to help me bury him.*

"Hands out of your pockets!" Mackenzie said in her hardest voice.

His forehead crumpled in confusion. Slowly, he raised his hands and licked his lips. She instructed him to come inside.

When he brushed past her, a chill encased her, as if the temperature in the room had plummeted. Mackenzie shut the door behind him.

He took off his coat deliberately, and her eyes made a quick inspection of his clothes. A dark green sweater and black jeans. No weapon tucked in his waistband.

Stinging tears disrupted her vision, but she refused to shed them. She told him to turn his pockets inside out and pull down his socks. Puzzled and mildly offended, he did.

He wasn't armed.

They stood glaring at each other in the living room. Mackenzie never lowered her gun. Her aim was glued to the middle of his forehead. If she pulled the trigger, she would kill him instantly.

He would die again. He would come back again.

"Micky, can we talk?"

"Who are you?" she whispered.

"Your father. Robert."

If *he* was alive, who had died that night? Who had she buried in the woods?

The possibility of him being a conman had crossed her mind. What if he was a lookalike? But he'd called her *Micky*. Only her father had called her Micky.

Holding the gun in one hand, she marched to the couch and tapped his coat. There was nothing in it except a bus ticket in the inside pocket.

*Portland.*

She clicked the safety on and tucked the gun in her waistband.

"You try to do anything stupid, and I'll put a bullet through your head." Mackenzie sounded out of breath.

He nodded and followed her into the kitchen area.

She took out a bottle of water from the refrigerator and downed it like a creature parched in the desert. She felt the coolness spread into her lungs and soothe her insides. She kept her gaze locked on the ghost of her past.

She had a billion questions, but her tongue was sticky and heavy in her mouth. There was one question above all that stopped her from showering him with the others.

How much did he know about that night?

"Talk," she demanded.

He chuckled. "I should have practiced before I came. How are you?"

Mackenzie's eyes darted all over his face. His eyes were narrow, like slits. There was no sign of an old major head injury in his appearance or speech. He looked exactly like he did all those years ago, only older. The sole blemish Mackenzie didn't recognize was a little scar on his chin. No one could look at him and imagine that his head had once curved inward, his eye swollen to the size of a golf ball.

"Robert Price went missing twenty years ago." Her voice was thick. "He was never found. Thirteen years ago, he was declared dead by the courts."

"I see." He perched on a stool at the kitchen island. "I left Washington and never looked back. Even changed my name. I knew I was nothing but a nuisance to you and your mother."

"Where did you go?"

"Everywhere," he replied vaguely. "Last few years, I was in rehab down in Dallas."

"Did you know that you were a missing person?"

He chuckled. The sound made the hair on Mackenzie's arms rise. "I didn't think anyone would care enough to look for me. That morning, while you were both asleep, I took some cash lying around the house and walked out."

Mackenzie remembered that day. She hadn't seen her father all day, but that wasn't unusual. She had just assumed he was sleeping off another hangover in his room. Later that night, Melody claimed to have killed her abusive husband as Mackenzie had stood trembling in the kitchen, staring at his barely recognizable corpse.

She wanted to ask him what he knew. But could she trust him? Would he lie? Would he threaten her? Something had clearly gone awfully wrong that night—and she didn't trust the man standing in front of her one bit.

"Why are you here now?"

"To be a family, of course." There was a glint in his eye. It made her heart rise up in her throat. He had been alive this entire time and showed up now—after *twenty years*.

"Took you a while to realize you wanted that," she snapped. "Where are you staying?"

"Miller Lodge."

Mackenzie nodded, but a sickening thought unfurled in her brain. How did he know where she lived? Had he been following her? He wore a small smile. But she knew his temper. She knew the damage those swinging fists could do.

"How did you find me?"

"I went back to our old house, but someone else is living there. I looked you up on the internet and asked around. Took me a few days, but Lakemore is still small. Not too difficult to find someone if you look hard enough."

*Had* he been following her?

Sweat trickled down the back of her neck. The air thickened between them. The shackles of fear held her eerily still. She felt like she was balanced on the tip of a sharp blade. One wrong move and she would find herself in a situation there would be no saving herself from. She stared at Robert. He had done nothing to threaten her until now. But she couldn't help feeling like there was danger behind that smile and the spark in his eyes.

"Micky? Are you okay?"

"Y-yes. I think you should go. It's getting late."

"Are you sure? You look pale. Where's your husband?"

"He's sleeping upstairs," she lied, not wanting to tell him she was alone in the house. "Give me your number. I'll call you when I'm ready to talk."

"I don't have a phone yet. Just call at the lodge. I'm going to stick around, Micky. We should reconnect, wouldn't that be nice?" He stood up and put on his coat. His nonchalance was unnerving. As if it were perfectly normal to show up twenty years later and "reconnect."

As soon as he left, Mackenzie sprinted to lock the door. Quickly, she ensured that all the doors and windows were locked and ran up to her bedroom, locking the door behind her.

She rehashed her meeting with Robert again and again—memorizing his words, his face, and his voice. Like she would find the hidden answers there. She couldn't shake the feeling that he knew more than he was saying. That he wasn't just here to be reunited as a family.

Her heart skittered and thumped wildly inside her chest. With trembling hands, she retrieved her service weapon and held it tight. She climbed into her bed and pulled the duvet up to her chin.

She held the gun close to her chest, the awful realization seeping into her bones. Her father was alive, which meant someone else had died that night. What wasn't Robert telling her? And why was he really back here?

# CHAPTER ONE

*November 20*

Detective Mackenzie Price killed the engine of her car and removed her sunglasses, studying her reflection in the rearview mirror. Her blazing red hair was pulled into a high ponytail. The dark circles under her eyes were concealed, the cracks in her lips covered in pink. She was tall, muscular and often imposing, always wearing a fierce expression on her face. "Mad Mack," as the team at Lakemore PD called her. They had coined the nickname during a particularly grueling case: the murder of a woman and her eleven-year-old son in their own home. Mack practically hadn't slept for the duration of the investigation and she damn near went mad. But she had brought the killer to justice, and that's what mattered.

Mackenzie's obsession with tidiness was another source of amusement to her co-workers, but that's how she liked it. She liked her appearance, desk, and life to be clean. But today she lacked her usual composure. Her face gave away her exhaustion, but she hadn't admitted defeat.

This was just another day. Another day trying to make Lakemore a better place.

Lakemore was a small Washington town, tucked right next to Olympia. It was stricken with crime and poverty, but united by its passion for football. The Sharks, Lakemore High School's football team, was Lakemore's identity, that *one thing* this fading town relied on. But Mackenzie's previous case had changed all that, exposing a disturbing history of rape and murder linked to the team that went back years. The previously revered Lakemore Sharks were in disgrace, and as the cases moved toward trial, there was a gaping hole in the fabric of Lakemore's community. The case had triggered a chain of events leading to riots and protests in town, and it was going to take time to heal. In truth, the process had barely begun.

Mackenzie climbed out of the car to be greeted by a chill nipping into her skin. The wintry air was difficult to inhale, like miniature icicles were scraping through her nostrils. She looked around the packed parking lot. Cars and tracks were covered in snow.

She liked winter better than summer; the biting winds helped fortify her composure. In the heat, she felt like her armor was melting away.

Lakemore usually had mild and wet winters, but in the last three days a shocking snowstorm had swept across the dwindling town. Heaps of snow and frozen lakes—everything Lakemore *never* prepared for.

Mackenzie shoved her numb hands in her pockets and jogged across the parking lot. The hedges around the building had been shaped into boxes and were now crowned with snow.

Inside, the station was crowded and noisy. Mackenzie weaved her way through the uniforms, nodding at the familiar faces.

The Investigations Division in Lakemore PD consisted of Special Investigations and the Detectives Unit. While the former looked into robberies, fraud, and drug- and gang-related crimes, the Detectives Unit was tasked with homicide, cold cases, missing persons, and felony assaults.

Mackenzie was part of the Detectives Unit, along with five fellow senior detectives and three junior ones, headed by the quirky but sharp Sergeant Jeff Sully.

"She returns!" Troy Clayton, a senior detective, announced to an empty office.

"Hey, Troy. Where is everyone?"

"The last couple of weeks have been a mess." He dragged his hands down his face.

Mackenzie looked at the state of the office. All the cubicles were littered with cups and files. The garbage was overfilling with empty takeout boxes and the stench of old Chinese food lingered in the air. Even Troy looked haggard. His mop-like hair fell unevenly over his forehead. "The FBI investigation into the department is fully underway."

Mackenzie winced inwardly. More fallout from the Lakemore Sharks case—the whole affair had reeked of police corruption. "Since when?"

"They got here a week ago."

"Right." She took off her coat and scarf.

"You still sick?"

"Sick?"

"Your flu."

She blinked in confusion. "Yeah. Much better now."

"And the wedding?"

"The wedding?"

He narrowed his eyes but a phone call diverted his attention.

Mackenzie sat at her desk, trying to gather her wits. She had been away for over three weeks—her longest break from work—traveling all around the country confirming her father's story. Now she was back and had clearly missed more than just the winter storm. She was ready to dive back in, except everything was in flux. Looking at the disarray around her, Mackenzie's heart started thudding wildly. She began fixing the little things she found out of place on her desk. She was determined not to let her work slip away from her. It was the only thing left in her control—the sole and lonely source of stability in her life.

Detective Nick Blackwood walked in. "You're back."

Nick was another senior detective in the Detectives Unit. For the last eight years, he had been not only Mackenzie's partner but also her best friend. Their friendship had weathered several storms, but they always managed to come out strong.

She eyed his cropped black hair, turning gray around the ears. "Working so hard is making you old."

"Can't say I missed you really," he teased.

"My *flu* is gone." She waggled her eyebrows at him.

When Troy left, he shrugged. "Had to come up with an excuse."

"There was a wedding?"

"I said you had a destination wedding. Normally, the flu doesn't last three weeks. So, where were you?"

"Around."

"Around?" Nick leaned against his desk. "I covered for you. Don't you think I should get more than that?"

"I went on a road trip to clear my head." It was only half a lie.

"Alright. Sterling showed up here *and* to my place."

Mackenzie winced. Sterling Brooks, assistant district attorney, was Mackenzie's husband of three years. Their marital bliss had shattered when Sterling had cheated on her earlier in the year. He had had a fling with a waitress who he'd hooked up with after a few drinks. It had taken Mackenzie a while to wrap her head around it and confront him. But when she did, she kicked him out of their house, wanting space and time to think. Now he seemed determined to earn her trust back.

"What did he want?"

"Looking for you. You didn't tell him where you were. He was panicking."

Mackenzie rolled her eyes. "Yeah. I was preoccupied."

"Did you make up your mind?"

"About what?"

"Sterling!" he said, exasperated. "Isn't that why you took off? To think things over?"

Mackenzie swallowed. She hadn't thought of him nearly as much as she should have. "Still deciding. Anyway, what did I miss?"

Nick's eyebrows dipped, assessing her. She met his scrutinizing eyes with a composure practiced and perfected over decades. Eventually, he let it go. "Crime's up. I just came from throwing a pickpocket in jail. That's how bad it's gotten. All departments are short-staffed. Peck's gone. We have a new lieutenant—Atlee Rivera. Transferred from Ohio."

She opened her mouth to inquire about Sully when the door to his office opened and a stranger's face poked out. The woman was middle-aged, with olive skin and dark hair pulled back from her square face. Her eyes were narrowed above her broad nose.

"Detective Price?" She cocked a brow.

"Yes."

"Could I see you in here, please?"

Mackenzie stepped into Sully's office. It was filled with packed boxes and papers—no place for whatever his latest hobby was.

"I'm Atlee Rivera." Atlee shook Mackenzie's hand. "Good grip."

"Thanks."

"Sorry about the mess!" She looked around the office and hopped over the boxes to get behind Sully's desk. "My office isn't ready, so all my things are here. Sergeant Sully's been kind enough to lend it to me. So, you're Mad Mack."

Mackenzie suppressed a groan. "You can call me Mack."

Atlee chuckled. "If they've given you a nickname, it's a compliment. It means you stand out. Worth remembering. I was in Savannah for a few years before moving to Ohio. They called me 'the Razor.'"

"Why?"

"I was cutthroat." She leaned back on her chair. "I had the chance to address this department a few days ago, but you were out sick?"

"Flu."

"From what I've heard you never take any time off, so you must have been really sick."

"All good now, ma'am." Mackenzie's smile was strained.

"Call me Lieutenant. Good job on your previous case. From what I hear, it changed a lot of things in this town."

"For the better," Mackenzie said, almost defensively.

"We'll see about that." A corner of Atlee's mouth raised in a half smile. "Justice doesn't always bring peace, unfortunately. Anyway, the reason I called you in was to introduce myself. I've been told that I'm the first female lieutenant in the history of Lakemore PD, and you are the only female senior detective in this unit. Police work is still considered a man's job, especially in small towns like Lakemore. I don't know about you, but I have dealt with my fair share of old-school thinking and boy's club culture. I won't make any assumptions about this office, but I wanted to let you know that I have an open door *and* an open-mind policy. If there's anything I can help you with, I'd like you to come to me."

She smiled warmly, but Mackenzie could detect a steely composure underneath. Instinctively, she could tell Rivera wasn't the kind of woman who needed to raise her voice to intimidate. A woman with clear intentions, who was not easily fazed. "Thank you. I'll keep that in mind."

Atlee nodded. "Glad that's settled, then."

There was a knock on the door, and Nick peered in. "Sorry to interrupt. Mack, we have to leave. Two bodies at Woodburn Park."

"Where's Sully?" Mackenzie asked, following him out and getting her jacket from her cubicle.

"Rounding up graffiti artists." Nick smirked.

"He's out on the field?"

"I think he's trying to make a good impression on the lieutenant."

"What do you think of her?" Mackenzie asked.

"She's hard to read. We'll see."

"Is the crime scene secured?"

"Yeah. Justin is holding the fort."

As they approached the exit to the building, sirens blared loudly. Several officers shot past them toward the parking lot. Mackenzie and Nick exchanged a bewildered look before shouldering their way outside.

Mackenzie's breath caught in her throat. A police squad car was on fire.

Fire trucks were turning round the corner, zipping past the traffic. As they entered the parking lot, the sirens drowned the drone of the crowd. Black smoke jetted upward. Even from several feet away, Mackenzie could feel the heat on her cheeks. The view of the lot behind the car rippled. Flames danced higher, licking the air. Suddenly, the windshield of the squad car cracked and shattered. An explosion, and chunks of the car fell to the ground, still on fire. The toasted car was disintegrating when the firefighters began dowsing it.

"What happened?" she whispered, turning to Nick.

He looked at her. "Lakemore happened."

# CHAPTER TWO

Mackenzie remembered coming to Woodburn Park as a child. It was a fleeting memory, like a vague dream on the brink of being forgotten. She recalled chasing her father along the edge of the lake. She closed her eyes and saw him from behind; he looked so much bigger and stronger. It must have been a time before the alcohol took over his life and brought him down brick by brick. She heard his laugh, cheery and guttural.

Woodburn Park had changed over the years. What was once a hangout spot for families was now abandoned and creepy. Westley River—one of the two major rivers in Lakemore—cut through Woodburn, opening into Crescent Lake before continuing on its way and finally draining into the sea at Riverview, a neighboring town. There were cabins in the park, but they were all rundown. The exodus had started when drugs came to the area, and the woods became a spot for dealing. Some teenagers were found having overdosed. Arrests were made. The police eventually cleaned up the area, drove away the dealers and users, but a bad reputation was more durable than a good one.

Now, Woodburn stood lonely. Safe, but haunted by the ghost of its treacherous past.

There was a single trail that ran through Woodburn and was used to access most of the cabins in woods. Before the drugs, it was used for hiking. Walking through the woods was difficult with wild thickets and shrubbery covering nearly every inch of ground.

Mackenzie scowled at her feet cracking a frozen silver puddle. The thin blanket of snow was crushed and brown under their feet as they walked. Weathered leaves hung from lifeless, barren branches. The cold came suddenly and would leave just as quickly. A blip in the otherwise predictable wet winter of Lakemore.

"How's Luna?"

"Good. I'm getting her for Christmas this year," Nick beamed.

"How come?"

He rubbed the back of his neck. "Shelly's going on a vacation with her boyfriend."

"She has a boyfriend? Since when?" Mackenzie almost slipped on a thin sheet of black ice. She gripped the mushy bark of a tree to balance herself. "Damn it."

"Few months now. If she's going on vacation with him, means it's serious."

Mackenzie dusted her muddy hands. "Ordered a background check on him?"

Nick turned and raised an eyebrow.

"What? This man might become Luna's stepfather."

"Already did it. He's a widower with only a few parking tickets to his name."

"How did his wife die?"

He threw back his head and laughed. "Are you seriously suspecting he killed his wife?"

Mackenzie shrugged innocently. "Maybe?"

"It was cancer."

Mackenzie could see the shore of the lake a dozen feet ahead of her. The frozen river upstream was pristine white from a distance. She spotted the yellow tape and the crime scene unit dressed in jackets. Detective Justin Armstrong, a junior detective, looked over the area with his binoculars. He had been with Lakemore PD two years and was often assigned to assist Mackenzie and Nick on their cases. His build was beefy but muscular, a moustache sat on his upper lip, and a contemplative frown always clouded his face. His discipline and mannerisms were military-like, and Mackenzie appreciated his unwavering focus.

The stretch of river meeting the lake was thawing and the brilliant wintry light made the surface glitter like crystals. As they got closer to the shallow bank, she saw the thin layer of ice on the surface was cracked. Pieces drifted away from each other, revealing the gushing water underneath.

"Detective Price," Justin tipped his head. "Welcome back, ma'am."

"Thanks, Justin. What do we have here?" She and Nick donned disposable suits, latex gloves and skullcaps before getting close to the crime scene.

Justin pointed at two men sitting on a boulder with blankets around their shaking bodies. "Those fishermen caught two bodies instead of fish around an hour ago. First they caught the victim wearing the blue sweater in fishing net. When they were rowing to the shore, their boat hit the other victim floating just under the ice."

"Any other witnesses?" Nick asked.

"None, sir. No one else is in the area. The cabins look unoccupied."

Nick made his way to speak to the spooked fishermen. Four personnel from the medical examiner's office huddled together, blocking Mackenzie's view of the bodies. Two of them collected samples from the soil and the bodies, while the third one made an inventory. The fourth person took pictures.

They moved, giving Mackenzie full view. Two women lay side by side on the shore, several feet apart. Their eyes were open, milky white and bloated. Their skin glistened like wax, matted with mud and sand and remnants of the lake. They both had long dark hair like tattered ropes, the same length, tangled with weeds and debris. One body was wrapped in a fishing net. Both barefoot, their skin was covered in bruises and cuts.

The woman in the net was dressed in jeans and a full-sleeved blue sweater, the other in a brown woolen dress and stockings. Their clothes were bloodied, the epicenter being their abdomens, but otherwise largely intact. There were some rips, likely from being underwater—no obvious signs of deliberate tearing or removal, which could have indicated sexual assault.

Mackenzie noted their similarities: bone structure, rosebud mouths, height, and build. They were bloated and their skin was clammy and translucent, a blue tinge coming from their veins.

"Did they have ID?" Mackenzie asked Justin.

"No. It's probably at the bottom of the lake somewhere."

Mackenzie nodded and continued staring at the women's faces. They looked too similar. Were they related? She wouldn't be surprised if they were twins. But being underwater had morphed their appearance.

"Looks like they were stabbed," Nick noted as he joined them. "No other major injuries visible that could lead to death. Sexual assault looks unlikely. They were thrown in the water instead of being positioned a certain way, so no ritualistic killing either. Robbery gone wrong?"

"I don't think so, sir. One of the bodies is wearing a wedding band and a necklace," Justin pointed out. "The necklace looks cheap, but the ring is probably gold."

"They look very similar, but they're bloated and have all these marks," Mackenzie said.

"Probably from the water. This lake is forty meters deep and pretty rocky at the bottom. There can be strong afternoon winds here, causing currents." Nick frowned. "I swear I've seen someone like them before."

"Where?"

"I don't know..." He shook his head and leaned on his haunches to get a closer look. "I've definitely seen this face somewhere."

He pulled out his phone and typed something. He handed it to Mackenzie. "One of them could be her?"

She stared at the picture. It was slightly pixelated, but the woman smiling at the camera bore an uncanny resemblance to both corpses. "Who is that?"

"Katy Becker."

"The social activist?" Mackenzie raised her eyebrows.

Katy Becker was a well-known name around Lakemore. The short, slender-framed woman had worked relentlessly to raise money to restore several state parks and construct homeless shelters around the city. She dodged direct media attention, preferring to work from behind the scenes, but was big on social media. Authorities knew her—or at least of her. Mackenzie had never spoken to the woman, but on several occasions they had been present at the same event. Last year, Katy had organized a protest outside city hall demanding better wages for schoolteachers. Mackenzie had been deployed to handle the crowd in case things spun out of control. She remembered watching Katy shouting slogans into a microphone. She was passionate and determined, everything Mackenzie prized in a citizen of Lakemore.

"Maybe it's someone who just looks like her?" she suggested.

"We should wait for Becky to confirm," Nick said, referring to the chief medical examiner. "But what a waste if it is her."

"Yeah, she's one of the few inspiring figures in Lakemore."

"Did you find the murder weapon?" Nick asked Justin.

"Nothing. Just them."

"Think they were murdered together?" He looked at Mackenzie.

"They were both stabbed in the abdomen. No other major injury marks. The stage of decomposition looks the same. Unlikely they were killed by separate people. When did the lake freeze?"

"Two days ago. Sunday. The bodies must have been dumped before that."

Mackenzie looked out over the broad expanse of the lake with frozen patches. Some cabins were visible along the shoreline. "Justin, can you check if there were any arrests made in this area in the last few days?"

"Drug activity?"

"Yeah, I haven't heard anything, but just to be sure."

"Yes, ma'am."

Chris, one of the forensic personnel, came up to them. "Detectives, we're going to take the bodies to the morgue now."

"Thanks, Chris. Do you know where Becky is?" Mackenzie asked.

"She's in court testifying on that mall shooting." He ducked out from under the yellow tape and removed the plastic covers on his shoes. "Okay, c'mon," he turned to his team. "Need a few hands here!" Together, they lifted the bodies and placed them in black body bags, then carried the gurneys all the way to the van parked at the edge of the woods.

Justin spoke with the fishermen and gave them his card. They looked relieved to be dismissed. While Nick and Justin discussed the details of keeping the crime scene secured for the next few days, Mackenzie wandered along the shore.

It was eerily quiet and desolate here. If she closed her eyes, she could hear the icy water tearing apart under the bright sun. All she could see in her mind's eye was the barren solitude of the park.

Were the women murdered here, or was this just the dumping ground? It was a good location to get rid of a body. Mackenzie couldn't think of a reason why the women would be here in the first place. They weren't dressed to go hiking—not that it was hiking season. Maybe there was still some minor drug activity in the area; Justin was checking on that. But their clothing and faces didn't show any obvious signs of them being addicts. Nor had she heard of any wrongdoing going down round here for a while.

But, until today, she hadn't seen a police squad car set on fire at the Lakemore PD headquarters either.

"Once we confirm their identity, we'll inform the next of kin," Nick said, joining her. "It's pretty, isn't it?"

"It is," she acknowledged. "In a creepy way. How long do you think before the rest of Lakemore burns it down?"

"People are angry, Mack. We all just have to be careful."

"Why?"

"We took away the only thing this town cared about," Nick commented dryly. He turned in a circle, taking in the area. "Most of this park is inaccessible because of the thick woods. Just the trail and cabins along it. If we can figure out where the bodies were dumped from..."

She pointed upstream. "The river runs from southeast, pouring into the lake here. The bodies could have been thrown into the river and brought to the lake by the currents, or directly into the lake. Both locations are accessible by the trail. We should check if anyone's filed a missing person report for Katy Becker."

"Good idea." Nick pulled out his phone. "Ready to go?"

Mackenzie wanted to stay surrounded by silence and stillness, so removed from the chaos in her life. She felt like she was in a snow globe, trapped and tucked away safely in artificially induced peace. But it just took a flick of the wrist to turn the globe over and disrupt it all.

Her phone vibrated. She knew it would be Sterling. He had been texting and leaving her voicemails.

"Can I meet you by the car in like five minutes? Want to make a quick phone call."

Nick pressed his lips in a thin line and nodded understanding. When he disappeared behind the frosty trees, she took out her phone. As she'd predicted, her husband had been worried about her. There were over ten voicemails from the last week alone.

She clenched the phone tight. She was still undecided about him. With an aching breath, she dialed the number to Miller Lodge and asked for Robert Price.

"Hello?" Her father's voice came on the phone.

"It's me."

"Micky!" he gasped. "I thought I would never hear from you. It's been weeks. I left messages."

"I was busy. Can we meet tonight?"

"Of course. Should I come to you?"

"No!" Mackenzie said abruptly. "I'll see you at seven."

"See you, Micky."

She hung up without saying goodbye and made her way back to the car. As she weaved her way through the icy Woodburn Park, she thought about the bodies that lurked beneath its tranquil surface, just like the demons that lurked beneath hers.

# CHAPTER THREE

Back at the station, Mackenzie fired up her computer and began looking into Katy Becker. There was no confirmation that either one of the victims was Katy, but the resemblance to the woman in the dress was uncanny. If she imagined Katy with glassy white eyes, a bloated face and a road map of veins on pale skin, she would look like the corpse. Or at least spookily similar.

Did Katy have a twin?

She checked Katy's social media accounts. Her Twitter account was active. She had over thirty thousand followers and posted regularly about important social and political issues. Her latest series of posts were calling attention to an impending unemployment crisis in Lakemore. A lot of people and businesses had lost money following the Lakemore Sharks' withdrawal from the Olympic Championship—a local football tournament between high school teams from neighboring towns in Washington. Over the last five decades, it had developed into a symbol of pride and prestige. But the Sharks out of the tournament meant no associated business for Lakemore.

Mackenzie felt a pang of discomfort. Lakemore's economy was heavily dependent on sport, if not entirely. Before she could go off-piste, she realized that Katy hadn't posted anything in the last six days, since the previous Wednesday.

She looked at her history. She always at least liked or retweeted a post every day. But Katy Becker had gone dark on Twitter.

Mackenzie leaned back on her chair and tapped a pen against her keyboard. Maybe it didn't mean anything. Maybe she was sick or on vacation.

She opened the file containing the crime scene pictures. Some of them were still being catalogued, but Mackenzie had requested to take whatever was ready.

She was impatient; she needed a project.

Only the mid-range pictures had been uploaded, but they were good enough to start with. Mackenzie gazed at the bodies. Except for the blood staining their clothes, nothing violent stood out. Compared to the naked and mutilated bodies she'd seen over the course of her career, these bodies were remarkably unviolated.

The likelihood of any sexual crime was low considering their clothes were intact. That could hint at a female culprit.

The victim she suspected to be Katy Becker wore a necklace with a Gemini locket. Mackenzie zoomed in and inspected her hand.

A wedding band.

The picture wasn't close-range, so she couldn't make out the details, but like Justin had pointed out, it looked like gold.

She looked for Katy's pictures on the internet. There were plenty, from her talking at forums to attending charity events she helped organize. Mackenzie saw a picture of Katy standing between two old ladies, her arms wrapped around their shoulders. Katy had written an article raising awareness for mental health problems among senior citizens. She was wearing a wedding ring that looked similar to the one in the crime scene photo.

Yet more evidence indicating that one of the bodies belonged to Katy Becker, but there was no confirmation yet, Mackenzie reminded herself. Becky planned to begin the autopsy later this evening. Mackenzie sighed at the pictures. Without a positive ID, there was nothing to go on. All she could do was wait and *hypothesize*.

"Mack?"

The voice jolted her upright. She turned to find her husband standing in her office. Sterling's chiseled jaw was dotted with spurting facial hair and his curly hair looked unkempt. Dressed in a crisp beige suit, his jacket draped over his arm and his other hand holding his briefcase, he looked spotless. But his strained expression gave away his distress. He stared at her with wide eyes.

Mackenzie was relieved that the office was empty. She stood up. "I was meaning to call you, but—"

"Do you have any idea how worried I've been?" His forehead bunched. "We haven't spoken in weeks!"

She licked her lips and looked around. Anyone could walk in at any time. "This really isn't the time or the place."

Sterling put his briefcase on Troy's desk and shook his head. "I don't care. You aren't returning my calls or my texts." He sank into a chair and held his head in his hands. Mackenzie stood over him, watching his chest move with every choppy breath he took. She could see tears pool in the corners of his eyes. She'd skimmed over the texts he'd sent her; she knew he cared. But he had cheated on her. He had been hurt that she didn't want children and had dealt with that hurt by having a meaningless fling.

Unless… was it really meaningless, or was he misleading her again? She brushed off the thought. Her husband wasn't malicious; he was weak.

She mustered up some kindness and took his hands. "I wanted to get away. I couldn't stay in that house."

"I understand. But you can't just get up and leave without telling anyone. Why didn't you answer my calls? All I got from you were vague texts." His eyes searched hers.

"I… I should have. I was angry, and I needed space—"

"I gave you space! I've been living in an Airbnb. I was worried something had happened to you. You can't just…" He shook his head incredulously. "You can't *leave* like this, Mack. I had to chase Nick for answers. I'm your husband!"

She kept quiet.

"I guess I don't have the right to ask anything from you now." Sterling squeezed her hands in his and hung his head low. She contemplated telling him about her father, but she didn't know where to even begin.

He stood up and picked up his suitcase and coat. "I wanted to check in on you. Good to know you're okay."

"Sterling."

He paused.

"I should have called you."

"Are you ready to talk to me?" he asked. "I really think we should talk, Mack. Now that you've had some time to think."

Mackenzie swallowed. "Of course."

"Tomorrow?"

"Sure."

"I'll come over after dinner." He checked his watch. "I should head out. I have a deposition to get to."

Sterling leaned in to give her a kiss on the cheek but froze, his lips hovering a few inches away. She held her breath. It felt natural but *wrong* at the same time. Instead, he pressed his lips softly against her temple.

When he left, Mackenzie dropped into her chair with a thud. Her phone rang, and she picked it up eagerly.

"Detective Price."

"No one has reported Katy Becker missing yet," Nick said.

"So this is someone who looks a lot like her and is wearing her wedding band?"

"It's the same as Katy's?"

"Yeah, I compared it to some pictures I found online. Looks an awful lot like hers."

"Maybe she took off like you did, so no one reported her missing."

She could hear the smile in his voice. "Subtle."

"Subtlety isn't my style. Did Chris send all of the crime scene photos?"

"Just mid-range. I'm more interested in the close-range ones. Long-range won't help. No car can get in that area."

"You're right. There were three cabins in view. They looked abandoned, but might be worth pursuing."

"I'll send Justin and Jenna to knock on some doors," Mackenzie said referring to two of the junior detectives in the unit. "Where are you?"

"Luna's ballet recital. We're getting dinner after. Want to join?"

"Can't. Got plans."

"Sterling?"

"Yeah," she lied.

As Mackenzie drove to Miller Lodge, she found herself punching the gas pedal too hard and clamping the steering wheel with too much force. She took the longer route to the lodge—avoiding the highways, instead sticking to the winding roads that cut through the middle of the city.

She looked out the window at the empty restaurants and bars. Melting snow dripped from the head jambs of the windows. Usually, they'd be packed around this time of the year, cheering on the Sharks. The streets were littered with relics of torn-down posters and cigarette butts. It was eerily quiet—no chants, no hoots, no curses. Even as the sun's piercing red orb set over the horizon, bathing the city in golden hues, there was nothing attractive about Lakemore tonight.

It was a shadow of what it could be.

Mackenzie couldn't say she was surprised to come back after three weeks and find her hometown changed drastically. Lakemore was a small community built on the fiction of football that connected and inspired people. When that fiction fractured, so did the town.

The humble lodge came into sight, situated at the end of a dirt road. She veered off the main street and found a parking spot. Killing the engine, she braced herself. The thought of seeing him in the flesh, alive, a second time made her sick to her stomach.

Setting her jaw, Mackenzie approached the building. There were only five cars parked in the lot. The two-story lodge was square and tired-looking. Paint peeled from the timber frame around the front door. Entering, Mackenzie cringed at the faded floral wallpaper and sagging furniture.

"I'm looking for Robert Price. Could you call him down, please?" Mackenzie said to the receptionist, a large woman with frizzy black hair, playing solitaire on her computer.

"Who are you?"

Mackenzie showed her badge. The woman rolled her eyes and muttered something about "shady business in her lodge." After phoning Robert to come downstairs, she smacked the receiver down.

"How long has he been staying here for?" Mackenzie inquired.

"About a month or so."

"How does he pay?"

She narrowed her eyes. "Is he in trouble? I don't want any criminals here."

"He's not. But I want to know anyway."

"Pays in cash. On time. Doesn't cause any trouble."

"Has anyone come to visit him?"

"You're the first one," she answered, disinterested.

Minutes later, Robert appeared in the reception. Mackenzie's heart rose up in her throat and her stomach contracted. For a moment, her peripheral vision blurred.

"It's nice to see you, Micky."

They took a seat in the living area by the open kitchen. An unbalanced wooden table separated them. An old man snored in a chair a few feet away.

"Ignore him. Marv has a room, but he likes to sleep here," Robert said. "Would you like something to eat?"

"No, I'm good."

"Okay, there isn't much here anyway." He smiled, looking embarrassed.

Mackenzie searched for that glazed look in his eyes, the sneer on his lips, and the red creeping up his neck. He had always been strung so tight, prowling around the house like he was looking for something, like nothing around him was enough.

But now Robert had peace in his eyes, a polite smile on his lips, and his fingers were interlaced on the table. It looked like he'd finally found whatever it was he had gone looking for.

"How are you paying for yourself?"

"I've worked at some random places over the years—shops, garages, anything where I could use my hands. I saved every dollar I could."

Mackenzie crossed her arms. "In Mexico."

"Y-yes." Surprise flickered in his eyes. "How'd you know?"

"I took a little trip to Dallas and visited every rehab center. There was no record of Robert Price. I took more time, showed your picture around. The doctors at one of the rehabs recognized you as Freddie Graham. You were in rehab for six years, discharged two months ago. Did some more digging, used my contacts and found out that *Freddie Graham* had spent around a decade in Mexico before that, after a stint in Vegas where he accumulated gambling debts. Why choose that name?"

"Freddie was a buddy of mine in Vegas." Robert's eyes drifted into the space behind Mackenzie. "He was a meek guy. An addict like I was, but not an angry soul. A few months later, he passed away. Drinking killed him. He didn't have any family, and I was in trouble."

"You stole his identity?"

He nodded. "Are you going to arrest me, Micky?"

"There are a lot of things I could throw you in jail for." Mackenzie couldn't quite hide the spite in her voice.

The sound of a vase smashing resonated in her ears. She was locked in her room. All she could hear was Robert shouting at Melody. An hour later, she saw Melody with a bandage around her head. It was the first time Mackenzie realized that her father used to hit her mother.

"I can't even begin to describe how…" His eyes fluttered like a butterfly's wings. "I'm so sorry, Micky. I… I'm so ashamed. I can't even bring myself to ask about Melody."

"Who were you running away from?"

"Loan sharks. I don't even know what to call them. They would just send these guys to beat me up." His mouth twitched. "How is Melody?"

"She's dead."

"*What*?" he gasped. "How? When?"

"Around twelve years ago."

His eyebrows stitched together. He looked around, not knowing what to do with himself. "What happened?"

"Car accident. She had a brain hemorrhage."

Robert sat back in his chair and dabbed his pink face with a handkerchief. "That's unbelievable. Who took care of you?"

Mackenzie gritted her teeth behind closed lips. A sizzle rippled through her veins, and she clenched her calves tight. "I'm not here to talk about me. How long before your savings run out?"

"Few more weeks at best. Will have to find some way to make money now."

"Are you planning on working?"

"I don't know who'll hire an old man."

She almost let out a wry laugh. He might have learned to control his addiction and diluted his violent tendencies, but she believed her father to be shrewd and manipulative. He had spent the last two decades on the run all over the country and across the border. He'd never tried contacting her before, never tried to wedge his way back into her life. But now that he was getting older and running out of money, he suddenly wanted a relationship with her.

"So you're a police officer. How did you decide that's what you wanted to do?"

"Long story." She took out a phone from her pocket and placed it on the table. "I came here to give you this. You should have one."

He picked it up. "You didn't have to..."

"It's fine."

"Thank you."

"I actually have to go." She checked her watch. "But I'd like to discuss a possible living arrangement with you. I need to talk to my husband first. I'll ring you tomorrow evening?"

"I'll be right here."

As Mackenzie walked to her car, she looked over her shoulder. Robert stood at the entrance, waving at her and smiling. She closed her eyes and revisited her first memory. Her father kneeled on the ground and planted seeds in the soil. From behind, she could see his cheeks lift higher as he smiled. She ran toward him and just when he turned his face, it vanished. His face was unclear. But she remembered his smile was more honest and open.

Driving away, Mackenzie's heart felt heavy as a boulder in her chest.

She didn't trust him. Something had gone horribly wrong that night, and he was the only other person left alive who might know what happened. She had installed a spying app on the phone she had given him. It would allow her to monitor his calls and texts, access his location, and check his online activities.

A plan was forming—a potentially dangerous one. But she reminded herself that she wasn't a little girl who hid from her father anymore. Today, she was a trained police officer, whereas he was just an old man. And she believed that it was important to keep your enemies close.

# CHAPTER FOUR

*November 21*

The hallway of the concrete building that housed the morgue was grimy and ugly, with sickening yellow-tiled walls and a gray limestone floor. It reminded Mackenzie of an abandoned hospital constructed during the Cold War era. She expected her grandmother to come around the corner at any moment, a grim expression on her face, informing her of the terrible news.

*"I'm sorry, Mack."*

*"What happened?"*

*"She lost control of the car. They don't think she's going to make it."*

A draft made the hairs on her arms stand up. She looked around, but there were no windows. This part of the basement was claustrophobic, clinical, but unsterile.

Nick noticed her shudder. "Must be a ventilation issue."

"All the money they spend on changing the windows, they can't fix the heating in here."

"Priorities." He opened the door to the examination room and let her in.

The room was a brightly lit massive rectangle, with a lot of open space. Unlike the hallway outside, it had been recently renovated. There was a sanitization station with lockers on the left and a wall-mounted dissection bench running along the right wall. There were four downdraft post-mortem tables situated in the center with pull-through fridges on the back wall. There were two doors at the other end of the room—one leading to the utility room used to reserve chemical solutions and instruments, and the other to the staff transit area.

Becky Sullivan, the medical examiner, stood between the two tables on which the women lay. Wearing her personal protective equipment, she turned off the voice-recording device around her neck.

"Jesus, Becks!" Nick scowled. "What's that smell?"

"Methane, hydrogen sulfide, and carbon dioxide. AKA gas," she said flatly. "This is nothing. You should smell a charred corpse."

Mackenzie took quick, short breaths, training her nose to adapt to the smell. They pulled on gloves and walked over to Becky.

The bodies came into view. They lay naked with their eyes closed, torsos and chests covered in white cloth. The trunk incision on their chest cavities had been sewn shut with the classic baseball stitch. Now that their faces were devoid of hair, dirt, and little particulates and had bright light shining on them, Mackenzie was certain about the resemblance.

The body on the left table surely belonged to Katy Becker. The one on the right looked significantly like her.

"Did you confirm identity?" Nick asked.

"That's Katy Becker." She lifted the tag on the body's toe to show the name. "I compared her to the pictures. The face structure and even eye color is an exact match. I'll bring in the next of kin for identification. The husband, I presume."

"Do you have to do a dental?"

Becky pulled open the whitened lips of Katy's corpse to reveal missing teeth along the upper gum. "Jane Doe over there doesn't have missing teeth. Katy's teeth were knocked out either during a struggle or deliberately."

"No one knows she's missing yet," Mackenzie said.

She inspected Jane Doe closely. Her face looked similar to Katy's but something was off about it. Mackenzie couldn't put a finger on it. The tissue distribution in her facial muscles looked odd, notwithstanding the effects of being submerged underwater. Mackenzie noticed slight scarring near the ears and under the eyes.

"These marks, what are they? They don't look like they're from being in the water."

"They're not. Those are from cosmetic procedures."

"Really?"

Becky pointed at the scars on the body. "Jane Doe had work done to her face. See these tiny scars along the hairline? To be honest, it's not my area of expertise, so I can't tell what exact procedures she had done."

"Could all these modifications have made her look more like Katy?" Nick asked.

"Looks like it. She's a natural blonde, but dyed her hair to a color that's a match for Katy's. Also, she was wearing colored contacts." Becky picked up a container on the tray next to the tables. Two lenses floated inside the solution. "Her eyes are actually blue, but she wore brown contacts. Katy has brown eyes."

Mackenzie's stomach flipped. She looked at Nick, who was clearly uneasy. Whatever this was, it was twisted and dark. Katy Becker had been killed along with a woman who went to great lengths to look like her. Who was this woman? Why did she take extensive measures to look like Katy?

"What do we know about this Jane Doe?" Mackenzie asked.

"Her teeth are in better condition; I'll do a dental. Her fingertips are too wrinkled for a reliable biometric identification."

"What about cause of death?"

Becky pulled down the sheets from their bodies to reveal the wounds on their torsos. The blood had been cleaned. They looked like clean cuts surrounded by some discoloration. "Katy has two stab wounds—one into her spleen and the other into her stomach. Jane Doe had a single stab wound into her lungs. There were no signs of drowning and the depth of these stab wounds would have killed them."

"Means they were already dead when they were dumped in the water," Nick said.

"Yup. Jane Doe was stabbed straight, right between two ribs. Clearly the killer knew how to strike and where. But with Katy, the stab wound into the spleen was shallow and at a downward angle." Becky traced the pattern on Katy's body. "The one into the stomach was what killed her. The weapon was thrust and then curved at an upward angle toward the ribcage and forced all the way in, as is indicated by the hilt mark. The blade is between three to four inches long. I'll need more time to come up with the exact shape and finish. My preliminary conclusion is that both were killed with the same weapon."

"Was it a knife?"

"Can't say for certain yet. Will have to look at the bone. But looks like it."

"Any other signs of a fight other than the teeth?" Mackenzie asked. "They seem to have enough knowledge about anatomy; that knife into the spleen looks like an aberration."

"It's hard to differentiate between defensive wounds and injuries from being in the water."

"Any sign of sexual assault?" Nick asked.

"Nothing on breasts or thighs. No bite marks. The clothes weren't torn; I'll send them to the crime lab..." She gestured behind her at the plastic bags containing their clothes. "No injuries in the pubic region. I didn't find any semen on the clothes, either."

"Can you detect semen underwater?"

"On clothes for up to three months. I'm concluding no sexual assault in this case."

"Our killer could be a woman," Mackenzie offered.

"Here's the kicker. Katy Becker was pregnant." Becky crossed her arms. "At least ten weeks from my estimation."

Mackenzie felt a burst of grief. She looked at Katy: cold, rigid, and decomposing. Her eyes flitted to her very slightly protruding stomach, and she felt bile rise in her throat. "How did you know?"

"Her cervix was higher than what I've seen in my experience. I got the results back an hour ago. RT-PCR detected beta hPL, confirming early stage pregnancy."

"Jeez, when did you start working today?" Nick asked.

"Five in the a.m."

"I wouldn't be proud of that," he muttered.

"My diener called in sick, so I didn't have much of a choice."

"*You* closed them back up?"

"Just like the old days. Felt young again."

It was possible that the killer hadn't known Katy was pregnant. But in Mackenzie's experience that wouldn't have stopped them. This wasn't a crime of passion. The killer had stabbed them with the intention of ending their lives.

"What about time of death?" she asked.

"Based on rate of decomposition and factoring in that they were underwater, I'd say less than a week."

"The lake and the river froze over on Sunday—the bodies would have been dumped before that," Nick mused. "We still don't know if the bodies were dumped directly in the lake or they came from the river."

"Another strange thing about our Jane Doe…" Becky shone the overhead light on the end of the table. She lifted the knees of one of the bodies—the one with the procedures done to her face—to reveal tattoos. "She has tattoos on the back of her knees."

Mackenzie and Nick bent and tilted their heads to get a good look.

"What is that?" Nick asked.

"39A and B75C."

What did these mean? They were like codes drilled into her body. Letters and numbers that seemingly made no sense.

Becky straightened Jane Doe's legs and pointed at the shins. Her clumped veins underneath the skin looked gray and decaying. "These are collapsed veins. Sign of a long-term intravenous drug user."

"She's a drug addict," Mackenzie said.

"A big one. I'll have to run another test to estimate which drug though."

This Jane Doe was a drug addict, had cosmetic procedures on her face, and had mysterious tattoos on the backs of her knees. Mackenzie stared at the clammy, swollen corpse—a big question mark.

"Anything else?" Nick asked.

"Not for now. I'll have more information on the murder weapon later."

"When can we bring in her husband to identify the body?"

"Just give me a heads up."

"Thanks, Becky."

The ME covered the bodies with the white cloths again and rolled the trolleys over to transport their bodies to the freezer. "Anytime."

As Mackenzie silently regarded their matching faces, she couldn't help but wonder about the fixation behind it. Why had Jane Doe gone to such great lengths to look like Katy?

# CHAPTER FIVE

Mackenzie gazed through the window of the moving car. The leafless trees were a blur of brown and gray. The sun shone through the branches. She had never seen Lakemore *look* so cold. The mountains of snow swept to the side of the roads were melting. The drooped branches of trees were beginning to coil back up as snow melted off them. The road ahead itself was caked with slush—suds of it flying as cars skidded over it.

She turned up the heat. "I've never seen it get this bad."

"Another storm is coming in the next few days," Nick said from the driver's seat.

Mackenzie looked at her phone again and opened the app that gave her information on Robert's activity. He hadn't called anyone or received or sent any text messages. His GPS location showed he had gone to the local market close to the lodge. Probably to buy some essentials.

She closed the app and continued her research into Katy Becker.

Katy had married her husband Cole Becker right after she earned her degree in sociology from the University of Washington. She grew up in Lakemore and had returned with a renewed sense of passion to build something. Cole was from Seattle. He moved to Lakemore with her and opened his own physiotherapy practice.

Mackenzie scrolled down her tweets and smirked. Katy was witty, but Mackenzie didn't know how she felt about Katy's entire life being splashed all over the internet for anyone to see. It certainly made Mackenzie's job easier, from tracking down logistical information to helping her understand Katy better, but it wasn't wise. She shared where she worked, which bars she went to. She even shared which gym she went to. It would have been so simple for someone to watch her.

Mackenzie wasn't on any social media. Sterling often suggested to her that it was a good way to maintain contact with her old friends from New York and the academy. She would always brush off the suggestion, too embarrassed to admit that she didn't have any friends except Nick.

She felt lightheaded and groped for a Gravol in the glove box.

"I told you reading makes motion sickness worse, Mack," Nick said, with an unlit cigarette dangling from his mouth. He had quit smoking, but it was his habit to fiddle around with cigarettes and lighters—especially if he was stressed or concentrating.

"I was doing research." She swallowed the pill dry and leaned against the leather headrest.

"What did you find?"

"Katy and Cole have been married for four years now. She likes to wake up with the sun. And he is allergic to peanuts."

"Vital information." He snuck a glance at her hands. "What happened with Sterling?"

Her chest tightened. "I don't know."

"You're still wearing your wedding band."

She hadn't even realized. Her wedding band had molded into her left hand over the last three years. It was part of her body. Suddenly, she felt it cinching her finger and weighing down her hand. Like it wasn't a part of her, but a burden she carried.

"Where did you go?"

"Dallas."

"Dallas?" The cigarette dropped from his mouth and landed on his lap. "Why?"

"Let's talk about this later." Mackenzie cracked her neck, regretting her slip of the tongue. She had to talk to Sterling first. But how much did she owe Sterling? Was he completely obliterated from her life and consideration because he had cheated on her? Nick didn't push the issue; he always knew when to stop. Her marital issues with Sterling were her private business, though Nick had unwittingly found himself right in the middle of it after he had stumbled upon the truth. But she didn't mind. A part of her found comfort in the fact that there was *someone* to talk with.

He turned the car into a street with brick townhouses on each side. The trees formed a lush canopy in spring, but now they stood thin and rigid, crisscrossing the sky above. Sheppard Hallows. It was one of the neighborhoods Mackenzie and Sterling had been considering when they were looking for a house to buy. The townhouses were modest, but each had a unique look—different windows, different paints. The minuscule efforts made by owners to add their personal touch. She'd imagined setting up a hammock there and reading. But Sterling said he felt the street was too claustrophobic, the houses too close together. He said he wanted more privacy. She knew he just wanted a bigger house.

Nick parked in front of the address—a corner house. "Someone's home." He nodded at the black Prius in the driveway.

Absentmindedly, Mackenzie fixed the pins in her hair and pulled her ponytail higher. She glanced at the little barbecue area in the front with cobbled tiles and patio furniture covered in snow. The white curtains fluttered behind the windows. Someone had seen them. Before they knocked on the door, it swung open.

A wiry man well under six feet, with chestnut-colored hair falling in his eyes, stood at the entrance. He wore a black tracksuit. Removing his earbuds, he frowned at them. "Can I help you?"

Nick flashed his badge. "We're from Lakemore PD. I'm Detective Blackwood. This is my partner, Detective Price. Are you Cole Becker?"

"Yes. What is this about?"

"Can we come inside?"

"Sure."

Mackenzie followed Cole and Nick inside. On the outside, their house was unassuming and old. But inside, it had been renovated with everything in white and chrome. Their furniture was glossy with straight lines and sharp edges. It wasn't ostentatious, but tasteful, and right up Mackenzie's alley. There was no clutter. On the coffee table, the newspaper and magazines were fanned at uniform angles.

"Is everything okay?" Cole asked.

Mackenzie sat on one of the black leather armchairs, preparing for the hardest part of her job. It was Nick's too. That's why he'd had a cigarette in his mouth on the ride over.

"We're very sorry to bring you this news," Mackenzie said, "but yesterday afternoon, we discovered two bodies at Woodburn Park."

Cole began to pale. His lips parted.

"We would like you to come with us to help identify one. We have reasons to suspect it's your wife."

"*Excuse me?*"

Nick shuffled in his seat. "I know this is difficult to process—"

"Is this a joke?" Cole's voice raised an octave.

"No, Mr. Becker. We—"

"I have no clue what you're talking about." He yanked at his hair and exhaled. "You almost gave me a heart attack. There has obviously been a mistake."

"Mr. Becker," Mackenzie tried again, "please try to understand. We have some questions and—"

He rolled his eyes. "She's not dead. She's upstairs." He craned his neck toward the staircase. "Katy! Katy!"

Mackenzie and Nick looked at each other in bemusement. Was Becky mistaken? Becky had never made a mistake, and they hadn't needed to rely on her entirely. The bodies were fresh. Once the faces were cleaned and were viewed under a bright light, there was no denying that one of them was Katy Becker. She even had the wedding band. She had been inactive on Twitter for the last week. Becky said she died within that timeframe, likely before Monday.

Was Cole mistaken? Maybe he *assumed* that she was upstairs. Maybe he had just returned from a trip somewhere. Mackenzie's brain raked over the various possibilities.

A floorboard creaked. She spun her head to see who it was.

Katy Becker glided down the stairs.

# CHAPTER SIX

Dressed in mismatched T-shirt and pajamas, Katy looked like she had just rolled out of bed. Her dark hair was pulled in a messy bun. Her brown eyes fluttered nervously at them.

Mackenzie jogged her memory and combed through all the pictures she'd seen of Katy online. She looked different. Her cheeks were sunken, and there were dark grooves under her eyes like she hadn't been sleeping well. Her lips looked like she'd been chewing on them.

Other than her bedraggled state, it was the same woman. Same height, same features, and same wedding band on her finger. It was the same woman lying in the morgue.

"Who are you?" Katy asked.

Cole stood up and guided Katy to sit on the couch. Was she ill? She certainly looked much thinner. "These are Detectives Blackwood and Price from the Lakemore PD."

"What?" she gasped. "What's happened?"

Nick opened and closed his mouth like a fish. But Mackenzie was quicker to recover. "We found two bodies at Woodburn Park. Until now, we thought that one of them was you."

"Oh my God." Katy's voice came out breathy.

"They were murdered a few days ago," Nick said warily.

Katy's neck turned red as she looked at Cole. "C-Cole…"

"They made a mistake," Cole assured her, rubbing her back. He turned to them with angry eyes. "My wife isn't feeling well.

I think you've done enough. If there's nothing else, then kindly see yourself out."

Mackenzie wasn't ready to leave yet. She gazed at Katy, who sat next to Cole like a frightened animal. The way she bowed her body into his. The way she winced whenever she glanced at Mackenzie and Nick. The way she looked like even the slightest sound would make her jump out of her skin.

They might have made a mistake in identifying the corpse, but there was a connection here. Katy's face had been found on two bodies. One was a replica and the other an uncanny resemblance.

"Do you have a twin?" she asked.

Her eyes widened. "N-not that I'm aware of."

"Any siblings?"

"No. Do we really have to do this?" Cole asked, impatient.

"We do." Mackenzie arched an eyebrow. "Two bodies were found and *both* of them have your wife's features."

Cole stuttered, "That's ridiculous."

Mackenzie would almost assume that Katy was a battered wife. That's where her mind went first whenever she encountered an unnerved woman clinging to a piqued man. But their interaction didn't seem unhealthy, just uncomfortable. Like they didn't know how to be around each other. Katy flinched when Cole rubbed her arm gently, like she wasn't used to being touched there. He opened his mouth to say something to her but didn't, like he wasn't used to soothing her. There was tenderness in the way they huddled together, but hesitation too.

It reminded her of the way Sterling had kissed her forehead yesterday.

"Katy, do you mind if I have a glass of water?" Mackenzie began to stand up.

"I..." Katy looked at Cole. "Sure."

Cole let Katy go reluctantly. She led the way, guiding Mackenzie to the open-plan kitchen behind the living room. Nick and Cole's hushed voices were indecipherable. Mackenzie plopped onto a stool and watched Katy stand on the other side of the kitchen island with her hands hanging down like she didn't know what to do with them.

"Water?" Mackenzie reminded her.

"Yeah… right."

She opened one of the bluish-gray cabinets behind her. There were plates and bowls inside it. She opened the one next to it and pulled out a glass. Filling it with tap water, she handed it to Mackenzie. "Here you go."

"Thanks. How long have you been living here?"

"We moved in soon after we got married."

"It's a lovely house. Did you decorate it yourself?"

"It was both of us," she shrugged.

"Do you have a cleaner? Your house is spick-and-span."

"Maria comes twice a week. Wednesdays and Sundays."

"My husband and I were looking at a house here. But he didn't like how they were so close together. Is that a problem?"

"No. The walls are thick."

Seconds ticked by in silence, and Mackenzie found herself surprised. The Katy she'd discovered on social media and who she'd seen at protests was outspoken and energetic. The Katy in front of her was reserved and jittery. Mackenzie had expected her to make more conversation. It was then that she noticed Katy was touching her belly a lot.

"You don't look too well."

"I… I'm pregnant," she sighed, sounding resigned. She perched on the stool on the other side of the kitchen island. "I'm nauseous *all* the time. And I'm hot and then I'm cold." She fanned the back of her neck. "I've never been so *uncomfortable* in my life."

Mackenzie nodded.

"I'm sorry," Katy said abruptly. "I didn't mean to—"

"Oh, don't worry about it. Congratulations."

She gave her a wan smile. "Thank you. Cole and I haven't told anyone yet. We've been planning to do something special to make the announcement. I don't know why I told you, but the last few days have been so crappy and then you showed up and gave us this news..."

"I'm sorry. That sounds rough. When did you find out?"

"Two weeks ago. All my energy has been sucked out of me." She gestured at her grubby appearance. "As you can tell, all I do is either stay in bed or have my head in the toilet."

Mackenzie decided to withhold that one of the murdered women had been pregnant for now. But a roiling sensation made her stomach sick. One Jane Doe dyed her hair, wore contacts and underwent medical procedures to look like Katy, and the other one was pregnant. This couldn't have been a coincidence.

"You haven't told *anyone* else?" Mackenzie pressed.

"My parents and my doctor, obviously."

"I hope you don't mind me asking, but was it a planned pregnancy?"

"No. Cole was just as taken aback as I was."

"How far along are you?"

"Thirteen weeks."

"I see. Has anything strange happened with you lately? Anyone threaten you? Or have you thought someone's been following you?"

"No."

"Any ex-boyfriends?"

She let out a dry laugh. "Cole and I got together freshman year of college. There was no one serious in high school. Those bodies had *my* face on them? *Both* of them?"

"Yes."

"Just one having my face doesn't make any sense. I don't know what to think about there being two."

"Do your parents live in town?"

"Why?"

"You said you're not aware of a twin. We'd like to talk to them, if possible."

She chewed on her lower lip, sucking it into her mouth. "Yeah, they live in Lakemore. In Nelson Heights. Charlotte and Frank Harris."

"And you've been in town this past week?"

"Yeah."

"Cole too?"

"Why?

"Standard questions."

"He left on Friday for a conference in Seattle." Her eyes got shifty. "But he came back early on Saturday. Said it wasn't really worth it."

Mackenzie looked over her shoulder at Nick, who was writing down something Cole was saying. As though he knew she was watching him, he looked up and nodded.

"Would you let me know what happens with your investigation?" She played with the hem of her sleeve, pulling at the loose threads.

Mackenzie looked at Katy's ring finger. "I will. Do you mind if I take a picture of your ring?"

"Why?"

"We found a similar ring on the body. I want to see if they're the same."

Katy presented her ring hand. Her fingers were bony and her knuckles a deep shade of pink. The only mark of adornment was the simple gold. Mackenzie took a photo with her phone.

After a few more routine questions, Mackenzie and Nick walked out the door. Cold mist hung in the air, forming a film over Mackenzie's face and hair. The sun was now eclipsed behind rolling gray skies, suggesting rain later.

"That has never happened to me before," Nick snorted, referring to Katy being found alive. "It was almost embarrassing."

"She's pregnant. Thirteen weeks."

"Cole told me." Nick spun on his heel and stopped in front of the car. "He said she's been sick all week and hasn't gone to work since last Tuesday. She even had to cancel an appointment with the gynecologist."

"There's a housekeeper that comes twice a week. We should talk to her. It looks like they're having trouble."

"You saw it too, huh?" Nick pulled out a pack of cigarettes and slapped it against his palm repeatedly. "Think it's the pregnancy?"

"Maybe. It was unplanned. They could just be adjusting to the news."

Mackenzie looked over her shoulder at the house again and the simmering tensions it sheltered. It was wedged beside a bluish-green painted house that already had Christmas decorations up—there was a light-up snowman in the yard. As she climbed back inside the car, she saw a movement behind the front window of a neighboring house on the right. She was certain she saw the face of a young woman peeking at them through the window. The peach-colored curtains flapped into stillness as the face disappeared.

It was just a curious neighbor. Mackenzie could imagine this neighborhood being a close community, what with the cramped houses. As they drove away, she thought about the pregnant Katy lookalike in the morgue and the pregnant Katy back in the house. Then there was the Jane Doe. Three women, all nearly identical. Two of them pregnant. Two of them murdered. Mackenzie had no idea what the connection was yet, but it turned her stomach just thinking about it.

# CHAPTER SEVEN

With a sigh of impatience, Mackenzie rummaged through another drawer in search of a pair of scissors. She had a habit of rearranging things mindlessly when she was deep in a thought. But things were never permanently displaced. They always found their way back to their original place. She realized now it was Sterling who was putting things back.

"Ugh!" She punched one of the drawers shut.

Sterling was arriving any minute now. Mackenzie had laid out a plate of chocolate-chip cookies. She stared at them now and felt like a complete idiot. What was she doing? She had considered getting Nick's opinion on how to handle this situation, on how to break the news to Sterling that her father had returned and she had a living arrangement in mind. But it felt wrong to share an intimate detail with anyone but her husband first.

She felt her skin flush. Why did she feel like she still owed Sterling anything?

She was rotating the wedding band on her finger when the bell rang.

"Don't you have your keys?" Mackenzie asked, opening the door. Sterling looked cleaner than yesterday. His sweater and slacks were ironed, and his hair was combed.

"I do. But I didn't want to just walk in. I thought maybe you'd..."

She left the door ajar to let him in and tuned his excuses out.

"I made cookies."

"Thanks." He picked one up and nibbled on it. "It's really good."

Mackenzie bit her tongue. She wanted to question if that was another lie, but the last thing she wanted to do was engage in a petty argument. She reminded herself that tonight's meeting had a specific purpose. Tonight their marriage had to take a backseat.

"Something happened few weeks ago," she started, and his face fell. "That night, after you left—"

"Mack," he swallowed hard and raised a hand. "Do I need to know this? I can look past it. I will never ask you anything, and we can j-just move on."

"What?" She stared at him blankly. When the meaning of his words sunk in, she widened her eyes. "Is *that* what you think? Just because you cheated means that I did, too? Not everyone is like *you*, Sterling."

"What else do you expect me to think when you started off like that?"

"You would have liked that, wouldn't you? Ease your conscience a little?"

He dragged his hands down his face. "Tell me what to do, Mack. Just tell me what I can do to fix this. I can't feel worse about this—"

"Try."

Sterling gave her a look that indicated he didn't recognize her anymore. Like he wasn't used to her being cruel. Mackenzie surprised herself in that moment. She dug her nails into the fabric of the couch. If she hadn't invested in good upholstery, she would have caused a tear.

"That's not why I called you here. I called you to tell you that my father got in touch with me again."

Sterling blanched. "Say that again?"

"My father," she enunciated. "A few weeks ago, he returned."

"*Returned*?" He raised his eyebrows. "That's… hasn't he been dead for over a decade?"

She nodded.

Sterling sat back on the couch. His arms went slack over his thighs. His eyes grew distant as his mind raced. "Where was he?"

"All over the place. Mexico at some point. That's why I left. I drove down to Portland then flew to Vegas and finally to Dallas to confirm his story."

"Confirm his story? You don't trust him. What did you find?"

"He was in Dallas in rehab for the last six years. He spent a decade in Mexico. I couldn't find out much about Vegas, but he went there twenty years ago so it was a long shot anyway."

"And you didn't tell me until now?"

Mackenzie pressed the heels of her hands into her eyelids. "Of course, you're making this about you."

"I'm not making this about myself. This is big, Mack. I don't get why you haven't said anything for weeks!"

"Why *I* didn't say anything? Really?" she snapped.

A muscle in his jaw ticked, but he maintained his cool. "What does he want from you?"

"A relationship."

"After twenty years?"

She pinched the sides of her waist and shrugged. She stood firmly, holding her ground. Heaviness pressing her ribs into her lungs. Part of her wanted to just give in to the tension and sink down to the ground. But she knew if she showed Sterling how much this was affecting her, he would make things harder for her.

"You told me he was never found. He just disappeared from home."

"Yes. He… um…" She cleared her throat. "He was unhappy and a drunk. He left us without bothering to say goodbye and then got involved in some bad stuff. That was that."

"This is all a little suspicious. Did he know people were looking for him?"

"He claims not. He was busy accumulating gambling debts in Vegas, from what I found out."

"Well, if he was a drunk then it wouldn't have been a big case. Not every disappearance makes the news."

"Sterling, please don't tell anyone about this. Not yet. Also... I want him to stay here. With me."

Sterling's eyes bugged out. "Are you out of your mind? You don't even know him!"

"He's living in a motel, and he's running out of money."

"*So*?" He looked at her, startled, and stood up. "He's a stranger. He's here to leech off you."

"I know that. What, do you think I'm an idiot?" Mackenzie snapped. "Frankly I'd rather have him right under my nose instead of running around town and potentially causing problems for me," she explained as Sterling paced back and forth. "This way I have control over the situation."

"What the hell are you talking about? What problems can he cause?"

What if her father knew what happened that night? What if he'd lied to Mackenzie? What if his plan was to blackmail her?

"I don't know. Talk to reporters? Make up lies about me and my mom?"

"If you think he's capable of doing that, you definitely shouldn't invite him to stay here. Help him out financially if you want to. Don't put yourself in danger."

"I'm a police officer. I can take care of myself."

Sterling looked around, frustrated, and clasped his hands behind his head. "That's not good enough. You don't know *anything* about him."

"I wasn't asking your permission!" she argued.

"You're my goddamn wife!" he shouted. Mackenzie felt a jolt of surprise. She'd rarely seen Sterling blow a fuse. "I'm not letting you live alone with a stranger!"

"Letting me?" She folded her arms. "Really?"

He groaned. "C'mon, Mack. You know what I meant! What would you do if you were in my place?"

His icy blue eyes met hers, staring daggers.

"You can't stop me. This is *our* house."

"Exactly. *Ours.* I have a say, too."

She raised her hands in defeat. "What do we do then? Should I move out and rent a two-bedroom?"

"Are you serious? You'd do all that for him? What exactly do you owe him?"

Her legs almost buckled at his words. She realized this was more than self-preservation. She thought she'd wronged her father, and she had carried his ghost with her all her life—whispering in her ear and never letting her forget.

This was her chance at redemption.

# CHAPTER EIGHT

*November 22*

"Mack!" Sergeant Jeff Sully grinned at her from behind his desk. "I haven't seen you since you got back. Happy Thanksgiving. How was the wedding?"

Sully's rounded belly looked more bloated and stretched than ever. The buttons of his shirt were ready to pop off anytime. The boxes from his offices had been cleared away, as had the files, but his desk was littered with poorly folded pieces of paper. Mackenzie noticed that all of them had words printed and realized they were department memos and newsletters.

"Great." She looked at his desk. "Origami?"

"Yes!" He picked up one of his creations—a poorly folded rabbit. "Very therapeutic. You should try it."

"Thought things were too busy around here."

"They were. That's why I need this now more than ever. Some departments were short-staffed, and as you know, people are agitated." He gestured at her to take a seat across from him. "But it's dying down now. You missed the worst part."

"I'm sorry I wasn't here."

He waved a dismissive hand. "Give yourself a break. I'm surprised you're not sunburned."

"Got a good sunscreen."

"Nick and Becky will be here in a sec." He put on his glasses and began folding another piece of paper. There was a manual on the table with instructions that he kept glancing at. "I saw Sterling a week ago at the courthouse. He didn't go with you?"

"He had work. I went alone."

"Good. Get that separation. I'm trying to send Pam off on a solo trip."

Mackenzie stifled a yawn. She had barely got any sleep after spending hours trying to convince Sterling that letting her father live with her wasn't dangerous. She didn't trust Robert and his "patient father wanting to make amends" act. Sterling's arguments were valid, but he didn't know the whole truth and what was at stake.

It had been extraordinarily difficult to put aside her issues with Sterling. Her ego screamed at her to kick him out, not give his opinion any importance. But she let him have his say and, after much deliberation, they had come to a compromise. Sterling would come over for dinner whenever Mackenzie was at home. It was his way of showing her father that even though they were separated, she wasn't alone. That someone had her back. The idea had briefly made her heart squeeze.

Maybe Sterling wasn't as bad as his mistake.

The door opened following a knock. Nick walked in, fixing his tie. "Sorry. Hope you weren't waiting too long." His mouth twitched to contain his smirk when he saw Sully trying to fold a perfect rabbit.

Becky followed him in with a thick file, raising her eyebrows at Sully. "Charming."

"Mock me all you want, but it's boosting my creativity. Anyway, lay it on me. I want to get out of here on time today. If I'm late for Thanksgiving, my wife will leave me."

"We don't have much right now, unfortunately," Mackenzie said. "Katy Becker's two doppelgangers—Jane Doe One and Jane Doe Two, I suppose—were found murdered at Woodburn Park. Becky estimates based on decomposition and the conditions of the water that they were murdered within the last week, before Sunday."

"Those fishermen found them on Tuesday?"

"Yeah, they went ice fishing for bluegill," Nick said. "We're going to get some assistance from patrol in combing that shoreline, but the area is huge. There are almost fifteen acres of woods around. Plus, with the weather, it's possible a lot of the evidence was lost."

"Tell them to continue looking. We might get lucky. It was just snow! It'll melt. Better than rainfall. You said doppelgangers. Did you locate Katy Becker?"

"Yep. She's at home. And pregnant, just like one of the victims."

Sully's hands froze, and he looked up at them. As Mackenzie explained the details of the similarities and peculiar coincidences, he set the paper aside and took off his glasses. "You're saying Jane Doe One is almost exactly like Katy, and Jane Doe Two was trying to be. Is the latter pregnant?"

"No."

"But she had tattoos," Nick showed him pictures. "A combination of numbers and letters inked on the back of her knees."

Sully glowered at them. "Any idea what these mean?"

"Looking into it."

"She also had signs of long-term drug use. I noted some bruises on her legs were a result of collapsed veins, most likely due to heroin use." Becky showed a picture of Jane Doe Two's shins under a bright light. Her twisty veins ran black and misshapen under her pale skin. "I did the hair follicle test but didn't detect any traces of heroin or any other drug. It could only mean that Jane Doe Two had stopped using recently."

"How far does the test go back?" Sully asked.

"Up to three months."

"Did Jane Doe One do drugs?"

"The test came back negative for her too. But she didn't have any physical signs of drug use so I wasn't expecting anything."

"Jane Doe Two was a junkie in recovery." Sully picked up her picture.

"Her DNA is not on any local or national database. Her dental records didn't find a match anywhere either," Nick said.

"There was no ID on her?"

He shook his head.

Mackenzie wasn't as hopeful, now that the DNA and dental records couldn't identify Jane Doe Two. At most they could print out posters urging the public to help with identification. But the face would still look bloated, unnatural and discolored. She was also a serious drug addict at some point, as was evident from her damaged veins. Based on Mackenzie's experience, it was unlikely that anyone would come forward.

"Jenna is going to ask around in hospitals. Maybe we'll find the doctor who performed this procedure," Nick suggested.

"I know a cosmetic surgeon," Becky said. "Dr. Rees Preston. He owns a private practice here. Used to be based in Seattle, I think. Anyway, I've met him a couple of times. I'd recommend asking him for his expert opinion. Maybe he'll nudge you in the right direction."

"Get on that," Sully instructed Mackenzie and Nick. "Think it's a coincidence they were found in Woodburn Park?"

"That place is clean now."

"Mack, this is Lakemore. No place is *clean*. There might be drug deals going on."

"Neither of them had drugs in their system, and Justin confirmed that no recent arrests have been made in the area. But the bodies both look like Katy. I think this is about her."

"Where are we on forensics?" Sully looked at Becky.

Becky displayed pictures of the bones taken under the microscope. The gray-colored cross-section pictures were labeled as belonging to Jane Doe One and Jane Doe Two, with arrows and circles marking the important findings. "Wound analysis was conducted using scanning electron microscopy and macroscopic observations. The V-shaped incisions in the kerf floor were found in both cases, verifying that the murder weapon was a knife. Jane Doe Two died from being stabbed in the lungs. The blade slid over the rib in a zigzag pattern indicative of a straight thrust. Jane Doe One had two stab wounds. The first thrust punctured the spleen, but it was made at a downward angle, nicking the rib and leaving a cone-shaped mark. The second stab killed her. The knife was thrust into her stomach up to the hilt and then curved upward, causing a hinge fracture of the rib." Becky's long finger tapped at a fragment partially detached from the rest of the bone. "This caused a small portion of the tip of the knife to break." She pulled out another picture showing a tiny piece caught in the ribcage.

Mackenzie frowned at the picture. "It was lodged inside her body."

"Yes. I took it out and ran a microscopic scan. The weapon has a satin finish. But I found something more interesting. Some of the markings on the bones were unusual. It was a single blade knife, but the tears it left in the tissues and organs were consistent with there being another blade."

"A gut hook blade," Mackenzie said just as Becky revealed a picture of the knife she believed to be the murder weapon. The end of the blade had a sharp hook curling back toward the shaft, technically resulting in two tips.

"You know your knives," she beamed.

"I used it for gutting fish in the summer." Sully pulled a gagging face. "Never picking up that hobby again."

"It's used for a lot of other things too," Mackenzie said. "Roofing, opening beer bottles."

Nick looked at Becky. "But you said you think the killer has some knowledge of human anatomy?"

"I believe so. He knew exactly where to strike them. Especially with Jane Doe Two. The stabbing was precise, in between the sternum ribs. And with Jane Doe One he knew to finish the job. If he'd left her after the first stabbing, she could have survived."

"Any idea about the physical characteristics of the assailant?" Sully asked.

"The killer is right-handed based on the distribution of the thrusts. Height is a little difficult to gauge because I have to factor in that there was a struggle involved. But I can confidently say he is between one point five to one point eight meters."

"So five-nine tops? That could be a man or a woman," Nick sighed. "Did you find any other trace evidence?"

"Some tests are still running, but don't be too hopeful. The clothes of the victims have been sent to Anthony at the crime lab. There's a backlog, might take weeks, even. They were underwater for days. That changes things. I found some textile fabric on that broken portion of the blade. It had blue and brown woolen strands from the clothes of the victims."

"The blade was found in Jane Doe Two, who was dressed in the blue sweater." Nick twirled a pen between his fingers. "This means that Jane Doe One was killed first. That's why the brown wool from her sweater dress ended up on the blade. And then Jane Doe Two was killed, leaving traces from both sets of clothes inside her."

Mackenzie imagined the struggle go down. The two Jane Does and an assailant. He killed Jane Doe One first, with precision and speed. Death would have been painful. Her lungs would have filled with blood. She would have dropped to her knees, choking, clutching her throat as blood flooded out of her mouth. Jane Doe Two was with her. The assailant stabbed her on the side but not with the correct technique. A struggle ensued, and he ended up striking her in the face, knocking out her teeth. Cutting into her stomach and curling the knife upward was the fatal blow. He knew that's what would kill her.

"Our killer could be a woman," Mackenzie pointed out. "Statistically unlikely, but there was no sexual assault."

Becky checked her watch. "I have to run and buy pie. I don't have any more updates. Is it okay if I leave?"

Sully dismissed her begrudgingly and tweaked the ends of his mustache. "When are you going to talk to Katy's parents?"

"Tomorrow morning," Mackenzie said.

"I have to apprise Rivera of the latest developments tomorrow. It will help if you have identified at least one of the victims." When he saw Mackenzie raise her eyebrow, he grunted. "You don't know her, Mack. This one is very hands-on."

"Are you hiring more detectives? We've needed someone since Bruce left."

"There is someone over at Port Angeles I have my eye on. Comes highly recommended. Has over five years of experience in the field. But I don't want to say anything right now. We'll see." Absentmindedly, Sully picked up a paper he'd just folded and grazed its edges. He kept brooding at the pictures of the corpses.

Mackenzie knew his mind was racing. "What are you thinking, Sully?"

Sully dropped the paper with a sigh. "I'm not sure about this."

"About what?"

"Jane Doe Two." His face was white as chalk. "Around sixteen years ago, there was a suicide. Hikers found the body of a woman in her early thirties washed up on the shore of the Fresco River. No signs of sexual assault. Her face had signs of cosmetic procedures."

The light fixture overhead hummed.

A fly buzzed.

Nick scratched his scruffy jaw.

"What happened?" Mackenzie asked.

"She was never identified. She was a drug addict like this one—that's all we knew. We never found out why she killed herself."

# CHAPTER NINE

Mackenzie trailed her fingertips over the crime scene photos of the blonde woman found dead by the shore sixteen years ago. She had accessed their record management system and printed out the case details. They stored digital files of the cold cases separately. Cold cases weren't considered "closed," it was just that were no active lines of inquiry. Considering they were never able to ID the woman, it was still a cold case.

The victim's frail body was curled in a ball, concealed by the growing shrubbery around her. She was dressed in a long, flowing white dress. Her lips were parted, her eyes half open. She hadn't been underwater long.

Her face and arms were covered in fresh lacerations. The coroner had concluded that they were sustained from her body being carried by the currents.

There was water in her lungs—drowning killed her. But why did she drown herself? Mackenzie knew those waters. They were famously tumultuous, being downstream of a dam. She closed her eyes and saw the unnamed woman sinking down into the black water. Her arms flailed wildly. Her hair floated around her like seaweed. The inky water dragged her down.

"That's an uncommon way to kill yourself," Nick said from her side.

"Maybe she didn't. What if someone pushed her off the bridge?"

"No. They have multiple witness accounts and a video of her jumping." He passed another part of the investigative report.

She read over the statements. "Some of them said she was standing and staring at the water for a few minutes before taking the leap. No one tried talking her out of it?"

"One person did. By the time he called for help she'd jumped."

"Just one?" Mackenzie was aghast.

"It's the bystander effect." Nick crossed his arms. "Sometimes people *don't* intervene if there's a group of people present."

Her heart sank as she recalled the theory. "They think that someone else will, or already has, and delay acting."

"Yep. Were there any drugs or alcohol in her system?"

"No," she confirmed. "Toxicology screen was clean. But she used to be an intravenous drug user based on the needle marks on her arms."

Nick paused. "An ex-addict. Like our Jane Doe Two."

"They ran the Fresco River woman's DNA but didn't find any matches."

He patted his pockets for a cigarette pack. Realizing he was out, he waggled his jaw. "Have they run it against updated databases?"

Mackenzie quickly skimmed the document. "A few years ago. Still no match. Do we still have the body?"

"Nope. Seven years ago it was released to a funeral home with a government contract."

"Damn it," she muttered. "They didn't find any ID on her. No tattoos. And it was ruled a suicide."

He tapped his finger against his lip. "Sixteen years ago, a drug addict with a surgically modified face committed suicide. And now, someone like that is murdered. What's the connection?"

Mackenzie showed him the ViCAP alert issued by the FBI sixteen years ago. Someone in Lakemore had called in a tip that the victim looked like her neighbor. "Carrie Breslow. She was thirty years old at the time. A schoolteacher. The police went to her house and found her alive, playing with her daughter. Her husband, Owen, is an engineer and was out of state at the time of the suicide."

"Sounds familiar, doesn't it?"

"Yup." She drummed her fingers on the edge of her desk. "I might have thought it a coincidence, but signs of cosmetic work? That's oddly specific. There has to be some other connection."

She took out disinfectant wipes from a drawer and began scrubbing her desk clean, to Nick's amusement.

"Do you want to ask Katy if she knows Carrie?"

Ignoring the teasing smile in his voice, she bent down and wiped the underside of her desk. "We can go now. I want to show Katy pictures of the clothes the victims were wearing. We should speak to Carrie too, if possible."

A quick search through their database coughed up Carrie Breslow's address. It was the same as before. Maybe she would know why a woman would go through the trouble of looking like her, only to kill herself.

# CHAPTER TEN

Mackenzie knocked loudly on the door and rocked back and forth on her heels.

"You sure you're okay?" Nick asked.

"How many more times will you ask me that?"

"Until you tell me the truth. You look like you're high on caffeine. Which you don't drink."

"It's the cold," she blurted. She had accidentally worn the wrong boots and the cold puddle water had seeped into her socks, threatening to freeze her toes. "Don't you have big Thanksgiving plans?"

"Yeah. Me and bourbon watching the parade rerun."

"You don't have Luna this year?"

"I have her for Christmas so she's spending today with Shelly."

Katy opened the door, looking healthier than the day before. Dressed in a baggy sweater and yoga pants, her hair looked untangled and her skin devoid of blackheads.

"Please come in."

"I like your earrings," Mackenzie said. "You look better today, Katy."

She touched her gold earrings and smiled. "Yeah, it's been a relatively good day. Cole made sure I did some yoga this morning."

"Sorry for disturbing you on Thanksgiving."

"Don't worry about it," Katy waved her hand. "I'm too weak to do anything really. And the smell of poultry makes me nauseous, so turkey is out of the question. We're just going to stay in and watch a movie."

Cole was in the kitchen chopping vegetables. Mackenzie's eyes flashed to the sharp knife in his hands. Cole was about the right height to be the killer, according to the range predicted by Becky. He took off his apron and greeted them with a nervous nod. "Did you find anything?"

"Not yet. We'll let you know." Mackenzie spotted a book of baby names on the table.

Katy followed her eyes and smiled brightly. "We're shortlisting some names for her."

"Her?" Nick asked.

"We'll find out in a couple of weeks." Cole put an arm around Katy.

"It's just a feeling I have. That it's a girl," Katy said softly.

Mackenzie's face fell. The intimate exchange between Katy and Cole couldn't be missed. The softness in their eyes and the nervous gulps they took. They were scared but happy. The good kind of butterflies. The kind Mackenzie had when she was about to marry Sterling.

"Do you know who those women are?" Cole asked.

"Not yet. We should have some answers by tonight," Mackenzie said. "I wanted to show you the clothes and jewelry the victims were wearing. Because they look like you, we're just ticking off some boxes."

"S-sure," Katy shuddered.

They sat down as Mackenzie pulled out the pictures of the sweater dress, wedding band, and necklace with a Gemini zodiac pendant. She handed them over. Katy's lips were pursed in concentration as she took her time. "That looks like my wedding band. The rest, I don't recognize."

"Wait," Cole said from her side. "Go back to the previous one. This dress!"

"What about it?"

"Katy, isn't this the one you bought a month ago from that factory outlet close to Everett?"

"Is it?" She looked again at the picture, and her eyes widened. "Oh my God! It looks exactly like that."

It was the dress Jane Doe One had been wearing, the pregnant doppelganger that could be Katy's twin.

"Do you want to check if you still have it?" Nick suggested.

Katy rushed up to her bedroom at lightning speed—a stark contrast from her slumbering the day before. They heard closet doors open and shut and footsteps shuffle. A few minutes later, Katy reappeared with a trembling chin.

"It's not there," she whispered.

She almost lost her balance on the stairs, and Cole hurried to hold her. "Careful."

"Are you sure you checked everywhere?" Mackenzie asked.

"Even the laundry room."

"Maybe you gave it to someone?"

"I didn't!" she cried. "What does this mean?"

Mackenzie and Nick looked at each other uneasily. Nick cleared his throat when he spoke. "It could be a coincidence, or someone could have been here."

"And stole my *clothes*?" She raised her eyebrows. Her eyes were teary and her knuckles red as she clutched Cole's shirt in her fists. "That's insane."

"We can get a patrol officer to guard your house," Nick offered.

"Please." Cole clenched his jaw.

"It will help if you can go through the house and make us a list of anything else you think might be missing," Mackenzie said. "There is another matter we'd like to discuss."

"Do you know anyone by the name Carrie Breslow?" Nick asked.

They shook their heads.

"Around sixteen years ago, a woman killed herself. She had undergone cosmetic procedures to look more like Carrie. Like in this case: one of the woman's faces was made to look like yours.

With surgery." Nick paused, giving them a moment to absorb the information.

Cole's jaw hung open. "*What*? I don't know what to think."

"We don't have enough information yet, but this is a big coincidence." Mackenzie looked at Katy. "Are you sure you haven't heard of this person?"

"No. I mean, yes. I'm s-sure I haven't." Her forehead crumpled. "Did they find out who that woman was?"

"No. It's a cold case. We're going to start looking into that and hopefully find a connection."

Mackenzie and Nick spent more time going over the Beckers' statements again and their activities over the past week. They didn't contradict anything they mentioned before. If anything, Katy was more verbose and confident.

Stepping outside, Mackenzie hugged her coat around her tighter. She was carefully navigating her way back to the car, avoiding the sporadic ice patches, when another movement caught her attention.

"What?" Nick followed her gaze to the bluish-green neighboring house, the one with the electric snowman already in the yard.

"We should talk to that neighbor." Mackenzie narrowed her eyes at the peach-colored curtain still fluttering.

"Why? Justin can gather the generic statements."

"She keeps peeking."

He rolled his eyes. "You're such a keeno. Okay."

After two rings, the door opened a few inches. A face appeared in the space. The woman's doe-like eyes flitted between Mackenzie and Nick. "Yes?"

Mackenzie flashed her badge. "Mind if we ask you some questions?"

She pressed her lips in a thin line and left the door ajar.

The layout of the house was a mirror reflection of the Beckers', except this house hadn't been renovated. The wooden tables had cabriole legs. The couch and armchairs were covered in dated upholstery with a flowery pattern. A grandfather clock stood imposingly in a corner. A shelf running along the length of one wall displayed miniature dollhouses.

The house was clean and the clutter was organized, but the sheer abundance of things irked Mackenzie. She stuffed her hands in her pockets.

"I'm Delilah Pine," the woman said and looked at Nick. "Would you like some tea?"

"No, thanks," Nick said.

She looked disappointed. She already had an elaborate tea set out—something Mackenzie would reserve for guests. "How can I help you?"

Delilah Pine reminded Mackenzie of an overflowing bucket of water. This woman had a lot to say but for now she was holding back. Mackenzie could see it in her twitchy eyes and trembling fists. But she was all about decorum. When she held the teacup, her pinkie finger stuck out straight.

"Are you friends with the Beckers?" Mackenzie asked.

"Not really. It's not like I didn't make an effort. When they moved here, I sent over lasagna. But when my husband died, they were the only ones who didn't even bother sending a casserole."

"Oh, I'm sorry for your loss," Nick said.

"Thank you. Are they in trouble? I've seen you visit twice."

Mackenzie was relieved that she wouldn't have to draw information out of Delilah. She looked eager to help. "Not exactly, Mrs. Pine. We found two bodies and just want to know what Cole and Katy know about it."

"*Bodies*?" The teacup almost tipped from her hand. She set it on the table and looked at Nick. "Like murder?"

"We're not at liberty to share much."

"Are they suspects?" Her eyes bugged out. "I knew Katy would end up getting involved in something."

"Why would you say that?"

"She's too opinionated. She doesn't have to be vocal about *everything*."

Sheppard Hallows had a reputation for being uptight. The middle-class community was respectable and safe. Acceptable topics of conversation probably included recipes, weather, the annual local art show, and football. Always football. Anything with a tinge of controversy would be understandably brushed aside, which is why politics, social issues, and global events were likely considered inappropriate. There was an unspoken rule in such neighborhoods, an implicit understanding. Their logic was to promote unity and *civility*.

"Did she get into a disagreement with anyone local?" Mackenzie asked.

"She can't get into disagreements with anyone because no one talks to her in this neighborhood," Delilah said, again addressing Nick.

Mackenzie and Nick exchanged a knowing look. Delilah was fishing for information. They'd also realized that Delilah answered only to Nick, even when Mackenzie was asking the questions.

"How are Cole and Katy otherwise, Mrs. Pine?" Mackenzie pressed. "Do you know anything about them?"

She smirked and looked at Nick. "They fight a lot."

"How do you know?" Nick asked.

"The walls are thin. I'm not a creep." She flipped her hair back. "You'll be surprised at the things you know if you keep your eyes and ears open."

She was baiting them with a little waggle of her eyebrows and a coy smile playing on her lips.

Nick leaned forward, performatively taking the bait. "Like what, Mrs. Pine?"

"Like the fact that Cole goes somewhere on Thursday and Saturday nights. And sometimes at other times, when Katy is either out at work or visiting her parents."

Mackenzie offered, "Maybe he goes to some class or the gym?"

She rolled her eyes. "My late husband was sleeping with his boss for around a year before he died. Trust me. I know how a man acts when he's going to a class versus going someplace he doesn't want to be followed."

"Did you ever follow him?" Nick asked.

"Of course not."

"Have you ever seen anyone you don't recognize visit them? Anyone suspicious?"

"No. Katy's family and the cleaner, Maria, are frequent visitors. Cole has a brother who lives on the east coast and visits on Thanksgiving with his partner. Katy's co-workers sometimes drop by with their spouses to celebrate happy hour."

She continued listing the people who visited the Beckers—and how often. It was clear Delilah was a shut-in. Mackenzie could sniff the staleness in the air.

"Well, thank you for your time." Nick stood up with Mackenzie. "If you think of anything else or see anything, please let us know."

Delilah shot up quickly. "You didn't give me your contact information."

"You can just call the police and ask for Detective Blackwood or Price," Nick said.

On their way to the car, Mackenzie let out the giggle she was holding.

"Shut up," he muttered.

"Why didn't you give her your card, Nick?" she asked, getting inside the car.

"Because I don't want to wake up with her standing by the foot of my bed with a knife."

He started the engine and turned up the heat. The hot air fanned Mackenzie's face, making her eyes droopy. "I almost asked if she likes you or if she likes men to be in charge."

"I almost asked how her husband died."

# CHAPTER ELEVEN

On their way back from the Beckers', Mackenzie and Nick visited Dr. Rees Preston, the cosmetic surgeon Becky had recommended they consult. Preston presided over a private practice in a medical complex that housed various other services. Located close to Forrest Hill, the few rich residents of Lakemore flocked to the place. It smelled like a spa. Preston's practice occupied the entire top floor. A koi pond was situated in the waiting area. Green vines dropped from the wall behind the reception desk. There was a skylight above, making the room bright and cheerful. Mackenzie was appreciating the appealing aromas and gentle babbling of the interior waterfall when she heard someone walking towards them.

When Mackenzie looked at him, she was slightly taken aback. Preston was a tall man with a strong build. He had broad shoulders that tapered into a narrow waist. His hair was thick, blond and glossy and his skin was sun-kissed without any blemishes. His nose was long and sharp, his face perfectly symmetrical, his eyes gray.

He looked like a Ken doll. Utterly handsome and molded into the kind of "perfection" the world was socially conditioned to recognize.

"You must be Detectives Price and Blackwood. Becky—Dr. Sullivan—told me you would visit. I'm Rees Preston." He offered his hand with a dazzling smile.

"Thank you for seeing us today," Nick said.

"It's a good thing to catch a break at work before heading into big family reunions. Trust me."

Preston led them into his minimalistic office. A series of photographs of a woman's face getting more enhanced were displayed on a wall. "Please take a seat. I met Becky at a conference in Seattle a few years ago. I made a joke about consulting on her cases. The offer was genuine, but it seems I should have been more sensitive in how I made it."

"So what kind of work do you do, exactly?" Nick asked, scooting along the couch.

"Any kind of enhancements." He gestured to the hanging pictures. "The stereotype holds true. Most of our clients are women above forty. It gets a bit repetitive sometimes. We also have a tie-up with Lakemore General and assist in plastics."

"And how many doctors are there in your practice?"

"Five, including myself. We have clients from across the state." His hypnotic eyes fixed on Mackenzie. "You have a striking face, Detective Price."

"Sorry?"

"You have an aquiline nose." His long fingers drummed the arms of the chair. "A prominent bridge and slightly curved. What laymen call a Roman nose. My mentor back in medical school told me that it was the best kind of nose to be born with. It combines elegance and power."

"We were hoping you could give us some information," Mackenzie cleared her throat and passed him the picture of Jane Doe Two's face.

Preston picked up the pictures and studied them curiously. His eyes narrowed into slits. "Interesting."

"Excuse me?"

"Becky said that this woman was made to look like someone else?"

"Yes." Mackenzie hesitated but showed him a picture of Katy on her phone. "Her."

Preston's eyes bounced between the two. "Yes. You can see some natural similarities between them."

"Like what?" Nick asked.

"The mental protuberance is similar." He traced Jane Doe's chin. "Both have a wide zygomatic arch and the same mandible angle. Complexion falls close on the spectrum."

"But these surgical enhancements were made to increase her likeness to Katy?"

Preston nodded. "That's right, Detective Blackwood, but this technique is outdated. *Crude*, even."

"What do you mean?" Mackenzie asked.

"Do you see this big incision along her hairline?" He pointed at it. "She got coronal brow lifts. They were popular in the eighties and the early nineties. Since then endoscopic lifts have taken over—they're far less invasive."

"Why would anyone use an old technique?"

"I don't know. It's frankly a little offensive—a touch unethical, even. I have to give it to this doctor, though." He cracked a hazy smile. "He's definitely skilled, just working with old knowledge. These alterations would make her look more like the subject. Do you see the differences in their eyebrow region?"

Katy's were higher and tighter. They nodded.

"The brow lift is a trick to make the patient's supra-orbital notches—in other words their eyebrow region—match."

"Was there any other work done?" Nick asked.

"There's a good chance that lip fillers were injected, since the thickness of their lips look exactly the same, which is very rare. I can't tell that from a picture. I'd have to look at the body for that. Their noses match too—both have a 'pinched tip' and nasal bridge of the same length. Highly unlikely for two people to have such similar features."

"But you can't tell just from looking if rhinoplasty was performed?"

"Oh, no. This was done well, that's why. Like I said, his technique is flawless, but he's using some old procedures. I'm speaking on the balance of probability, based on seeing the similarities side by side."

"But the coronal brow lift is obvious because of the scar?"

"Yes, yes. Those take time to fade away. It was likely the last procedure conducted on her."

"There were multiple?"

He smiled. "Oh, yes. Spanning months, I'd predict."

Nick showed him pictures of the suicide victim, Jane Doe Three, and Carrie Breslow. "Sorry, this is really old so the quality isn't good. But she also had work done to her face to make her look like *this* woman."

Preston frowned and spent no more than a minute assessing them. "Good effort, but careless. He's removed too much cartilage during rhinoplasty, which is why their noses still look noticeably different."

"Do you think they were conducted by the same person?" Mackenzie asked.

"I honestly can't say."

They asked some routine questions and verified that none of the women were clients of the practice.

Outside the clinic, Nick took a cigarette case from his pocket and played with it absentmindedly. It had been a gift from Mackenzie a few years ago. "Either this doctor doesn't know better or he didn't get access to what he needed."

"These endoscopic brow lifts started coming in in the nineties. The suicide happened in 2003. The timeline makes sense. I can believe some surgeons take time to adopt new techniques," Mackenzie said.

"If we can find this doctor, we can find out who is taking these women to him."

"And like Preston said, it could be different surgeons."

"What I don't get is the sixteen-year gap in between. Chances are that it's the same person, right?"

"Could be. What if there isn't a sixteen-year gap?"

Nick nodded, understanding what Mackenzie meant. What if there were others out there? Scores of women who had been surgically enhanced to look like someone else? It wasn't just the cold air that made Mackenzie shiver as they walked back to the car.

# CHAPTER TWELVE

A starless night fell over Lakemore. The black sky felt like rock above, trapping the town in a cave. As Mackenzie's feet pounded the gravel and she pushed her body forward, puffs of gray rose around her. Slivers of moonlight leaked through the cracks in the thick soot-like clouds suspended above the sky.

Mackenzie looked ahead at the empty street. The concrete glistened under the streetlights. A spooky, ominous chill enveloped her.

Usually, she went for runs in the mornings. There was always some activity around her. If not a garbage truck then at least the birds chirping. Now, Lakemore stood still and claustrophobic under an opaque sky that seemed to hang lower than usual. Like it was trying to crush the diminishing town.

Mackenzie's thighs burned. She took a different route—away from Hidden Lake. Far away. She didn't know whose bones were buried there. She didn't want to know.

Eight years after he "disappeared," Melody had filed a petition with the county court to declare Robert dead. The petition was approved. Robert Price had been missing for eight years. He hadn't contacted any family or friends. The police were unable to locate him. Now that he had shown up, it would lead to a lot of paperwork, with insurance companies getting involved. It could open up an investigation with the police. If Melody had received any social security benefits then the FBI could get involved, too. Companies might even choose to sue Robert.

Mackenzie had no clue what had happened to Robert's assets. She didn't know if he'd had any. She didn't even know who their estate lawyer was. She had only been twelve years old, completely oblivious to how complicated the adult world was. Melody had taken care of everything. The house was sold off three years after Robert "died." When Mackenzie turned eighteen, she was able to access a trust fund set up for her. It had been enough money for her to never worry about college. Not that she needed to—she had a full scholarship. She used that money to pay for her share of the down payment for the house. Growing up, she was acutely aware of their limited means and humble lifestyle. It had struck her as odd that she had come into a fairly large amount of money.

In short, Robert being back would lead to a mess. Mackenzie wasn't even sure what the exact procedure would be like. She had never dealt with someone returning from the dead. But she knew it would lead to questions.

She stopped abruptly. How much more could she lie? How long before the truth came out? She had been checking Robert's phone activity religiously. Still nothing suspicious. He read a lot and rented a lot of movies. The only person he contacted was her.

*Do you want to meet today? It's Thanksgiving.*

*Busy. Tomorrow.*

Mackenzie had considered looking into who had died that night. She knew where to start. She could look up the people who went missing in Lakemore twenty years ago—assuming that the man on her kitchen floor was from Lakemore. Then she could follow up on those cases; her unit was in charge of cold cases as well. But, contrary to popular belief, it wasn't easy for police officers and detectives to access old records. They had to have a solid reason and official permission—like she'd had for the Jane Doe Three records that morning. They weren't allowed to search through databases out of curiosity. If Mackenzie went down that road, she'd have to come clean, lose her reputation and potentially even her job.

Even if there was some way to cut through the red tape—call in a favor or lie—was she ready to find out the truth about that night? What if she found out the identity of that man? What if he had a family? What if they were still waiting for him to come home?

Her throat tightened. Her breath came out in painful hiccups. A force tugged at her ribcage, pulling it inward into her heart. She dropped to her knees. She hadn't felt like this in a while. She looked around her. The emptiness of her surroundings inflated a sense of doom. She was alone in this.

She didn't have the strength to run back. Her tongue was dry and heavy in her mouth. A sudden wave of fatigue overcame her. Home was too far away. Realizing she was only a five-minute walk from Nick's place, she decided to stop by to catch her breath.

Her skin was flushed and matted with sweat by the time she was knocking on his door.

Nick opened the door and frowned. "What the hell's wrong with you?"

"I-I ran," she panted.

"I can tell. That's why I asked."

"Can I come in?"

He moved aside to let her in. She went straight to the kitchen and poured herself a glass of water. As she guzzled the liquid, she felt his eyes on her back.

"Sorry for showing up unannounced."

"Are you having a breakdown?" He narrowed his eyes at her.

"No!" she said defensively, then sighed. "I don't know."

He leaned against the refrigerator and crossed his arms. "Well, are you going to tell me?"

"I... I shouldn't."

"This has nothing to do with Sterling, does it?"

She shook her head.

"What is it?"

"Can you promise not to tell anyone?"

"Why? Did you kill someone?" His lips curled in a mocking smile.

Mackenzie flustered. She grabbed the edge of the counter behind her. Nick's eyes raked over her. "Mack... what happened?"

She licked her lips. "My father's back."

The words poured out of her. How her father had returned. How she had spent weeks confirming his story in Dallas and Vegas. How she was going to invite him to live with her. The truth about the last few weeks, built on lies from twenty years ago.

Fifteen minutes later, they were sitting in Nick's living room. She pressed the cold white wine bottle to her forehead. He turned a glass of bourbon in his hands, catching the light refracting through the sculpted glass.

"Does he have a bank account?" Nick asked.

Mackenzie frowned at the strange question. "I don't think so. He's using cash."

"Under his real name at the motel, though? Not Freddie whatever?"

"Yeah."

"Has he talked to anyone except for you?"

"Apparently not. Perhaps some other customers at the motel? Why are you asking these questions?"

"He should continue to stay off the radar. Avoid anything that would require him to produce paperwork." He scratched his temple. "If he goes to the bank or anything, it would lead to an unnecessary investigation."

"So you won't tell anyone?"

He looked at her in disbelief. "Of course not! This is personal. You've got a lot to figure out. Best do it without any interference. But if anything strange happens, you'll tell me, right?"

She nodded.

"You should get a paternity test."

"Paternity test?" She pulled a face. There was no need to. She knew what her father looked like.

"He has a ridiculous backstory about gambling debts and Mexico—"

"Which I confirmed. Not all of it. Trail kind of goes cold in Vegas, but it was so long ago."

"I know. But we're now investigating a case with twins. You should confirm it."

"That's bizarre."

"As bizarre as your father showing up at your doorstep after twenty years?" he challenged.

Mackenzie swallowed hard and nodded stiffly. It was a logical suggestion. The next reasonable step to take in a situation like this. As a trained detective, she knew to confirm every piece of information, not to rely on words and memory.

Then why was she resisting?

# CHAPTER THIRTEEN

*November 23*

There was a storm coming in two days. Just when the snow had melted enough to reveal the hidden green and brown hues of the town, fresh blankets of snow were on the way to swallow Lakemore up again. As a result, people were beginning to stock up on supplies. Mackenzie climbed out of the car and jogged through the numbing air to the grocery store. It was packed for a Friday morning. She took off her gloves and grabbed a cart, her eyes scanning the customers for her father.

She hated grocery shopping. It was Sterling's responsibility. Mackenzie's job was to keep the house clean, whereas her husband was in charge of the kitchen and anything kitchen-related. She baked, but cooking and grocery shopping weren't her domain. Now she had to adapt to this new life.

Absentmindedly, she threw items into her cart, more focused on finding Robert. She spotted him in the meat section. She threaded through the crowd and some glaring customers. Picking up ground beef, she pretended to look engrossed, knowing he would notice her anytime.

"Micky?" he said.

She jerked and feigned surprise. "Oh! What are you doing here?"

Robert shrugged, "What everyone's doing I guess. How come you're here? This store is far from your place."

"Yeah, I thought I should pick up some stuff on my way to work."

The truth was she had followed him, tracking his location through the app. She had wondered if he was meeting someone, but he was by himself.

"Your mother used to take care of these things," he reminisced, his fingers twitching, as they walked around together. "I feel very guilty, Micky. Was she better after I left?"

Mackenzie didn't know. Robert looked at her, clearly hoping she would say yes. "I-I don't know. After you left, she sent me to New York to live with my grandmother. Did you never think of contacting her after you left?"

He stilled. "No. I thought of you and her often. But it was better for me to stay away. To give you the life you deserved."

Mackenzie's eyes stung as she held back tears. Those years in New York had been lonely. Her grandmother had done the best she could, but then she got cancer and was frequently in and out of the hospital. Mackenzie had to grow up and take care of the house. She drifted away from her friends, whose crises around boys and test scores seemed unimportant to her. And then there was Melody.

*Mom, when are you coming to visit?*

*I have to cancel again. Sorry. Next time. I promise.*

"Why did Mel send you to New York?" Robert asked. They tiptoed around each other, trying to gather little pieces of each other's lives.

"She wanted to keep me away from the 'circus,' she said. With the authorities and Lakemore being even smaller than it is now. And New York had better schools."

"Good call. She stayed here the entire time?"

"Yeah."

"You must have missed her terribly."

The last conversation she had with her mother was so vivid. Melody had come to see Mackenzie after a year apart. Her mother's touch had felt so foreign to her.

*"Grandma got cancer and had chemo. And instead of coming here to help, you let the entire responsibility fall on your teenage daughter."*

*"Your father's cousin turned up. She thought I kept him isolated and that I was abusive. The police got interested, and I had to stick around to make sure that we were safe."*

*"Do you regret it? Do I remind you of what we did? Is that why you've been avoiding me? Because you feel guilty?"*

Sharing the secret of burying Robert in the woods had driven them further apart. In a twisted way, she'd thought that it would bring them closer together, but it had just made them more distrustful of one another.

Turns out she was right not to trust Melody. Looking at her father, very much alive, she wondered who her mother had truly been. Had Mackenzie been sent away, not because she was too traumatized to continue living in Lakemore, but because Melody was guarding a secret? The thought made the back of her neck break into a cold sweat.

She turned to face Robert. "Actually, I was meaning to talk to you later, but might as well do it now. I'd like you to live with me."

Robert's eyes widened. "Really?"

It had struck her how naive he must think she was. Inviting trouble inside her home—a man who did nothing but beat her mother after drinking too much. But she wanted him right under her nose. She straightened and gave him the firm look she had mastered over the years. The sharp gaze and hard face that made people wilt.

"Yes. That is, if you're comfortable. There's a guest room where you can stay. I've spoken with my husband as well. We are separated, but he's still a part of my life."

"I see." He eyed her cautiously. "If you're sure about this..."

"I am. You can move in tonight."

"I'd like for us to be a family. Thank you."

The word *family* made her queasy, as did the thought of living with Robert again after years of having his memory taunt her at every turn and remind her what she had done. She left the store, bidding him farewell and praying she wasn't making a big mistake.

Mackenzie was never a fan of jigsaw puzzles growing up. In hindsight, it made sense. She liked to solve problems, but she needed more than to simply piece information together. She wanted to know *why*. She liked stakes.

The pictures of the tattoos on Jane Doe Two's body lay in her lap. *What odd places for a tattoo*, she thought. Not that Mackenzie was particularly au fait with tattoo culture, but she reckoned these locations on the body were uncommon. They weren't private either, easily exposed if the legs weren't covered. Why had she got them? Who was this woman?

"39A" on the back of her left knee.

"B75C" on the back of her right knee.

Mackenzie had seen flowers, waves, skulls, and even words like "breathe" inked on skin. She had never come across a random bag of letters and numbers. Sometimes reformed prisoners would get their prison number tattooed, but this wasn't that. If Jane Doe Two had ever been to prison, her DNA would have shown up on the national index. Her tattoos didn't correspond to a date, either. But they must be important.

Hopelessly, she typed the codes into a search engine. The internet yielded nothing useful, as expected.

Jane Doe Two had been a heavy drug user. What if the codes on her body corresponded to the chemical compound or serial number of some drug? But the codes weren't structured right.

There should be four numbers representing the labeler and product code and the last three digits standing for a package code. Still, Mackenzie checked the NDC Directory.

Nothing.

It hit her that the numbers and letters could be jumbled. She noted down the letters and digits on a piece of paper. Why would Jane Doe Two go to so much trouble? If she tattooed these on her body, then they must mean something. It certainly wasn't for aesthetic purposes.

A faint sound drew her attention. She turned around to find Finn, another senior detective in the unit, watching the expert analysis on some big football game. He sighed dejectedly and closed the tab. When he left the office, his feet dragged and his shoulders were slumped. Mackenzie knew it had nothing to do with work. She could tell that even the little things not going his way were getting on his nerves. He wasn't the only one feeling that way; she felt it too.

"Detective Price." Lieutenant Rivera appeared by her side. Mackenzie almost shot up but Rivera gestured for her to remain seated. "Sully discussed the case with me yesterday. Any new updates?"

"Jane Doe One is Katy's twin, but Katy didn't know about her."

"You're going to talk to her parents?"

"Yeah. Today."

"In Nelson Heights?" Rivera placed her elbow on the cubicle wall separating Mackenzie and Troy's spaces.

"Yep." Mackenzie restrained a smile. Sully was right. Her working style was a lot different from the former lieutenant's. "We also talked to their neighbor yesterday. She thinks the husband is having an affair."

Rivera raised her eyebrows. "That's not a shocker."

Mackenzie felt the back of her neck warm. Rivera's eyes swept over her.

"Keep me apprised," Rivera said after a heartbeat.

Mackenzie gave her a grudging smile. She knew that her boss had caught her moment of vulnerability. Rivera was good at reading people; it was a job requirement. But it flustered Mackenzie that she had become easy to read. That was unacceptable to her.

"The suicide from sixteen years ago. Where are you on that?"

"We have Carrie Breslow's address, but she and her husband are on vacation. She was the person Jane Doe Three's face was modeled on."

"What do you think?" She tipped her chin.

"It's too early to form any conclusions. Katy said she hasn't heard that name before."

"We have Jane Doe Three's DNA on file and our Jane Doe's. Tell Becky to run a familial DNA test. The victims could be related."

# CHAPTER FOURTEEN

Nelson Heights was a gated community on the edge of Lakemore. It was a short drive from this side of the town to Olympia, and the neighborhood attracted old people and families with special needs who needed easy access to the vastly better hospitals and services in the larger city. It housed the only two retirement homes in town and had apartment complexes as opposed to houses—to encourage interactions and activities.

A few years ago, Mackenzie had moved her grandmother, Eleanor, from New York to a retirement home here. The last time she had been here was after they'd called to tell her Eleanor had passed away in her sleep.

Katy's mother, Charlotte Harris, reminded Mackenzie a lot of her grandmother. Not only did they both have a strapping physique, but also a firm calmness on their face.

Charlotte's husband, Frank, was quiet, bored, and grumpy. Occasionally, he looked out the window through his horn-rimmed glasses, searching for something interesting. Then his eyes trailed back around his apartment with the same monotony. Mackenzie couldn't tell if he didn't want to talk to *them* or to *anyone*.

"Cole told us what happened," Charlotte said in her throaty voice. "Please have some cucumber sandwiches."

"Don't mind me." Nick picked up two and stuffed them into his mouth.

"Have you talked to Katy?" Mackenzie asked.

"Briefly. She wasn't feeling well again, so we decided not to impose on Thanksgiving and did something with our friends instead. Difficult pregnancies run in the family." Charlotte held her husband's hand. "You said that one of the bodies was entirely identical to Katy?"

"Yes. She looks *exactly* like her."

Her words pulled Frank into the conversation. His face was ashen. "Oh my God."

Charlotte pinched the bridge of her nose and closed her eyes.

"What happened?" Mackenzie asked.

Frank looked at Charlotte almost helplessly. Like he was used to her taking charge. When she looked up at Mackenzie and Nick, her eyes were bloodshot. "I… that was Kim. Katy's twin. We gave her up a very long time ago."

"Why?"

"She was always different." Charlotte took out a handkerchief from her pocket and dabbed her eyes. "Even when she was just two years old, she had this temper. She would smear her dirty diapers over furniture and bang her head against the wall. Her outbursts became more aggressive, and when she was three years old, I took her to a doctor." Her eyes turned ghostly. "At first, it was ADHD and then she was bipolar and then borderline personality disorder and then split personality disorder."

"At the age of three?" Nick asked.

"It happens. Katy was badly affected by all this. Most of the time, Kim's anger was directed at her. She would scratch Katy hard enough to draw blood, punch her, kick her…"

"And then cry inconsolably out of guilt," Frank added.

"We tried *everything*." Charlotte's nostrils flared. "When the twins were four years old, I became pregnant again. Kim didn't improve with age or medication. One day, she threw a tantrum and pushed me down the stairs. *On purpose.* I was eight months pregnant. I lost my son."

Mackenzie had never dealt with a sociopathic child in her career, but she found it hard to believe a four-year-old could hurt someone like that on purpose.

"I'm the only one who knew what she was," Charlotte said, noticing Mackenzie's look of disbelief. "She was becoming impossible to deal with and dangerous to Katy. We had to keep Kim away from her. My brother and his wife didn't have children of their own and desperately wanted one. We were honest about Kim's condition to them, but my sister-in-law was a psychiatrist. She convinced us that perhaps a change in environment would help her."

"We agreed," Frank pitched in. "It gave me some relief that her sister-in-law was qualified, and that Kim would still stay in the family."

Charlotte continued, "We used to visit her when she was living with them. We never took Katy. It was best not to confuse her, especially since Kim wasn't ready to come back into our lives. But when Kim turned nine and still showed no signs of improvement, my sister-in-law suggested the best course of action was to get her admitted to a treatment center. She was too much for them to handle. I'm surprised and grateful that they cared for her for five years. My sister-in-law's training helped. Unfortunately, when Kim was fourteen years old, she ran away."

"From the treatment center?" Nick asked.

"Yes. She could be very charming if she wanted to be. Probably sweet-talked the security guard," Charlotte scowled. "We never found her. We didn't know what happened to her… until now."

"Katy doesn't remember her at all?"

"We used to discourage their interaction to protect Katy. And when Kim went away, it was easier to lie to Katy that Kim was her imaginary friend. She's a *good* girl. She doesn't deserve to live with this burden. Though she always said that she felt like something was missing from her life."

Frank had checked out of the conversation again and stared outside. His hand went limp in Charlotte's. Mackenzie wondered if that was his way of coping. It couldn't have been an easy decision to part with a child. And then that child disappeared. Did he feel guilty for what became of her?

"You never told anyone about Kim?" Mackenzie asked.

"No. A year after Kim was admitted, we packed our bags and moved from Oklahoma to Washington to prevent Katy finding out about her from someone else. The center kept us informed; they had to. But her treatment was going nowhere. We gave up hope."

"Did you visit her at the center?"

"Not after we moved." Charlotte blinked away her tears. "I know it seems heartless to you, Detective. But you have no idea how painful it was to realize that we had to let go."

Charlotte and Frank gave the name of the treatment facility in Oklahoma City where they'd admitted Kim. They also said that Katy's behavior hadn't been entirely unusual, just that her phone calls had been more sporadic in the last few days.

"What do you think of Cole?" Mackenzie asked.

"He's a good husband. He's always kind to us and takes care of Katy. He's a very good physiotherapist. Fixed Frank's sciatica."

"Have Cole and Katy ever had any problems?" Nick asked.

"Every marriage has problems." Charlotte rolled her eyes. "They fight, they make up."

"Do you know anyone by the name Carrie Breslow?"

"Carrie Breslow?" She looked at Frank, who shrugged. "No. Should we?"

"It's alright. If you think of anything, please let us know. We'll be in touch either way." He handed her his card.

"I'm sure whatever Kim was involved in has nothing to do with Katy. This is all nothing but a terrible coincidence. I'd hate for Katy to be troubled by this."

As they left the apartment, a spine-tingling thought came to Mackenzie. She didn't believe any of this to be a coincidence. There was a reason why Kim ended up in Lakemore. That reason had to be Katy.

# CHAPTER FIFTEEN

Mackenzie stuffed her mouth with another dumpling. The rich taste exploded in her mouth. Sterling sat next to her and fiddled with his watch; he hadn't touched the food. She'd ordered Chinese for dinner, unable and unwilling to cook. Sterling would leave right after anyway. Robert was already fifteen minutes late. She knew she should have waited before she started eating. But she'd been polite enough already.

"Is he even coming?" Sterling asked, irritated.

She set down her chopsticks. "You can leave if you have somewhere else to be. I didn't ask you to come tonight."

He ignored her jab. "I'm just saying. He did walk out and not bother to check in for twenty years."

"He gets to live here rent-free and eat my food. He'll be here." She resumed eating, surprised at how detached she sounded.

"That doesn't bother you?"

"Anger comes when expectations are defied, Sterling." She dunked the dumpling in rice vinegar. "And I have none."

"Have you thought about us?" he asked gently, placing his hand on hers. His finger grazed over her wedding band. The corners of his eyes creased with relief.

"I need more time." Her voice broke, and she withdrew her hand from underneath his.

"How much time?"

She gritted her teeth. "You shouldn't complain. It means that I still give our relationship enough importance to actually *think* before doing something drastic. How many drinks did it take you to hook up with someone else?"

He winced like he'd been punched. "I… I was asking because a colleague of mine is subletting his apartment January onward. I have to let him know soon if I want it."

"I'll let you know soon, then."

The bell rang, and Mackenzie jumped out of her chair to answer the door.

"Sorry, Micky." Robert tottered inside with his small suitcase. "It started raining, and the bus got delayed."

She helped him take off his raincoat. "I ordered Chinese."

"That's very nice. Where should I put this suitcase?"

"I'll show you your room after dinner. Leave it in the foyer for now. This is Sterling Brooks. My husband."

Sterling stood up like the courteous man he was. He offered his hand. "Sir."

"Oh." Robert looked surprised for a moment, like Sterling wasn't what he'd expected. Mackenzie wondered if it was Sterling's icy blue eyes against his dark skin. The contrast threw a lot of people off. "How do you do?"

After exchanging meaningless pleasantries, they sat at the dining table. Sterling watched Robert's movements like a hawk.

"Mack told me you lived in Mexico for some time?"

"A decade."

"I went to Cancun in college but didn't get a chance to explore much."

"I lived in Tepic. It's on the west side. Beautiful city. Good architecture." He struggled with the chopsticks. The greasy dumpling kept slipping. He gave up and used a fork instead.

"Is it dangerous?"

"Oh, yes. Gang violence. They're always fighting for territory. What do you do?"

"I'm an assistant district attorney."

"Is that how you met Micky? Through work?"

"Yeah. Six years ago."

"I'm so proud of Micky. I never thought she'd be a cop." He chuckled nervously.

"What did she like growing up?"

"Math and science."

"Not surprised. She always has her nose in some science book."

Mackenzie tuned out their mundane conversation. Her stomach flipped when they laughed together. This was a bad idea. What was she thinking—having dinner with a man who hit her mother on a daily basis and her husband who didn't think twice before screwing someone else?

She felt sick. Beads of sweat popped up all over her back. Her gut felt hot, like it had been torched with gasoline.

"You okay, Micky?"

"Y-yeah." She cleared her throat. "I'll just get some juice. Do you two want anything? Beer? Wine?"

"I don't drink anymore."

"Oh. Right." She remembered his years at rehab. "Sterling?"

"I'm good, babe."

*Babe.*

She went to the kitchen. Their conversation resumed. She opened the door to the fridge and pressed her body into it, feeling the cold seep through her clothes.

Her father was obviously taking advantage of her. And now Sterling would use this to weasel his way back into her good books. Maybe involving Sterling had not been wise. This was her personal business. She was marching deeper into the belly of disarray and could feel everything falling apart. She hoped her decisions were sound: biding her time and playing nice with her father to find out what he knew.

Today her house was filled with the laughter of her husband and father. The miracle had happened that everyone prays for.

Someone missing for decades, presumed to be dead, had returned. But there was another house out there that was filled with loss and despair. A family who'll never have their miracle. A family who'll never have closure.

It was all Mackenzie's fault.

"Mack? Where did you go to?" Sterling's voice came from the dining room.

"Coming!" She returned to the table.

"Micky, what's it like being a police officer?"

"It's okay. Keeps life interesting."

"I bet. Do you have a partner?"

"Yeah. Nick Blackwood."

"Hmm. So what do you solve? Murders?"

"Yes."

"Sounds dangerous."

She shrugged. "If everyone's done eating, I'll clean up."

"I'll help," Sterling said.

"Yeah, Micky. Me too."

"No!" she almost yelled. They froze and stared at her. "I mean... I like to clean. Sterling, why don't you show him the guest room?"

Luckily, no one protested. Robert was a stranger. A stranger she'd invited to live with her.

"What the hell am I doing?" she muttered, collecting the takeout boxes.

She picked up the fork and glass Robert had used and quickly placed them inside a sealed plastic bag.

# CHAPTER SIXTEEN

*November 24*

"Tell me if you see anything," Nick said. He went behind the television and adjusted some wires. The portable screen blinked with static. There was a flicker of the frame of a video on screen.

"Stop!" Mackenzie called out. The screen displayed a pixelated image of a parking lot.

"Cool." He fell on the chair next to her in the conference room.

"Why are you wearing jeans?"

His ears turned red. "All my suits have gone for dry cleaning."

"I don't think I've ever seen you in jeans. It's either pants or sweatpants."

"Focus, Mack."

She grinned, and they watched the CCTV footage in silence. Woodburn Park didn't have an official parking lot. There were two open spaces by the edge of the park—one by the east side and the other on the west side. One of them lined the inlet ponds that also served as runoff. The other used to have a hotdog stand and an ice cream truck when Mackenzie was a kid. Now, it was empty.

They didn't have sophisticated cameras, but fortunately for Mackenzie and Nick there were traffic lights close enough to offer a view. Jenna had retrieved footage from Monday night to the Saturday night before the bodies were found. They sat and watched the blurry videos of shadows and slivers of cars driving by. The footage from the two cameras played on the split screen. Three hours in, no car had parked in those spots.

"How was the family dinner?" Nick leaned back in his chair and crossed his ankle over his knee.

"Awkward."

"Your father's just at home now? No supervision?"

"He's a senior citizen. He doesn't need supervision," she said defensively. When Nick didn't say anything, she knew he was watching her, and she knew what he meant. "I have no cash or jewelry at home. And you know I don't own any other guns. My service weapon's always with me."

"Did you ask Becky to do a paternity test?"

"I brought the samples in. Becky's going to drive here for a meeting with Sully on another case. I'll just catch her then."

Her eyes never left the screen. It was mundane to comb through hours of footage and her gut told her that they wouldn't find anything useful here. But it was a matter of crossing the "t"s and dotting the "i"s. A huge chunk of the job involved dreary legwork.

The timestamp showed hours ticking past, but no car or person swung by. Just as Mackenzie had expected. The park stretched out for acres. With no designated parking lots, people parked anywhere around the edge. Patrol was searching the trail in the park, prioritizing the shoreline of the lake, to identify where the bodies were dumped in, but the weather was slowing them down. All Mackenzie and Nick could do was hope for a lucky break.

"I found the suicide video tape in the evidence locker." Mackenzie handed it to him.

Nick played it on the screen. The footage was gray and grainy from a traffic light. Cars zipped by on the bridge over the Fresco River. The timestamp showed it was three in the afternoon. Ten minutes later, a woman came into frame wearing a white flowing dress.

"There she is." Nick leaned forward.

She stood at the railing, looking at the water below. Some people walked past her, throwing glances and looking back, but no one stopped to talk to her.

"No one cares," Mackenzie said.

At seventeen minutes past three, she swung one leg over the railing and then another. There wasn't much space. Just enough. She leaned forward but kept her arms coiled over the railing behind her.

More people took notice. Two people walking by paused for a bit and observed her. Like they were contemplating. But they didn't talk to her. After hovering for a minute or so, they continued walking. The bystander effect. Someone else would stop her. Why should they get involved in someone else's mess?

Three minutes later, a man stopped and tried talking to her. They couldn't make out his face or any identifying features. He took out his phone and started dialing when suddenly the woman jumped.

Mackenzie gasped. The man rushed forward and leaned over the railing, still on the phone. Others joined him. Minutes later, the police came, but the water was deep and tumultuous. It was too late.

"Who was that guy?" Mackenzie asked.

"A good Samaritan. The police questioned him."

"No one pushed her or had a gun on her. Definitely looks like a suicide."

"I'll go through the detective's notes and see if there were any suspects."

"Yeah. Is there a possibility that she was blackmailed?" But something told Mackenzie she hadn't been. The woman didn't look around like she was scared. She just stared at the water in which her death was written.

"Did you hear from Justin?"

"Not yet." Mackenzie checked her phone again. "He did get in touch with the center in Oklahoma City, but it will take time for them to send their records to us."

"Katy didn't remember Kim." He interlaced his fingers behind his head. "But did Kim remember Katy?"

"I think she would have. She stayed with an aunt and uncle until she was nine and her parents visited her. They would have talked about Katy. And then at the center she had counseling sessions round the clock. They must have mentioned her family and tried to understand her thought process, right?"

He shrugged. "I honestly don't know how these places work. I feel bad for her. Sociopathic children—don't come across them very often."

"Do you think she resented Katy?"

A look of brief bemusement crossed his face before he spoke. "Resented the twin that got to stay at home with her family and live a normal life. Why not?"

"She ran away, meaning she wasn't happy there."

"Who would be, in a mental institution?"

"*Treatment center*," she corrected him.

"Yeah, okay." He took out a lighter from his pocket and shook it close to his ear, listening to the lighter fluid lap inside it. "She ran away but never contacted her family. Guess she was mad at them."

"They also moved, remember? Maybe she didn't know where they were."

"Kim knew Katy existed. She must have come to Lakemore looking for her."

Mackenzie nodded. "Either that or it was one damn big coincidence. Kim ran away from a center in Oklahoma City more than a decade ago and ends up two thousand miles away in this small-ass town in Washington where her twin sister just happens to be? Seems unlikely. So, we assume she comes to Lakemore to look for Katy and her family. But she didn't contact them?"

"Maybe she was going to," Nick suggested. "She was just observing her at first."

This wasn't a normal woman. Kim Harris had been a violent toddler who had pushed her pregnant mother down the stairs. Even the doctors didn't know how to label her. Being admitted to a treatment center at the age of nine and spending all those formative years away from a healthy family environment must have taken its toll. Had she gotten better or worse?

Mackenzie's insides clenched. "What if Kim was the one who took Katy's dress?"

The hand playing with the lighter froze. "Why?"

"I don't know."

"Think Cole was in on it?"

"Having an affair with his wife's twin? That's weird."

"Twin fantasies are pretty common, Mack." He grinned.

"Shut up!" She smacked him on the arm. "Be serious."

"Whatever Kim was up to with Katy could be unrelated to her murder. And who the hell is that other woman?"

Mackenzie exhaled. They weren't getting anywhere. She stretched out her limbs and paused the video. "I had a strange thought."

"What?"

"I wondered if Kim's plan was to replace Katy."

"What do you mean?"

"Like maybe she took her clothes. She was wearing the same wedding ring. A simple gold band. Even their hairstyle was the same, Nick. What other reason could there be?"

"Yeah..." He tapped his lip. "But where does our Jane Doe factor in?"

"I don't know," she said, resigned. "Maybe she and Kim knew each other? They were clearly together when they were murdered; we found a part of Jane Doe's clothing *inside* Kim. It must have come from the knife the guy used to stab them."

Nick groaned and dragged his hands down his face. "Okay. Let's break this down. There are too many things. We should pin

Katy as our focus point and go from there. She maintains a public profile. She's active on social media and organizes events across town. It's possible she caught someone's attention."

Mackenzie straightened her back. "I'll extract her social media history and get pictures and videos of her rallies, fundraisers, etcetera. Maybe we'll catch a break there."

There was a knock on the glass door of the conference room, and Jenna, the other junior detective in their unit, poked her head in. "Got a minute?"

Nick waved her in.

"Justin and I looked into the three cabins around the lake. They belong to the same guy. Blake Richie, a mechanic who owns a couple garages around town. He said he bought them years ago and has been trying to sell them off, but no one wants to buy anything in Woodburn Park. He doesn't use them or even maintain them."

"Homeless people must break in all the time then," Mackenzie said.

"Especially in winter. Patrol said they've chased homeless people out of those cabins many times over the years. But they never had any drugs on them so no arrests were made."

Nick pressed his lips in a thin line. "Poor guys were just looking for a place to crash."

"The troopers patrol the park often?" Mackenzie asked.

"Sometimes. Just to make sure nothing is going on. When they caught them there, they increased their patrols in winter. But they said they come in around January and February," Jenna replied.

"But this year was different. There was a big storm way earlier than usual. Maybe some people had snuck in. Did you ask if they checked earlier?"

Jenna gave her standard look. The half roll of eyes and wiggle of shoulders with a condescending smirk on the lips. "Of course I did. But the storm was unpredictable and so short. There were no patrols."

"What about the other cabins at the park? Are all of them abandoned?"

"Some."

"Can you label them on a map?"

She twirled a strand of her hair and shrugged. "Sure. Anything else?"

"Yes, you were checking with hospitals to see if anyone recognizes Jane Doe Two. Any luck?"

"Not in Lakemore. I'm going to check with hospitals in Olympia and Tacoma."

"Keep at it." Mackenzie turned around.

Mackenzie and Jenna didn't always see eye to eye, which Mackenzie felt like a waste considering they were the only two female detectives in the unit. But Jenna had an attitude problem everyone was aware of. She didn't like learning or being challenged in any way.

As soon as Jenna left, Nick let out a breathy chuckle. "It's always fun to watch you and Jenna. So much tension."

She rolled her eyes. "I don't know why she has that sour-lemon face."

"Sour lemon?"

"That's what Troy calls it. She makes that face like she's sucking on a sour lemon when she talks to me."

"If it helps, she makes that face whenever she talks to any woman."

"It doesn't." Mackenzie gave him a tight smile and checked her phone. There was a message from Justin.

*Carrie Breslow and her husband came back last night.*

"The Breslows are in the city again. Ready to go?"

# CHAPTER SEVENTEEN

Carrie Breslow's house looked like the perfect picture of happiness. The front yard was blanketed with a thin sheet of snow. Two children ran around, throwing snowballs at each other. Even from inside the car, Mackenzie could hear the chirping of their laughter and innocent giggles. The Breslow house wasn't lavish. But it looked like it was enough. Gray clouds bowled into the sky, casting a shroud over their fun. The front door opened, and a woman with dirty blonde hair called the children inside.

The first observation Mackenzie made about Carrie Breslow was that she looked nothing like Katy Becker. While she had already known this from the pictures of the dead woman from years ago, Mackenzie had wondered if in person their similarities would magnify. But she couldn't look more different to Katy—her face was squarer, her forehead bigger.

"That's Carrie Breslow," Nick confirmed.

"This suicide victim, she must have already looked like Carrie. Cosmetic procedures can't change the face entirely. Whoever she was, she looked like her a little bit and then enhanced herself to look more like her. Just like our Jane Doe."

"The question is why?"

Questions clamored in Mackenzie's brain. She looked at the house again. The children rushed to Carrie and wrapped their little arms around her legs. She ushered them inside. "Maybe she wanted Carrie's life. She saw Carrie had stability and accomplishments, and she envied that."

They climbed out of the car to be met by howling wind, casting small flecks of snow adrift. Carrie saw them approach before she closed the door and stepped outside.

She stuffed her hands inside her coat. "Can I help you?" When they flashed their badges, a frown marred her face.

"We just have some questions for you," Nick said. "Around sixteen years ago—"

"Oh! God. Not that again," she groaned. "Of course. Why else would the cops come to me?"

"You remember what happened?" Mackenzie asked.

"How can I forget?" she scoffed half-heartedly. "I was only thirty years old, and the cops showed up to tell my husband that I might have jumped off a bridge."

Mackenzie's eyes jerked to Nick. "And what happened?"

"A lot of questioning. I had no idea who that woman was or why she looked so much like me."

When they fell silent, her face creased in wariness. "Why do you care after all these years? Did you find out who she was?"

"No." Nick licked his lips. "It happened again."

Carrie's eyes went wide like saucers. "Oh my God."

"Yeah, so if you know anything…"

She rubbed her chest and mulled. "I'm thinking. But—"

The door to her house swung open. A man with a wizened neck and a cowlick marched toward them wearing a friendly smile. "Carrie! When is Sue coming to pick them up? They're causing a ruckus!" He paused, looking at Mackenzie and Nick. "Oh, I'm sorry. Hello, I'm Owen."

"Honey, these detectives are from Lakemore PD," Carrie said.

"Oh, dear. What did she do?" He laughed.

"It's about that suicide." She pressed him with a look.

Owen's mouth parted—understanding crossing his face. "I see. That was awful."

"We just wanted to know if Mrs. Breslow has any more information," Mackenzie explained.

"I'm sorry; it was so long ago. I didn't know anything back then, and I don't know anything now."

"Was anyone following you? Any ex-boyfriend threatening you?"

Carrie shrugged. "No. Life was normal."

"Were any of your belongings missing?"

If Katy's dress was taken, then maybe something of Carrie's was missing too. But Katy's dress was found on Kim, not on Jane Doe. Which is why, when Carrie shook her head, Mackenzie wasn't very surprised.

"Did you reopen the case?" Owen asked. "I thought it was ruled a suicide."

"It was. But it's happened again. Another woman is dead, and she'd had work done to her face to look like someone else. Not Carrie this time."

"You don't say!" He gasped and turned to Carrie. "Think that creep is back in town?"

"What creep?" Mackenzie asked, alert. Maybe he knew something.

"I don't think that was anything, Owen." Carrie flicked her hand.

"The police questioned this one guy—" Owen said.

"They just interviewed him, but nothing came out of it," Carrie interrupted. "He was a bit strange. I'd see him around a little too often. He stared a lot, you know. Word spread."

"That's Lakemore," Owen shrugged and slung an arm around Carrie's shoulders. "Gossip and crime spread faster than the speed of light. And rain," he added when the first fat drop landed on the tip of his nose. He gestured at them to take cover under the porch. The gray skies dimmed into a darker shade. Thick droplets splattered on the ground. "Strangest winter in all my years here."

"What was his name?" Nick asked.

"Steven something… Boyle! Steven Boyle," Owen replied.

"Does he still live around here?"

"Oh, no. I don't know where he went." Carrie clicked her tongue. "I heard the rumors ruined his career. That he was fired from his job and socially exiled."

"The police suspected that he became obsessed with Carrie," Owen chipped in. "Happens more often than you think, they said." His eyebrows formed a knot as he pulled his wife closer. "I wish I was around more during the investigation, but I was dividing my time between here and Henderson."

"Not your fault, Owen. Work is work." She patted his chest like they had had the same argument several times.

"Why did the police question him?"

"He worked at Lakemore General Hospital," Owen said. "Carrie had gone to him a bunch of times to get a childhood scar removed. He was a cosmetic surgeon."

# CHAPTER EIGHTEEN

On their way back to work, Mackenzie looked up Steven Boyle on her phone, ignoring Nick's protests about her motion sickness.

"He studied in Seattle at the University of Washington and also taught there for a few years before moving to Lakemore," Mackenzie read aloud.

"He didn't make the news for the suicide?" Nick asked.

"No. Why would he? No one was arrested." She opened the case file in her lap.

"I don't remember coming across his name."

Mackenzie skimmed through the notes of the detective in charge at the time. "Me neither. Because it's in the footnotes, easy to miss." She found Steve Boyle's name scribbled at the bottom. "He was never a *suspect*, since it was just a suicide. They interviewed him, trying to find out the identity of their Jane Doe, not because they accused him of foul play. But that went nowhere."

Mackenzie found a picture of him on a website that listed his publications in medical journals. "Wow."

"What?"

"He has good citations. Did a lot of research. The last article he published was twenty years ago though."

"What kind of research?"

Mackenzie skimmed over the list of articles and noticed two words popping up frequently. "'Hyaluronic acid' is a popular topic with him." She clicked on one article. "It's some molecule that's good for the skin. Some articles on facial reconstruction methods, injections, and reviews on topics like psychology behind body perfection and ugliness."

"We should talk to him."

By the time they reached the station, the rain had died just as suddenly as it had started. The asphalt was glistening. As she climbed out of the car, she noticed the perimeter of the lot had been barricaded. No doubt after the unfortunate incident of the squad car being set on fire. She wondered if they'd caught who was responsible for that. She spotted Becky standing behind a hedge. Mackenzie grabbed the plastic bags from the glove box and jogged toward her.

"I'll catch up with you," she shot at Nick. He looked at the plastic bag and nodded, before walking away.

Becky stood with her back pressed against a concrete wall, sucking on a cigarette.

"You started smoking too?" Mackenzie asked.

She rolled her eyes. "Save the judgment, Mack. Not in the mood."

"Jeez. Sorry." She raised her hands.

"What's that in your hand?"

"I needed a favor, but not if you're in an asshole mood."

A throaty laugh ripped out of her and soon became a cough. She bent down, clutching her chest.

Mackenzie patted her back. "I told you." She took the cigarette from her hand and crushed it under her boot. "You've been working long hours in the lab."

"You're a workaholic too."

"Yeah, but it's not usual for you. Did your meeting with Sully tank or something?"

Becky crossed her arms. "I'm thinking of leaving Garrett."

As soon as Becky said the words, a brief moment of satisfaction surged through Mackenzie. She hated herself for it, but she found solace in the fact that her marriage wasn't the only one that was on thin ice. "How did you know that you should leave him?"

Becky narrowed her eyes. "*That's* what you're asking me? Not 'why?' or 'what happened?', but how I knew?"

"Sorry." Mackenzie flushed. "Bad wording. I meant *why.*"

"Nothing happened," she sighed. "We've just been fighting a lot. And then he accused me of working too much when he has twelve-hour shifts at the hospital."

"I'm sorry."

"Does Sterling ever complain that you work too much?"

He hadn't. Not once. He teased her about it from time to time, but they never criticized or discouraged each other's careers. She shook her head gingerly.

"He's a good husband. What favor did you want?"

"This is off the books. Would you do it?"

Becky smirked. "Ballsy. Sure."

"Can you run a paternity test on these?" She handed her the bag. "The glass and fork have the same DNA and that Q-tip has the other one."

"Paternity test? What's going on?"

"I can't say yet. Will you do it?" When Becky continued staring at her, she added, "It's for a friend. He has suspicions about his kid."

"Do you want me to run it through any database?"

"No. Just a paternity test is enough. When could you have the results by?"

"Tomorrow."

"Working all night again?"

"Just proving him right."

Lakemore's weather was more familiar now.

Wet and not snowy.

It was a welcome reprieve in between the two storms. The late afternoon was glum, with gloomy skies and rapid rain. As the patches of snow shrunk, the town bore more greenery.

Mackenzie pulled up in front of a rickety one-story house with a tin roof. The front yard had drying ropes with clothes getting drenched. An overweight woman tottered out of the house carrying a bucket. She began removing the clothes.

Mackenzie cast her eyes over the yard as she approached. The garden was modest. Neatly cut grass, no trees, but clusters of cosmos grew around the perimeter.

The woman was new to gardening.

"Maria?" Mackenzie offered her the cover of her umbrella. "I'm Detective Price. From Lakemore PD. I called ahead."

Maria scowled. "Yeah… yeah. Just let me finish this."

The way her hands moved told Mackenzie that she was a robust worker. Even with a round belly and rounder hips, she was muscled and strong. She also clearly didn't like being disturbed. Embracing the bucket in her arms, she gestured for Mackenzie to follow her to the rusty walls and sharp edges of the porch.

Maria patted her neck dry with a towel. "Mrs. Becker called me and told me what happened."

"She did?"

"Yes."

"You shouldn't leave your pots of cosmos outside during the rain. They don't like excess water."

"I see." Maria frowned, with a gleam of approval in her eyes. "Thanks for the tip. I don't know how to help you."

"Have you noticed anything unusual with the Beckers?"

"Unusual how?"

"Anything out of the ordinary."

"I don't want to lose my job. Mrs. Becker pays me generously."

"This conversation is confidential, Maria." Mackenzie shivered against the cold breeze. "You won't get in any trouble."

"I don't know who to trust in this town anymore." Her face was hard as stone.

"What do you mean?"

A muscle in her jaw ticked. "My husband was laid off." When Mackenzie didn't speak, she continued, "We used to have good jobs and good healthcare plans. Now, my husband and most of his friends are out of work. Do you see that house over there? With the pink fence?"

Mackenzie followed her gaze to another downtrodden house.

"Our friend, Enzo, lives there. He's a single father. He burned his hand by accident when baking his little girl a birthday cake. Days later, it got infected. He went to the emergency room. One tube of an antibiotic cream and a five-minute consultation with the nurse is going to cost him a thousand dollars. He doesn't have insurance because he lost his job too—through no fault of his. He worked for Samuel Perez. You think whoever takes over Perez's companies is going to stick around? In *this* town? That means even fewer jobs to go around."

Her stomach clenched at Maria's cutting words. Perez had been the local boy made good, a hugely successful businessman, until Mackenzie had exposed his past during the Lakemore Sharks case. "I'm sorry. But we have to do the right thing."

"You didn't have to take down the entire town in the process."

"Lakemore *will* recover," she said earnestly. "I'm sorry you're suffering, but the government is working on several welfare programs and with time—"

"The *government* does nothing," she shot back. "The rich walk away with probation and community service for the same crimes that the poor end up spending decades in prison for."

Her eyes glided over Mackenzie's appearance. And Mackenzie knew what she saw. A woman with expensive-looking clothes, conditioned hair, painted lips, and mascaraed lashes. A woman who didn't belong in this debilitated neighborhood, even though she'd grown up in a house only three streets away.

Maria's scorching gaze could burn a hole through her. "Optimism and morality are luxuries the poor can't afford too easily.

We just want to feed and educate our children. But I don't expect *you* to understand."

Maria turned to go inside. Mackenzie knew she had lost her. She tried a different approach to reel her back in. "Katy's life is in danger."

"*What?*"

She nodded. Maria cared about her employer. It was evident from her parted lips and the knot between her eyebrows. "Someone's after her. So if you know anything. If you care about her..."

She did. Mackenzie could see it. But she didn't push. Maria's shoulders fell. "Wednesday last week, I went there at three in the afternoon. Mrs. Becker opened the door, but she looked very upset. She was almost shaking."

"Did she say anything?"

"She told me to go home and that she didn't need me to clean that day."

"Has she ever done that before?"

"No. Never. She looked frightened. She kept looking over her shoulder and was blocking the view. I thought there was someone else inside with her. She didn't want me to see who it was. I asked her if she was okay. She was acting so agitated, but she put cash in my hands and shooed me away. Is she really in danger?"

Mackenzie didn't know. While she strongly suspected that Katy was, there was no proof. Still, she found herself nodding. "How's Cole? Any fights between them?"

"A few times."

"Anything catch your attention?"

She grunted. "I'm a cleaner. People are wary around me. In case I steal or gossip."

"Thank you, Maria. Please let me know if you think of anything else." She handed over her contact information.

Maria nodded stiffly and went back inside the house. Back in the car, Mackenzie glanced at the house with the pink fence. The collateral damage from bringing justice.

Everything in this town came at a price.

# CHAPTER NINETEEN

*November 25*

The Detectives Unit handled all the missing persons cases in Lakemore, so gaining access to first incident reports of any woman reported missing was straightforward. Mackenzie had gone back six months. Of course, maybe Jane Doe Two wasn't reported missing. Maybe she was never missing. There were no signs that the victims were held captive. No ligature marks.

Did Jane Doe Two want to look like Katy? Or had this been forced upon her?

But why would she want to look like Katy? Was she trying to impress someone with a perverse obsession? Or maybe *she* was the one who was obsessed?

Mackenzie picked up Katy's picture: a candid shot from a fundraiser she had organized. She was smiling at an old lady. Her cheeks had more color. She was dolled-up, wearing a silk green dress and pearl earrings.

Mackenzie went over the reports. There were four women reported missing in the last six months who matched Jane Doe Two's description. But none of these women had any tattoos. Jane Doe Two could have gotten the tattoos after she disappeared. However, going over the descriptions of the missing women, it was clear that none of them was the one she was looking for.

Mackenzie growled. Too many unknowns.

"You sound like a demon when you growl," Troy quipped from her side.

She chucked an eraser at him. "What are you doing?"

"Going over witness statements. Are you okay?"

"Yeah," she sulked. "Three women with the same face. Unexplained medical procedures. A sixteen-year-old suicide. Run-of-the-mill stuff."

"Is that why you forgot to clip your nails?"

She frowned and looked at her nails; they were long and uneven. Her stomach flipped. She always took care of her nails. She even oiled them. The first signs of coming apart were always small and subtle. What else wasn't she paying attention to?

"Relax, Mack. I'm pulling your leg. Normal people sometimes let their nails grow out."

"Yeah." She felt her face redden and went back to reading the reports.

Two out of the four missing women were in abusive relationships—according to statements from neighbors and friends and families—and showed signs of abuse. Healing bruises on their bodies. One even had a sling on. Mackenzie crossed them out. Jane Doe Two displayed no signs of torture or abuse of any sort.

Then there was one woman who was a natural redhead. Unlike Jane Doe Two, a natural blonde, who dyed her hair black.

The last woman was a blonde who disappeared three months ago. She lived in Lakemore but was last seen driving to Olympia, so the police there had taken over. She was generally flighty, didn't use drugs, according to her husband, and had left two children behind.

Mackenzie stared at the picture. Could she be their second Jane Doe? Jane Doe Two had stopped using drugs at least three months ago and had damaged veins. Surely, this missing woman's husband would know what her legs looked like? Maybe he didn't tell the police because he didn't want her to get into trouble. Or maybe he himself was a heroin user too and didn't want to lose his kids to social services.

But then she read that the missing woman had a chipped tooth. This wasn't their Jane Doe.

"Troy, you have a tattoo, right?"

Troy flashed her a charming smile and rolled up his sleeve. A spider web with flowers covered his bicep. "I would have made it bigger. But, oh, the stigma."

She showed him the pictures of Jane Doe's tattoos. "Do these mean anything to you? In your tattoo world?"

"Tattoo *world*?" He grinned. "No. Haven't seen anything like it. Is this some kind of code?"

"Apparently. How many tattoo parlors are there in the city?"

He bobbed his head and tallied them. "Six legal ones, I think. There'll always be some guys inking people from their basements without a license."

Nick walked into the office with pink cheeks.

"Did you let your daughter put makeup on you again?" Troy whistled.

Nick playfully slapped the back of Troy's head with a file. "It's cold, you jackass. If I liked harsh winters, I would have lived on the east coast. What the hell's going on this year?"

"Bet Mad Mack feels right at home. Was New York worse than this?"

"Yes. Your nuts would have fallen off," she deadpanned.

Nick laughed, and Troy shook his head, amused. "Speaking of nuts, Finn and I have a suspect to tail. Catch you guys later."

"Did you get anything useful from Cole's colleagues?" Mackenzie asked Nick when they were left alone.

"His partners are a couple. Neither of them has seen Cole with anyone else. There's also an assistant and receptionist. They all said that Cole has been acting normally."

"Nothing stuck out?" She was disappointed.

"Well..." Nick trailed off before finding his voice. "Cole works strictly from nine to four on weekdays. His assistant showed me his calendar. He goes to the gym on the weekend, in the mornings. At most he'll do phone consultations with clients out of hours."

She remembered Delilah's statement. "So where has he been going in the evenings when Katy works late?"

"Not to work. What did Maria say?"

Mackenzie repeated Maria's story about Katy's suspicious behavior on Wednesday. "It could be unrelated to the murder?"

Nick's face was pensive. "Or the Beckers are lying to us."

Her computer chimed with a notification. It was an email from Becky. *Working Sundays too, Becky?* Her breath lodged in her throat, wondering if it was the results of the paternity test. But it was the familial DNA test she'd requested to compare Jane Doe Two and Kim's DNA against the suicide victim's DNA already on file.

"It's not a match." Mackenzie sighed.

"The victims aren't related?"

"Nope."

"Why *them*?" Nick wondered aloud. Mackenzie's eyes drifted to Katy and Carrie's pictures as the same question blared in her mind like a siren.

Justin walked into the office, tipping his head. "Ma'am. Sir."

"Yes, Justin?" Mackenzie sighed, exasperated at his unnecessary salutes. "Got anything?"

"I tracked down that doctor, Steven Boyle. He changed his name to Steven Brennan after the suicide, which is why we couldn't find him through the DMV records. He's in a nursing home in Olympia. We could drive there now."

"I have Luna for a couple of hours. Keep me updated?" Nick said.

Mackenzie picked up her keys, ready to brave the worsening weather. "Will do."

# CHAPTER TWENTY

The nursing home in Olympia wasn't too far from Nelson Heights, where Katy Becker's parents lived.

Mackenzie and Justin approached a cream-colored reception desk, behind which stood a man who looked to be in his mid-twenties. When they showed their credentials, his lips parted. "Oh, um. Yes. What is this regarding?"

Justin looked at Mackenzie expectantly, but she gave him an encouraging nod and let him take the lead. She was almost certain she saw him smile briefly under his bushy mustache. "We need to speak with Steven Brennan."

A woman in blue medical scrubs overheard him. "Steven has dementia. I'm Shanice. One of the nurses here."

"I understand, but it's important." Justin adjusted his belt buckle.

"Sure. Come along."

They followed her into a wide hallway with French windows overlooking a plush green courtyard on one side. The other wall was lined with posters giving information on the importance of elderly mental health and the various activities the home organized for its residents.

"Thanks for that," Justin muttered gruffly.

"You're going to be leading the big cases very soon."

Shanice led them into an airy room bathed in yellow light with bookshelves set into the walls. Two residents sat on couches, playing chess. There was one man in a wheelchair, facing the window. His shoulders were hunched, his bald head partially covered by strings of white hair. His shriveled cheeks hung low, as if trying to drag his eyes down too.

"Steven?" Shanice crouched next to him and placed her hand on his. "These are detectives from Lakemore PD. They want to talk to you. Is that okay?"

He made a gurgling sound, which apparently translated to approval.

"Dr. Brennan?" Justin asked. But Steven didn't respond. Shanice shrugged helplessly. "Dr. *Boyle*?"

Steven's hands twitched like he had been electrocuted. He swiveled his head to look at Justin worriedly. "Did you not get my check? Should I write you another one?"

Justin looked at Mackenzie. "I did."

Steven turned to Mackenzie with a scowl. "Oh. It's you again, Sofia. Always crying. Or sleeping."

It was clear that Steven wasn't going to be of much help. When Mackenzie realized her presence was agitating him, she moved out of his vision and closer to Shanice. "Is he always like this?"

"Yes. He's one of our worst patients."

"How old is he?"

"Seventy-one. But he looks a lot older. His dementia started early and progressed rapidly."

Justin showed him a picture of Carrie Breslow. Mackenzie paid closer attention. When a rambling Steven saw the screen, a dark look crossed his face. "Do you recognize her, sir?"

"Carrie."

He remembered her. Her face had the power to wrench him out of his state. Mackenzie wasn't surprised; it had been a significant event in his life. Enough for him to leave town and change his name.

"Do you remember what happened?" Justin prodded.

Steven ran his fingers over the face in the photo. But it didn't seem like a romantic gesture. More like adulation. "Role model. Good woman. *Ideal.*"

"Do you remember that suicide?"

He sucked air through his teeth. "Bad day. There were floods, you know. So many people died. All I wanted was to live in peace. But the flood killed them all."

Justin shook his head at Mackenzie. This was a lost cause. Steven went back to mumbling to himself. Chasing down leads related to a sixteen-year-old suicide had grim prospects already.

"I told you he wouldn't be able to help," Shanice whispered.

"Does he have any family?" Justin inquired.

"No. He's what we call an elderly orphan."

"Are there any moments he's lucid?" Justin pressed. "Has he ever said anything then? Does he talk about a particular person, maybe?"

"Just his wife, Sofia. She died many years ago. He talks about how she was weak, addicted to drugs, and a hermit, and all he wanted was for her to be *perfect*. It's a little odd."

"Has anyone ever visited him?"

"Never..." Shanice's eyes narrowed like she was trying to remember something. "But I think around a year ago, someone sent him a gift."

"A gift?" Mackenzie repeated.

"Yes. It was just dropped off at the door with 'For Steven B' scribbled on the wrapper. There was no stamp or sender's information on it."

"Do you still have it?"

"It's in his room. I'll be right back." Shanice gestured for them to wait, before slipping away.

"Strange way to drop off a gift," Mackenzie said to Justin. "Just leaving it at the door without any information."

Shanice returned, holding a thick pen. "This is it. Sorry, we threw away the wrapping paper."

Mackenzie took the pen from her. It looked expensive—painted in gleaming red and silver. There were two symbols on it. One consisted of a golden snake winding around a staff. On the other side lines had been engraved into the pen—artfully, if slightly messy.

"Looks like fine craftsmanship." Mackenzie twirled it in her fingers.

Justin nodded. "Someone went to a lot of trouble, but then didn't bother to visit?"

"Happens more than you'd think," Shanice said sadly. "People feel guilty for not showing up, so they send gifts."

A gift that Steven was unlikely to be able to use, in his state. Mackenzie regarded the frail, bony man staring vacantly out of the window, the answers they needed locked away deep in his brain.

# CHAPTER TWENTY-ONE

Back at the station, Mackenzie shivered, climbing out of the car. The brewing cold was seeping into her bones. The weather seemed to have taken a complete turn from Olympia to Lakemore, even though they shared a border. While Olympia had been cool and rainy, Lakemore was dry and chilly. This winter it felt like Lakemore was in a bubble.

"Ma'am?" Justin said gruffly at her side, looking at his phone. "The psychiatric center and social services will send over Kim's files. I was able to track the detective in Oklahoma PD who was in charge of finding Kim."

"What did they say?"

"He said that it's considered a cold case. They don't have any active lines of inquiry and all the leads have dried up. They… they assumed that she was probably dead somewhere, he says, being so mentally unstable."

"I see." She suppressed a sigh. Their line of work had hardened them. It was so common to see the ugliness of human nature that it was nearly impossible not to become a little crass. "Can you do one more thing?" She forwarded him pictures of the tattoos.

"These were found on Jane Doe Two." Justin glared at the picture, like his intensity would cause the tattoos to reveal their mystery. "These numbers and letters don't make sense to me. But can you check with the tattoo parlors in the city? Maybe we'll get a hit."

"Yes, ma'am."

When they got inside, Mackenzie heard an angry female voice.

"Absolutely not! I call every day and no one's taking me seriously!"

"Please calm down, ma'am." A uniformed cop was trying to placate her.

The woman was much older than Mackenzie, with dirty blonde hair that looked unkempt and rough. Her face was aged, lines running down her puffy cheeks and crinkly neck. However, she dressed young. A ratty T-shirt, hot-pink yoga pants and cheap jewelry around her neck and fingers. She glared at the officer with her raccoon-like eyes. "They're right about the cops in this town. It's been a week since I've heard from you!"

The officer tried to maintain his cool, despite growing uncomfortable from the attention the woman was attracting. Everyone at the station watched them. "The detective will be right with you, ma'am."

"May I help you?" Mackenzie asked.

The woman's eyes landed on Mackenzie but before she could reply, Finn darted right past her. "Michelle, I'm here to help you. Come upstairs with me."

"You've been doing *nothing*. Where is my daughter? Why are you here and not out there looking for her?"

Since Finn had her handled, Mackenzie walked past them, flashing him a sympathetic look. He guided the woman away, pressing his lips in a hard line. She realized how she and her colleagues had hardened too. It was the only way to survive. She'd learned from Sully. Too much empathy made a detective unfit for the job.

In her cubicle, she stared out the window. It wasn't too bad yet, but tonight they were expecting a confetti of snow.

*What was Robert doing?*

The dinner on Friday night with Sterling had been awkward. After Sterling left, Robert had retreated to his room and hit the sack early. He said he hadn't slept on a comfortable bed in a long time. It left Mackenzie wondering what his endgame was. Was he biding his time and earning her trust before doing something drastic? But what could he possibly want from her?

She took out the pen that was gifted to Steven at the nursing home and placed it on her desk.

The golden symbol of the snake and rod was clearly an original part of the pen. It was the Rod of Asclepius—adopted as the symbol of medicine and healing.

But the strange lines on the other side looked like someone had carved them into the pen with a blade. They were rough and jagged. They didn't particularly look like anything. There were two squares interconnected by two lines with little lines extending out of the points of the squares, like branches.

She looked up the pen online, entering its basic description, and found several stores that sold it. It was expensive, worth a hundred dollars. Since it was easily available, it would be impossible to track who purchased it.

Her phone rang. Nick.

"How's Luna?"

Nick snorted. "Too full of ice cream." Luna shrieked her protest in the background. "What happened with Boyle?"

She updated him on their visit. "Interesting. Who sent the pen to him?"

"No clue." She picked it up. "It's readily available online. It would be damn near impossible to track down the sender."

"Too bad. Could be nothing. Let's wait on the Kim files. Her life has been a question mark—she could have been involved in something. Maybe that's where the answer lies."

# CHAPTER TWENTY-TWO

Mackenzie had never seen Sully act this civilized in a bar. Not that Sully was a disruptive and unruly drunk, just that her sergeant was a sloppy drinker. He'd sit quietly in a corner, slurring, and grinning cheek to cheek even if no one had said anything remotely funny. His bushy mustache would often drip with beer.

Now, he looked more dignified and responsive. Mackenzie realized that it was because he had stopped after his first glass of beer. Their new lieutenant sitting next to him seemed to be the reason.

The bar was relatively empty, even for a Sunday. There was a group of construction workers by the pool table, and couples sat at tables scattered throughout. But the noise levels didn't match the number of people. The construction guys were contemplative and spoke in whispers. The television played an NBA game that no one was really watching. Eyes would mindlessly drift to the screen and stayed glued. But there was no spark in them. No interest. They would just as easily look away.

"Who was that woman at the station today?" Mackenzie asked Finn. "Looked pretty intense."

He shook his head. "Her thirty-year-old daughter left a letter saying that she's going away. But she doesn't believe it."

"Oh." Unfortunately, at least half of the missing persons in Lakemore were runaways; it was a town to escape. And understandably, families had a tough time buying it. "What did she look like?"

"According to the picture, she has short black hair, around one-seventy centimeters..."

"Okay." Not their Jane Doe, then.

"I told forensics to do a handwriting analysis on the letter for the mom's peace of mind, but my hands are tied. There are only so many resources I can waste, given the evidence."

"I get it. Hopefully, it will be a match, and she'll come around."

Finn smiled gratefully then changed the subject, jutting his thumb at his partner. "Mack, do you know that Troy doesn't know how to parallel park?"

"Shut up. I do." Troy scowled and took a swig of his beer.

"There was enough space for *two* cars. And it took him ten minutes to figure it out."

"Jeez, Troy. How did you pass your driving test?" Mackenzie quipped.

"Charm. She was fifteen years older than me and very obviously a cougar."

Mackenzie groaned, but he seemed very proud of himself.

"So, tell me, Nick," Rivera said. "How did you catch Lakemore's most notorious serial killer?"

Mackenzie hid her smile behind her glass of wine. Nick didn't like discussing that case. It had propelled his career at a young age. All the police departments in Washington knew Nick for catching one of the state's most infamous serial killers, but he didn't like the attention; it was one of the reasons he was never by his senator father's side during campaign season.

"It was a team effort."

"I read all about it in Ohio." Rivera tucked her hand under her chin. "How did you figure it out?"

"I talked to him." Nick swallowed hard. "He started sending letters. We knew who he was, but didn't have anything against him."

She looked intrigued. "Every detective dreams of a case like that one. Straight out of a movie."

"What was your most memorable case, Lieutenant?" Mackenzie jumped in, shifting the focus from Nick, much to his gratitude.

"My third year as a detective in Savannah." She stroked her chin. "A couple was found shot in their apartment. Their nine-year-old son was hiding in the closet. We found gunpowder on his hands and clothes."

"He killed them?"

"Yes. Later, he admitted it, too."

"Why?"

"He wanted to know if TV shows portrayed gunshots accurately or not."

"That's some messed-up shit," Sully muttered, and finished his beer.

Was Kim like that too? "Maybe you can help us profile in our cases," Mackenzie suggested.

"Of course. I'd like to say that I know Peck had a different style. As a lieutenant, I have a lot of teams to oversee, but homicide is my passion. I like to be more involved." She slammed her hands on the table. "No more shoptalk. How about we order another round on me?"

Hoots. Guffaws. Glasses raised. And Sully's sleepy beam of appreciation.

The waitress wasn't paying them any attention, so Mackenzie hopped off her chair to go place the order at the bar.

"Can we get another pitcher for the table over there?" She hitched her thumb in its direction.

"Sure thing," the bartender said. "Anything else?"

"Another glass of the merlot, please?"

"Yeah. Just give me a minute."

She placed her elbows on the counter and then jerked them away. It was grimy and sticky, matted with spilled drinks that hadn't been cleaned up. Next to her, one of the construction workers was sitting at the bar, away from his group. His face was hidden behind graying dreadlocks. His calloused finger trailed over the hardhat in his lap.

"This one's on me, Billy." The bartender slid him a drink.

"Pitying me already?"

"It's a tough situation, man. Sorry."

"It was going to the biggest contract of our lives. I feel like I let the boys down," Billy gestured to the group by the pool table.

"It's not your fault. And they didn't cancel the construction, right? It's just postponed." The barman's deft hands made two more cocktails, and he passed them to the waitress.

"Yeah, but they didn't give us a date. It's all up in the air. Who knows."

Lakemore's college team was supposed to be getting a brand-new football stadium with higher capacity, but construction had been postponed pending the FBI investigation. Mackenzie had read that it was supposed to bring at least two hundred jobs to the town.

"Bullshit, if you ask me," the bartender said, opening a bottle of merlot. "Why should the entire town pay?"

Billy shrugged.

Mackenzie lingered, considering telling them something similar to what she'd said to Maria, but ultimately decided against it. She returned to the table, feeling glum. Everyone was telling Rivera stories about Captain Murphy falling asleep in briefings and going on incoherent rants. She laughed politely.

"How are things with your dad?" Nick asked in a low voice.

"Awkward. But overall fine, I guess. He keeps asking me about the state of my marriage."

"And what is the status again?"

"Complicated." Her own voice sounded bleak to her. "Sterling's planning to come over for dinner almost every night to show *support*."

Nick smirked. "Of course he is."

"Yeah. There's just too much on my plate."

"What do you call him? Dad? Robert?" Nick asked.

Mackenzie hesitated. "I don't. I avoid addressing him."

"What did you talk about last night?"

"Not much. He asked about how I met Sterling, about my day. I kind of avoided him."

Nick nodded like he understood.

Her phone pinged with a message from Becky. Before she opened the notification, her heart lurched. She knew Robert was her father. But a part of her hoped that he wasn't; that he was an imposter and that the man she had buried that night had been her abusive father.

The thought itself gutted her. She had spent the last twenty years feeling guilty for burying her father, but now she was hoping that she had. The alternative was so much worse.

With trembling fingers, she unlocked her phone and opened Becky's text.

*That paternity test was positive. He's the father.*

Blood roared in her ears. She tossed her phone on the table with a thud and gulped down the wine. She felt Nick watching her curiously. She was usually careful when drinking wine; careful not to get stains on her teeth, careful not to get too drunk. But tonight, she just couldn't bring herself to care.

# CHAPTER TWENTY-THREE

By the time Mackenzie returned home she was slightly buzzed. After a few glasses of wine, she had called a cab. When she climbed out, icy wind slapped her face. Her skin immediately began to crack. Luckily the alcohol kept her insides warm as she jogged across the driveway to the front door. She had the urge to talk more, move more, clean more, read more, just do everything *more*. This kind of jitteriness was foreign to her. When she reached the door, she paused. Looking over her shoulder, the unforgiving storm with flurries of swirling white seemed more inviting than her home.

She knew her father and Sterling were inside. The two people she didn't want to lose control in front of. But her voice of reason was too faint for her to pay attention to for once. When she entered the house, she heard some movie playing in the living room.

"Mack?" Sterling said. "Where were you?"

"Happy hour with the new boss." She avoided his gaze and put away her jacket.

"Are you drunk?"

"Shit." She didn't realize it was obvious. But then she looked up at the mirror in the foyer. Her red hair was disheveled. Her pale skin flushed pink. And her red lipstick was wiped out. "I'm just a little tipsy."

"But you never get tipsy." He was horrified, like she was a different person.

Behind him, Robert sat on the couch. There were explosions on the flat screen and guns blazing. But the silence in the room was much more deafening. Robert paused the movie. He played with his hands, not knowing where to look.

"It was just two glasses of wine." *On an empty stomach.* She rolled her eyes and headed to the kitchen to drink water. She should have eaten more.

But Sterling gently held her elbow. "Mack, you're not *this.*"

A giggle sputtered out of her throat. Sterling stared at her with wide eyes like she was a lunatic. Robert slipped out of the room quietly, giving them space. "Sterling, you should hold yourself to the same standard you hold me to."

"That's not what I meant." He released her.

"Hypocrite."

"I'm concerned."

"Why?" She filled a glass with tap water and whispered, "Are you concerned that I slept with somebody else, like you did?"

"No!" He flinched, like the thought itself disgusted him. "I'm concerned that everything's a little too much for you. Your father, your line of work, our issues—"

"We don't have issues. *You* have issues. *You* are the one who decided to have a fling instead of communicating with me."

He pulled at his hair. "I think we should see a marriage counselor."

"Give me a break!" Her stomach grumbled loudly.

"I made mushroom ravioli." He pointed at the large pot on the stove.

"Why?"

"Because you don't have any food at home."

"Ugh!" Mackenzie growled and covered her face. "Why are you doing this, Sterling? What are you trying to prove? How nice you are? How caring you are?"

"No. I'm just helping you out."

"I didn't ask for your help!"

"You don't *need* to ask me."

She fluctuated between wanting to slap him for hurting her and to hug him for loving her. Two years ago, Mackenzie had caught a nasty infection. She had to take ten days off work. Sterling's best friend was getting married in London, and he was a groomsman. He could have easily gone for five days and flown back. Mackenzie was an adult and able to move around. Nick was there to check on her. She had told Sterling that if it made him feel better, he could stock her freezer with food. It was only a matter of five days.

But Sterling refused to leave her side. He missed the wedding. He skipped work. He didn't let her move a finger and nursed her back to health.

"I think you should go," she croaked.

"Mack…"

She looked outside at the new onslaught of snow. "Sleep on the couch. It's getting bad outside. But leave early in the morning. I need to take a shower and sleep this off."

"Okay. Just eat something before you go to bed."

She nodded and went to her bedroom. Launching herself onto the bed, she cried into her pillow.

## *November 26*

The white noise of the blender filled Mackenzie's empty kitchen. Sterling had left by the time she came downstairs. She regretted not being able to go on a run early in the morning. It was not just the fresh blanket of snow, but the fact that she was irritable and ultrasensitive to sounds and light.

A hangover. Her first one. At the age of thirty-two. She didn't know whether to be proud or ashamed.

The contents of her stomach threatened to swim up to her throat. The only thing that was missing was a headache.

"Micky?"

She looked at him, startled, still not used to having him around.

"Sorry," Robert raised his hands. "Didn't mean to scare ya there."

"It's okay."

"I wanted to talk to you." He perched on a stool by the kitchen island.

Mackenzie braced herself. Did he know something more about that night? Did he trust her enough now to share it with her?

"About last night."

Her shoulders fell.

He scratched his ear and sighed heavily. "I know alcoholism is genetic. And I'd hate if you've been struggling because of me."

Mackenzie flipped the blender off with more force than required. Her face clenched into a stone-like hardness. "Excuse me?"

Robert stuttered. She knew he'd never seen this side of her. He remembered her as the meek girl who hid in her bedroom and ate the rotten eggs he'd cooked while crying. She had grown a spiky exterior over the years. "M-Micky... I'm sorry. I didn't mean to—"

"I appreciate your concern. But I'm not an alcoholic." Her tone was clipped. She began pouring her smoothie into her thermos.

"Thank you for having me here," he said after a moment of silence. "I know I don't deserve it."

His face looked heartfelt. She didn't remember him looking like this—eyes glistening with moisture, nostrils flickering, the corners of his lips pulled down. Even when he had flashes of conscience back then, his eyes would be shifty, his voice curt. Like he didn't like admitting his mistakes and apologizing.

Could someone really change this much?

Mackenzie found herself shrugging.

"I didn't want to be a burden, so I found a job."

She stilled. "A job?" Did he tell them his real name? Give his social? Did they need paperwork? "Why didn't you ask me first?"

"I thought I didn't need to—"

"No!" A sudden wave of panic swarmed over her chest. "You were legally dead. If you… it might lead to complications. Unnecessary digging into your past."

That was enough to make him understand. "It's not a *legit* job. I gave my name as Charles. I'll be paid in cash for working four times a week. It's all under the table."

"What job is this?"

"One of Blake Richie's garages. It's walking distance from here. You mentioned him the other day, remember?"

Mackenzie remembered distinctly. He'd casually asked how her day went and she had casually answered that they hadn't made much progress except to track the ownership of some cabins to a mechanic. He'd asked the name of the mechanic. And she had given him the name, not thinking much of it.

She had withheld all other information. But he'd latched on to the minute detail she accidentally let slip and used it to his advantage.

"Did I do something wrong?" he asked.

She grimaced and drummed her fingers on the edge of the counter. "No."

"Are you sure? You look mad. I swear, I just wanted to help out. He's not some murder suspect, is he?"

She felt like a cornered animal. Why did she open her mouth? She was so used to talking about her day with Sterling. But Sterling understood lines of professionalism and appropriate behavior. Her desperate eyes searched for something to clean, something to control.

She picked up the blender and started to wash it with her hands, despite having a dishwasher. As the green paste began to detach itself from the walls of the blender, she felt her body lighten.

"He's not," she said, giving him her back. "But please don't discuss anything I tell you there. I'm on an active case."

"Understood."

Some green clumps were stuck to the lid that weren't coming off. She had to use her fingernails to scrape them off. When she was done, she looked at her caked fingernails to assess the damage.

Except they weren't coated in green. They were red and black. Like the dried blood on the pan Melody had struck him with.

"Ah!" she screamed and jumped back. The blender slipped from her hold and crashed into the sink with a loud clunk.

"Micky!" Robert was instantly at her side. "What happened?"

She looked at her hands again. They were green. "I… I thought I cut myself on the blade."

"Did you?" He tried to inspect, but she moved away. "Sorry."

She stumbled back and grabbed her thermos. "I have to go to work."

"Are you sure you're okay? You look really pale."

She nodded vaguely. It was difficult to breathe. Like the air had become toxic. When she flung open the door and stepped outside, she inhaled deeply. She jogged to her car and threw a quick glance at her front yard.

The wilted flowers were covered in snow. She had clearly neglected her little garden.

She climbed inside the car and turned on the engine. Her phone rang. It was Nick.

"What's up?"

"Mack, you need to come to the Beckers' right away."

"What happened?" She punched the accelerator.

"Katy was abducted."

# CHAPTER TWENTY-FOUR

Mackenzie parked her car haphazardly next to the squad cars in front of the Beckers'. The curious neighbors had crawled out of their houses to inspect what was happening. They stood in their yards, whispering among themselves.

Nick was talking to one of the officers in the front yard.

"Mack!" Nick called her over. "This is Peterson. The first responding officer."

"The dispatcher got a call at 8:23 a.m.," Peterson said. "I was close enough and arrived at 8:31 a.m. The husband was sitting on the steps leading to the front door. We went inside the house, and there were clear signs of a struggle."

"There's a patrol officer assigned to keep an eye on the house," Mackenzie said. "Where was he?"

"He came back at around 8:30 a.m., ma'am. Said he takes a breakfast break every day from eight to eight thirty." He tipped his chin at the young patrol officer with an army haircut and red ears being interviewed by Justin.

"I'll be inside."

She ducked under the yellow tape secured across the front door. The red armchair on the way to the staircase was tipped over. The rug in the living room had shifted, as evidenced by the deep grooves misaligned with the legs of the coffee table. A lamp had toppled over, the bulb smashed on the hardwood floor. This was a crime scene. One of the officers carried Katy's scarf and pajamas in a plastic bag—scent articles in case they needed search dogs. Another one clicked pictures. Mackenzie's eyes scanned the house—no blood. There was a broken plate on the kitchen floor. The door that opened to the backyard was off the kitchen. The window had been smashed in. The glass pieces were cluttered on the inside of the house, meaning someone had broken it from the outside, trying to get in.

"We believe that's how he got inside the house," Justin came to her side. "And probably how he left too."

"Are any items missing?"

"The husband is upstairs going over the inventory."

"When did Cole last see her?"

"She was still sleeping when he left for his run at 7:45 a.m."

"And the patrol officer was outside?"

"Jenkins? Yes," he huffed. "He's a good kid."

"He knew when to come." She crossed her arms. "It's no coincidence he came when Jenkins was on a break."

"He's probably been watching Katy," he agreed.

Katy might have been feeling sick these past few days, but she was an active, adult woman. It would have taken a considerable amount of strength to abduct her from her house in such an aggressive manner. The abductor was likely to be a man, based on the method and statistics. Mackenzie imagined a woman would have lured Katy somehow, been more strategic.

Mackenzie's insides curdled. First Kim and the doppelganger, and now Katy. Would Katy be dead soon too?

"What's behind the house?" She headed to the door, careful not to touch anything or step on the glass. Peering through the broken window in the door, she saw a frozen creek and woods draped in snow on the other side. "Where do these woods lead to?"

"They're shallow on this side and run a little deep if you head west from here."

"To the highway, right?"

"Yes." Justin frowned. "Directly to Olympia."

"Call the department of transportation and see if we can get anything from the traffic lights. Did the dispatch center enter her information into NCIC?"

"Yes, ma'am."

She imagined how it played out. The back door rattled loudly. He must have checked to see if it was open. When it wasn't, he smashed his elbow through the window of the door, snaked his arm inside and twisted the knob. The action would have made a loud sound. Did that wake Katy up? Was she already awake? She came running down the stairs, wondering where the noise was coming from. She saw him and screamed. He tried chasing her around the living room. The chair fell. The table moved. Finally, he grabbed her. She struggled in his arms. But he was stronger. The plate came crashing down from the counter as he took her out the way he got in, leaving the door slightly ajar.

Mackenzie looked over at one of the crime scene investigators dusting for prints.

If the killer had planned to take Katy when he knew the patrol officer would be on a break, then he would likely have been careful enough to wear gloves.

"Mack," Nick came back inside and edged past the moving bodies. "Delilah Pine reported she heard shouting and furniture toppling."

"She didn't call 911?"

"She thought that Cole returned early from his run and they had got into a fight. It wasn't until the cops showed up that she realized Katy was missing."

A few hours later, Mackenzie and Nick were going over Jenkins' initial contact report. Justin had prepared a briefing too, including statements from all the witnesses. Patrol had ventured into the woods, hoping to find a clue left behind. No car could be brought into the woods. The only plausible explanation was that the man took one of the exits off the highway, left his car there and then embarked into the woods on foot. Unfortunately, the freshly falling snow obscured any footprints.

The positioning of the houses made it such that the only person who would have had a clear view of the backyard would be Delilah. But she hadn't seen anything. And neither had any other neighbor.

"Have we sent out her description?" Rivera asked. Her nose was buried deep in one of the reports.

Mackenzie and Nick confirmed they had. Cole had verified that Katy was dressed in gray pajamas and a white T-shirt. She was wearing no accessories.

"Cole said her phone's missing," Mackenzie said.

Rivera looked up. Her glasses rested on the bridge of her thick nose. "If there was a struggle, then when did he find the time to take her phone?"

"It must be on her," Sully grumbled from her side. "She heard the noise and grabbed her phone to dial 911."

"Or her phone has something on it. When will you get the records from the phone company?"

"Waiting for a judge to sign the warrant," Nick said. "But we're tracking her phone. It was last active in the house at eight this morning. If it's turned on for long enough, we'll find out where it is."

"Let's hope he doesn't destroy the phone," Rivera said. "Make sure the crime scene investigators go through that house with a fine-toothed comb. If there was a struggle, there could be some DNA. Hair strands or blood."

Sully sighed, exasperated. "Can anyone confirm Cole's alibi?"

"Not yet," Nick admitted. "You think he's behind this?"

He raised his eyebrows. "He's been fighting with his wife. Has a temper. Probably having an affair."

"What, you think he knew about the twin? Killed her and the other one?"

"Not necessarily. He might not have killed the others, but maybe he saw them as a way of getting rid of Katy."

"We should get his phone records too," Mackenzie said.

"If Cole wanted to get rid of his wife, then this has been one hell of a setup." Nick ran a hand through his hair. "And how do Carrie and the suicide victim factor in? If they do at all."

"I think the murders are related to the twin," Sully said. "God knows what life she led before finding her way here."

Rivera closed the file and removed her glasses. She glared at Mackenzie and Nick with piercing eyes. "Regardless of Cole's involvement, we can all agree that there's something very disturbing about this case. We have a dead twin, an arbitrary old suicide, not to mention an unidentified body in our morgue with mysterious tattoos. Katy has been abducted and going by what we know, there's a high chance she'll be dead soon, if not already. We have our work cut out for us."

# CHAPTER TWENTY-FIVE

"Am I in an alternate universe?" Troy left a dramatic pause.

"What?"

His mocking eyes slid over Mackenzie. She looked down and almost swallowed her tongue. She was dressed in her running gear. Her red hair was frizzy and jutting out in every direction. She touched her face, realizing that she hadn't done her makeup.

"Don't look so devastated, Mad Mack," Troy smiled. "You don't look scary today."

She knew he meant it as a compliment, which is why she flashed him a tight smile. But inside, a harrowing feeling brewed. Her armor was chipped. It felt like just a matter of time until it came crashing down completely.

She turned to see Nick with a pack of cigarettes in his hand and a grimace marring his face. He stared at the pack for ticking seconds, contemplating giving in to the poisonous habit. She could have nagged him, but she didn't. His eyebrows stitched together in a knot. With that, he tossed the pack in the trash can.

Mackenzie's phone pinged with a message from Justin.

*Checked with all the tattoo parlors. Nothing.*

"Justin couldn't find the tattoo parlor," she sighed.

"She could've gotten it outside of Lakemore." Nick picked up his steaming coffee mug and pressed it against his head.

"I'm going to get a head start on the posters for Katy," she said, preparing to send a request to the Washington State Patrol Missing and Unidentified Persons Unit.

Nick checked his phone. "I'll talk to patrol and go over their plan."

Mackenzie nodded. Suddenly the door to their office opened, and a uniformed cop walked in, followed by Charlotte Harris.

"Detectives, she really wanted to see you."

"Thanks, Jerry."

Charlotte chewed on her dry lips. Her striking face seemed to have aged a decade since the last time Mackenzie had seen her.

"You go ahead, Nick. I'll touch base with you later."

"Detective Price," Charlotte's voice was breathy. "Cole told us what happened."

"Yes… I'm sorry, Charlotte. Can you think of anyone who wanted to hurt Katy?"

A sob sputtered out of her throat, and she clasped her mouth to muffle it. Tears streamed down her cheeks. "N-no. She's so good. Sh-she has dedicated her life to helping others."

Mackenzie raised a hand to comfort her, but dropped it to her side. "Could I get you some water?"

"No! No!" Charlotte sniffed and set her face straight. "I want you to bring back my daughter."

"Charlotte, when was the last time you talked with Katy?"

"I called her yesterday evening. I'd wanted to take her to church in the morning. She's been so stressed with everything. I thought it would help her. But she'd declined by text, so I called instead."

"And how did she sound?"

"Fine. Just tired and sleepy."

"And the last time you met her?"

"I… I think more than a week ago."

"What about Cole?" she asked deliberately.

Charlotte narrowed her eyes. "Do you think *Cole* has something to do with this? He's broken."

"I'm sorry, Charlotte, but his behavior has been unusual."

She looked cynical. "Really? I… I don't know what to believe. He seems fine to me."

"Where's Frank?"

"At home. He's been ringing our friends. Maybe someone knows *something*. Do you think this could be related to Kim?" Charlotte asked warily.

"Why would you say that?"

She looked irritated. "I don't know what kind of things Kim could have gotten involved in."

"We'll look into everything. Meanwhile, if anything happens or you think of something, please contact us."

"Please find her. She's my everything."

# CHAPTER TWENTY-SIX

*November 28*

There was no news of Katy Becker. It had been two days. The Washington State Patrol was on it. She was all over the local news, posters had been strung up around the city. They had also approached the Sheriff's Office, asking for assistance in searching the woods—especially with Woodburn Park still being on the list of places to search. The Sheriff's Office often collaborated with the Lakemore PD, especially with missing persons, as they knew the woods well. But it wasn't in Mackenzie's control how much help they could offer. They were stretched thin too because of budget issues and the FBI investigation.

Yesterday the storm had subsided, allowing more manpower to venture into the woods, but they had found nothing. Jenna had confirmed that no hospitals in Tacoma or Olympia claimed to recognize Jane Doe Two or the work done to her face. The doctor could be anywhere in Washington, or maybe even out of state. Mackenzie and Nick were hoping to track their culprit through him. But that approach was proving to be fruitless.

Jane Doe Two's identity and the old suicide loomed like bad omens over the case. Mackenzie was just heading home after a frustrating day's work when her phone rang.

"Nick? What's up?"

"Crime scene investigators found a man's footprints in the backyard. They were under an overhang so weren't covered by snow."

"That's good! Maybe the crime lab can get something out of it. I went over the cameras from the department of transportation. The nearest exit to the Beckers' has a car wash and a Wendy's. But no camera covers the entire area."

"So nothing?"

"Nada," she said. "This guy's too smart. Only one pair of footprints?"

"Yep. My two cents? He used chloroform on her and carried her. Stuffed her in the trunk and drove off."

"That way no one would hear her scream for help," Mackenzie said. "What about the footprint? Any specification?"

"It was too faint."

Her phone pinged with a notification. "Oh, they sent us Katy and Cole's phone records."

"Yeah, I just got them too."

"I'll go over Cole's. You go over Katy's."

"Yeah. Also, remember that conference Cole returned early from that weekend?"

Mackenzie recalled Katy's statement that Cole had left for Seattle on the Friday before the bodies were found, but came back Saturday, claiming that the conference wasn't worth his time. "What about it?"

"I was just following a hunch. There was a conference for physiotherapists in Seattle that weekend. I called them and Cole never even registered for it, let alone attended."

Mackenzie bit the inside of her cheek. "Where did he go, then?"

"He's definitely hiding something. Anyway, I'll see you tomorrow."

Sterling couldn't make dinner that night, so it was just Mackenzie and her father.

"What do you say to takeout?" said Robert. "My treat."

"Sure. Thanks." She still didn't trust him, but she appreciated the gesture, especially if it meant she didn't need to cook.

Later, they watched a sitcom, munching on pizza. To anyone else, they would probably have looked like a normal family. Except that Mackenzie sat at the opposite end of the couch, curled up in a ball. Occasionally, her father snickered good-naturedly. The sound was familiar. She knew him in her bones; he had created her. But she couldn't shake the feeling that he was a stranger in her house.

Mackenzie got up abruptly.

"I've got some cleaning to do," she said, and headed to the kitchen.

The lemony scent of her homemade disinfectant solution trickled up her nose, comforting her. Through the window, she watched her father go into the garden and stand there. He looked up at the twilight sky—swirls of pink against a dusky purple slowly dimming into velvety darkness.

Later that night, the wind howled like an angry ghost haunting the streets of Lakemore. Mackenzie lay awake in her bed, staring at the crown molding. Shadows danced across the ceiling from the window. She focused on the shadow of the tree swaying and bending at unnatural angles. Like it would snap anytime. It was a tree, not a branch. But the winds were strong. The leafy tree had been reduced to barrenness after the fall. It looked dead, but still it moved wildly.

Mackenzie clutched the edge of the blanket, disturbed by the image and the wind. She had locked her door from the inside but still didn't feel safe. She tried everything to fall asleep—counted sheep, lit a scented candle, even listened to soothing music. But two hours later, she was wide awake. Her brain was buzzing even though she couldn't focus on anything concrete.

She looked to Sterling's side of the bed and swallowed hard.

It was two in the morning.

She dragged her feet to the bathroom to take another shower. Spending the entire day crammed in the office reviewing the security cameras around Sheppard Hallows had left her grimy, with sore muscles.

She reckoned feeling clean would soothe her jangled nerves. After the shower, she wiped the steamed-up mirror and studied her reflection.

She looked so exhausted.

*You have to help me bury him.* Melody's voice hissed in her ears. Everything that had happened came crashing into her like a wave. She might not have bashed that man's skull in like Melody did, but she had denied him dignity and justice.

Was it even in self-defense, like Melody had claimed?

Mackenzie's breathing came loud and strong. She gripped the sink hard enough to leave grooves on her skin.

She looked up, expecting to find her pallid reflection, but for a moment saw her mother instead. They looked so similar. She hated it.

Her hand curled into a fist, and she punched the mirror.

# CHAPTER TWENTY-SEVEN

*November 29*

The phone company had sent Cole's records for the last month. Fortunately for them, the provider saved text messages for a month before deleting them, giving Mackenzie and Nick full access to his communication.

Delilah said that Cole went somewhere on Thursday and Saturday nights. Mackenzie spent the next hour going through call logs and text messages. There was one number that showed up more frequently—and it didn't belong to Katy or his office. Cole called that number during his lunch hour and after work. She highlighted the entries. Their conversations would last from one minute to thirty minutes. They could call the company for the customer data.

She clicked on the transcripts of his text messages and searched for messages exchanged with the mysterious number. There were very few messages compared to the phone calls.

If Cole were hiding an affair, then it would make sense not to text much. She combed through the texts, looking for a clue. But most of them were too general to provide any information on their relationship or the identity of the person.

*Call you back.*

*See you later.*

*Good luck.*

*Did you check it out?*

*No.*

*Me too.*

But then she found one text from Cole.

*Not now, Ana.*

The critical seventy-two-hour window had passed, and there was no news of Katy Becker.

"I don't know what Lakemore's true enemy is—crime or the weather." Nick entered the conference room chucking off his coat, which was dusted with snow.

Jenna spread a map of Woodburn Park on the table. "I'll need more time tracking all the owners of these properties. The records haven't been well maintained. There are also illegal constructions deeper into the woods, slightly further from the trail."

"Like what?" Nick asked.

"Sheds and small lodges. The woods are vast and dense. Hard to regulate. It might take weeks to cover the area, especially if we keep getting blizzards every second day."

The patrol had been focused on the trail, trying to decipher where the bodies were dumped from, looking for a clue that might have been left behind. But if they had to expand deeper into the woods, which were usually inaccessible and difficult to navigate, a thorough search would take months.

"There was nothing in Katy's call and text logs," Nick said, filling a cup with coffee from the espresso machine. "In fact, she hasn't been that active at all in the last couple weeks. Coffee?"

"Yes, please." Mackenzie extended her arm to him. Nick paused. Justin raised his eyebrows.

"Really?" said Nick.

She ground her jaw. "I didn't sleep last night."

"Yeah, I can tell." He smirked and gave her his mug.

The comment made her uneasy. She knew she looked rough; her skin was dry and her eyelids felt swollen. She took a hesitant sip and hated it.

"Anyway, Cole has been talking to *Ana* a lot," Mackenzie said. "Their texts didn't give anything away. We'll have to call the company to get her information."

Justin took the printout of the call logs from her and headed for the door. "On it."

"We still haven't confirmed Cole's alibi for when Katy was taken, have we?"

"Nope," Nick said.

"Why don't we just ask Cole who Ana is?" Jenna shrugged.

Sully came in carrying a laptop.

"Uh oh," Mackenzie muttered under her breath. Sully was pouting and glaring at them. He set the laptop on the table and played a video.

"*Lakemore PD was too focused on harassing me and my wife instead of solving the murders of two women. Now, my wife is missing.*" Cole was carrying grocery bags and climbing out of his car.

"*Do the police have any leads? Is it true your wife was pregnant?*" A journalist followed him.

He dismissed her. "*Ask the cops. That is if they're done sitting on their asses.*"

Sully closed the laptop sharply, sending papers on the table flying away. "Why is it that every case you two handle ends up making the news?"

"You can't blame us for the Perez case," Nick argued.

"Fine. But why can't you stop this physiotherapist trashing us in the media?"

"Free speech?" Mackenzie gave him a weak smile.

Sully crossed his arms. "The FBI is investigating possible corruption in Lakemore. The mayor's office isn't their only focus. They're also looking into Captain Murphy and some retired cops."

"Murphy has been here for a very long time. How old is he again?" Nick asked.

"This is a serious matter, Nick," Sully reprimanded him. "Not that I have ever given a damn about what people think, but these are critical times. Rivera just blasted me."

"She doesn't know how this town works. Lakemore is small. Our cases end up getting coverage," Mackenzie said.

"When you get my job, Mack, feel free to tell the brass off."

She raised her hands in surrender.

"Cole's lawyered up," Nick said. "He's denying us access."

"Well, that doesn't make him look good," Sully huffed. "Where are we on Katy's status?"

"The weather has slowed us down a bit. Still no news."

"Her phone hasn't been switched on?"

"Nope."

"I'm in the wrong line of work." He pinched the bridge of his nose. "Tell me if anything changes."

After he left, Nick turned to Mackenzie. "You were checking her social media accounts, right? Anything there?"

"Not yet." Her shoulders slumped. "It took me days to get through her Twitter alone. Now I'm going through her Facebook pictures. *Hundreds* of pictures."

"Yeah…" He eyed her coffee. "You're not drinking more, are you?"

"I don't want to throw up, so no." She pushed it in his direction.

Justin knocked on the door and stuck his head in. "I got a name. That number belongs to Anastasia Hunter."

# CHAPTER TWENTY-EIGHT

Mackenzie was certain of two things. First, that loyalty was dead; and second, that all the clouds were magically attracted to Lakemore. She drummed her fidgety fingers on the steering wheel and blew out a breath. Her head felt heavy. Her sleep had been disjointed these last few days.

"What are you annoyed at?" Nick asked.

"Cheating husbands," she muttered, and bit her tongue.

To her surprise, Nick snorted. "Sorry, I wasn't expecting you to be honest."

She turned her eyes to Cole, sitting in the cafe by the window. Mackenzie and Nick were parked on the other side of the street. Delilah Pine had informed them that Cole was leaving home on Thursday afternoons or evenings. This time, Mackenzie and Nick had been ready to follow him.

"Anastasia Hunter has a clean record. A Stepford wife, *apparently*," Nick said, and then paused. "Mack? Are you paying attention?"

"Yes."

"Now that you know that your dad *is* your dad, how's it going?"

"I think I'll order sushi for dinner."

"Is that your way of changing the topic?" Nick gorged on a donut. Crumbs fell into his lap and he brushed them off.

"Please don't dirty up my car. There are napkins in the glove box."

He opened it and took some out. "Who puts napkins in the glove box?"

"Someone who spends a lot of time with you." She scowled at the tidbits on the floor.

"Maybe he's just drinking coffee alone?"

"She'll show up," Mackenzie asserted, and turned down the heater.

"The holiday party is coming up," Nick reminded her. "Are you bringing your dad?"

She had forgotten about that. "I… I don't know. Should I? You said he should keep a low profile."

"Yeah, I meant officially. Avoid banks and anything that would require him to produce paperwork. Easy enough when he's like, what? Late sixties? Seventy?"

She hadn't told him that her father had found a part-time job at one of Blake Richie's garages. She was embarrassed that her father had been an opportunist. "Yeah."

"Your call."

"I guess I could."

"Will you bring Sterling?" He took out a cigarette and popped it in his mouth. He looked ahead at the cafe casually.

"I don't want to. I'm hoping he'll be busy so that we can avoid an awkward conversation."

A woman with reddish-brown hair walked into the cafe and went to Cole's table. He stood up and kissed her on the lips.

"She's here."

They climbed out of the car with their umbrellas. Mackenzie shivered in her leather jacket. A car zipped by, spraying water on Mackenzie's feet.

"Shit!" She groaned as the water soaked into her shoes.

They crossed the street and entered the cafe. Cole and Anastasia were sitting together, looking out at the rain. Cole was in the middle of a sentence when he spotted them. The blood drained from his face.

"I-I…" He stood up. "D-detectives…"

"Mr. Becker." Mackenzie smiled sardonically at Anastasia. "Mrs. Hunter."

Anastasia looked at Cole nervously.

"I'll call my lawyer right now." Cole took out his phone from his pocket.

"I think it's in your best interests if you don't make this difficult for us." Mackenzie couldn't keep the spite out of her voice. "Otherwise, we'll have to go to a lot of people with our questions, including Mr. Hunter."

Anastasia paled. "How did you…? Oh, Cole. Please…"

Cole nodded and sat down with a clenched jaw.

"You're not looking good, Cole." Nick took a seat and folded his arms on the table. "Your wife is missing. And you have motive."

"He doesn't!" Anastasia pleaded. "We don't want to hurt Katy."

Mackenzie raised an eyebrow at Cole. With a slump of his shoulders, he gave in. "I never intended to leave Katy. And Anastasia doesn't want to leave her husband either."

"I don't understand," Nick said.

"We…" Anastasia pressed her lips together. "Cole and I like each other. But we also love our spouses."

"You love your husband, but you cheat on him?" Mackenzie asked sharply as she also sat down.

"I don't expect you to understand."

"Our priority is our marriages. Anastasia has a son. And Katy's pregnant." The tip of Cole's nose turned red. "I shouldn't have left her alone that morning."

"You went to meet Anastasia?" Nick asked.

Cole squeezed his eyes shut and nodded. "I did. I go running at that time, but this time Anastasia decided to join me." When he opened his eyes, they were bloodshot. "I know I'm breaking Katy's trust, but that doesn't mean that I want her *dead.* If I wanted to leave Katy, I would have. I love her. I just… I just have feelings for Anastasia too."

"We know you didn't go to any conference in Seattle that weekend. Where were you?" Mackenzie demanded.

"We decided to go away for a weekend," Anastasia answered. "We left Friday morning, but the next morning my son got sick, so we had to leave."

"You and Katy have been having problems. Is it because of your affair?" Nick asked.

"Who did you hear that from? Delilah? That woman is crazy. She exaggerates."

Mackenzie raised an eyebrow. "Who says we heard it from Delilah?"

Anastasia's pager trilled. "Shoot. I have to go." She placed a kiss on Cole's cheek like it was instinct and then blushed, looking down. "Detectives, you can talk to me whenever you want to. But *please* don't tell my husband about this."

When Nick nodded, she sighed in relief and scurried away toward her car.

"Who else knows about your affair?" Mackenzie asked.

"No one. We're discreet. If you don't have any more questions, then I should go. My lawyer instructed me not to talk to you at all."

"Don't discuss the case with the media."

"If talking to the media keeps Katy's face out there, then I'll do it."

"You're walking a thin line. You reveal too much and that'll hurt Katy. We'll be in touch," Nick warned in a hard voice.

Cole nodded and stood up. "Just find my wife before it's too late."

The pitter-patter of the rain grew louder. Back at the station, Nick leaned back in his chair with a sigh. "I don't get it."

A muscle ticked in Mackenzie's jaw. "If he's so worried about his wife, then why is he meeting his girlfriend for coffee at a time like this?"

Nick opened his mouth to reply but seeing Mackenzie's face, he closed it. She wondered what her expression gave away. "He may be cheating on Katy, but that doesn't necessarily mean he wanted to hurt her," he said gently. "Then we have Kim and Jane Doe in our morgue."

"What if he killed Kim, thinking it was Katy? And Jane Doe got in the way?" Mackenzie mused.

"Jesus. Imagine the shock he would have had when he came home and found Katy alive. So, what, he kills the lookalikes by mistake, realizes it could be an opportunity to pin it on a random serial killer and abducts Katy?" Nick looked unconvinced. "Seems pretty extreme. And what about the person who did that to Jane Doe's face?"

"We don't know that the procedures have anything to do with the murders. And I'm not saying Cole murdered all three of them, necessarily. But he could have abducted Katy. He has motive. I don't buy all that crap about loving their spouses and not wanting to leave them."

"His alibi for the abduction is Anastasia. She could be in on it," Nick agreed.

"Let's keep an eye on them."

Later that afternoon, Mackenzie finally got a chance to drive to the crime lab in Seattle to hand over the mysterious pen that had been gifted to Steven Boyle/Brennan anonymously. With Katy missing and the pen quite possibly having nothing to do with the case, the item had taken a backseat. But Mackenzie wanted to be thorough.

She was on her way to Anthony's fusty office when she saw him through the window in the lab. Clumps of white hair on a mostly hairless head peering into a microscope. She tapped on the glass.

Anthony Wallace looked up with a pout, disliking being interrupted.

"What are you doing here, Mack?" He closed the door behind him and stuffed his latex gloves in the pocket of his lab coat.

She handed him the plastic bag containing the pen. "Can you find anything on this?"

"Why wasn't this collected by the CSI? Related to that woman you're looking for?"

"Not exactly. It's not evidence or from a crime scene. I'm not even sure what you can get from this..."

"Prints? DNA?"

"It's been compromised. Sitting out for at least a year. It looks like someone carved those lines into it. What does that mean?"

Anthony inspected it with a frown. "Come with me."

Mackenzie followed him into his office, baffled. He went behind his desk, pulled out a notepad and started scribbling. She rocked back and forth on her heels, unsure of what he was up to, but his brows were knitted and his lips pursed in concentration. The large bookcase behind his desk seemed to be filled with more books than the last time she was here. She noticed the frame slightly drooping and bending from the weight. It was only a matter of time before it collapsed.

"You need a new shelf. That thing could fall anytime."

"When it does, I'll find a new one," he mumbled.

"What are you doing?"

He tore the sheet off the notepad and slid it toward Mackenzie. He had drawn a molecular structure on it, complete with the symbols for hydrogen and oxygen.

"It's the chemical structure for hyaluronic acid. That's what was engraved on the pen," Anthony announced with a smirk.

Mackenzie compared the markings to Anthony's drawing. It was a match.

"It's a polymer, excellent for your skin," Anthony went on. "Heavily used in dermatology treatments. Properties include wound healing, tissue hydration, and decreasing wrinkles. It's also the ingredient used in lip fillers."

It was also the same molecule that had featured so heavily in Steven Boyle's research. Whoever sent the gift must have been familiar with his work, enough to add a personal touch. Mackenzie's scalp prickled. She had a feeling that if they could track down the sender, they would be able to identify their Jane Does.

# CHAPTER TWENTY-NINE

*November 30*

Mackenzie massaged her eyelids, clicking away on the computer. The glare from the screen made the back of her eyes throb. Despite it still being early, she'd lost track of how long she had been sitting in front of it. It was good—necessary—to take breaks. But it was hard to stop once she started.

Katy Becker had been snatched from her home. Mackenzie couldn't afford to take a break.

She had been scouring the internet and Katy's social media accounts to look for anyone suspicious. Katy put herself out in the world. She photographed herself eating breakfast, striking yoga poses, reading a book, pouting at work, as well as views from evening strolls, the song she was listening to, and her "makeup free" selfies in bed.

To Mackenzie, it was excessive. But she knew this was a lot of people's world today. Willingly giving glimpses into their lives. Regardless of the creeps who might be watching.

She scrolled through the comments on one of Katy's Instagram posts.

*Damn. I'd like those red lips wrapped around my d**k.*

Disgust unfolded in her gut. It was a sixteen-year-old boy.

The more she dug, the more comments she found. There were equally revolting remarks but no account that commented on all the posts regularly. They were sporadic. And with over a thousand followers on Instagram alone, this was an uphill battle.

Mackenzie leaned back on her chair and cracked her neck. Her scalp felt itchy, and she wondered when she'd last washed her hair. She twirled a strand around her finger. Stringy and dull, with forked ends. Pushing her hair behind her ears, she browsed the pictures of events Katy had attended.

The pictures began to blur into one another. People smiling at the camera—she couldn't differentiate between what was genuine or forced. Even faces began to blend into each other. She kept her eyes focused on Katy, who was full of zest and sparkle—a formidable contrast to her current self.

Mackenzie's repetitive tapping on the keyboard stopped.

A man dressed in a blue T-shirt and baseball cap was standing in the background of a picture of Katy posing with an old woman.

Mackenzie frowned and went back a few pictures. He was in all of them. His face was mostly hidden due to the cap and downward tilting of his face. Even as Katy moved around the venue—at one point to speak on stage—he hovered close by. His posture was always unassuming, and Mackenzie wondered if his repeated presence was a coincidence, but there was a reason this man had stood out to her. Where everyone mingled with each other dressed up in formal clothes, he alone was in casual clothes. Plus, he was always facing Katy.

"Who the hell are you?" she muttered, searching for a picture that would show his face. But then something caught her eye. The guests at the event were wearing sticky name tags. She found a picture of him, drinking from a cup and looking over his shoulder at Katy. The nametag was visible. She downloaded the picture and zoomed in.

*Robbie Elfman.*

Mackenzie checked the Washington State Identification System database for criminal history and got a hit. He was a forty-year-old man convicted of unwanted pursuit of another person and harassment—twice in the last six years. His arrest offenses included several misdemeanors. There were no known sex offender registrations. He had been in and out of prison a couple of times. He had been out almost a year now after serving nine months in county jail.

She pulled up his photograph from DMV records. A cherub-like face marred by a sneer. He had curly brown hair, black beady eyes and unruly facial hair that looked like it would flap in the wind.

She searched him on social media. He was on Instagram, without a profile picture, and followed only one person: Katy Becker.

Mackenzie's brain crackled with energy. This was a solid lead—a man with a criminal past of stalking who seemed to be obsessed with Katy. Could he have something to do with the murders? Did he take Katy?

Fatigue slammed into her, followed by a squeaky howl released by her stomach. The corner of Troy's mouth lifted as he pretended to be engrossed in the report he was reading.

"Shut it."

"I didn't say anything." He chuckled.

Mackenzie fished out change from a drawer and headed to the vending machine. She needed a soda and some chocolate to wake her up after another sleepless night. Her usual smoothie wasn't quite cutting it today.

She was playing with the change in her hands when a familiar voice hauled her attention to the television.

"*We are joined by the most famous reporter in Lakemore.*" Debbie, the anchor, smiled at the camera, her face caked in makeup. "*The man who broke the story that took Lakemore by storm. Vincent Hawkins, welcome.*"

The camera panned out to accommodate a guffawing Vincent in the frame. His gray hair had been cut short, but the thin mustache capping his lips was intact. He was dressed in a beige suit, unlike the casual jeans and T-shirt he wore when he'd visited Mackenzie a few months ago.

"*Thank you for having me, Deb.*"

"*Did you anticipate that this story would blow up like this?*"

"*Of course I did.*" He shrugged. "*As it should. Lakemore put its trust in the wrong people. The public needed to know.*"

"*But the path to justice is complicated.*"

Vincent nodded. "*It often is. But that should never stop anyone from doing what's right.*"

Mackenzie selected a Sprite and a Milky Way and went back to her office. It was wise to stay away from the news. It stressed her out. Back in her chair, she munched on the candy. She checked her watch. Nick was dropping off Luna at school. He was about to return anytime.

She noted Robbie Elfman's information and his address—a man with a history of stalking women, appearing to orbit around Katy. They needed to pay him a visit.

# CHAPTER THIRTY

Robbie Elfman lived a five-minute walk from Woodburn Park. The single-story house was painted an ugly blue, with cabling from nearby poles dangling loose when it reached the roofline. An old Impala with dents and scratches stood in the driveway. The neighborhood was fraught with poverty and dread. Even after several knocks, no one opened the door.

"His car's here," Nick said.

"He could've—"

There was a sound on the other side of the door. "Someone's home." Mackenzie moved to a window and peered inside. A shadow scurried across the hallway.

"The back door!" she yelled.

Nick circled around the house, Mackenzie right behind him. A door squeaked open and shut. A round man with curly brown hair stumbled toward the thick spread of trees behind the house.

"Lakemore PD! Stop!"

The man ignored them, but struggled to run fast as his loose pants kept slipping down his waist.

Nick launched himself forward and tackled him. The man face-planted on the ground with a growl. Nick tried restraining him, but the man got to his knees and swung a fist, landing a glancing blow.

Mackenzie grabbed the man from behind and, using her entire strength, tossed him onto his side. He crashed into the ground with a groan. Before he could recover, she pulled out handcuffs and slipped them round his wrists.

"Robbie Elfman, you're under arrest for battery against a police officer. You have the right to remain silent. Anything you say can and will be used against you in a court of law—"

"Please, no! I'm sorry! I'm sorry! I just got out of jail." He writhed on the ground. Mackenzie pressed a knee into his lower back to keep him down. "You punched my partner, you asshole."

"I panicked! It was a reflex. Please. My record is screwed up already."

She looked at Nick. He had a bloody nose. He took out his handkerchief and gestured for her to go easy on him. "Will you cooperate with us?"

"I know nothing!"

"Will you?" She tightened the cuffs.

"Okay, okay. Fine."

She pulled him up by the back of his collar. The stench of cigarettes overwhelmed her nostrils. "You want to tell us why you ran away?"

Robbie shivered in the crisp winter air. "Because I saw on the news that Katy Becker was abducted."

"And?" Nick raised his eyebrows. "What do you know about that?"

He licked his lips. "Nothing. But I knew you wouldn't like what you'll find in there."

Robbie signaled to his house with a resigned look on his face.

Mackenzie dragged him over to the house with Nick on her heels. She didn't know what to prepare for. Was Katy inside?

She kicked open the door. When it slammed into the wall, a puff of dust blew into their faces. But once the dust settled, the sight in front of them was appalling.

Wires ran across the living room with Katy's pictures hanging from them. The walls were covered in her pictures too. Her face was everywhere.

"What the hell?" Nick muttered.

"I told you!" Robbie's skin was mottled red. "It looks bad."

She instructed him to sit on a chair. "I'm going to check your house. Is that okay?"

"You need a search warrant, right?"

"Not if you give us permission."

"And what if I don't?"

Mackenzie raised her eyebrow. He recoiled. "Okay! Fine! Go ahead!"

Nick stayed with him, making sure that he didn't run while Mackenzie navigated her way through his small house. She had to duck and push the photographs out of her way. Katy was everywhere. One wire had at least thirty copies of the same picture hanging on it. She recognized some others from her social media accounts. None of them looked like surveillance pictures. She checked his closets, the bathroom, and the tiny kitchen.

Katy wasn't in this house.

"You're obsessed with her." Mackenzie's tone was curt when she returned to the living room.

"I'm not *obsessed* with her. I *love* her."

Nick sighed, exasperated. "We checked your record, Robbie. You've been in love with a lot of women over the years."

"*This* time it's real," he insisted. "*She's* special."

"Do you know where she is?"

"No!"

"Where were you on Monday morning?" Mackenzie asked.

"Here."

"Can anyone vouch for you?"

He pressed his lips in a hard line. "No. I want a lawyer. I don't like how I'm being treated. This is harassment."

"Funny. Because I can arrest you for a lot of things right now," Mackenzie said.

"How long have you been following Katy for?" Nick demanded.

"I don't *follow* her. I like to look at her," he hissed through his teeth.

Mackenzie got in his face, towering over his pudgy, short frame, and placed her strong arms on her either side of him. "Cut the crap, Robbie. We have evidence of you following her around like a puppy dog. Since when?"

He wilted. "April. I was driving past this vigil outside city hall after that cop was shot dead. She was standing next to the cop's mother. I saw her… and I fell for her compassion."

"Have you ever tried to contact her?"

"No."

"You know where she lives?"

Robbie grunted and looked at Nick helplessly. "I… yes. But that doesn't mean I took her!"

Nick furrowed his eyebrows. "Have you ever been to her house?"

"Y-yes." He hung his head low. "Only when she was there. I never went inside. It was nice to watch her sit in the front yard and read."

"Does she know about you?"

A dreamy look crossed his face. "No. She's married. She's the best person I know. I never wanted to confuse her."

"What do you do for a living, Robbie?" Mackenzie asked.

"I'm in between jobs."

"When was the last time you had a job?"

"Two months ago. I was a busboy, but they gave me the can for taking too many smoke breaks."

She jutted her thumb behind her. "You got a fancy PC setup."

"So?" he glowered.

"When did you buy it?"

"Few months ago." He shrugged.

"How did you afford it?"

Robbie pursed his lips and gritted his teeth. "My grandmother left me some inheritance. I used part of it."

"How much inheritance?"

"Around ten grand."

"Do you have any proof of that?"

"No. Just take me for my word."

Mackenzie eyed him. Sweat collected on his upper lip and on the tips of his brown beard. He rocked back and forth on the chair, his hands still secured behind his back. His beady eyes looked smaller than they had in his DMV picture. He was clearly a delusional man with a history of stalking women. He couldn't hold down a job and lived in a dusty house that desperately needed more ventilation and fewer pictures of Katy.

He was unstable and alienated. But did that make him violent?

"You know we'll go through your financial statements, right?" she spat out. "And if you're lying, I'll haul your ass into jail myself."

"I… I responded to an ad." His voice was tinged with guilt. "It looks bad."

"What ad?"

"I'll show it to you. Have to dig through that drawer."

Mackenzie released the cuffs but hovered close as he scrambled to a chest of drawers.

"He's a nutjob," Nick whispered.

"This was the ad." He handed them the small piece of paper sheepishly. "It was on the dark web. I printed it out."

Mackenzie took it, and her heart stopped.

*Looking for a woman who looks like her and wants a fresh start in life.*

There was a picture of Katy Becker below and more details promising a healthy lifestyle.

"When was this?" Nick was the first of them to recover.

"May."

"And you had to *deliver* a lookalike?"

Robbie rolled his eyes. "You make it sound like trafficking. It's common. We like Katy but can't be with her, so we like to become friends with someone like her."

"*We*?" The word sounded like an accusation coming out of Mackenzie's mouth.

"People like me, who fall in love with someone from afar."

"You found someone?"

He rubbed the back of his neck. "Yeah... yeah, I did. Bella Fox. She's from Riverview. It was consensual. I didn't force her into anything. She had issues of her own. Pretty sure she did heroin."

Bella Fox. They finally had a name for their Jane Doe.

"How did you find her?" Mackenzie asked.

"On a prostitution website." His face colored crimson. "It's the best place to look for girls. There's a lot of variety."

"Who did you give her to?"

"I don't know. I was supposed to drop her off at Crescent Lake in Woodburn Park on June first, at noon. I did, and I never saw her again."

Mackenzie's blood fizzed with anger. She crumpled the paper in her hand. He took a woman with a drug problem and dropped her off in those woods and months later she was murdered. Unfortunately, there was no surveillance there. Lakemore hid dark secrets in the woods. She knew that only too well.

"How did you get the money? Deposited to your bank account?" Nick asked.

"Bitcoin. Which I sold."

The dark web was a bottomless black box.

"We're going to take your hard drive."

"You need a warrant."

"Not if we have your consent, Robbie."

Robbie looked between them and fidgeted. Sighing, he unplugged his laptop and handed it to them.

"You're coming with us to the station, Robbie." Mackenzie nudged him forward.

He looked appalled. "What? No! I didn't do anything. I don't even know what happened to her!"

"We have to take your formal statement. Will you cooperate or are you going to make this hard?"

He sulked and grabbed his jacket before stepping out with them. Nick locked him in the backseat and turned to Mackenzie. "I'll ask Clint to crack this open, but he'll need assistance."

Their IT guy was good, but his caseload was heavy. "Maybe Andrea from Special Investigations can help him."

"Good call. At least we have a name now. Bella Fox."

"This ad changes things."

As Nick pulled out of Robbie's driveway, Mackenzie's mind raced. Someone had paid Robbie Elfman thousands of dollars in bitcoin to get a girl who looked like Katy Becker. Bella Fox, a troubled young woman with a drug problem, was dropped off in Woodburn Park by Crescent Lake. A few months later, her body washed up on the shore of Westley River along with Kim's, her face surgically enhanced to look more like Katy. Both women had been murdered together in the last two weeks. They needed to find Katy, before she became the next victim.

# CHAPTER THIRTY-ONE

"We're looking for a gut hook knife," Mackenzie announced to the uniformed cops who had accompanied her to Robbie Elfman's house to execute a search warrant. "But bag anything you feel is out of place."

They nodded and began turning the place inside out. Emptying out drawers, tearing open mattresses, rummaging through piles of clothes. Most of their efforts were concentrated around the kitchen, but Mackenzie had instructed them to keep an eye out for a secret place—anywhere a knife could be stashed.

Robbie Elfman had spent hours being questioned and was then charged for trafficking. After all, he had received payment for providing a "service," which was finding and delivering a woman. He had been assigned a public prosecutor and with his record it was likely he would spend a good amount of time in jail. Robbie was willing to cooperate, getting spooked when told that the girl was found murdered. He'd even provided a detailed sketch of her before the procedures. But he maintained his innocence in both the murders and the surgery, swearing blind his only role had been to deliver Bella.

Mackenzie looked out the window of Robbie's home. Lakemore was like a ghost town, buried in blinding white snow, the dense woods looming menacingly in the background. The nightly blizzards had held the town hostage and Mackenzie couldn't recall the last time she had seen it so dead.

She thought of Bella, bought and sold like chattel, and her chest tightened. What had she and Kim been involved in? And where was Katy now?

Her phone rang. "Hey."

"Anything yet?" Nick asked.

"Just started. Will let you know. Anything in Riverview?"

"Yeah, I contacted Kevin in Riverview PD and forwarded him the sketch Robbie gave us of Bella. None of their missing persons match the description." Papers shuffled in the background. "And no Bella Fox was reported missing either."

Mackenzie paced the room. "Okay, Robbie said she was a prostitute, right? And we know she was a drug addict. It's possible no one reported her."

"It's going to be an uphill battle. But hopefully we'll retrieve something from his laptop, and we can go from there."

"Bella Fox could be her work name. Prostitutes often don't use their real name."

"Good point. I'll get on it."

Mackenzie hung up soon after and focused on sifting through Robbie's place. She thought again of the pictures of Katy, decorating every surface. Could they really believe he'd had no other involvement? He was clearly obsessed; no doubt he would have welcomed the prospect of making replicas of the woman he "loved." By all accounts he lacked the expertise to do it alone, but was there someone else? Mackenzie thought of the gift Steven had received. A fan of Steven's work; most likely someone with medical knowledge. They needed to find out who had sent that pen.

It was hours before Mackenzie and the team of officers finished digging through Robbie's place. They had searched it from top to bottom, but there was nothing more to be found. Empty-handed and disappointed, Mackenzie headed back to the station.

*

"Go home, Mad Mack," Sully grumbled without really meaning it. He shook his head when she didn't reply and walked out the door, leaving her alone. It was eleven. The floor was empty. Motion-sensitive lights in the hallway turned off.

Mackenzie sat alone at her desk in the silence. She had spent the rest of the day after the search going over the evidence they had gathered again. She had Katy's and Cole's phone records, forensics reports on Kim and Bella, Robbie's history, the crime scene unit pictures from Katy's abduction, and the ad looking for a woman who resembled Katy. Everything she knew about the case was right in front of her. But something important was escaping her notice; something was hiding in plain sight.

Clint and Andrea were still working with Robbie's laptop. Kim's files from the center would be received tomorrow. Maybe the answer lay in her history? What if *Kim* had put out the ad in an effort to look for Katy? Mackenzie quickly dismissed the idea. Katy's entire life was all over social media for anyone to see. Kim wouldn't have needed to resort to such extreme measures just to find her.

Mackenzie clicked her pen incessantly. The sound kept her tethered to the case. In the silence, it was too easy for her mind to float away; she'd hear Melody's shallow breathing in her ears. She'd hear the sound of dirt hitting the ground, as her mother buried a man Mackenzie had never met.

Her ringing phone startled her.

"Hello?" she answered without looking.

"Mack, I know you're working late tonight, did you get a chance to eat? I could bring you something," Sterling said.

"No. I'm good."

"It's getting really bad out there. Do you want me to pick you up? I know you don't like driving in the snow."

Her chest squeezed. "Please don't."

"Don't what?"

"I'll talk to you later." She hung up. He called back again but she declined it. She was still hopping mad at him, still gutted by his betrayal.

Mackenzie let her long tresses be free. She stretched and moved around, trying to relax.

What if what she was looking for was not in the physical evidence? She stopped and took out her notebook. There had to be something in her notes; she wrote everything down. Maybe she'd missed something in a witness statement, or her own observations. She settled down and started to read.

An hour later, she was still rereading and going over her meetings with everyone from the case. She had Katy's Twitter account open. Some of her followers were tagging her and asking her questions—others directing them to the news reports of her disappearance.

She stared at Katy's profile picture, her confident and carefree smile such a contrast from the woman she'd met. It was as if the pregnancy was sucking the life out of her. Or maybe her public persona was just that—a persona. A facade.

Her eye caught on Katy's earrings in the picture. They were crystal teardrops. She looked at the pictures of her room. On a side table, next to the lamp, sat some gold earrings. It was the same pair Mackenzie had complimented the other day. She took out a magnifying glass and inspected them closely. They were clip-on.

She reviewed Katy's pictures on all her social media channels. Finally, she found a selfie with Cole in which she wasn't wearing any earrings. Mackenzie zoomed in on the picture and used her magnifying glass. Her breath hitched.

Katy's ears were pierced.

But then why was she wearing clip-on earrings the other day?

Mackenzie's heart sped up. She closed her eyes and began connecting the dots. At her first meeting with Katy Becker, she appeared so different and skittish from what Mackenzie had come to expect. She opened the wrong cupboard to take out the glasses. She claimed the walls were thick when Delilah Pine said they weren't. She acted jumpy with Cole. Her statements and assertions were weak and unsure. She cancelled her appointment with her gynecologist. She didn't recognize her sweater dress until Cole pointed it out. She wasn't posting anything on social media. She wasn't leaving her house. She wasn't talking to her mother as frequently.

"Oh my God," Mackenzie whispered to no one.

The woman they'd talked to wasn't Katy Becker. She was Kim Harris. *Kim* had been abducted. The real Katy Becker had been lying dead in their morgue all this time.

# CHAPTER THIRTY-TWO

*December 1*

Mackenzie had walked in sketchy neighborhoods and dark alleys alone. Her work had taken her into the homes of violent criminals—into the very belly of nightmares.

But what scared most people didn't scare her much. There was only one spot in Lakemore that she had managed to avoid until now. And it wasn't the woods behind Hidden Lake. It was her childhood home. For the first time in twenty years, she found herself there.

It was a spontaneous decision. She was on her way to work and on a whim decided to take a quick detour.

She rolled down the window of her car and studied her old house. It looked smaller than she remembered. The white color of the wooden planks had faded into a yellowish tinge. The porch steps that always creaked under her weight were cracked. But the porch railing was new and freshly painted. Mackenzie didn't remember the balusters being straight and symmetrical. The entire front yard had been paved. There was no car parked close by and no smoke coming out of the flue.

Mackenzie let out a shuddering breath. Despite its rickety appearance, there was no place more menacing. It was a house that had eaten away at her innocence. It was where she used to console her abused mother, until she walked in one day to find a battered corpse in the kitchen. It was unfair how the bad always overshadowed the good. It stuck for longer. She raked her brain for one good memory.

She saw it. A vague image of a man wearing gardening gloves. A tiny Mackenzie with red pigtails running toward him. She must have been not even four years old. He turned around and hoisted her up in the air. She yelped and giggled. The blurry imagery dissipated into thin air.

Mackenzie's heart soared. Tears welled her eyes. That house wasn't all evil. It still had an echo of something good.

Mackenzie and Nick stared at Katy's picture placed on Sully's desk. It was a professional headshot—she wore a cream blouse and had her dark hair tied in a ponytail, stray locks falling down artfully. But she had laughed a little too much at the camera, as though she had let out a nervous chuckle. The picture came off as candid, capturing her sparkling personality. It was almost as if the woman didn't have an unlikeable bone in her body. She helped the less fortunate, used her voice to raise important issues, and inspired fairness and compassion in communities. A dwindling town like Lakemore needed someone like her. And now she had left behind her parents and husband.

"Are we sure about this?" Sully arched an eyebrow.

"I swung by the Beckers' on my way," Mackenzie said. "Cole let me dig around their master bedroom. None of her earrings are clip-on other than the gold ones she wore when we visited her."

"I called Becky to confirm. The body's ears are pierced." Nick shoved his hands in his pockets and leaned back against the wall.

"Becky was right when she said that the body belonged to Katy," Sully brooded. "Did you tell anyone about this?"

Mackenzie shook her head.

"Good. Don't."

"Why not?" Nick asked.

"A woman who was institutionalized at the age of four for being violent returns and starts living in place of her twin, who was murdered. Do you see where I'm going with this?"

"You think Kim murdered Katy? Then what about Bella?"

"Who the hell knows the kind of craziness Kim got involved in after she ran away. Especially given her history, I wouldn't be surprised if she was part of it, but something went wrong."

Mackenzie tapped a pen against her lip. "I wonder if Kim confronted Katy."

"Maybe that's what Maria stumbled into on that Wednesday. Katy wasn't letting her inside the house. Was it so Maria didn't see Kim?" Nick proposed.

Sully adjusted his belt buckle. "Riverview PD got nothing on Bella?"

"Nope," Nick confirmed. "Justin's on it. What about the pen?"

Mackenzie leaned her hip on the edge of his desk. "Anthony said that he'll run tests on it, but it will be a while before he gets around to it because of the backlog. But the chemical structure of an ingredient used in lip injections was engraved on it."

"What ingredient?"

"Hyaluronic acid. Steven Boyle published a lot of papers on its benefits in medical journals. It was the focus of his research."

Sully sat back. "Interesting. It's almost like a tribute to his work."

"Looks like it. Can't confirm a connection to the murders and the ad, though."

"Is Robbie cooperating?"

"He's still maintaining he knows nothing more. But given his history and mental instability, we can't take him on his word alone."

"Someone is picking up women, getting their faces altered, and then doing what with them?"

There was a knock on the door and an officer delivered Sully a box. He hopped off his seat and tore it open with childlike wonder. He dismissed them soon after.

Leaving the office, Nick clapped Mackenzie's back. "Nice work on the earrings!"

She teemed with satisfaction. After a very long time, she had had her first good night's sleep.

As they passed Finn's cubicle, Mackenzie heard him talking gently to someone.

"Michelle, the handwriting is a match."

The woman who had been yelling at him the other day sat on a chair next to him, clutching the beads of her long necklace. "She wouldn't disappear like this!"

"I'm sorry, but she wrote this note. We have confirmation. And her roommate gave a statement that Alison was planning to change her lifestyle."

"She wouldn't leave Oliver."

Finn hung his head low and rubbed the back of his neck. "Come with me. Let's get you some coffee."

The woman gritted her teeth and jerked her bag off Finn's desk, spilling a file on the floor. Ignoring the mess she'd created, she paraded out of the office with Finn tailing her, shaking his head.

"What was that?" Nick asked.

"Denial," Mackenzie answered with a heavy heart.

Clint came into their office with a sense of urgency. "Katy's phone just turned on."

# CHAPTER THIRTY-THREE

Mackenzie's strides were confident in the shallow woods not more than two miles from Crescent Lake. She paused behind a huge fir tree and peeked around it at a cabin made of wooden planks and a shingle roof. She checked her gun was loaded.

She turned off the safety, held the weapon ready and approached the unassuming cabin, acutely aware of her surroundings. Her boots digging into the deep snow, a soft breeze ruffling the few leaves left on the branches, the sound of a stream bubbling nearby. Nick stood behind another tree a few feet away from her. Making eye contact, they nodded at each other and moved forward.

Justin and another deputy approached the cabin from the other side. They didn't know what they were walking into. But four armed police officers were a good bet.

Mackenzie's stomach whirred with anticipation.

Her eyes made quick work of the cabin. There was no vehicle in sight. No fresh footprints in the snow, at least in front of the cabin. Curtains blocked all the windows. The patio furniture on the deck was covered with a tarp. Azalea bushes were planted below the deck rail—a fussy plant. Initial assessment concluded that the cabin appeared to be unoccupied. So how did Katy's phone end up here?

Mackenzie noticed the front door was slightly ajar. She directed Nick's attention to the door. He nodded. Then she heard a sound. They froze.

Something fell and clattered on the ground. Then there were footsteps.

A man emerged from behind the cabin, walking along the right side to the front, carrying logs under his arm. As soon as he saw them, he dropped the logs.

"Lakemore PD! Freeze!" Nick commanded in his deep voice. Mackenzie gestured to Justin and the deputy to circle around the property.

The man raised his hands in the air. "I didn't do anything!"

"On your knees!" Mackenzie jogged closer.

The man was average build, with reddish-brown hair and beard. His eyebrows and nose were pierced. He dug his knees into the ground and stared up at them with wide eyes. "What's going on?"

Mackenzie checked his pockets. They were empty. "He's fine."

They lowered their guns.

"Can someone please tell me what's happening?" His face creased with worry.

"Stand up." Nick put his gun back in its holster. "What's your name?"

"Ben Harlan."

"The property is undisturbed. No signs of anyone else," Justin said.

"You live here?" Mackenzie asked.

"Sometimes."

"Can we search the cabin?"

"Why?"

"We're looking into a woman's abduction. Her phone was located near here. This cabin is the only one in the area."

"A phone? Why didn't you just say that?"

"What do you mean?" Nick frowned.

"I found one earlier." He hitched his thumb to the cabin. "Do you want it? Come on in."

Mackenzie looked around the cabin. The faint smell of bacon strips tickled her nostrils. The furniture was old and dusty. Harlan's suitcase was parked against the wall by the entrance. A squiggly staircase was the only way upstairs. On the other side was another door that led to the back yard. There was nothing out of the ordinary about the cabin. Except the heating hadn't been turned up all the way.

Harlan walked to the coffee table. He picked up a phone from the empty fruit bowl there and handed it to them. "Is this the one?"

Nick pulled out his handkerchief and took the phone from him. It had a cracked screen and mud had got inside the cover with a map of Washington for a design. It matched the description of Katy Becker's phone, which they now knew had been in Kim's possession when the latter was abducted.

"Yup." Nick gave it to Justin, who carefully placed it in an evidence bag. "It was damaged when you found it?"

"Yeah. I figured someone dropped it." He scratched his ear. "Am I in trouble?"

"Not if you're telling the truth," Mackenzie said.

"I didn't know some woman was missing."

"When did you come here?"

"Two days ago."

"Why?"

"I… my girlfriend broke up with me," he admitted bashfully. "I needed time to clear my head. Thought I should get in touch with nature and everything."

"Did you do anything with the phone?" Nick asked.

"Like what?"

"I don't know. Go through it?"

"It's locked."

"Can you show us where you found it?"

"Yeah, sure."

It was along the shore of a creek. The ice on the surface had fractured and melted. Ben pointed at some rocks. "It was here."

Mackenzie knelt and assessed the rocks and the ground, searching for other clues. There was nothing. No blood. She stood up and looked at the thick trees threatening to swallow her. "Have you seen anyone else in these woods?"

"No. The cabins are so spaced apart. It's quiet anyway, what with the weather."

"Did you hear anything?"

"The woods always make strange sounds. But nothing out of the ordinary."

"When exactly did you find the phone?"

"At around ten o'clock, on my way back to the cabin. I was just walking around and stopped to catch my breath and noticed it lodged between those two rocks."

Mackenzie shot Justin a knowing look. He tipped his head in a salute and started taking Ben Harlan's details.

"Kim was here at some point," Nick said. "With Katy's phone on her."

"I'll check if this guy has a criminal record."

"I'll get some officers to scope the area."

"She could be anywhere." Mackenzie couldn't keep the dread out of her voice. She didn't know what exactly they were looking for—Kim, or Kim's body.

# CHAPTER THIRTY-FOUR

Riverview was what Lakemore would be if it were not for football. Both towns tucked next to Olympia were on the poorer side and rainy. But Riverview had nothing to unite the people. It reminded Mackenzie of a giant halfway house; a patch of land where delinquents crashed together and had no sense of community or attachment.

Nick killed the engine in yet another dingy neighborhood. Riverview was a string of bad neighborhoods and this one was where Justin had tracked Bella Fox's address. Her real name was Isabella Fabio.

When Mackenzie climbed out of the car, her nostrils were assaulted with the smell of piss. Potholes led the way to a dilapidated-looking apartment building. Dumpsters filled to the brim sat outside, infusing the air with a foul smell. A group of cats scurried around them, digging for food.

"You promised me twenty dollars!" a woman screamed from the balcony above at a man walking out of the building.

He was buckling his belt and zipping up his pants when he turned around and shouted back at her. "That handy wasn't worth it!"

"Screw you!" She picked up a flowerpot and aimed it at him. It crashed inches away from his head.

He seethed. "You're crazy!"

The woman went back inside. The man almost bumped into Mackenzie and Nick. His teeth were blackened and chipped. Meth use.

"So this is where Bella lived?"

Unsurprisingly enough, the elevators weren't working. It was a nine-floor climb. The stairs were covered in stains. They walked past doors with a lot of curses being thrown around behind them. Mackenzie only hoped that no child lived in this building.

"That's the apartment," Nick confirmed on his phone and knocked.

The same woman yelling from the balcony opened the door in a quick motion. Mascara was smeared around her eyes—an obvious sign she had been crying. Her strawberry-blonde hair was disheveled and pinned in a giant bun on the top of her head. There were holes in her ratty T-shirt. Her bare legs showed signs of drug use. Needle marks and dark veins.

"Who the hell are you?"

Mackenzie showed her badge, and the woman almost stumbled back. She pressed a hand to her forehead. "Can you give me a minute?"

"Sure," she nodded.

The door closed, and sounds of footsteps pounding and things falling trickled through.

"Hiding drugs?" Nick asked.

"Yep."

The door opened again. "Come in."

The apartment was surprisingly airy and light. The balcony door was open, allowing a breeze to filter inside. The furniture was tattered, obviously picked up from yard sales or the street. Magazines and makeup products were spread on a table. There was a tiny kitchen in one corner without any utensils, only paper cups and takeout boxes. There was no personal touch to the apartment. No pictures. No paintings.

"Why are you here?" She curled up on an armchair and covered her body with a blanket.

"What's your name?" Nick asked.

"Jasmine," she said dryly.

"You live with Isabella Fabio, right?"

"Bella, you mean. I used to. She moved out in the summer. Without warning," she added spitefully. "Took me over a month to find another roommate."

"Were you in contact with her after she moved out?"

"Nope."

"She's dead," Mackenzie said.

Jasmine's face didn't change. "Sucks."

Mackenzie and Nick exchanged a look. Mackenzie was usually prepared for shock or remorse. It was instinct to jump into comforting mode: the soft tone, the reassuring words, the gentle eyes.

"You obviously weren't close," Nick commented.

She raised a brow. "We weren't. And it's common in our business for girls to turn up dead. Overdosed in a ditch."

"She was murdered," Mackenzie stressed, hoping Jasmine would understand the gravity of the situation.

"Oh." Jasmine took a quivering breath. "Must have gone sour."

"With who? Was there some angry client in the picture?"

"I don't know exactly. We didn't talk much. And there are always some hot-headed dudes, but she left because she said she found a long-term placement with a client."

"Did she tell you his name?" Nick pushed. "Leave an address?"

"No. All I know is that she said someone wanted to keep her long-term. That's why she was moving out. I was kind of jealous. I tried finding out who but never did. She was secretive about it."

Someone had placed an advertisement, searching for a girl who looked like Katy/Kim. Robbie had found Bella and delivered her to that person, by dropping her off at Woodburn Park. Bella must have imagined that she would make good money. And maybe she was. But then why did he kill her? Was that his plan all along?

"Do you know Robbie Elfman?" Mackenzie asked.

"Never heard of him. Was that the client?"

"We don't know. Did you find it strange that she was going away to be with someone?"

"Not at all," Jasmine snorted. "You see everything in our business. Hasn't happened to me, but sometimes someone wants you for more than just a night. And honestly, I would have gone too if I were in her place. Bad luck that the guy turned out to be a psycho."

"She was troubled, right? Into drugs?" Mackenzie asked.

Jasmine's eyes flitted between them, like she was contemplating her answer. "She was using heroin. It's common."

Mackenzie took out her cell and pulled up a picture of the tattoos on the inside of Bella's knees. The jumbled letters and numbers that didn't seem to mean anything. She showed the picture to Jasmine. "Bella got these tattoos. Do you know what they mean?"

Jasmine frowned at the phone. "No way..."

A burst of energy shot through Mackenzie. Maybe Jasmine knew what they meant. Maybe it was a clue.

"That can't be her."

"What do you mean?"

"Bella was allergic to tattoo ink." Jasmine rolled her eyes. "Last year, we went to get tattoos together, and she had a bad reaction when they did a test spot. I had to take her to the hospital. Hives all over her skin. The doctor told her to stay away from tattoo ink. Something about the metal in it."

A frown marred Nick's face. Mackenzie knew the questions flying through his head. How was that possible? Had Robbie given them the wrong name to throw them off? Was there a chance that their victim *wasn't* Bella Fox?

"Could Bella have been forced into getting a tattoo?" Mackenzie whispered to Nick.

"If she had a reaction bad enough to go to the hospital, I don't think anyone would force it on her. It would draw more attention." Nick put on latex gloves and turned to Jasmine. "Do you still have her stuff?"

"I threw out most of her crap she left behind the day after she moved out. I think there might be some stuff left in the dresser." She guided them to Bella's old bedroom and opened the drawer of a scruffy dresser with a cracked mirror. There were a few earrings, a comb, a razor, and a toothbrush. Nick picked up the toothbrush and placed it in a plastic bag. "Let's get Becky to do a DNA match with the body."

On their way out, Mackenzie showed Jasmine a picture of Katy. "Ever seen her before? Or her and Bella together?"

"Huh," Jasmine's eyes widened. "I haven't, but are they related? They look so similar."

Mackenzie sighed. "You have no idea."

# CHAPTER THIRTY-FIVE

## *December 2*

The next morning icy winds blew through Lakemore and snowflakes danced in the air, impairing Mackenzie's ability to drive confidently. Through the windshield, all she could see was swirling white with a splinter of light weaving through gray clouds. Many welcomed the change from the usual drizzle, but heavy snowfall was the last thing the detectives needed in the search for Kim Harris.

The patrol that was searching Woodburn Park had moved to the woods where Ben Harlan's property was located. Since Katy's phone had last been active in that region, and it was assumed that Kim had had the phone in her possession, Lakemore PD deemed it fit to give those woods priority. Mackenzie would have liked to continue the search of Woodburn at the same time, but Sully had sourly reminded her that they didn't have the resources.

*"I agree the other woods get priority, but I still want some officers combing through Woodburn."*

*"Mack, this isn't the FBI or a big city like Seattle. We don't have enough resources. And we don't even know exactly what we're looking for in there."*

*"Surely there's something you can do? We need to find Kim ASAP."*

*"I can't magic up money, Mack. There are other departments and squads too. Let the patrol finish searching through the woods first. Then they can move back to Woodburn. That's the best you're going to get."*

The patrol had almost finished searching, but still there was no sign of Kim. Apart from the phone, it was like she was never there. It made searching Woodburn Park even more urgent, but the weather was their enemy.

Meanwhile, they were left with several questions only Kim could answer. Why had she and Katy swapped places? What was her connection to Bella? Mackenzie thought of Charlotte's conviction that Kim had been born evil. Mackenzie didn't really believe in evil, but she could understand jealousy and revenge. Had that driven Kim to kill her sister?

Mackenzie pulled up in front of the station and jogged inside, late for an important meeting. The team was already working on a Sunday, so she didn't want to keep them waiting. Sergeant Curtis, who headed the Special Investigations Unit, had decided to spare Andrea temporarily to help Clint with Robbie Elfman's laptop. Having to deal with prostitution rings and narcotics, that unit had more experience with the dark web than the Detectives Unit. Apparently, Clint and Andrea had some news to share.

Mackenzie dusted off the snow lodged in her hair and took her seat. Clint, the tallest person in Lakemore PD, had a slim face and the neck of a giraffe. "Is anyone else going to join us?"

Mackenzie looked around—Nick, Justin, Sully, and Andrea. She wondered if he was referring to Lieutenant Rivera, but caught him looking through the glass wall to the hallway.

Captain Murphy walked past the conference room lazily with a toothpick in his mouth.

"This case doesn't involve rich men of the town." Nick flashed everyone a sarcastic smile.

"I would reprimand you, but he *is* a useless sack," Sully admitted in a rare moment of honesty. There were budget sheets spread in front of him as he strived to multitask. "I spoke to him five minutes ago—he thinks he left his credit card in his office on Friday, that's why he's here."

There were repressed snorts of laughter round the room.

"What do you guys have?" Mackenzie asked, getting them back on topic.

"Robbie Elfman used a website where people put out ads looking for illegal stuff to buy and sell. Kind of like a dark-web version of eBay," Andrea explained. "It's mostly for drugs like cocaine, flakka, LSD, meth. But there are some ads looking for prostitutes into some specific kink. Once you respond to the ad, you can chat with the person who put out the ad and work out the details. The website either hides or erases the chat."

"So we don't know who Robbie was talking to?" Nick asked.

"No," Andrea confirmed. "We couldn't find any information on the account that put out the ad. There are ways to go about it, but it will take much longer, and I can't guarantee results. That's the risk with the dark web."

"But you said you have something?

"Yes." Clint passed around a folder to everyone in the room. "We found more ads like the one Robbie answered, buried on that website. Based on the content and language, we're certain it was posted by the same person."

Mackenzie opened the file. There were copies of the ads printed out.

There were five in total.

Three had been posted between February 2014 and August 2015, each showing the face of a different woman and the tagline, "Looking for a woman who looks like her and wants a fresh start in life." Mackenzie didn't recognize any of the women until she came to the fourth one, from December 2017: Katy Becker—the one that Robbie had come across and responded to in May 2018.

And there was a fifth advertisement. It had been taken out just four months before, for yet another woman.

Andrea blew on the lens of her glasses.

Tires screeched as a car passed by outside.

The electric heater whirred.

"What the hell is this?" Mackenzie whispered.

A different woman's face, but the same information every time. Each one promised a better life: personal coaching, rehabilitation, and, most chillingly, a whole new identity. The first ad made specific reference to a woman "in Seattle or the surrounding area," but that had been cut from the subsequent posts.

"Robbie supplied Bella—for now we're assuming she is Bella, though Becky is going to do a DNA test—who then underwent surgery to look even more like Katy. Almost a replica, I'd say. If you look from afar," Mackenzie said. "And there's been another ad since." She looked at the one taken out in July, with the picture of another beautiful woman smiling at the camera. "Does each new ad mean that he got his doppelganger?"

"If he did, then where are these other women now?" Nick asked. "And how does Sully's old suicide fit in? How long has he been doing this?"

"We have to track down the women featured in the ads. They might need to be warned."

"We moved Mack's grandmother from New York to a retirement home here a few years ago," Sterling told Robert over dinner later that night.

Mackenzie rolled her eyes and took another sip of wine, ignoring Sterling's wary glance.

"I'd never had the opportunity to meet Eleanor," Robert confessed.

She paused. "What?"

She didn't remember her grandmother visiting them in Lakemore, but she found it odd that Eleanor never met the man Melody had married and had a child with.

"She was against us because of my… addiction." Robert turned red. "For a long time, Mel was estranged from her mother.

They reconnected soon after Micky was born, but Eleanor hated my guts."

Mackenzie remembered Eleanor's disgusted face whenever she spoke of Robert. She'd also eavesdropped on Eleanor chiding Melody over the phone for staying in Lakemore to supposedly look for Robert.

*He's not worth it. Come to New York.*

"How was Eleanor?" Robert asked.

"She was the strongest woman I knew. She had several rounds of chemo, but she was always there for me."

Robert looked down at his food, embarrassed. The rest of the dinner was mostly spent with Sterling and Robert talking about mundane things. When they were done, Robert insisted on rinsing the dishes and loading the dishwasher.

Mackenzie watched her aging father's hunched back, working sincerely. She was still convinced he was hiding something. But her diligent spying on his phone had yielded nothing suspicious.

Could someone actually change? Was he a different person now?

"Mack, I'm going to leave," Sterling said from the door. "See you tomorrow?"

"No."

He frowned. "What?"

She dropped her voice. "You were coming for dinner because you thought he was dangerous and you wanted to show him that I have backup. I don't think that's necessary anymore."

"You trust him because you shared a few nice meals together?" Sterling was incredulous.

"No. But you've made your point. I don't think he's going to murder me in my sleep."

Sterling looked distraught, but then he cracked a grin, pointing at a dent in the wall. "Do you remember when we got back from our honeymoon, and you tricked me into thinking that someone was in the house?"

Mackenzie couldn't help smiling at the memory. She had pushed Sterling out of bed, thrust a baseball bat in his hands and ushered him away. "And when I jumped you, you squeaked like a mouse and ruined my wall."

"Not like a *mouse*."

Her fingers grazed the little dimple in the wall, their laughter still ringing in her ears. Spending time with Sterling again had left her feeling conflicted. Being in Robert's company, they never talked about their problems. It was like the good old days. But just when she felt like she was slipping—due to nostalgia and loneliness—the reminder of what he'd done would crash into her.

"You should go, Sterling. Goodnight." She choked back sudden tears, closing the door behind him.

"Micky?" Robert asked, returning to the living room. "Do you want to watch *The Princess Bride*? It used to be your favorite."

"I have work to do…"

He gave her a disappointed smile and turned away to go to bed.

"Wait," she said almost reluctantly. "I can work downstairs. Put the movie on."

This time his smile reached his eyes. Mackenzie let out a breath and tried to loosen the knot in her chest. She just needed to take it one day at a time.

# CHAPTER THIRTY-SIX

*December 3*

Mackenzie dialed the number for Detective Ethan Spitz, one of her few contacts in the Seattle PD. They had worked together two years ago when there had been a trail of bodies starting from Seattle and ending in Lakemore. She felt comfortable speaking to him, trusting his technique and an instinct that matched her own. He also had ten years of experience over her. She had learned a lot from him.

"Spitz." His rich baritone reverberated, with the hum of an engine in the background.

"Ethan, this is Mackenzie Price. Is this a bad time?"

"Oh, hey, Mack. Haven't heard from you in a while. More bodies?" His laugh was grating.

She folded her lips over her teeth and chuckled. "It's not what you think. This is kind of an odd one."

"Wait. Hold on." She heard him swerve. "I'm back. What do you have?"

"I'm emailing you some information." She typed deftly on her computer. "Still carrying your laptop on you?"

"Always." Sounds of scuffling and movement. "What is this?"

"Advertisements taken out on the dark web. The second to last has two bodies tied to it here, and a missing person, but the first mentions Seattle specifically. I'm hoping our killer was keeping things really local, but I need your input now."

"Sounds like a real bastard. What do the ads say?"

Mackenzie explained the situation to him. The medical procedures, the murders. The sixteen-year-old suicide that was somehow connected. How they had a lot of questions, and not a lot of answers. Through the phone, she could almost hear the wheels whirring in his brain. "Could you cross-reference the photos I've sent with missing women who fit the profile? Young women addicted to drugs?"

He sighed. "It's a big city. We have a lot of missing cases. And if these women are from the wrong side of the tracks then they might not even be reported missing."

Like Bella.

"Can you still check?"

"Of course. I'm already on it. I'll call you back."

Mackenzie smiled to herself. The fifty-year-old veteran had a sense of urgency that she admired. All the years in the force hadn't tired him; Spitz was still as keen as any police officer on their first day of the job. He called her back half an hour later.

"Okay, I think I got one. Our case is Tamara Wilson. She's been missing for almost two years. She's a prostitute and was a heroin user. Looks like the African American woman in one of your ads."

"Any progress made on the case? Any suspects?"

"Not yet. Like I said, it's common for prostitutes to go missing in a city this size and damn near impossible to get people to talk. But let me speak to the squad. We have new information now. Might find something."

After working out more details, Mackenzie hung up, feeling slightly more optimistic. It sounded like Tamara was a good match for one of the missing women, and she trusted Spitz to look into the others.

Mackenzie accessed Washington State Patrol's missing person database and pulled out the information of the four missing women in Lakemore in the last six months. She had gone over them before when trying to identify Bella, but now there was a possibility they were linked to the latest ad.

Nick joined her, and they studied the ad. It featured a woman with red hair like Mackenzie's, a long face, and pale skin. She was attractive, but nothing stood out about her. They compared her to the missing women.

"Well, it's not this one." She indicated one woman, who looked significantly older than the redhead.

"Maybe with a bit of Botox, though? Imagine her younger—their bone structure is similar," Nick offered. "What about that one?"

"The blonde?"

"Yeah, Bella was a blonde but she dyed her hair. Wouldn't they look similar if she dyed her hair too?"

Mackenzie tried picturing the woman's face with a different hair color. "I guess… Okay, we can remove this one." She pointed at one of the pictures. "She's mixed race, looks too different."

"Yeah." Nick scratched his head. "But any of these remaining three women *could* be a potential doppelganger?"

Mackenzie tapped her finger on the mouse, staring at the screen. The three missing women looked somewhat similar to the woman in the latest ad, but not exactly. "We should ask Dr. Preston. Maybe he can point us in the right direction. I *could* see all of them looking a lot like her if they got some work done."

"Good idea. We need an expert's eye. I'll call him."

While Nick made the phone call, Mackenzie's attention wandered over to Finn's empty cubicle. She recalled the heartbroken mother whose young daughter had run away, and picked up her phone.

Finn answered after two rings. "Mack?"

"You know that woman whose daughter left her a note? The one who came to the office the other day?"

He scoffed, "Of course. Michelle. She's been sending me dozens of messages. What about her?"

"Can you send me a picture of her daughter?"

There was a beat of silence. "Why? Did you find something?"

"I don't know. I'll update you later."

She hung up. Seconds later, Finn texted her the picture Michelle had provided. At first glance, the young woman looked a lot like the woman in the latest ad. But more so than the other women? *Probably? Maybe?* It all felt too speculative.

Nick turned to her. "Preston's at a café. He's asked us to meet him there."

The café was situated inside an old industrial building. When Mackenzie saw the ugly concrete building with smoky skies behind it, she never expected to find a quaint, artful café inside. Wooden tables were placed either side of a koi pond. The walls were adorned with pictures showing Lakemore's history from the early 1800s to the present.

They spotted Rees Preston seated in a corner, reading the newspaper with a cup of tea or coffee. Seeing them, he put the paper away and waved good-naturedly.

Mackenzie was once again caught off guard by his handsome face and dazzling smile.

"Interesting place," Nick commented.

"I accidentally discovered it a few years ago. Reminds me how you can find beauty in places you least expect." He glanced at Mackenzie. "Wouldn't you agree, Detective Price?"

'Oh, I... Yes, I suppose." Mackenzie didn't know what else to say. Preston's charm had rendered her uncharacteristically tongue-tied, much to her frustration. She saw Nick swallow a grin.

"We were hoping you could help us, Dr. Preston." Nick showed him the pictures on his phone. "These are three women who have been reported missing in Lakemore in the past six months." He took out a printout of the woman who was featured in the latest ad. "We narrowed them down based on their similarity to this woman."

Preston looked at her picture and then at the phone. "I see..."

"We want to know if you think any of these missing women could be surgically made to look even more like this woman."

"There's another one?"

Nick nodded mutely.

Preston spent a minute zooming in on each picture and then studying the photo in his hand. "None of them."

"Really?"

He returned the photo and phone to Nick. "Their basic features might be similar, but not similar enough that cosmetic procedures could match their faces as closely as in the other case you showed me. The first woman has a very large forehead. The second one's eyes are too far apart. And the last one's too old—Botox would only enhance the difference."

Mackenzie pulled out her own phone. "What about this one, Dr. Preston? Could she be the one?"

Preston looked at the picture and nodded vehemently. "That's the one. She has the same pupillary distance and a slightly cleft chin. Her jaw is wider but that can be easily fixed with jaw reduction surgery."

Alison Gable. A Lakemore local whose mother had sat every single day at the station demanding her voice be heard. Another woman who had been lured into a trap much like Bella had been. Mackenzie's blood ran cold. Going by what they knew, it could only be a matter of time before they had another body on their hands.

# CHAPTER THIRTY-SEVEN

Alison Gable's mother, Michelle, had become a familiar face around the Lakemore PD station. She was short, round-faced, and dressed in bright clothes. Gold costume jewelry hung low from her neck. "Please, come on in. I'm glad someone's finally taking me seriously."

Michelle led Mackenzie and Nick inside her cramped one-bedroom apartment. The hardwood floor was partly covered by a stained rug with a flowery pattern and a leather couch with tears in it. The walls were a dirty yellow, black curtains pulled back to allow light from one tiny window. Mackenzie was overcome with claustrophobia. But she focused her attention on the young woman standing in front of her, smacking gum and twirling her purple-streaked hair around her fingers nervously.

"This is Lila." Michelle gestured to the girl. "She's a friend of Alison's. When you called me, I convinced her to talk to the cops."

Lila rolled her eyes and looked away, making it clear she didn't want to be there.

"Can you confirm the last time you spoke to Alison?" Nick looked at Michelle.

"November first," Michelle said firmly, like she'd been through the answers multiple times, which she probably had. "She seemed to be in a good mood and mentioned nothing out of the blue, which is why when she left me the letter the next day, I was surprised."

"Do you have it to hand?"

She raced to the kitchen counter and picked up a piece of paper. "The other detective returned it to me after he verified that it was Alison's handwriting."

Mackenzie stood on her toes to peek over Nick's shoulders at the letter.

*I'm leaving for a while. But I promise I'll be back and get in touch in two weeks. Please take care of Oliver and yourself. I love you both. Talk to you soon.*

Mackenzie noted Michelle's heaving chest, damp hands rubbing each other, and worry lines deepening on her forehead.

"Did she often handwrite notes, rather than texting or calling?" Nick inquired.

"No, but like I told your colleague, she broke her phone a while back and didn't have money to buy a new one."

Nick turned to Lila. "Do you have any idea where she went?"

Lila let out a long exhale and crossed her arms. "I don't want to get in trouble."

"Lila, how do you and Alison know each other?" Mackenzie asked.

"We're..." Lila blushed. "We're sex workers."

"Oh God," Michelle groaned and looked away, shaking her head.

"Who do you work for?"

"Nobody. We're... freelancers. We both look pretty similar. People often think we're sisters. Some customers want... both of us together. Like a twin fantasy."

Mackenzie surveyed Lila's legs and arms—both covered even though it was swelteringly hot inside. She kept scratching her arms. Her young face was caked in makeup, but Mackenzie could see the pallor underneath.

"Was Alison doing drugs?"

"Yes," Lila admitted reluctantly. "It's easy to fall into them in our line of work. But she never sold. It's a disease, you know. No one wants to be on drugs. It eats away at your body."

Nick looked at Mackenzie, both of them thinking the same thing. "Do you know anyone by the name of Bella Fox, or Isabella Fabio?"

Lila shook her head.

"Lila, I think you want to help us. It's clear you care about Alison, otherwise you wouldn't be here," Nick said.

Her eyes fluttered to keep the tears away. "She's a good person. She had tried so hard over the last few years to get off drugs. And it's not like people like us can afford nice rehab with fancy doctors to help us. She really wanted a fresh start. But with our work, it's not easy. It's not just the drugs, but in a small town like Lakemore you run into customers all the time. It's easy to get into trouble with the cops and once you're in the system or on their radar it follows you forever."

"She went somewhere to get that fresh start?" Nick echoed the tagline from the ad. The ad that had lured prostitutes addicted to drugs into a sense of security.

"There was this ad on the dark web." Lila sniffled. "She went on there all the time to buy drugs. The ad had a picture of some woman and was looking for someone who looked like her. We figured it was someone with a fetish who wanted a keep, you know? Those jobs can pay real well, so Alison suggested we both respond. We sent a picture of us together, but the guy responded saying that he was only interested in Alison. He said she'd be more *appropriate*. They talked some more, and she said that he'd convinced her that he would help her get off drugs and give her a new identity. Then she left."

"Do you know where she went to meet him?"

"It was somewhere in Woodburn Park, around that broken bridge, but she didn't tell me where exactly." Lila shrugged. "She said she'd get in touch in a few days and would be back. That's the last time I heard from her."

Mackenzie recalled how Robbie had dropped Bella by Crescent Lake in Woodburn Park. Different location. Something was there, but the harsh winter and snowstorms had created a dent in the effort to search the woods thoroughly. And it didn't help that the park was so gigantic to begin with.

"Did this person want anything in exchange for helping?" Nick asked.

"Alison told me that he didn't say anything, but she assumed that he'd probably want sex. Isn't that what all men want?"

"Are you sure that they were male?" Mackenzie asked.

Lila's eyebrows furrowed. "Why wouldn't he be? His username was Steven, but that'll be fake."

*Another tribute to Steven Boyle?* It couldn't be a coincidence.

A cry disrupted Mackenzie's thoughts. Michelle went briskly into another room and emerged with a baby in her arms. Dressed in a yellow onesie, he was easily under a year old.

"This is Oliver," Michelle said. Behind her there was a framed picture of Alison cradling Oliver when he was a newborn. Her pinkie finger touched his mouth. He was asleep, but her eyes were full of wonderment. Like she couldn't believe that she could love someone that much.

This was what Sterling wanted. A child. For the first time in her life, Mackenzie wondered why she didn't feel that way. Why she didn't want to love another person to the point that her heart felt like it was bursting at the seams.

"There's no *way* that Alison wouldn't contact me in so long." Michelle's eyes brimmed with tears. "She had issues, but she loves Oliver more than anything. Whatever she was trying to do, it was for him. And I'm not his mom. He misses her. Alison would never do this. Please. Please find her."

# CHAPTER THIRTY-EIGHT

*December 5*

It was a bustling morning at the station. With the holidays right around the corner, there was renewed ambition to wrap up cases and get all the paperwork in place. Mackenzie was one of the few people who were planning on working through the holidays as she usually did, despite the drunk Santas she would be forced to deal with.

Mackenzie and Nick had spent the last day going over the statements of Alison's friends and acquaintances and confirming them. No one seemed to know anything. They had tracked her last movements before she disappeared based on her credit card activity, but there was nothing there that could lead them to her.

In the conference room, Nick drummed his jittery fingers on the table and stared at his laptop. Mackenzie waltzed in and presented him with a cup of coffee.

His eyes lit up. "Bless you. Where did you find this?"

"Downstairs. I bribed Officer Fields."

"Their cappuccino machine is much better than ours." He took a sip and grinned. "When I retire, I'll have my own coffee farm."

Mackenzie raised an eyebrow at the house Nick was making with cigarettes. "And I thought you were concentrating on something important."

"I was." He showed her his screen. "Alison was last seen by Lila, right before the latter left for work. There was no surveillance in her dingy apartment building, but there's this convenience store across the street with a camera that could give a view of the apartment building. But the camera isn't set to record, only to view."

"That's a bummer." She sat next to him and drummed her fingers on the table. "I believe she planned to stay in touch. Which means she's being prevented from doing so."

Nick nodded. "What about Bella? Any more on her?"

"Becky should have the DNA results soon," Mackenzie said.

While they were waiting to get confirmation on whether their Jane Doe Two was actually Bella or not, Clint had finished his analysis on Katy's phone. They already had her call log and texts, but her phone had no suspicious pictures or files. However, her email, which was logged in, revealed an interesting correspondence that had caught their attention. Katy had been arguing with a "Derek Lee" for the last few weeks. The vague emails went from Katy asking him to reconsider his stance, to warning him about his actions being unethical.

Nick checked the time. "Derek Lee should be here any minute now."

"Why was she talking to a hotelier?" Mackenzie wondered.

"We're going to find out." Nick tipped his chin toward the door. A uniformed officer escorted Derek Lee to the conference room. His white hair fell like a sheet to his shoulders. His leathery skin sagged around his eyes and jawline, making him look a bit like a basset hound. Despite his old age, he had the physique of a lumberjack.

"Thank you for meeting us, Mr. Lee," Mackenzie said as Derek slid onto the chair across from them.

"Why am I here? I'm a busy man." He checked his phone before putting it back in his pocket.

"Do you know Katy Becker?"

Derek rolled his eyes. "That pain in the ass. What about her?"

"She's missing," Nick said.

He raised his eyebrows and sat back, making an undecipherable sound.

"Our team accessed her email, and we came across your correspondence with her."

"I see." He rubbed his fingertips together.

Mackenzie leaned forward. "Can you elaborate on that?"

"Am I a suspect?"

"You're not in an interrogation room."

He nodded and placed his elbows on the table. "I'm a hotelier. I'm looking to expand in Lakemore. The town has untapped potential. Plenty of people from across Washington flock here to watch a game and end up staying a weekend. It's a good time for me to invest. With the riots, the prices have never been lower."

Lakemore suffered a setback, and the vultures descended to make their profits.

"How does Katy factor into this?" Nick frowned.

He sighed. "I wanted to build in Woodburn Park. I've been lobbying, and have a few supporters in the city council. That park is wasted today. But Katy wanted to build a homeless shelter there."

"But Woodburn Park is massive. Both of you could use it."

"The woods are dense, and the soil is hard. Only a fraction of it would allow construction without removing too many trees and requiring too much equipment. There are regulations. And even if that leaves enough space for both, no one is going to want to stay at my hotel when there's a homeless shelter that close!"

Mackenzie understood Derek's concerns. He was a businessman. He was doing his job. But she couldn't help but feel drawn to Katy's actions. There were so people few in this world whose actions were dictated by selflessness.

"When was the last time you met Katy?" she asked.

He hesitated, thinking it through. "November sixteenth. It was a Friday night. She showed up unannounced on my doorstep."

"What did she say?"

"We discussed work, and then she said that she would leave Woodburn Park alone but needed money in cash."

Mackenzie glanced at Nick. Why would Katy need money suddenly? And why would she try to leverage it from Lee?

"What exactly happened?" Nick urged him to continue.

"Look, she wasn't happy to be there. I can tell you that." His eyebrows drew together. "I almost felt bad for her. I had offered her money before—funding, for another project that would keep her away from Woodburn, but she'd rejected it. I was happy that she had come to her senses, but she looked very conflicted. It was obvious that she didn't want to take the money like this—and I was uncomfortable about being asked for cash, too. I'm no crook. I asked her if she was being blackmailed or something, but all she said was that there was some emergency."

"Did you give her the money?"

"I had offered her fifty grand, previously. But she said she only needed thirty-five, which made me worry the money wasn't intended for one of her projects."

Mackenzie had to suppress a snort. She had no doubt Lee was dressing up the exchange to make himself look better, but she believed the basic structure was accurate.

"Her reputation preceded her, though. I said I didn't have that much cash lying around the house, so I told her to meet me the next morning, and we'd take care of the paperwork in good time."

*Thirty-five thousand dollars.* Mackenzie chewed her lip, deep in thought. They had come across no evidence that Katy was being blackmailed or was in any situation that would require a huge chunk of money.

"Where did you meet her?" she asked.

Derek looked around and stroked his chin. "I have a cabin in Woodburn Park. It's something of an office for the project. I keep some money there, so I told her to meet me in the morning. I waited, but she never showed up."

What other secrets did Woodburn Park hide? Why hadn't Katy shown up?

Mackenzie pulled out a map of the park and asked him to locate his cabin. It was situated away from the shore but downstream of where the bodies had been recovered.

After asking more routine questions, they dismissed him.

"What the hell did Katy need thirty-five grand for?" Nick flicked the end of a cigarette.

But another thought was simmering inside Mackenzie's mind. "We don't know when exactly Kim took Katy's place."

"Maybe Kim went to Derek, posing as Katy, because she wanted money?"

"Or Katy went to Derek because Kim was threatening her?"

Nick took out his cigarette case and placed the unlit tube back inside. "Could be either. Thirty-five grand's a lot of money. Plenty have killed for less."

# CHAPTER THIRTY-NINE

It was Mackenzie's first time in Rivera's office. The new lieutenant liked to keep her office crisp, minimalistic, and scented. The only splash of color was a cactus sitting on the windowsill. Rivera didn't keep anything personal in her office—not even a picture of her family, just like Mackenzie's cubicle. While Troy had a picture of his fiancée, Ella, pinned to his desk, and Nick had a framed drawing Luna had made of them, Mackenzie's desk had no signs of Sterling. One of her instructors at the academy had told her that women had to make an extra effort to project their toughness, especially in a field like police work.

*Mack, a family picture on a man's desk means he's responsible, but on a woman's desk it means she's too emotional.*

As Rivera flipped through the pages of their case file, her face was a blank canvas. Unflinching and sharp. "Do we think someone's after prostitutes?" She looked up at Mackenzie and Nick.

"Not specifically," Nick said. "The ad is targeting vulnerable women looking for a change. It just happens to be the case that the victims we confirmed are all prostitutes."

"We still haven't told Katy's family about the switch," Mackenzie piped up. "Charlotte Harris and Cole Becker have been calling regularly, asking us if we're any closer to finding where Katy is. It's not right. We have to tell them that Katy's dead, Lieutenant."

"I understand, but we have another missing woman. Alison. I don't want anything jeopardizing that. And we don't know the extent of Kim's involvement. It will take one leak to alert whoever has them."

Mackenzie looked at Nick, who shrugged helplessly. Both of them were uncomfortable about lying to the family of the victim, even a cheating scumbag like Cole. Every time Mackenzie lied, it ate away at her a little bit.

Rivera sensed their discomfort. She took off her glasses and placed her elbows on the desk. "At this point in the investigation, we have a lot more questions than answers. We might be sure about the switch, but we haven't *proven* it. In a case this sensitive, we have to be sure of everything. Our job is to bring justice to Katy and find Kim and Alison alive. Keep your eye on the ball. And I don't want to remind you that this department is under investigation by the FBI. We can't afford any more mistakes. We will tell them, but now's not the time."

Mackenzie nodded reluctantly. They were all under heavy scrutiny. Every move was being watched and every decision would come under review. This was the problem with dishonesty—it affected everyone.

"Good. The crime lab sent their reports today. Anything on that gift left for Steven?"

"Yes." Mackenzie opened the attachment on her phone. "Anthony said we got lucky; there was trace evidence found in the engraved markings. Ryegrass, brome, manure, chromium-vanadium steel, and horse hair."

"That's a stable." Rivera raised an eyebrow.

"That's what it seems like. The steel could be whatever was used to carve the pen with, according to Anthony."

"So the gift was in a stable at one point, or the tool used to engrave it was. That doesn't really help narrow it down. No idea who bought the pen?"

"It's widely available online," Nick shrugged.

Rivera pressed her lips in a hard line. "Alright. Pursue the Derek Lee lead. He was present at Woodburn Park."

Back in her cubicle, Mackenzie skimmed over the pages in Kim's files from the treatment center again. She had read them as soon as she had received them, spending hours digging into the explorations done of Kim's mind. Since her admission at the tender age of nine, Kim's moods were erratic, swinging from demure and calm to seething and destructive. But one thing was constant: her grudge.

*Do you miss your parents?*

*No.*

*Are you angry with them?*

*Wouldn't you be?*

*How do you feel about your twin, Katy?*

*The one who didn't get sent away? What do you think?*

Over the years, her outbursts had decreased. In her final two years before she ran away, she hadn't displayed violent tendencies. But her social skills had been severely hampered. She suffered from depression as well.

The more Mackenzie tried to plow through Kim's life, looking for answers, the more complicated the woman she'd met became.

"Anything on your end?" Nick bounced a stress ball against the wall.

She held a sneeze. "Not really. She was furious with her parents. Understandably so. And there's no evidence linking her to anything criminal."

"Are you catching a cold?"

"Allergies." She took out a Kleenex and blew her nose. "What about you?"

"Healthy as a horse."

"Nick…"

The case was a giant and messy ball of interwoven thoughts inside her head. She tried catching any theories she conjured up, like they could be the key to solve the puzzle.

"You know, you'd think Cole would notice that his wife wasn't his wife," Nick said.

Mackenzie winced. "I'm sure he would have eventually, but she'd been with him for like, what? Ten days? And he's hardly going to jump to the conclusion that she's been replaced with a twin he never knew about. Plus, he's having an affair. He's clearly not very attentive to her."

Nick gave Mackenzie a searching look, but she remained unflappable. The phone on his desk rang. "Detective Blackwood."

A calm but rapid stream of information came down the line.

"Are you sure? Okay, thank you for your cooperation." He hung up with a sigh.

"What's up?" She wheeled into his cubicle.

"Lee's alibis check out. He was on a conference call when Kim was snatched, and after waiting for Katy to show up, he spent most of the day at the country club with friends."

"To be honest, I have my doubts about Derek. He may have had motive to kill Katy, but what about the others?"

"Yup. Another dead end." He checked his watch and frowned. "Right. Have to go for lunch with Shelly and her boyfriend."

"*Really*?"

He pulled on his coat. "She wants us to get along. Build a rapport. I guess I do too."

"That's fair. You're the father of her child."

"It's complicated."

"Are you getting jealous?"

"Over Shelly?" He looked at her in disbelief.

"No. Over Luna. She might get a stepdad."

Nick gave her a thin smile before leaving, but didn't answer.

Mackenzie stared at Kim's file. Her life was a big question mark. But an even bigger question mark was the sick operation she and her sister had got involved in, either intentionally or not. The clock was ticking. Kim and Alison had been missing for weeks now—if they didn't pick up a better trail soon, the case could go cold.

*Then what? We wait for the next ad to appear?*

Her phone vibrated with a message from Becky.

*DNA was a match. Jane Doe Two is Isabella Fabio.*

Mackenzie was relieved Bella hadn't just been another wild goose chase. But this didn't explain the tattoos on her knees, and her apparent allergies to the ink.

She looked over the crime scene unit's report on the Beckers' house again. Shoe casting showed the perpetrator had size ten. Then something caught her eye.

The soil sample from the shoe print had been analyzed.

Mass spectrometry identified dark-brown gravelly loam soil, which was typical of Washington State. But there were high levels of vinegar in the soil obtained from the footprints.

"Vinegar?" she whispered.

Mackenzie checked the samples taken from around the shoe for comparison, and there were no traces of vinegar. She sat back in her chair, contemplating. Why would the bottom of shoes have traces of vinegar?

It could mean nothing. But something was odd about it. Could this person maybe work at a restaurant? Still, how would vinegar end up on the bottom of their shoes?

The memory struck her like a wrecking ball. Ben Harlan had azalea bushes growing around his cabin. Those shrubs thrived in acidic conditions, and as such it was common practice to add vinegar to the water when hosing them.

Mackenzie grabbed her Glock and jacket. Her pulse raced. She was about to dash out when she saw Nick's empty cubicle. She called him on her way out and left a voicemail.

"I'm going to follow up on a lead. Ben Harlan's cabin. I found some evidence in the forensics report that could link him to Kim's abduction."

# CHAPTER FORTY

Mackenzie parked at the edge of the woods closest to Ben Harlan's property. Her spine stiffened as she entered the woods. The ground was moist under her feet, soil sticking to the bottom of her shoes. The deeper she went, the more dizzying the woods got. Bright sunlight weaved uninhibited between the leafless branches zigzagging the blue sky. The lack of wind made the woods eerily still. But even as the sunny afternoon melted off the snow that had cloaked everything in sight, the bite in the air still lingered. Her breaths formed little clouds that dissipated quickly as she passed by some cabins and small sheds. She walked in a straight line with confident strides. The last time she was here, she had memorized the path. When she heard the faint bubbling of a creek, she turned right. A few minutes later, Ben's cabin came into view.

She halted. Her eyes and ears strained for activity. There was none. Still treading noiselessly, she inched closer, reaching the flowers in the front yard. She kneeled and padded the soil in the bed. Scooping a little in her palm, she took a sniff.

Vinegar.

Ben Harlan could have easily lied about finding the cell by the creek. They had searched the cabin, but not very thoroughly, considering his cooperation after attaining the phone.

She pulled out her cell to call for backup. But there was no service.

"Shit."

Stuffing her cell back in her pocket, she took out her gun. The door was unlocked. *Strange.* It squeaked against the hinge. Mackenzie waited, but there was no sound of any activity. She stepped inside with her gun pointing ahead.

The space looked unassuming. Ben's suitcase was still parked in the corner. No smell of food. Nothing sitting on the stove. The sink was filled with dirty dishes. Her neck moved in quick and jerky movements, like Ben could come out of nowhere.

There were no hiding spots in sight. She eyed the twisting staircase dead ahead of her. Bracing herself, she took one step at a time, trying not to make any sound. Ben could still be in the cabin. Maybe in one of the bedrooms. There was a narrow corridor at the top of the stairs with two doors on either side.

Mackenzie looked over her shoulder, making sure no one was at the bottom of the stairs. Maybe Ben was out. She twisted the knob on the first door to her right. As the sound punctured the silence, her heart came to a racing halt.

Sweat pooled in her tailbone.

There was a click. She turned on instinct. But before she registered anything, something slammed into the side of her skull. Blinding pain shot through her. Her gun slipped from her grip. Her legs buckled, and she came crashing down to the floor, clutching her throbbing head.

Her vision swam as tears sprung to her eyes. She saw sports shoes and the hem of blue jeans. Then everything went black.

# CHAPTER FORTY-ONE

The cold wood against her cheek. The smell of damp air. Rope scratching against her wrists.

"Detective Price?" a woman's voice whispered.

Mackenzie's eyes fluttered open. Kim's face hovered over her. Her thick eyebrows pulled together tautly, lips quivering.

"Kim…"

Her eyes widened briefly. "You know."

Mackenzie tried nodding, but her head was too heavy on her shoulders. She was curled in a ball. Her arms were tied behind her back with a rope, her feet bound together by tape. A single light bulb dangled above. There was a clothes rail above their heads, along it some stray hangers.

Mackenzie pulled herself up and rested her back against the wall. Her lungs coughed up bits of dust. "Where are we?"

"Ben's cabin. We're inside a closet," Kim said. "How did you know I'm Kim?"

"Your ears aren't pierced."

Mackenzie felt something on her cheek. She stuck out her tongue and tasted the sticky liquid, already knowing what it was. Blood. She tried to reach for her pockets weakly.

"He took your phone and your gun."

*Dammit.* Why did she come here alone? Why didn't she bring Justin or Nick with her? She had planned to confirm if this lead was solid or not and then call for backup. She didn't realize that there would be no service.

"How long was I out for?"

"Around ten minutes."

*That's not good.* Her eyes flitted to Kim, who looked even scrawnier than before. Her cheeks had lost color and looked sunken. She was dressed in gray sweatpants and a white T-shirt. The clothes she was wearing the morning of her abduction, according to Cole's statement. Her long neck had red marks. "Who is he?"

Kim glanced at the door and swallowed hard. "My ex-boyfriend."

Mackenzie dragged her body closer to Kim. Her throat was dry like sandpaper. The light above made her squint, sending pain pulsing behind her eyes. "I… we have to get out."

"*How*? The closet automatically locks from the outside when it's shut. He installed a special lock."

Kim's feet were also bound by tape. They had to start somewhere. "I'll try to tear that with my teeth, okay?"

Kim nodded.

Mackenzie leaned down, wrapped her teeth around the tape, and pulled. Her head throbbed, and her eyes felt droopy. Blinking was a chore. She wondered if she had brain damage and kept wiggling her toes to make sure she still could.

She grunted, trying to tear the tape. Kim sobbed. It was what gave her the motivation to continue. Even injured, she was the police officer. It was her responsibility to take care of Kim.

The tape ripped. Relief flooded through her. There was some progress.

Kim wormed her legs out of confinement. "I'll help you."

Mackenzie sighed and leaned against the wall, as Kim bent over to tear the tape from her ankles. Her eyes searched for a weapon she could use. The small closet was empty. Kim said the door would be locked from the outside. "Did Ben kill your sister?"

Kim paused. "I don't know."

Mackenzie felt like she was intoxicated. Unmoored and woozy. The only thing that tethered her to her reality was the pain in her head that was slowly seeping down the back of her neck.

"Did you hurt Katy?"

"No!" Kim bit through the tape binding Mackenzie's ankles.

"Then what happened?"

"I met Ben four years ago when I was at a very low point. He… hit me. But I don't know why I stayed."

"And then you ended it?"

"Yes, I'd had enough and wanted to get my life together. I got out of the relationship, cut off toxic friends, and found a stable job. I decided to look for my sister. For the first time in my life, I was in a good place and proud of myself. I was ready to meet Katy and have a family."

"So you came to Lakemore looking for her?"

"Yes."

"Not your parents?"

Kim sighed. "I… I don't blame them for putting me in that institution. But I haven't forgiven them for not visiting me after they moved. I don't think I ever can. They abandoned me."

Mackenzie nodded, understanding. The vivid memories of spending months waiting for Melody to visit her only for her to cancel last minute were still raw. She had only seen her mother once or twice a year after her move to New York.

"How did you find her?"

She gulped. "It took me weeks to track her down. I was living in Scottsdale, but went back to Oklahoma, found old neighbors, asked around. I… I thought maybe we could reconnect. It's not like I have anyone else."

"Can you turn around? I want to see how he's made the knot."

Kim twisted and revealed bony arms covered in maroon bruises. They made Mackenzie's stomach contract. But she pushed it aside and readjusted her focus on how to get out. This is what the bottom line was in training. It was about compartmentalizing just as much as knowing the tricks. "Okay, I think I got this. Turn back."

Mackenzie had memorized the knot. She positioned her back against Kim's, her hands fumbling to untie the rope. "Ben followed you to Lakemore?"

"I realized it when I got here. He had been stalking me this entire time, demanding money, and it scared the hell out of me."

"And did Katy know about you?"

"No. I met her on Monday of the week she went missing. She was shocked when she saw me, and hurt." Her voice broke at the last words. "It took her a few days to come around; she confessed that she always felt like a part of her was missing. Twin telepathy, I suppose," Kim scoffed dryly. "She wanted to call our parents and confront them, but I begged her not to. I was almost embarrassed, because of Ben. They'd given up a troubled child before, and she was back in their lives bringing trouble *again*. I didn't want to be a disappointment. I wanted to show them, especially my mother, that I… that I wasn't what they thought of me anymore."

Mackenzie began loosening the knot. "You said Ben wanted money? That's why he was harassing you?"

"He used to take away whatever money I made to spend on booze and hookers. He couldn't keep a job. When I left him, I took the money I was owed. It was at least thirty grand. He wanted it back, but I spent it on rent and a car and paying back some friends. Katy offered to help me. She thought it was the least she could do for me after what our parents did. And I guess it was in her nature too, right? Always helping people. She decided to give me money so that I could pay Ben."

"Did she give it to you?"

"She said she needed to arrange the money first and didn't want her husband finding out."

"Why not?"

"I don't know. She didn't say. But it was obvious she didn't trust him. Cole was supposed to be away that weekend, for work. I'd been living at a motel. She suggested I spend the weekend at her place. I agreed, figuring it'd be safer. She told our parents that she was away for the weekend so there was no risk of me being discovered. I came to stay with her on Friday morning. That night she left to get the money, but she returned without it. She told me that someone had promised to pay her the next morning. She didn't tell me who. The plan was that she'd hand me the money on Saturday and then I could get Ben off my back. Except Katy never returned when she left to collect the money. Then Cole was home early; his trip got cut short. He thought I was Katy and asked me if I had taken my prenatal vitamins and made an appointment with the OB/GYN. That's when it hit me why Katy looked so sick and nauseous. And I… I played along. The next day, I ordered a wedding ring from eBay. Luckily, it was just a simple gold band so easy to find. I just… I was so scared and confused that Katy hadn't returned. I'm so sorry. I didn't know what to do! It happened so quickly."

Katy had gone to Derek Lee on Friday to ask for money. He had asked her to meet him the next morning at Woodburn Park. But he claimed she never showed up, and he had alibis for the rest of that weekend.

Mackenzie freed Kim's wrists from the rope. She almost toppled over in the process.

"Detective? Are you okay?"

She didn't respond. The searing pain was dripping down her spine now. It frightened her to think how much damage Ben had done. She was at the brink of passing out, but she couldn't. The next thing she knew, Kim was untying her.

"Ben has your gun. And you're hurt. Is it safe for us to go out like this?"

Mackenzie recalled that she'd left a message with Nick, telling him where she was. It was only a matter of time before he'd look for her. Once he realized that she wasn't answering her phone, he'd come.

"We need a weapon." She looked around at the empty closet space. The hangers. She hoisted herself up and plucked one off the rail. "Kim, who else knew about the switch?"

"I didn't tell anyone else. Katy didn't either. She respected the fact that it was my decision whether to come clean to our parents, considering what they did. I was very grateful. I bought her a necklace after she invited me to spend the weekend with her. The one with the Gemini locket."

"Why didn't you say anything to us before?"

"Because I thought you'd suspect *me*!" Tears welled in her eyes. "You'd think I killed Katy to take her place. I know I was a problematic child, but I'm not like that anymore. I didn't know who to trust. And Ben was *still* out there. I figured I'd lie about miscarrying the child, leave Cole, and just live as Katy to stay safe."

"Does the name Bella Fox ring any bells?"

"Who?"

"That's the woman who was found dead with Katy."

"I haven't heard that name before."

"Have you seen anyone else here? Any other woman?" Mackenzie implored her to think. "Heard any other voices?"

Kim shook her head. "He just slips me food and a bucket from time to time. I don't know."

Mackenzie inspected the hanger and smacked it against her palm. It was plastic and wouldn't do any damage—maybe it could be used to gouge at an eye, but only if she overpowered Harlan first. Her mind raced to come up with a plan. Even if she managed to break down the door, there would be a sound, possibly alerting him. But what other option did she have?

Gravity felt stronger than ever before. Her head still pounded. And now her spine felt too stiff.

A door opened and shut outside the closet. Footsteps got closer.

"He's here," Kim mouthed.

The air thickened and pressed into Mackenzie's skin like deadweight. They had to get out of here alive. She braced herself against the wall and directed her fading strength into her fists. She was going to launch herself at Ben when he opened the door.

*No.* That wasn't smart. He had a gun. And she still couldn't see straight.

Mackenzie gnashed her teeth. There was only one way to get out of this.

Deftly, she pulled Kim down and tucked her feet under her hips, hoping that Ben wouldn't notice she was free. Kim understood and put her arms behind her. Mackenzie assumed the same position.

*Click.*

The door to the closet opened with a screech. Ben stood there holding Mackenzie's gun.

"You shouldn't have come here, Detective Price," Ben said, the light from the bulb making his piercings gleam.

"You took her from the Beckers'. You followed her."

Ben remained silent. His wild eyes and the Glock in his hands were trained on Mackenzie. He hadn't killed her immediately, and that was a positive sign. There was a way out of this.

"Who knows you're here?" Ben dodged the question. "Tell me!"

"The entire Lakemore PD," Mackenzie exaggerated. Ben's face went pale. "If I'm not back in time, they'll know to come here and look for *you*."

"You're lying."

"You think I'd come here and not tell anyone?"

"I can just tell them that you're not here."

"They've traced my cell, Ben. If you kill me, you'll be in deep shit."

His eyes flew between her and Kim. Then there was a sharp knock on the door downstairs. Ben's neck jerked. Mackenzie breathed a sigh of relief.

"Lakemore PD! Open up!" Nick's faint voice wafted up the stairs.

Ben's hand gripped the gun tighter. He shifted on his heels.

"Lakemore PD! Open the door!" Nick shouted again and banged on the door of the cabin.

For a moment, indecisiveness was suspended in the air. The only sound was Kim's loud and erratic breathing. Mackenzie could taste freedom on the tip of her tongue. It was so close. But Ben was a big obstacle standing in the way. A bigger obstacle was her fading strength. She kept flexing her fists but her grip was weak.

The door crashed open. Mackenzie knew the protocol.

Ben yanked her by the back of her collar, his nostrils flaring when he realized that she wasn't bound anymore. But there was no time to do anything. The police were inside his house.

"Come with me!" he growled and dragged Mackenzie with him.

She looked back at Kim and gestured toward the door, which was about to lock from the outside if it swung shut. Kim nodded in understanding and crawled forward.

In the commotion, Ben didn't notice that the door never clicked shut. He pressed the gun into the side of Mackenzie's throat and pushed her down the stairs.

Nick came into view. He was standing in the middle of the living room holding a gun. A dark look crossed his face when he saw Mackenzie's bloodied face and the gun to her neck.

Had he come alone?

"Drop the gun, or I'll blow her head off," Ben instructed when they reached the bottom of the stairs.

Nick hesitated and gave Mackenzie a meaningful look. He wasn't here alone. She looked around discreetly, but couldn't see anyone in sight. Then she caught a reflection in one of the windows of a woman coming in the back door. It wasn't Jenna. This woman had a tall and sturdy frame.

It was Lieutenant Rivera.

Nick put his gun on the floor. "Mack, are you okay?"

Mackenzie nodded. But Nick was dubious. Her eyes glazed over the scene, and her knees threatened to collapse. She knew she wasn't going to be of much help.

"Kick it over here," Ben ordered. Nick did what he said, his eyes darting up the stairs. Mackenzie swayed to catch a glimpse behind them. Kim was climbing down soundlessly, barefooted, carrying a lamp.

*No.*

Mackenzie wanted to yell at Kim to run back upstairs. Now that Rivera was closing in behind Ben, they had their element of surprise. They could take Ben down. But if she alerted Ben to Kim's presence in any way then he might panic and shoot her.

Nick's jaw clenched, but he couldn't gesture to Kim to turn around either. Not when Ben had him pinned with a look. "Ben, calm down. Let's talk."

"If you don't leave right now, then I'll kill her. I'll kill *both* of them."

Kim reached the bottom of the stairs, holding the lamp like a weapon, ready to swing it across Ben's head. Rivera only spotted her then. Mackenzie saw Rivera's reflection pause. But Rivera was behind Kim. There was no way Kim could see Rivera. Unless Rivera made some sound.

The situation was disastrous.

Then came a sound. A loose floorboard creaked under Kim's foot.

Mackenzie's heart sank.

Ben turned around, his grip on Mackenzie loosening enough for her to wrench herself free. Kim lunged at him, swinging the lamp and aiming for his head. But the gun went off.

A beat of silence.

Kim's back curved out like she had been sucker punched. Jets of scarlet sprayed out of her abdomen. She tripped on her feet, staggering backward. When her limp body dropped to the floor, dust billowed in the air.

The lamp crashed to the ground, and the room sprang to life.

Another gunshot. A bullet pierced Mackenzie's skin just above her collarbone. She rolled on the floor and shrieked.

Two more gunshots.

From her peripheral vision, she saw Ben collapse on the floor. Blood was soaking through the layers of her jacket. She knew it was a flesh wound. But her whole shoulder throbbed in a dull ache before going rigid.

Kim lay on the floor, her dimming eyes watching Mackenzie. She coughed like a broken motor. Blood trickled out of her mouth.

Mackenzie crawled toward her. Her knees slipped in blood. Whose blood? Kim or Ben's? Her own? She couldn't tell. Ignoring the jab at the base of her skull, she reached Kim and looked at her stomach. The epicenter of the carnage.

"Kim!" Mackenzie was startled by her own voice. She placed her palm on Kim's stomach to contain the bleeding. "Keep your eyes open!"

Faintly, she heard Nick call an ambulance.

Kim's blinks were languishing. She tried to speak.

"Hush. Help is coming. Conserve your strength. Please," Mackenzie begged.

Rivera kneeled on the other side and pressed her fingers on Kim's neck, checking her pulse. She looked up at Mackenzie with pursed lips. "She needs surgery immediately."

"Kim! Stay with us!"

"Detective Price. You're injured. I'll take over." Rivera gently removed Mackenzie's hands and pressed her own into Kim's wound.

Tears streamed down Mackenzie's face. She felt Nick's hand on her face and shoulder. Hiccups caused little tremors in her throat. She looked at her hands. Her fingers were sticky with congealing blood.

# CHAPTER FORTY-TWO

The white light above Mackenzie was sharp and blazing. Even with her eyes closed, it was burning her corneas. When she came round, she was in the hospital with tubes going into her skin. Her head was wrapped in a bandage. Her right arm was in a sling.

"Shit," she grumbled.

"Easy," a young nurse with pink hair said from her side. "How're you feeling, Detective Price?"

"My head hurts."

She placed a pen in her pocket. "Fortunately, your CT scan shows no signs of internal bleeding or swelling. You have suffered a bad concussion, and the back of your head will be tender for a few days. And you have a flesh wound in your trapezius muscle from the bullet. You're lucky it missed the clavicle."

"All my injuries are external?"

"Yes. Just monitor your symptoms for a while. If anything changes, come back immediately."

Mackenzie shifted. "Can I leave now?"

"Let me talk to the doctor."

As soon as the nurse left, Mackenzie dropped her head on the pillow and groaned. The room smelled like antiseptic and fresh paint. She noted the gleaming white walls; a sharp contrast to the yellow tiles over her head.

A crack ran through the middle of one tile. She glared at the sliver of blackness. Like the force of her stare could pry it further open. She blinked and the vision of Kim collapsing on the floor swarmed her mind. When she opened her eyes, they were brimming with tears.

What had she done? She had tried calling for backup. But she shouldn't have gone alone in the first place.

There were mutters and burbles outside the door. Quickly, she wiped her tears and sat up on the bed. No one could know Mad Mack cried.

Sully walked in first, followed by Nick, who wore a scowl on his face.

"How're you, Mack?" Sully pulled a chair from the corner and perched on it.

"Peachy."

His unibrow rose. "We need to talk."

Nick made a point of exhaling loudly and leaned against the wall with his hands in his pockets. Sully rolled his eyes, ignoring him. "Kim didn't make it. She died in surgery."

Mackenzie schooled her face to maintain composure. Saliva pooled in her mouth. The muscles in her throat went rigid, unable to move and swallow.

"Ben Harlan was shot dead on the scene by Lieutenant Rivera."

Her eyes darted to Nick. Sensing she was watching him, he gave her an empathetic look.

"When you're discharged, we're going to need you to do a walkthrough. Can you do that?" Sully asked.

Mackenzie nodded. Her quirky sergeant usually carried a sense of humor or disinterest—anything to dilute the seriousness of their profession. She had often wondered if it was a management technique. But today was one of the rare times his face was pinched in hardness.

"Why did you go there?" Sully asked.

"I… I suspected Ben after reading that there were traces of vinegar in the shoe casting they lifted."

"Vinegar?"

"Yes. I thought it was odd that there was vinegar on the bottom of the shoes. Then I remembered that I saw these flowers at Ben's cabin that grow better in acidic soil."

"And you decided to go alone?"

Mackenzie's voice was thick. "It wasn't a solid lead. As soon as I confirmed that the soil smelled like vinegar, I tried calling for backup, but I didn't have signal."

"You had no business going alone in the first place. You could have brought along Justin. Or someone from patrol."

"I didn't think it would get this bad."

"What the hell were you expecting if you thought he'd abducted that woman?" he hollered.

"Sully," Nick interjected. "It was a bad call, but is this really necessary?"

"It sure as hell is," he snapped. "I have the prime suspect and another victim dead. Not to mention a detective injured."

The gunshot rang in Mackenzie's ears. "Are you okay?" Nick stepped forward. His hands curled on the edge of the bed, his knuckles whitening.

"Yes." She shook her head. "It was a bad call, Sully. I made a mistake. I underestimated how dangerous the situation could get. I was worried he'd move her to a different location or kill her if I waited any longer. What do we do next? Did they find anyone else in that cabin?"

Sully huffed. "No. Just Kim. *You* need to undergo a psych evaluation. You'll be issued another gun, since your Glock is evidence now. And you're off for the rest of the week."

She straightened. "It's only a flesh wound."

"You have a concussion. You need to take it easy for at least seventy-two hours."

"But—"

"No." He wagged his finger. "This time you will follow protocol. I'm protecting you, Mack. You have no idea how mad the brass is.

Rivera is seething. The FBI is investigating corruption and now we're sending the message that we're negligent."

She looked at Nick helplessly, but he shrugged. How was she supposed to stay away for the rest of the week? "What about the case?"

"Nick can go at it alone."

"I have updates."

"Give them to Nick." Sully's tone was stern and unyielding.

Mackenzie stared at him defiantly. "Look, I know I messed up. But I want to be useful. That's the only way I can still fix this."

Sully leaned forward. The lines in his forehead dug deep. "You'll be useful when I'm convinced you have rested and can make sound decisions. You made a rookie mistake by going alone. And now you have a concussion. Rest."

She almost swallowed her tongue. She didn't appreciate being treated like a child or a novice. But her actions had led her here. Her stupid, stupid actions. She sighed, resigned, and looked away.

After Sully left the room, Nick spoke. "Give him time. Things are in flux at work."

"I screwed up," she blurted and punched the mattress. Pain shot up her injured arm, and she flinched. "Ouch."

"Don't be an idiot. Focus on getting better. But give me your update now, while you're awake."

Mackenzie rehashed her conversation with Kim.

"Katy was going to pay Ben off, after she collected the money on Saturday?"

She nodded and recalled the nervous flitting of Kim's eyes. The sweat oozing out of her pores. The blood trickling out of her skin. Mackenzie shoved the image away.

Nick pressed his mouth in a flat line. "Could Kim be lying?"

"Why?"

"It would be a pretty genius idea. To replace Katy and pin the whole thing on the abusive ex."

Mackenzie frowned. "No. I believed her. She looked sincere."

His eyes searched hers, like he wanted to say something. She egged him on. "What?"

"You're feeling guilty." He ran a hand through his hair. "Over her death. It's fair. But that might make you biased."

"In her favor?"

He nodded.

Her hands were itchy and restless in her lap. She wanted to clean something. But what could she clean in a sterile hospital room?

"Sterling's going to be here soon."

Her eyes popped out. "*What*?"

"He's your emergency contact."

Mackenzie pulled a face. Of course he was. Their lives were still integrated. Kicking him out of their house meant nothing. "What about Alison?"

"Ben could be holding her somewhere else. I'll look into it and send you regular updates. Just rest."

But Mackenzie couldn't rest. Kim was dead, and so was Ben, which meant they were no closer to finding Alison—if she was even still alive.

# CHAPTER FORTY-THREE

*December 6*

The spoon slightly wobbled in Sterling's hand. The tip of his tongue poked out, resting on his upper lip. Mackenzie opened her mouth, and he shoved in a spoonful of soup.

She swallowed the burning liquid. The tangy taste coated her tongue. "Did you make this?"

He nodded silently and pouted at the bowl. Sterling was in an introspective mood. He had shown up frantic at the hospital, his tie askew and his eyes bloodshot. The only news he'd received was that Mackenzie had been shot.

"Is it okay?" he asked.

"Yeah. But I can eat soup myself. My elbow moves just fine."

His eyebrows dipped. "No, let me."

They were seated on the couch in the living room. Her father paced in the kitchen with a ticking jaw. His hands were balled into fists and trembling. "Is someone after you, Micky?" he asked suddenly.

Her head jerked in his direction. "No. Why would you say that?"

"You were shot."

"By a suspect. I'm a police officer."

He licked his lips. "Right. Of course."

It was Mackenzie's first day "off-duty," and she was already close to losing her mind. She had texted Nick for updates. He'd reminded her that it was nine in the morning.

Four hours later, her mind was buzzing with the events of yesterday. She couldn't sit still, couldn't stop tucking her hair behind her ears, and couldn't stop wiping her hands on her jeans.

Robert accidentally dropped a fork on the floor when emptying the dishwasher. To Mackenzie it sounded like the bullet barreling out of Ben's gun and into Kim's stomach. She jumped at the sound and cowered into Sterling.

"Mack!" Sterling's voice sounded far-off, like it was coming from the end of a tunnel.

She recoiled away from him. "Sterling, I'm fine."

"You have a bad concussion. There's swelling on the back of your head."

"I'm functional. And it's not like I'm living alone."

He opened his mouth to argue but closed it, his eyes flickering over to Robert in the kitchen. As if Robert sensed they needed privacy, he mumbled some excuse and left the room. She tucked her hand under her chin and shook her head.

"Mack, I'm ready to spend the rest of my life earning back your trust. I'll do *anything*."

"That'll be a sad marriage," she commented dryly. His face fell at her words. "Sorry."

"Mack," he clasped her hand in his. "I love you. Please."

He hadn't said those words to her since she asked him to leave their house. And those simple words messed with her head. She looked up at her husband, who had taken a backseat at a big trial he'd been preparing for months. He was supposed to be first chair. Instead, he was here, taking care of her. He never hesitated in giving, without her ever having to ask.

"I don't know, Sterling."

"We can take this slow. Maybe I could spend some nights here. Just don't close the door on us. I can't imagine my life without you."

Mackenzie was exhausted. Her body had gone through a wringer—head mildly pounding and arm sore and stiff. She couldn't tuck away the image of Kim being shot. And she was living with her father, who was back from the dead and possibly harboring secrets.

Deflated, she rested her head on his shoulder. For one moment, she wanted to forget that her life was a shambles. She just wanted security. Sterling kept stroking her hand, quietly, while she wrestled with the idea of giving him another chance.

"I need to rest," she said after a few minutes, and stood up. "I'll think about it. About you moving back in."

"Thank you."

Mackenzie locked the bedroom door behind her and slumped down. She'd never felt so confused in her life. Sterling had felt like the one thing she had going for her. She could take him back, but at what cost? Could she ever trust him again?

A sluggish roll crept up her body, starting in her toes and making its way up to her eyelids. Seconds later, her head was on the pillow, and she was snoring away.

Minutes after that, she was running wildly through the woods behind Hidden Lake. She was panting and puffing—her lungs squeezing painfully in her chest.

Speckles of light guided her through the dark woods. She ran around the thick trees, hopped over the bulging roots and thickets.

Suddenly, she saw Sterling on her left, watching her with dead eyes. "I'm sorry, Mack. We can make this work."

Then she saw her father. He was old but wore his flowery shirt from back in the day. "Micky, give me a chance. Haven't I proven myself to you? We can move on together."

She turned in the opposite direction, away from his looming presence that cut into her soul.

In her peripheral vision, she saw Kim Harris. A bullet wound in her abdomen. Her entire torso was red—a jarring color against the black and blue of the woods. "You owe me."

Mackenzie stopped dead in her tracks. In front of her, Katy appeared. Her face was invisible behind a thick cloud of leaves. "All I did my entire life was help people. I just wanted to do right by Kim."

Alison appeared in another corner. "I would never leave my son. Please, give him back his mother."

Mackenzie dragged her fingers through her soiled hair. They surrounded her. She decided to run back but something held her ankle.

A man's hand had extended out of the ground. It held Mackenzie and immobilized her.

A scream was stuck in her throat.

"Ignorance is bliss, Mackenzie."

She looked up and found Melody standing on the other side of the grave, holding the same shovel from that night. She swung the shovel against Mackenzie's head.

A crack.

Black.

Mackenzie woke up with a stir, her nightmare fading like smoke. The doctor had prescribed her a mild painkiller to get through the first night, but now she was wide awake and restless to get some work done.

Even though Nick was on top of it, the more heads and hands, the better for Alison.

Clint and Andrea were monitoring that shady website to check for more ads, but nothing new had popped up. They were still trying to hunt down who paid Robbie in Bitcoin. And the patrol was still underway at Woodburn.

Ben Harlan seemed like the obvious suspect for the murders, yet his role in the bigger operation felt unlikely. He was unhinged, an abusive drunk, but he didn't fit the profile. His only concern seemed to be Kim and the money. She'd let Nick check that box off, though.

Mackenzie logged in and scoured over all the files again. From the medical examiner's report on Katy and Bella, to old case notes on the suicide and records of Alison's last movements. She hoped that something would catch her eye, but going over the facts of the case again, she felt more and more baffled.

She was certain that Steven Boyle had had something to do with the suicide. Could the victim have been his drug-addicted wife, Sofia,—the one he talked about? Could he have surgically changed his own wife to look more like Carrie Breslow? She recalled how the nurse at the retirement home had told them that Steven had looked down on his wife for being a shut-in and an addict.

Years later, someone was doing something similar, using *his* name on the dark web. Someone had sent him a gift—an expensive pen with a molecule's structure engraved on it. A symbol that would have meant something to Steven, had he been in his right mind.

Then there was Bella's tattoo—except Jasmine was adamant that Bella was allergic to the ink.

Mackenzie had planned to follow up on this before the vinegar had caught her attention and distracted her. Now, she looked up all the reasons one might have an allergic reaction to tattoos. The most obvious explanation was metal hypersensitivity, as a result of heavy metals present in tattoo ink. It was more commonly associated with colored ink—especially red ink—as it contained rust, but even black ink contained metals.

She scratched her head, her brain scouring for alternatives. Realizing she was out, she shot Becky a message.

*Is it a good time to talk?*

Becky was a night owl, so Mackenzie was certain she wasn't asleep at midnight. But she and her husband were having problems. As Mackenzie waited for a reply, her mind imagined what their issues looked like. Did they scream and shout like Melody and Robert? Or were their cold silences bursting with tension and grudges, like with Mackenzie and Sterling?

Her phone buzzed—a call from Becky.

"How's the concussion, Mack?"

"Not too bad. I wanted to talk about one of the victims, Bella Fox. The one with the tattoos?"

"Oh yeah, the former drug addict." Mackenzie heard water gush out of a faucet and then Becky gulping. "What about her?"

"Tracked down her roommate. She said that the last time Bella tried to get tattoos, she had a severe allergic reaction and had to be taken to a hospital."

Becky was silent for a beat. "Okay…"

"The doctor told her not to get inked because of the allergy." Mackenzie dragged her hands down her face, drowsiness intensifying. "Can you extract the ink from the body and check its composition to confirm what kind of ink was used?"

Becky chuckled. "Doesn't work that way, Mack. Tattoo removal means destroying it."

"Then I don't know what to think. She had to be taken to the hospital when she tried getting tattoos before."

"Hmmm…" A chair scraped against tiles. "I read somewhere about something known as vegan ink, I think. I don't know anything about it but worth checking out."

"Okay, will do. Thanks, Becky."

"No problem."

Mackenzie disconnected the call and searched vegan ink. Traditional ink was generally iron heavy and used animal products as carriers. Bella's tattoos were black. Non-toxic versions of blank ink used carbon or logwood, and purified water and witch hazel for carriers. The information washed over Mackenzie. But then she came across some articles on how vegan friendly, non-toxic ink offered an alternative to people who were allergic to the ingredients found in traditional ink.

A glimmer of hope pulsed through Mackenzie. Her eyes were drooping, sleep coming back to her in full force. But she couldn't sleep *now*. She needed to scratch this itch, needed to get one step closer before the paths twisted away from her again.

She hunted for tattoo parlors that used "non-toxic" and "vegan" ink. There were no hits for Lakemore or Riverview. She expanded the search. There were six parlors fairly nearby that offered vegan ink services. Bella could have gone to any of them. Mackenzie noted down their addresses.

Maybe one of them was where Bella went. Maybe they would know what her tattoo meant.

# CHAPTER FORTY-FOUR

*December 7*

Mackenzie turned the key in the ignition and felt the pulsating car still. Driving had taken a toll on her shoulder. She had tried to keep her arm braced, but the little movements had accumulated and left her muscle sore and throbbing.

The bandage was still wrapped around her head—it was the last day she had to wear it. The swelling had reduced. She had displayed no symptoms as a result of the concussion. Just one more day and then at least her hair wouldn't be drenched in sweat. She grazed the back of her head and winced at the wetness pooling along the edge of the bandage.

She grabbed her bag and climbed out of the car. It was a rare sunny afternoon in Lakemore, with clear blue skies. But even as she put on her sunglasses, she felt a chill hanging in the air.

She pounded her fist on the door. The sound of footsteps grew clearer. The thick wooden door flung open, and Nick gave her a brittle smile. "You lasted a day away. Color me surprised."

"Move."

He grunted and let her in. Dressed in sweatpants in the middle of the day, he shrugged when Mackenzie cocked an eyebrow at him. "I wasn't expecting company. Who told you I was here, anyway?"

"Troy."

"That little shit. Come on." He led her to his office—or his *lair*, as Mackenzie called it. The square room was windowless, with dark wooden paneling. A vintage twin pedestal desk stood with several monitors on top. The wall opposite was crowded with pictures and copies of reports. There was no chair to sit on. Just a thick rug splayed in the middle with yellow elephants embroidered on it. It was brash and out of place. But Nick's mother had made it before she passed away.

Mackenzie was surprised at the unexpected effects the claustrophobic room had on her. Devoid of any distractions and stifled with investigation details, this room allowed her to submerge completely in a case.

She glanced over the pictures of Katy and Bella's bodies, Kim, Cole, Carrie, Alison, Ben, and Robbie pinned to the wall along with the ads. Her eyes froze on the crime scene pictures from Ben's cabin. A pool of blood photographed from every angle.

Thick and grotesque.

"Anything on Ben? Any connection to the ads?" she asked doubtfully.

Nick faced the wall where all the clues were pinned. The middle of the wall displayed the timeline of the cases. Starting from the suicide of their Jane Doe sixteen years ago to the deaths of Kim Harris and Ben Harlan. "Ben's alibi is airtight for that weekend. He spent Friday night getting drunk and Saturday in the hospital for alcohol poisoning."

"Are you sure?"

Nick tapped at a piece of paper clipped to the board. "Hospital sent a record of his stay. He was discharged in the evening. Clint is going through Ben's phone and laptop to see if he put out the ads. I don't think he'll find anything either."

She dropped her bag on the ground and sat cross-legged on the floor.

He froze and narrowed his eyes. "What are you doing?"

She shrugged innocently. "Helping."

"You're on leave."

"You don't have to tell Sully."

His gray eyes drilled into hers like their sharpness could change her mind. But she was stubborn. When the corners of her mouth quivered, he rolled his eyes and sat on the floor with her. "How are you doing?"

"Fine." Her tone was curt.

"Don't beat yourself up over what happened too much."

Saliva thickened in her throat. "I'm the reason she's dead."

"*Ben* is the reason she's dead," he scolded.

"Because I made a mistake."

"I don't know why you're so hard on yourself, Mack."

*You have to help me bury him.*

She smoothed her hair over her scalp repeatedly and unnecessarily—it was already glued to her skull with sweat.

He looked over at the wall. A dark shadow crossed his face. "The body count doubled weeks into the case."

Mackenzie chewed her lips in contemplation. Ben Harlan was impulsive and manipulative. She recalled his lopsided smile when he had fooled her and Nick into thinking he was an innocent bystander. A harmless fellow who had been heartbroken and wanted to explore the mysterious woods of Lakemore. But there was a twisted, even lethal, side to him.

"Becky finished the autopsy on the bodies," Nick said out of the blue. "Kim wasn't pregnant, unsurprisingly."

"We're still keeping the switch from the family?"

He nodded, clearly peeved by their boss's orders. "Next of kin identification isn't reliable because they're twins, so we have to wait for DNA testing."

"Kim told me that she was Kim. What possible reason would she have to lie?"

"None that I can see, but this is more for Katy. We need DNA validation to confirm her identity. Especially when we have another victim who looks a lot like her. Rivera is being very strict about protocol, especially after you..."

"Messed up big time?"

"No," he said reassuringly. "Made a mistake and then got unlucky. Anyway, yeah. Just going by the book now. Even if it feels a little redundant. But that's bureaucracy."

"How long will Becky take to confirm the identities?"

"Standard DNA testing doesn't differentiate between identical twins. Becky said it requires a deeper exploration of the DNA to pinpoint mutations, as their genetic code is the same. She's not an expert and doesn't have access to the resources, so we're sending the samples to a lab in Seattle."

"That's going to take several days."

"Could even be weeks depending on backlog." Nick's frustrated expression shifted to one of concern as he looked at Mackenzie. "Hey, you look like hell. Do you want a drink?"

Mackenzie shot him a look. "It's noon."

Nick shrugged and went to the mini fridge he kept in his office and took out two beers. "I don't have wine. You'll have to make do with this."

"Why are you out of wine?" She took a swig and suppressed a gag.

"You finished it, Mack."

"Oops."

Nick sat across from her and scrutinized her with curious eyes. "So you just didn't do any work yesterday?"

She scraped the label on the bottle and shrugged innocently. "Nope."

"I don't buy it."

She looked up and found him flashing her a triumphant smile. Like he was familiar with all the gears and wheels in her brain. "I did some browsing and made *one* phone call, to Becky."

"Of course, you did."

She told him about her research and the six parlors in close vicinity, where Bella could have gotten her tattoos.

Nick took a swig, visibly amused. "Hand over the names. I'll ask Justin to check them out."

"I can do that too," Mackenzie protested like a petulant child. What else was she supposed to do for the next few days?

"Mack, I'm worried about you." His forehead bunched. "That shooting was screwed up, and you had a bad concussion. Take it easy, okay?"

She wanted to confide in him that work was the only thing keeping her from breaking down. She was conflicted in her feelings for Sterling; too embarrassed to admit even to herself that she was considering letting him move back in. Then there was her father, who had snuck up on her out of nowhere. It was like exercising after a long time. At first it was painful, leaving her sore, but then one day, it stopped hurting. Their relationship was slowly unfolding, but Mackenzie had to quash that feeling. She had to keep the distance between them. He was still the man who had beaten her mother every day. And someone else was buried out in the woods. Mackenzie still hadn't made any attempt to find out who he was. She had to try and find out what her father knew. No excuses.

"Earth to Mack."

She took out her phone and sent him the list of parlors. "Here you go. Can you at least keep me updated?"

"Of course." He made a face. "Do you want to talk about something?"

Before she could answer, his phone chirped. He glared at it with a deep frown and shot up, moving fast around his office. His bare feet scuffled through sheets of paper lying idly on the floor to get to his computer.

Keys clacked.

Mackenzie followed up eagerly. "What?"

Nick opened an email and skimmed it. "Clint found some deleted files on Robbie Elfman's computer. There's an info dump on a lot of women."

"Not a huge shock, given his history. He was also in prison for stalking and harassment."

Nick opened his mouth but closed it and turned off the monitor. "Time for you to go home, Mack. I have to get to work."

"What did you find? There's something on it, isn't there?" Her pulse jumped, knowing her partner's ticks well.

A satisfied smirk and a twitch in his eye. "You're on medical leave. Have patience. Besides, I'll see you tonight?"

"What?"

"The holiday party, Mack. I reminded you a few days ago."

"Oh! God, yes." She scratched her head. "I totally forgot that's tonight. It's still happening?"

Nick shrugged. "Sully said it's only three hours, and we could all use a break. Rescheduling it is going to be a pain with everyone getting busy with their families soon enough. Oh, and remember to bring your contribution."

Every year at the holiday party Lakemore PD collected donations to support a charity. This year it was to help families of fallen firefighters. Mackenzie nodded, discomfort clawing at her skin. She didn't want to bring Sterling to the party. Nor was she ready to take her father. That was unnecessary. She would be going alone.

"I'll be there." She smiled tight.

# CHAPTER FORTY-FIVE

Troy and Finn were in charge of the decorations, just like the last few years. There was a fake Christmas tree in the middle of the office, twinkling with lights and ornaments. It was tradition. Christmas lights were strung up around the room; a shelf converted to a table held snacks and alcohol. Instead of candy canes, there were hanging white reapers. A disco ball and lights lit up the room, casting shapes and silhouettes that rippled over skins and surfaces. A strange mix of Christmas and Halloween. Troy and Finn called it a theme party. But Mackenzie and the rest of them knew the pair were too lazy to buy new decorations each year.

Everyone from the Detectives Unit was present, with families. Sully sat in a corner dressed as Santa Claus with a lazy grin on his face—an empty bottle of wine next to his feet. Mackenzie took a shuddering breath, waving hello at everyone.

"Where's Sterling?" Pam, Sully's chatty wife with a bob cut, cornered Mackenzie. "You look lovely, by the way."

Mackenzie looked down at her simple red dress, feeling self-conscious. "Thank you. He's busy. He's sorry he couldn't make it."

"Oh, that's a shame. I really like him. You two are such a handsome couple."

Mackenzie plastered on a fake smile that almost hurt her face and nodded. She tried not to think of the awkward conversation she'd had with Sterling earlier that evening, when she'd told him not to come. "I'm going to take a lap, but I'll catch up with you later."

"Sure, honey."

Nick sat on a chair patiently while Luna painted on his eyelids with a lipstick.

"I think hot pink would suit his skin color more." Mackenzie ruffled Luna's hair from behind.

"Don't give her more ideas." Nick's eyes were closed, his arms crossed.

Luna spun around and beamed. She wrapped her chubby hands around Mackenzie's waist and squeezed her tightly. "Merry Christmas, Aunty Mack."

"You too, Luna." She kissed the top of her head. "Are you excited to spend the holidays with your dad?"

"Yes. He's more fun than Mom and doesn't keep a swear jar."

Mackenzie picked up a drink, chuckling. Nick raised an eyebrow at her glass. Her cheeks felt flushed already, and there was a slight sway in her step. Her facial muscles were not as controlled as she liked them to be. She'd had a glass of wine before coming, despite the fact she was still taking painkillers for her injuries.

After all, it was a party.

Her eyes darted to the bowl marked "donations," containing envelopes.

"Oh shit." She pressed her hand against her forehead. "I left my contribution at home. I had it on the kitchen island, but then I opened a bottle of wine and I… forgot."

"You can hand it in later." Nick slapped her back. "It's a little embarrassing but not a big deal."

"Thanks." She rolled her eyes. "I feel bad. Maybe I can just quickly drive home and come back."

Her phone vibrated with a message. It was from her father.

*Come downstairs, Micky. I'm at the station.*

What the hell was he doing here? Mackenzie felt the effects of the alcohol melt away, her body going rigid. She put her glass away and rushed out of the office, her heart skittering wildly in her chest.

Was he in trouble? Was he hurt? Her mind reeled with possibilities. When she saw him standing in the lobby, smiling, irritation took over.

"What are you doing here?" she whispered, unable to keep the edge out of her voice.

Robert's smile faded. "I'm sorry, Micky. I saw you left this in the kitchen." He took out the envelope from his pocket. "You mentioned it was important. I thought I should drop it off."

She took it from him and looked around warily.

"Okay, then." He pressed his lips in a thin line. "I'll just go. Have fun tonight."

Robert had been doing this lately—small, nice gestures here and there—to prove that he wasn't the man Mackenzie remembered, that he had truly changed. But she didn't appreciate his timing this time, even if his blatant disappointment did make her feel a little guilty.

"Hey, Mad Mack! Do you know where Murphy keeps his scotch collection?" Troy came from behind her and paused, looking at Robert. "Hello sir, I'm Troy Clayton."

Robert shook his hand. "Robert Price."

"Her dad? Nice to meet you!"

Mackenzie's colleagues didn't know much about her personal life. All they knew was that her father wasn't in the picture and her mother had died. Robert Price had gone missing twenty years ago. Even if old timers like Sully remembered the case, she had prepared an answer: Her father had walked out on them but had reappeared to make amends. It wasn't a complete lie, and no one would have to know what really transpired that night twenty years ago.

"Aren't you joining us?" Troy asked good-naturedly.

Robert blinked rapidly, his face turning red. "No, I was just here to drop something off. I should leave."

"It's a holiday party! Everyone's family is here. I'm sure you'll have a great time."

Mackenzie wanted the earth to swallow her. Her two worlds were clashing in front of her, and there was nothing she could do to stop it without rousing suspicion or coming off as rude. And Robert was hurt by her reaction—she could tell from the expression in his eyes.

"It's okay. You can come up for a bit," Mackenzie offered reluctantly.

"If it's okay with you."

Mackenzie entered the elevator flanked by her father, who was supposed to be dead, and her clueless coworker, who chewed Robert's ear off with small talk.

As the elevator glided up, she kept her ears tuned to Robert, praying he didn't reveal anything suspicious. Fortunately, she trusted Robert enough to maintain the facade. His penchant for self-preservation meant he'd be careful.

When they joined the party, Mackenzie placed her contribution in the bowl.

Luna came up to them and frowned at Robert. "Who are you?"

"This is my father. Robert."

Robert leaned down to shake Luna's hand. Nick's eyes popped open and settled on Mackenzie. She gave him a forced smile and did the introductions, not missing the corners of his eyes tightening ever so slightly. She knew Nick was assessing her father. But Robert had perfected his manners. They made small talk, and Mackenzie grabbed another drink to give her the courage to get through the night without losing her mind.

Luna pulled on the hem of her dress, demanding attention. "I have a question."

"Yes?"

"Why is this called a *holiday* party not a Christmas party?"

Mackenzie tucked her hair behind her ear, wondering if it were a trick question. "Because we're celebrating all the holidays around this time, like Hanukkah."

Luna looked around, deadpan. "Then why are there only Christmas decorations and Christmas songs?"

"Okay, Luna." Nick tugged her back by her pigtails. "Enough questions for today."

"Looking good, Detective Blackwood." Rivera joined them, and turned to Mackenzie. "How're you doing now?"

"Better, thank you."

Mackenzie didn't like something about Rivera's expression. Maybe it was her whitened knuckles holding the glass. Or the strained smile plastered on her lips. Or her ballooned nostrils. She wondered if Rivera was still unhappy with her. Mackenzie knew that she had disappointed her new boss, especially after Rivera had essentially tried to take her under her wing.

Mad Mack had been reckless.

She grabbed her father's elbow and turned him around to diffuse the tension. "This is my father, Robert Price. This is Lieutenant Atlee Rivera."

Rivera's eyes flitted to Robert. "Nice to meet you."

"Ah! You too." He offered his hand. "Lovely party."

"Thank you. Can I get you a drink?"

"I don't drink."

Silence lingered in their little corner. The air felt frailer than usual. None of them were talkers. Nick was preoccupied, humoring Luna by allowing his face to be used as a canvas. Mackenzie let out an easy breath when Sully's wife Pam joined them, setting into motion some conversations.

An hour later, Mackenzie sat in a corner with a bowl of chips in her lap. Pam and Troy kept Robert engaged. It was easier to breathe not having to worry about entertaining him.

"Not feeling the Christmas cheer?" Nick perched on the desk next to her.

"I never do," she muttered, fiddling with the candy. "When I was six years old, my mom told me that Santa wasn't real."

"Sounds like a practical lady."

She laughed. "I don't know about that."

"You're laughing more than usual."

She looked at him with a straight face. "You're not the only one who has had a few drinks."

"I didn't know your father was coming."

She watched him mingle with her co-workers and felt almost nauseated. "I didn't either. He came to give me the envelope I'd left at home and then Troy caught us. I couldn't think of an excuse."

"Detective Price. Detective Blackwood." Justin acknowledged them, tipping his head.

"Relax, Justin. We're off duty. Take a chill pill," Mackenzie drawled. "You did a good job hunting down Bella, by the way. In case I didn't tell you before."

"Did you find anything on Elisa James?" Nick asked Justin.

"Got her address, sir."

"Who is Elisa James?" Mackenzie asked, sitting up straighter.

"Someone on Robbie's computer we need to talk to," Nick said.

"Do you want to go now?"

"No! We're both basically hammered. And… you're still on leave."

"I was hoping you'd forget that part."

"No chance." He clinked his beer bottle with Justin and took a swig.

A few minutes later, there was a commotion at the entrance of the office. Some beefy men dressed in suits had entered wearing distrustful expressions. Sully woke up with a stir and wiped the drool off his chin.

"Is that the FBI?" Mackenzie asked.

Nick put away his beer bottle and straightened his already straight tie. "No. That's my dad."

She raised her eyebrows. "He's *here*?"

He gave her a flat look and left to greet his father. Senator Alan Blackwood was shorter than Nick, trim in a midnight-blue suit, with a thick mane of gray hair on his head. Though she had been friends with Nick for eight years, Mackenzie had never had the opportunity to meet Alan. He was understandably a busy man. Nick didn't resemble his father much, but when he smiled, shaking Lieutenant Rivera's hand, she saw the likeness.

Luna tore away from the group of children and sprinted toward her grandfather. Her pigtails oscillating almost comically. Mackenzie stayed behind and watched Alan, Nick, and Luna together.

Her heart scraped a little even though a reluctant smile tugged at her lips. They were so normal. She caught Robert watching her, almost forlorn. Like he knew what she was thinking. Because he was thinking the same thing.

"This is Mack," Nick gestured for Mackenzie to come over. "My partner I've told you about."

"Ah, yes! Have heard great things," Alan smiled. "Happy holidays."

"You too, sir."

"Please, call me Alan." His face faltered as his eyes searched hers. "You know, you look like someone I knew a very long time ago."

"Oh. I don't know…"

He frowned. "What was your name again?"

"Mackenzie Price," she said slowly.

He raised his eyebrows and touched his fist to his mouth. "Are you by any chance related to Melody Price?"

Mackenzie's heart skipped a beat. Blood drained from her face. But there were eyes on her. Everyone except for the children had surrounded them, wanting to greet the senator. "Y-yes. She was my mother."

"I can't believe I didn't make the connection before. You look so much like her. And Nick and Luna always called you Mack, so..."

"Wait—how do you know them?" Nick asked the question Mackenzie couldn't find her voice for.

"We were old family friends when we lived in Salem. Me not so much, but your mother and Melody were good friends. In fact, you went to the hospital when Mackenzie was born. You insisted on holding her, but you were only five. You threw a big tantrum."

Troy almost spat out his drink and beamed. "*Really*?"

Mackenzie drew a blank and looked at Nick from the corner of her eye. His cheeks glowed pink, visibly embarrassed.

"We moved a few months after that, to Seattle. What a small world." Alan chuckled.

"Oh my God, please. I have so many questions." Troy grinned.

"You must know my father, then," Mackenzie said.

Robert nodded vaguely at Alan, avoiding meeting his eyes. Mackenzie reckoned he was ashamed. Robert was always known for being deadbeat. A drunk who stayed at home while his wife worked hard to afford his addiction and fill their stomachs.

Alan's lips parted, and a knot formed between his eyebrows. "Yes, of course." He offered his hand. "It's been a long time."

"It's good to see you," Robert replied shakily.

Mackenzie didn't miss their guarded reactions to each other. Almost like they were gauging each other before a duel. Something was amiss.

Soon Luna pulled her away to question her on why people killed each other. Mackenzie noticed how Robert made an active effort to avoid Alan for the remainder of the night, while Alan kept throwing cautionary glances at Robert, like he was trying to make up his mind about him.

She couldn't shake off the feeling that the two men had history.

# CHAPTER FORTY-SIX

## *December 8*

Mackenzie had messaged Justin inquiring how many tattoo parlors he had checked out. Justin had crossed off four out of six and was on his way to the fifth one. She messaged him back:

*I can look into the last one. Already in Kent on an errand.*

It was a lie, and her junior detective knew it. Mackenzie bit her nails, waiting for Justin's reply. The bubble appeared and disappeared repeatedly, indicating that he was struggling to type a message. He no doubt disapproved of her working while on medical leave, but she had forged a good working relationship with Justin. She trusted him not to tell anyone, just like she knew he wouldn't argue with her. She felt guilty for putting him in an awkward position, but she knew the flak would ultimately come her way if anyone found out. The reply was what she expected:

*Yes, ma'am.*

Mackenzie's fingers drummed the wheel as her eyes scanned for another parking space. There was a parking lot a few blocks ahead, but the price was ridiculous, especially considering the neighborhood. She was convinced she would get robbed there.

The street had few shops lining either side. They were shabby and discolored with broken windows, signs hanging off, newspapers patching up the holes in walls, and stinking garbage bags collecting at their doorstep. Cars in need of urgent wash and repair blocked portions of the narrow street. Even the streetlights were bent at awkward angles, with missing bulbs.

"Hey! Don't you dare hit him!" A woman dressed in a tight fluorescent-green dress stepped in front of the car, and bent to pick up a cat from the street. "I'll sue your ass!"

The woman retreated to her group of friends. All of them were dressed for a night out, except their eyes were bloodshot and mascara gathered in the corners. One of the women counted a thick stash of cash with a cigarette dangling loosely from her lips.

Mackenzie climbed out of the car and headed for the parlor.

It was a dead end. The two tattoo artists didn't recognize Bella or her tattoos. She left, disappointed, and thought about expanding their search to Seattle.

She was walking back to her car when she spotted a faded sign reading *Inkphoria* above a cracked window. No light and no activity came from inside. The space was empty—just stained walls and floor—with a little blackboard with instructions written in chalk to go inside and then down a flight of stairs.

She hesitated for a heartbeat but entered the shop and started downstairs. The bottom of the staircase was pitch black, slashed by a sliver of light from underneath a door. The walls and stairs began to rattle with vibrations from some techno music. The door didn't have a knob. Mackenzie pushed it slightly, and it swung open smoothly.

The room was bathed in red light. It was larger than she had anticipated. Intricate designs adorned the walls—abstract ink patterns churning in water or smoke, a flower birthing a dragon, a woman being held captive by vines and branches. The clinical smell of disinfectants and antibiotics was welcome. Mackenzie could finally feel her lungs expand freely. Shelves housed various tattoo supplies, from sterilization equipment like gloves and rubbing alcohol to products like needle bars, soldering guns, and disposable razors.

On her right side, a woman lay on a chair with her top lifted. A burly man leaned over her with an electric tattoo machine in his hands. "Do you have an appointment?" he asked without looking behind him.

"No," Mackenzie said.

"Make one and come back."

The woman on the chair let out a high-pitched giggle.

"Lakemore PD. Got some questions for you."

The man froze. He put his machine away on a tray and turned around on the stool. His long hair was tied in a bun, and a thick beard obscured his jaw. "This is a licensed shop."

"Good to know. What's your name?"

He took off his black gloves. "Liam. What do you want?"

"Do you use non-toxic, vegan ink?"

"Yeah, you want one?"

"I couldn't find your shop on the internet."

"I don't keep a website. Rely on word of mouth."

Liam was unfazed by her. It wasn't unusual, considering the dicey neighborhood. The most undaunted witnesses and suspects came from such places. They were desensitized to the police. Even the woman he was inking was on her phone now, disinterested.

Mackenzie pulled out her own phone and showed him a close-up picture of Bella's tattoos. "Recognize these?"

Liam glanced at them for a mere second. "Yes. The girl in trouble?"

"She's dead."

"I see." His eyebrows dipped low, like it was a mild inconvenience.

"Did you know her?"

"No. Just saw her when she came in. Said traditional ink gave her hives so she was looking for other options."

"Did she come alone?"

"Yes. What happened to her?"

"How did she pay?" Mackenzie dodged the question.

"Cash."

"You remember anything about her?"

He scoffed. "Of course I do. That was the worst thing I've inked on anyone."

"Why?"

"Those letters and numbers. I asked her several times if she wanted some kind of design around them, but she was adamant to keep them like that. Said that she wanted it to be taken seriously in case something went wrong."

Mackenzie became alert. "Did she say what might go wrong?"

"Nah, she was secretive. And honestly, none of my business." He raised his hands in surrender. "But she paid, so I didn't say no."

The tattoo meant something then. Bella had been in danger—and she knew it.

"When did she come in?"

"About two months ago."

"And did she say anything else? Anything odd?"

He sighed. "Other than that she wanted the tattoo on the back of her knees? I don't know… Wait, oh yeah. She told me to change the order of the numbers and letters."

"Do you have the original sequence?" Mackenzie asked, her pulse ticking faster.

Liam picked up a thick book from one of the stands and set it on a table, under a lamp. He flipped through the pages, as Mackenzie looked over. It was a collection of all the designs he had done. "Here it is." He stopped at one of the pages. A picture of the tattoo alongside a sequence of numbers and letters written by hand.

CBA3759. As opposed to the tattoos—39A on the back of the left knee and B75C on the right.

Mackenzie touched the page. It was obviously important, considering what Bella had said. "Can I take these?"

"Sure." Liam shrugged and took them from the book. "It's nothing I'm proud of anyway. Just a habit of documenting everything."

Mackenzie held the paper—the numbers and letters looking more magnetic in the red glow of the room. She scraped her memory. But this sequence hadn't turned up anywhere that she could recall. Not in the investigation into the Breslow doppelganger suicide. Not in Kim's old files from the center. Not in anything related to Alison or Katy.

"Thanks. Let me know if you think of anything else or if anyone contacts you about her." She gave him her card. He tossed it dismissively on the needle tray and turned back to his client.

Strong winds flapped around her as she walked back to the car.

"It's not a license plate," Mackenzie mumbled to herself, staring at the paper, like suddenly it would make sense.

The streets had emptied, making this tiny nook of Kent reminiscent of a ghost town. How had Bella even got here? The fact that she was able to travel so far suggested she hadn't been held captive, but if these women were free to go, where were they? Where was Alison? Unless... Had Bella had done something to earn their captor's trust? Something that gave her the freedom to get a tattoo; a *clue*? If only Mackenzie could decipher it. She thought about Robbie Elfman's computer. Clint had found something more on it. Something to do with women.

Could the codes be related that? Perhaps Bella wasn't the only woman Robbie had supplied.

# CHAPTER FORTY-SEVEN

Wearing her gardening overalls, Mackenzie stepped out into her front yard. The sky was bathed in copper hues and streaks of peach. A mellow breeze kissed her skin. The snow had mostly melted away now, the clusters of blizzards a thing of the past. Mackenzie looked around her garden. She had at least found time in the last few days to tend to it, and it was looking far healthier despite the winter season. Her favorite tree, the weeping willow, stood firm and unyielding. A solid presence in her life.

Robert was kneeling with his back to her. He grunted, pulling out weeds from the soil. She closed her eyes. The image of her father—a young man—kneeling and planting seeds in the soil flashed in her mind. His strong hands were covered in mud. Wind played in his hair. The corners of his cheeks lifted.

He had looked so different back then.

"Micky!" her father said.

"Yeah, I wanted to clean up a bit." She grabbed a bow rake.

Robert paused briefly before continuing. "Yesterday was fun."

She began gathering the loose debris around her garden. They worked in comfortable silence against the birds chirping and leaves flapping. Occasionally, she looked over at her father. She was so used to seeing a sneer on his face. He looked at peace now; often he was almost nervous that he'd unnerve her.

Darkness loomed over their heads, and she looked up. Vivid gray clouds churned overhead. Humidity cinched the air. The sky looked thick and imposing, ready to pop. A thunderstorm was coming.

Her phone rang. "Hello?"

"Is this Detective Mackenzie Price?"

"Yes?" she answered, unable to recognize the voice.

"This is Alan Blackwood. Nick gave me your number. I hope I didn't disturb you."

"Oh, of course not." She kneeled down and looked closely at the soil. "How can I help you, Senator Blackwood?"

"I don't know how to say this…"

Mackenzie froze. "Is everything okay?"

"Yes, yes. I didn't want to say anything yesterday evening and cause a scene. But it's very important for you to know this."

Her skin crawled. Her next breath got lodged in her throat. She knew this had something to do with her father.

"What is it?" she whispered.

Alan spoke after a beat. "The man with you is not Robert Price."

Leaves flapped.

The wind hissed.

Weeds scrunched as they were yanked out by their roots.

Numbness spread over her body like wildfire. The only part of her that had any sensation was her heart, which was tearing at the seams. Her brain hadn't absorbed the meaning of his words. But her body had reacted to them. It had reacted to them like they were the truth.

"A-are you s-sure?" Her voice was breathy.

"One hundred percent certain. I'm so sorry, Mackenzie. But I remember your parents very well. That man isn't your father. Nick told me he's living with you. You should know this. I don't know who that man is. He might be dangerous."

The phone fell from her limp grip. Her brain had been turned to mush. She didn't know what to think, what to do. DNA testing had proven that he was her father. She had remembered his face and his voice. He had called her Micky and known things about her childhood.

*You have to help me bury him.*

Her father leaned down next to her. His face inches away. He looked up at the sky with a look of wonderment, like he was savoring the air. A straitjacket of terror immobilized her when he spoke the words he often said to her when she was a child.

"Can you smell the thunder, Micky?"

Lightning forked the sky. Blackness swirled, visceral and hungry. The entire town of Lakemore had become a shadow. The thunderstorm had arrived with a vengeance, the overwhelmed ground already heavy with thawing snow. Power lines had come down and flash flooding had swamped the supply, leaving large areas of the town in darkness. Ankle-deep water collected on the roads. The sound of pouring rain was deafening.

Still, Mackenzie could hear the faint scrape of the shovel against the soil.

*Three hundred and fourteen.*

*Three hundred and fifteen.*

*Three hundred and sixteen.*

*Three hundred and seventeen.*

She halted and looked down at her boots, covered in dirt and twigs. A shiver travelled up from her toes, rattling the vertebrae in her spine, to the back of her neck. Despite the near pitch-blackness, she knew she was in the right spot. She had counted right and taken the measured steps from the backyard of a house that didn't belong to her anymore. Lightning flashed, and she caught a glimpse of herself as a twelve-year-old, sitting on the ground.

She was alone in the haunting woods behind Hidden Lake. But fear couldn't latch on to her. Nothing could.

A strange sensation filled Mackenzie's mouth—like it was stuffed with cotton. Water droplets fell heavy on her eyelashes, forcing her to keep her eyelids down. She picked up the shovel and started digging.

*You have to help me bury him.*

*The man with you is not Robert Price.*

Someone was here. Someone's bones were here. Someone had lied. Was it her mother or her memory? Had she fabricated what had happened that night? Had she misplaced important details over the years?

Nothing stopped her. Not the cold making her teeth chatter. Not the spasm in her tender shoulder. Not the rainwater swallowing her feet. Not the frightening reality of being alone in the woods.

She kept digging deeper and deeper. She didn't know how many hours went by—or maybe time had frozen still. All her feelings and thoughts were muffled.

She had plowed far deeper than she remembered Melody digging. A wider hole too, not the narrow strip her mother had tunneled into the ground. There was no evidence of a body there. No bones. No white cloth.

Mackenzie fell to her knees. Her eyes stayed hooked to the dark hole in the ground. Her body swayed like she was on rocking waves. She had never felt this unmoored. Something had snatched her away from her body, her senses. She was floating like a fading memory.

"There's no body here, Micky."

Mackenzie didn't even flinch at the sound. She merely looked up at her father, who had clearly followed her. His face was illuminated by the lantern he carried.

"What's your name?"

"Charles."

# CHAPTER FORTY-EIGHT

*Charles.* The same name he had given at the garage where he worked part-time.

The hole she had dug separated her from the man who was her father, and a stranger. The light from the lantern cast a glow around them.

"Micky... let's go back home."

"*No.*" She sucked in a sharp breath through her teeth. Her hands scooped mud into her fists, squeezing the earth. "Tell me everything. I knew you were hiding something since the day you showed up."

Charles licked his lips and looked around. "It's not safe here."

"Tell me everything. *Now.*" She instinctively reached for the shovel again. As though hitting him would be a wise idea. He didn't even wince, but watched her with pity. How pathetic she must look in his eyes; a prisoner of her past, a puppet of her mother.

"I *am* your father," Charles said warily.

"She was married to Robert Price."

"Yes. Not to me. Robert and Melody separated when you were four years old."

A ray of light trickled its way through the thick darkness surrounding them. Mackenzie saw the back of a man kneeling. His hair fluttering in the wind. His hands in the soil. His back was broad and muscular. It was the first memory she had of her father. But something changed. She heard a voice.

*"Daddy!"*

He turned around. A different face. It was a little blurry. But the basic features were visible, like seeing a face through a fogged mirror. A handsome face—strong jawline, long nose, and thick eyebrows. A little red-haired girl rammed into him. He picked her up effortlessly and kissed the top of her head.

"Melody ran away with you." Charles's voice disrupted the image. It cracked into pieces, and the darkness swallowed them. "Robert wouldn't give Melody a divorce when their problems started. There were custody issues to work out. But he was in the navy. He spent months away every year, so he would never get custody of you."

"This can't be possible," she cried. "I don't remember him."

Charles crouched across from her. "You were just four years old when you last saw him, Micky. You were so young. Melody never even kept a picture of Robert. You didn't see his face once when Melody took you and left."

It shouldn't have mattered. How could she forget an entire person in her life? But had she forgotten him?

"I'm sure you'll have *some* memories, if you think hard."

She felt like someone was using a cheese grater on her brain. Whenever she blinked, she caught something faint but tangible. She was in bed and a man was reading her a story. A man hoisted her up in the air and then caught her again. It was like trying to grab ashes.

"Micky, you were four," he implored her to understand. "When your mother moved to Lakemore, I moved too. We decided to be a family. After all, I was your biological father. Melody and I had been together for a while behind Robert's back."

"N-no. It can't be like this."

His nostrils flared. "Melody and Robert lived in Salem. Almost two hundred miles away from Lakemore. She decided to move here because she had some old friends. She had spent a few years here when she was a child. She thought it would be nice to go to a familiar place with a support system."

Mackenzie remembered a touch on her forehead. Like someone was checking if she had a fever. Absentmindedly, she pressed her palm there now, as if the hand would still be there.

"But she called *you* Robert."

"Because her friends here had known that she had married a Robert Price and had a child with him. As did her mother, Eleanor. But they'd never met Robert. Nobody had. They had eloped, didn't even have a wedding. She wanted to avoid a scandal. Lakemore is a small town. Back then it was very conservative, too. She didn't want people to gossip that she was with another man. She thought it'd be easier if people here just believed that I was Robert. I didn't care about anything as long as I got my booze. No one here knew what he looked like. It was also for you. You forgot over the years, but the first year away from Robert was difficult for you. She believed if she forced me into his place, the transition would be easier." His face looked haunted. "Melody was not who you thought she was. She was a far more complicated woman. And I was so lost in my drinking, Micky, I never really gave much thought to what she was doing to you."

Charles's words danced around her head. They made her want to shed her tingling skin. All this time, she thought her mother had been an innocent victim, but what had she done? What had Melody made *her* do?

"Did Robert know about you?"

"He didn't. Whenever he was back from the ship, he searched for you and Melody. A year before he died, he resigned from the navy so that he could focus his efforts on finding you. That night… that night… he tracked us down. He was livid that she had run away with you, that he hadn't seen his child in *eight* years. She had left a note for him, so even the police didn't help him look for you. Things got out of hand, and Melody ended up killing him. She didn't mean to. But then you came home earlier than expected. We didn't know what to do. Melody told me to hide."

The shoes behind the curtain—a little detail wiped over the years and overshadowed by everything else that had happened that night.

*You have to help me bury him.*

Realizing that she hadn't buried an abusive husband but a stranger sent Mackenzie into a downward spiral. But she hadn't buried a stranger, even. She had buried a good man, a father who *wanted* her.

Tears streamed down her cheeks. A fog of grief consumed her. She looked around for *something*. She didn't know what to do. It was a suffocating realization that there was nothing left to do. That night had sealed her fate.

"Where did his body go? We buried him here."

"Your behavior concerned Melody. She was worried you might spill to someone. After sending you off to New York, she moved the body so that you would be discredited if you told anyone."

"Where?"

"I don't know. I was keeping a low profile when the police got involved. It was complicated enough. Robert Price had also been reported missing by his family in Salem when he didn't return."

"How many lies did she tell?"

"I don't know, Micky. The truth was that after that night, we had a big falling out," he admitted. "I didn't like how she had involved you. She said she didn't have a choice. But still… it wasn't right. She never told me where she buried him. And then I left for Vegas. Everything I told you about my last twenty years is true."

"D-did he know? That I wasn't his?"

"I don't think so."

"I should have remembered him," she whispered, her voice hoarse from crying.

"Your childhood was traumatic, Micky. And then that night, it damaged you. You suppressed parts of it. It happens, but now that you know, it will come back to you."

She touched her hair—a faint memory of Robert braiding it, tugging on it when he was done.

"Why didn't you tell me?"

Charles closed his eyes. When they opened, there were tears pooling in them. "I took so much from you. Your childhood. I wanted to spare you more suffering. It was the least I could do. What I never anticipated was that I'd run into someone from the past. Thought twenty years was a long time for people to forget everything."

The *real* Robert Price was also her father—a good parent who Melody had kept away. "I can't believe I did this. I buried him. I… I buried him."

"You didn't know! That night wasn't your fault. *She* coerced you."

But Mackenzie wasn't listening. There was a brick wall in her ears. For the first time in her life, she didn't feel guilty for being relieved at Melody's fate. "Why did you come back?"

"I'm an old man, Micky. I just wanted to be with family. I-I'm so sorry for everything. You didn't deserve this. Nobody does."

"You need to leave."

Silence.

Wind rustled in the trees around them—the only witnesses to her crime, and now the truth. Charles's shoulders slumped. There was no flicker of surprise on his face. "Micky, *please*."

She looked up. The clouds thinned and floated away to bare the moon. From the corner of her eye, she saw a man's hand drift up and point at the sky.

*M-o-o-n, Mack.*

"No. I don't want to see you ever again. Go back, pack your bags and leave by tomorrow morning." She wobbled, standing up, zapping back into the present. "I'll give you some money if you need it. But you need to stay away from me forever."

Charles opened his mouth to argue but wisely didn't. Mackenzie wondered what he saw in her. If her madness and devastation was palpable. Walking out of the woods, she felt like she was dragging a pile of tires behind her.

It was the weight of the truth.

# CHAPTER FORTY-NINE

## *December 9*

Mackenzie wiped the fogged-up mirror above the sink. Dark circles caked her eyes. Her eyelashes stuck together in clumps. She put on her makeup, remembering how it was Melody who had taught her to hide behind layers of foundation and color. There were still so many unanswered questions—how had Melody handled the authorities? It was clear why she had sent Mackenzie away. And where was Robert's body now? Did Charles really not know?

She took a quivering breath. There was only one way to keep it together—to lock everything up in a drawer in her brain. Apparently, she had done exactly that growing up, without even realizing it. Tucked away the fading memories of Robert somewhere deep down.

She couldn't help but see the parallel between her and Katy. Both of them had lost someone important at four years old. Over the years, Katy's parents erased all memory of Kim, but Katy had always felt something was missing. An echo. That's what Robert had been reduced to over the years. Melody had done everything in her power to remove his traces—uprooted them from Salem, kept his family away, and never even kept a photograph of him. But Mackenzie cherished the first memory she had of her father. She had thought that memory in the garden was of Charles, but it was of Robert. She found some solace in the fact that she hadn't completely forgotten him. He was still there.

*

Mackenzie was stuck in traffic. A gridlock of cars covered the expanse of the highway, the flooding causing havoc. She turned on the radio but even the signal was poor.

Nick's car was straight ahead. She wondered if he knew she was following him.

Drumming her fingers to a random rhythm on the wheel, her mind wandered. She glanced at the car next to her. A middle-aged man stared ahead at the traffic. His young kid was in a car seat in the back, playing with a miniature-sized football. The father looked at his son through the rearview mirror and smiled with twinkling eyes.

A honk pulled her out of her trance. The cars were moving. She continued to tail Nick. He turned off the highway, entering a commercial complex with a mixture of warehouses, small offices, and other businesses. More concrete than green. A not uncommon sight.

Nick parked his car and got out. He waved at Mackenzie with a mocking smile.

*He knew.*

Sighing, she parked next to him and climbed out.

"You followed me." His voice boomed over the clashing rain.

"You wouldn't take me with you."

"You're on leave. It's just one more day, Mack. You're back tomorrow," he reminded her for the millionth time.

"I'm here to observe, not participate."

Nick pressed his lips together. "Go home."

"Please. I can't stay away. Throw me a bone."

Nick looked conflicted. Mackenzie suppressed the urge to stomp her feet in protest. He wagged a finger in her face. "You're not going to ask any questions."

"Deal."

"I'm taking the lead here."

"Done."

"And if you go back on your word, I'll personally haul your ass out of there and make sure you drive back home."

"Understood."

The corners of his mouth twitched in amusement. She knew he liked having her around.

"Why are we here?" she asked.

"Remember I told you how Elfman had information on a lot of women on his computer?"

"Yeah."

"One of them is Elisa James. She's currently working at the laser hair-removal clinic over there."

"He stalked her?"

They started walking together toward one of the buildings. "No. He *dated* her." He handed Mackenzie his phone. "Scroll through these."

She swiped over a series of photos. Elisa James had a scrawny face with hollowed cheeks, but full lips. Her light brown hair had highlights and fell to her chin. Some were selfies of her and Robbie Elfman, and others were photographs of her at restaurants, curled up on the couch with a book, or grilling in the backyard. In all of them, she smiled at the camera, content at being snapped.

"I can't picture Robbie dating anyone," Mackenzie said, feeling a little queasy at the thought.

The man she'd met was a delusional stalker living in a near-derelict house with Katy's picture plastered to every wall. Not exactly boyfriend material.

"Maybe he hadn't gone full psycho back then," Nick said as they entered a clinic with blinding white walls and furniture. A cheery receptionist guided them into another room.

Mackenzie tailed Nick, knowing he'd meant every word and intending to let him lead. She analyzed the laser clinic, its walls showing pictures of smooth legs and arms. There was a shelf with skincare products—various serums and creams, including a collection of hyaluronic acid serums. A common ingredient in a dermatological clinic.

"Where's she from?" Mackenzie asked.

"Thirty-one-year-old from Olympia. Went to nursing school in Seattle. No record."

"Nursing school?"

"She's a registered cosmetic nurse." Nick gave her a knowing look. "Worked at the practice of a facial cosmetic surgeon for two years."

"She could have picked up some skills in that time," Mackenzie said. "But enough to perform the actual procedures?"

Since Jenna's hunt for the doctor had turned up dry, they had considered the alternative. There was a chance that maybe their perpetrator was performing the enhancement themselves, instead of taking the women to a professional.

Elisa James entered the room wearing scrubs and carrying a file. Her short hair was pulled back in a ponytail, highlighting the splatter of freckles on her cheeks.

Nick made the introductions, with Mackenzie giving her a curt nod. She was strictly here to observe; Nick was already going out on a limb for her.

"I need to talk to you about Robbie Elfman. You were in a relationship with him?"

Elisa's eyes flicked between Nick and Mackenzie. Her grip on the file tightened. "What about him?"

"How long were you involved for?"

"Around six months. Five years ago, I think."

Mackenzie couldn't fathom why someone like Elisa, an educated woman and seemingly well put together, would date someone like Robbie.

"Don't take this the wrong way, but you and Robbie are… very different," Nick said, clearly thinking the same thing. "How did you meet?"

She shrugged. "We met at a bar one night and just hit it off. He's kind of a fixer-upper, but he would always go out of his way to help me out, take care of things for me, or just listen. I needed that."

"Can I ask why the relationship ended?"

"He's kind of a sheep. And he got really clingy."

Mackenzie leaned against the wall, taking in Elisa's glossy hair and manicured nails. A stark contrast to Robbie's squalid appearance. But there was something about her expression that rubbed Mackenzie the wrong way. No spark of nostalgia when she spoke of Robbie and no hint of nervousness speaking to the police. Not that Mackenzie hadn't dealt with her share of witnesses with a tough exterior to crack, but there was no toughness to Elisa. There was only detachment. Her relationship with him was brief and a long time ago; Mackenzie believed she had moved on.

"Did Robbie ever do anything strange or scary?" Nick asked.

She pursed her lips. "He was too clingy, too attentive. Liked to watch me sleep. It frightened me, but he never hurt me."

Nick dabbed his pockets, mindlessly. Mackenzie knew it was his tick—something was bothering him. "He didn't follow you around or harass you after you broke up?"

"He showed up a couple of times, at my place of work at the time. I didn't press charges because I felt bad for him. He's bad at being on his own."

"And when was the last time you were in contact with him?"

"Three months after we broke up." She paused. "I had a rough childhood. It's probably why I gravitated toward him. It was a mistake."

When Nick ended his inquiry, Elisa extended her hand to Mackenzie. "Nice meeting you, Detective Price."

"You too," she murmured.

When Elisa reached the door, she turned around, her face curious. "What did Robbie do?"

"He's facing a stalking and harassment charge. We're just looking into his past behavior."

"Too bad. Good luck." She shut the door behind her.

"What?" Mackenzie asked Nick, who was staring at the chair Elisa had been sitting on.

A muscle in his jaw pounded. "Took her long enough to ask why we were here, didn't it? I have to head to Seattle to knock on some doors with Ethan Spitz. I would say don't rush back to the office until you're well, but I assume I'll be seeing you tomorrow?"

"Bright and early."

# CHAPTER FIFTY

## *December 10*

With her medical leave behind her, Mackenzie felt confident when she walked into the station. Mindlessly, she nodded at the bustling officers greeting her. Mindfully, she ignored the lingering stares directed at her.

"Wow." Troy's eyes went wide. "That concussion really did a number on you."

"Shut up," she grumbled, and dropped her bag on her desk.

"Okay, now I'm *really* concerned." Troy spun around and nudged her to face him with his foot. "Seriously. I've never had a concussion. Did your brain rewire? Even your face looks different."

She was about to retort, when a familiar sight clouded her peripheral vision. She almost didn't recognize him at first. But that grating laughter was unmistakably Bruce Stephens, a retired detective. His appearance was radically different. He was wearing a peacoat, and underneath a fedora his once-white hair was dyed black. His pale skin had turned bronze.

Troy followed her alarmed gaze and snickered. "I know, right? That's what having a twenty-something girlfriend does to you when you're over sixty."

"Why is he here? I thought he was on some world tour?"

"The FBI hauled him back here for questioning."

The word was that the FBI was busy looking into the mayor's office. Being at the bottom of the totem pole, Mackenzie didn't know the details of their investigation. There were rumors and theories shared over lunches and smoke breaks. But facts were molded with notions, making everything unreliable. It was almost a relief not to see the FBI hovering around them. Out of sight, out of mind.

"Mad Mack!" Bruce guffawed. "I'm glad I caught you. Heard you were on suspension?"

"*Medical leave.*" She gritted her teeth, but gave him a cursory hug. They had worked together for years. "How's the world across the Pacific?"

"Oh, it's glorious!" he boasted. "You know, there's this village in Kenya called *Umoja*, where only women are allowed to live. It was founded by some rape survivors and has become a home to women escaping child marriage, domestic violence, genital mutilation, and so on. It's *fascinating*. Heartbreaking, but amazing what these women have done." He took out a necklace from his pocket. It was a string with vividly colored circular beads. "This is for you."

"For me?" She took the necklace, puzzled.

"There's this woman there. She told me her story under the *tree of speech*, where they get together to make decisions." His forefinger lightly traced his thin lips while his eyes stayed glued to the necklace. "When she was twelve years old, her parents sold her to a fifty-year-old man. He would beat and rape her. A year later, she gave birth to a son. It took her three years to escape her husband. And it was after several failed attempts. Let's just say, she lost an eye and the ability to bear more children."

Mackenzie's heart squeezed. "Did she make this?"

"Yes. She's training to be a doctor, you know. An impressive woman."

"Why did you give me this?" Her voice was small.

Bruce smiled, like they shared a secret. "She had this look of determination on her face. I've only seen that look on one other person in my life."

She looked at the bright necklace in her fingers, feeling suddenly that this was the most valuable thing she owned. "Thanks."

Troy interjected. "No gifts for us from Kenya, Stephens?"

"A donkey reminded me of you, Troy. Unfortunately, I wasn't allowed to bring it with me."

He laughed. "And now you owe me a beer. What did the FBI ask you?"

"They're interested in seeing if there were any leaks from this office and if anyone buried Sharks-related complaints and cases. They were looking into uniform, but based on their questions, I think now they're turning their focus to the crime lab."

"Really?"

"Anything's possible with that case."

Mackenzie stuffed the necklace in her pocket. "It's like one day we realized that everyone in this town is corrupt."

"Except you," Troy teased. "You're incorruptible."

She couldn't even find it in her to give him a disingenuous smile. The weight of the necklace in her pocket was heavy. A jarring reminder of what Bruce saw in her—and what she knew a lot of people did. No matter how hard life tried to pull her down, she knew she had to keep standing tall. Failure wasn't an option.

The door to Sully's office opened, and Nick gestured for her to come in.

"See you later, Bruce."

Inside Sully's office, Nick was sitting on a chair with an exasperated look on his face. It took her a second to spot Sully. He was bent down behind his desk, only the bulging arch of his back visible. She heard him grunt and leaned over to find him fiddling with gravity boots.

"You decided to exercise, Sergeant?"

Sully gave up and straightened. "I got tricked into this."

"How come?"

"Pam told me to buy these, and I got all excited thinking they make you feel like you're in reduced gravity or something. But now I spent all this money I have to make use of them."

"You thought they'd help you *float*?" Nick chuckled.

Sully ignored him and looked at Mackenzie. "You look better."

"Thanks."

"Do you want to tell her, Nick? Or should I?"

She looked between them. "Tell me what?"

"I was in Seattle helping out Ethan Spitz." Nick crumpled an unlit cigarette in his palm. "He had interviewed Tamara Wilson's sister, but that was a dead end. He needed help running down some leads, like her pimp and her clients. But either they don't know anything, or they don't want to talk."

Mackenzie clicked her tongue.

"According to the statements from Alison's mother and friend, Alison went voluntarily, so did Bella. Maybe all of them did—" Sully started before Nick interrupted him.

"But one of them turned up murdered. And the woman she was modeled on. That doesn't bode well for the others, does it?"

Mackenzie skimmed through the details of the women whose faces were featured in the ads. All were in their thirties. Three were white and one was African American. Clint was able to identify them by running a reverse image search. One was a nurse, one a firefighter, another ran an educational institute for children with special needs, and the other was in legal aid. Each woman was accomplished and attractive.

"I have something too," Mackenzie said.

"What do you mean? You were supposed to be on leave." Sully's eyes narrowed.

She updated them on her conversation with Becky and her short trip to the tattoo parlor in Kent. Sully's scowl deepened. She had continued to work on the case despite being told not to.

It might not have been an official violation, since she wasn't on suspension, but it was insubordination, nonetheless.

"The original sequence was CBA3759. Bella rearranged it to 39A behind the left knee and B75C behind the right, and said it was to be taken seriously in case something went wrong," Mackenzie informed them. "But I have no idea what it means."

Nick wrote out the code on a piece of paper and pressed his lips together. "CBA stands for Cascadian Banking Association."

"Yeah, I thought that, but then what are those four digits?"

"It's a safety deposit box," Sully said gruffly. "I have one with them, and it's a four-digit number."

"Bella was keeping something inside it, then," Mackenzie beamed. "She must have changed the sequence to hide it from whoever she was in danger from."

Nick agreed. "They have a branch in Lakemore and in Riverview. I'll call both."

"I'll start getting the warrant ready."

"Go ahead. Keep me in the loop. We have a few days of reprieve before the snow hits again. I'll dispatch patrol to start looking into Woodburn again," Sully said. "Thin ice, Mack. Thin ice."

But Mackenzie wasn't focusing on Sully's warning. All she could think about was what Bella had left them in the safety deposit box and whether it would lead them to Alison.

# CHAPTER FIFTY-ONE

CBA confirmed the box was held at their Lakemore branch. Nick had already called ahead and informed the branch manager that they were coming in to inquire about a safety deposit box of a murder victim.

A green carpet covered the floor and tellers stood behind glass counters. There was a seating area across from the row of counters, and private rooms further in the back. Fluorescent lights cast a brighter than comfortable glow around the room. Screens mounted on the walls displayed advertisements for mortgages and student loans.

Mackenzie thought of all the assets she shared with Sterling. She hadn't even begun to fathom how much work would be involved in divorcing him.

"Good day?" Nick's voice was like a bucket of cold water on her thoughts.

"What?"

He pointed at her fingernails. They were cherry red with rounded edges and cuticles pushed back. "I did them myself last night." She caught her reflection in one of the gleaming screens. She looked like herself after a very long time. Straight red hair pulled back in a high ponytail, devoid of any baby hair; an ironed blue pantsuit; hands moisturized and nails maintained; lips painted a light shade of pink; and eyes sharp and piercing.

Nick smirked. She appreciated him not probing.

Her phone buzzed.

*Micky, I'm staying at the Miller Lodge. I know you don't want anything to do with me, but I hope you change your mind. I'm not going anywhere.*

Mackenzie ignored her father's message. She knew he'd gone straight there after she kicked him out. She may not want anything to do with him, but she was still tracking his every move.

A skinny man dressed in a tweed suit with a nose like a pig's snout marched toward them. "Detective Price?"

"Yes, you must be Mr. Lester. We talked on the phone. This is my partner, Detective Blackwood. Here's the warrant."

Lester glanced at it. "It's unfortunate what happened. I didn't know her, but she was one of our customers. Please follow me. I'll direct you to where we have the safety deposit boxes."

"Do you know when Isabella rented the safety deposit box from you?" Mackenzie inquired.

"I checked after speaking with you. It was in early October. She also opened a bank account with us, which was used to pay for the renting of the deposit box."

"And how many times did she come to open the box?" Nick asked.

"Just once, when she first rented it."

They turned a corner, and the hustle and bustle of the bank became muted. There was a maroon-colored door at the end of the hallway, with orbs of light casting onto the marble floor leading up to it. "Is that what she looked like?" Mackenzie opened the picture of Bella in the morgue on her phone. "Just to warn you, the image may be distressing."

Lester's stoic expression barely faltered as he glanced at the photo.

"Yes, that's her."

This meant that Bella had undergone procedures sometime between June and October.

"Any odd activities in her bank account? Suspicious deposits?" Nick asked.

Lester opened the door with a key. "No. I'll give you her bank details, but her account had around a thousand dollars. No withdrawals and no deposits after the initial set-up."

The room beyond the door had a table in the center. The walls were lined emerald-green boxes. Lester found the correct box, brought it to the table and unlocked it.

Mackenzie put on latex gloves and instructed Lester not to touch the contents. He obeyed and stood off to one side with his hands folded in front of him. Mackenzie's senses spiked as she approached the box. She didn't know what she expected to find inside.

It was another, smaller box—rusty and old. Her finger traced the lid and found the little catch. Fortunately, there wasn't a lock, so they were saved the trouble of breaking it open. She twisted the catch.

Her heart skipped a beat. Photographs. Five of them.

Three were of a dilapidated shed surrounded by thick woods. The pictures were taken from different angles. It was small, made of badly painted wooden planks. The roof was uneven. There was a door with a handle made of rusted iron. Scratch marks and discoloration covered the outer walls.

It looked old, and the work of a novice.

The last two pictures made them freeze. They were of the inside—made clear by the same door as featured in the three pictures giving the external view. One interior picture was of a tray with surgical instruments—clamps, forceps, needles, speculums, and several other items Mackenzie didn't recognize. The last picture was of what looked like a makeshift operating table, with bulbs above it. A shelf was visible behind it that housed vials and bottles.

"What the hell is this?" Nick gasped.

"This is where Bella underwent the cosmetic procedures."

# CHAPTER FIFTY-TWO

"*Lakemore PD is being tight-lipped about what exactly led to the demise of the beloved Lakemore social activist, Katy Becker.*" The anchor's face, splattered with excessive makeup, popped up on the screen. "*The police still consider the case to be open, but refuse to divulge more information. It seems like a bad winter and blowback from the Sharks' withdrawal aren't the only problems in Lakemore. There is another girl missing. Michelle Gable, thank you for joining us.*"

The camera panned to Michelle, sitting next to Debbie, the anchor. Michelle was fidgeting with a handkerchief.

"*Your daughter, Alison Gable, is missing, but you claim that Lakemore PD don't consider her a missing person?*"

"*No… she left of her own will. But she hasn't contacted me like she promised.*"

"*And have the police made any progress?*"

"*I…*" Michelle looked around helplessly. "*I don't know. They are looking into her, I know that.*"

"*But you feel that Lakemore PD aren't taking her disappearance seriously enough?*" Debbie was egging Michelle on. It was obvious that she was using her to further her own agenda.

But then Michelle's eyes narrowed and she set her jaw. She straightened and stared at the camera, all her nervousness evaporated. "*I'm here to let everyone know that my daughter Alison Gable is missing and might be in danger.*" She displayed her picture and the camera zoomed in. "*This is Alison. She has a one-year-old son waiting for her. If anyone knows anything, please let the police know. I know they're doing their best."*

Mackenzie closed the video on her computer, her muscles tense with stress. She was grateful for the support, and felt a pang of guilt for not having kept Michelle updated.

She made a quick phone call to her, reassuring her that they were following a lead and were that much closer to finding Alison.

Mackenzie and Nick had made copies of the pictures they'd found in Bella's security deposit box and distributed them to the patrol team searching the park. They didn't know where this shed was located, but Woodburn Park seemed like a good starting point. How long it would take to find it was beyond their control. Those woods were huge.

They had also sent the pictures to the Sheriff's Office. Sometimes the SO assisted them with cases, and the deputies there knew the terrain and wooded areas of the county like the backs of their hands. They might catch a lucky break with them on board.

"Mack!" Nick poked his head over her cubicle wall. "Got the video footage from the bank."

Mackenzie followed him with a renewed sense of purpose. "Does Clint need to clean it up?"

"Nah, the quality is good. Even though it's black-and-white." He angled the monitor toward her. The first camera was inside the bank, placed behind the tellers, overlooking the clients coming to their desks. The stamp showing the date and time were at the bottom. Nick clicked on a button, and the video started playing in fast forward, with people moving in and out of frame none too smoothly. For several minutes, they watched the hours go by on the video. Mackenzie's eyes never left the screen. Like a blink would cause Bella to slip away from them. They also weren't sure exactly how Bella would look. They knew what she looked like before the procedures and what she looked like after. But Dr.

Preston had said that multiple procedures had taken place. She could also be bandaged.

Just when Mackenzie lost hope, a girl wearing a blouse appeared. "That's her!"

Nick paused the video and scrutinized it. "Looks a hell of a lot like Katy."

"Seems like by October she was done with most of the procedures. Maybe some minor corrections were remaining we can't spot now."

Nick cracked his neck. "She didn't intend to take Katy's place or anything. She opened the account in her own name."

Mackenzie played the video. For the next few minutes, they watched Bella talk to the teller, show her ID, and sign some documents.

Her motivation was still a black hole—one of the key pieces in an investigation was missing. Nick played the video from the other camera. The frame showcased the entrance to the bank with a partial view of the street. They adjusted the timestamp to see when Bella would have entered and exited the bank.

When Bella exited the bank, she stood close to the door, looking at the street and checking her watch. "Looks like she's waiting for someone."

Then Bella's hand went up in a wave. She stepped forward, to the edge of the frame, and opened a car door.

Mackenzie rubbed her fingertips in anticipation. Like the truth had brushed against her, and she was craving it again. She was so close.

Bella climbed inside the car and vanished from view.

"Damn it," she muttered. "The car isn't in the frame. Is there any other camera?"

"No. This is the best shot we have." Nick flicked a pen and pinched the bridge of his nose.

All the enthusiasm drained from her.

"You know what I find strange?" Nick wondered aloud. "No one mistook her for Katy. She's walking around Lakemore with her face."

"Maybe she didn't go out that often."

"Or she wasn't *let* out that often." He gave her a knowing look.

"She got a tattoo and opened a bank account within months of Robbie delivering her."

"And she waved at whoever picked her up." Nick tapped the monitor. "Not the signs of someone held against their will."

Captors didn't allow their victims this level of freedom. Unless they were confident that they'd brainwashed their victims enough.

Mackenzie sat back in her chair and wheeled back to her cubicle. They were going in circles, and there were lives out there hanging in the balance—and a mother and child waiting for Alison to come home.

Later that night, Mackenzie sat across from Sterling, nerves jangling. Her shoulder wasn't sore anymore. The swelling in the back of her head had gone down. But her insides were wound up tight. She stared at her husband's handsome face, preparing for a conversation she never thought she'd have when they'd exchanged vows three years ago.

"Mack? What's this about?" Sterling sounded hopeful. "Have you thought more about me moving back in?"

Mackenzie felt her ears burn. She licked her lips and cleared her throat. When she looked at him, his face fell. He knew where this was going.

"What can I do to make this work? Give me something." His eyes searched hers.

"Sterling, you broke my trust once. What's stopping you from doing it again?"

"I did it once. It doesn't mean that I'll do it again."

A knot formed in her chest. Tears tickled the back of her throat, and she swallowed incessantly. "I know you believe that now. But that doesn't make it true. What you did is something I can't get past."

He ran his hands through his hair, his eyes wild and desperate. He came around the kitchen island and held her hands. "Please, Mack. I'm so sorry. What we have is *good.* I'm a lawyer; you're a cop. We have seen how ugly marriages can get."

"It *was* good." She didn't wrench her hands free. A part of her wanted to comfort her crying husband. A part of her wanted to feel his touch one last time before she put the final nail in this relationship and walked away for good. Something was breaking inside her. And she blamed him for making her feel this way.

"I'll make it better."

"We're going to have disagreements down the road. And every time you step out of the house, I'll wonder if you're going to screw someone else because you're mad at me."

He exhaled and dropped her hands. Heavy silence sat between them. She watched his face contort with helplessness. She couldn't look away from his fingers. Long, thick, and dark with a splatter of hair on the knuckles. She inched her hand forward to touch him again. It was a delicate moment. A weak moment. And it was obliterated when she realized he was watching her, waiting for her to touch him.

"What changed, Mack? I thought we had a chance."

She wiped a tear trickling down her cheek. "I can't be with someone I don't trust. And I know myself. I'm not one of those who can learn to trust again."

What happened with her father was a harsh reminder. After Melody's stinging betrayal, Mackenzie had realized that she was never going to be able to work it out with Sterling.

"You're a good person, Sterling." She kissed his cheek. "But love isn't enough. This marriage is over."

Sterling stood in the kitchen, immobilized. She walked away, her breath tearing in her throat, but knowing that she had made the right decision.

# CHAPTER FIFTY-THREE

*December 11*

"I like Burt. I bet it's going to be him," Troy mused.

"Yeah, except he's failed his detective exam *twice*." Finn rolled his eyes. "My money is on Leslie. She's sharp as a tack."

"I don't know if we can handle that much estrogen around here, especially with a female lieutenant too."

Mackenzie turned her head to pin Troy with a glare. Except he was looking at her with a big smile on his face. She picked up an eraser and threw it at his head. It smacked his temple and bounced back into her hand.

"Ouch!" he whined. "You know I said that just to piss you off, right?"

"I know. And you succeeded."

Finn guffawed.

Sully was going to bring in a new detective. Bruce Stephens' empty cubicle next to Ned was finally going to be occupied. Naturally, everyone was curious. But Sully was secretive. Mackenzie was looking forward to the new addition. The unit was often stretched too thin. But change was always uneasy. At least to her. The start of the year, she had a stable marriage and work life. Her father had been her constant companion in her mind. But it was something she could control, something that was *predictable*.

Now everything was different.

She got a message on her phone and looked back at Nick. "John Newman's here. From the Sheriff's Office. Maybe they've got something on the shed."

"Let's hope so. I'm losing my mind." He picked up his coffee mug and walked out with Mackenzie.

John Newman was a rugged and strapping deputy sheriff dressed in khaki uniform. He was at least ten years older than Mackenzie and always wore a bone-melting smile on his face. He wasn't married and had no intention to change that. He always reminded her of a stranger who whispered tantalizing promises at a bar.

Nick shook his hand. "John, haven't seen you in a while."

"It's been a rough couple of months." His voice was throaty. His mischievous eyes flew to Mackenzie. "Heard it's been bad for you guys too."

"It can always get worse in Lakemore. That's the silver lining." She glanced at the envelope in his hand. "You have something for us?"

"Yeah, we received copies of those photos." He opened the envelope and rifled through them. "I was looking over them last night and found something."

Mackenzie's muscles constricted in hope. She crossed her arms and leaned forward. John showed her the picture of the shed from the outside. "Do you see this cross section of the chopped down tree?" It was situated next to the shed. One of the angles captured the tree rings. "The height and diameter are small, but the rings are broad in the center and then progressively become very narrow."

"So it's a really old tree?" Nick raised an eyebrow.

"One of the oldest you'll find in Woodburn Park. It's a western red cedar. Like the ones around it. I know where this is." He tapped on the picture.

"What are we waiting for? Let's go now," Mackenzie said.

*

Thunder rumbled so loudly that Mackenzie was convinced the ground underneath her shook. Her feet snapped over the remnants of ice and snow. The day was gray and gloomy. Leaves further restricted sunlight from pouring into the woods. The temperature had dropped drastically from the previous day, floating around a cold thirty-seven degrees. She shivered, following John, who seemed to know the way as they veered off the trail into the forest thicket.

"How's the kid?" John asked Nick.

"Getting too curious about my job."

He laughed. "Maybe she should start her training now. A future detective."

Mackenzie grinned and eyed Nick. He had paled at the prospect. But she knew him. If that was what Luna wanted, he wouldn't discourage her. He would just suffer alone in silence, start smoking again, and sneakily tail her on the job.

"There it is." John pointed ahead of him.

A shed was concealed behind the growing trees. This part of the woods had relatively even ground—no protruding roots or moss-covered branches. It was cleaner but cluttered. The trees were huddled a lot closer, forcing them to maneuver with greater difficulty.

"This is probably one of those illegal constructions Jenna was talking about," Nick said.

As they approached, Mackenzie realized that the shed was bigger than expected, the size of a studio apartment. There was no other structure. It stood alone.

Isolated and terrifying.

They took out their gloves and examined the structure. It looked exactly like it did in the pictures. A clandestine shed with chipped paint, rusted iron, and dated design. Concealed in a tiny nook of the woods.

John circled it.

"No visible footprints," Nick noted.

"Rain and snow took care of that," Mackenzie mumbled, inching closer to the door.

A sudden gust of wind whooshed around her. The hairs on the back of her neck rose. She extended her hand in front of her. A spooky sensation coiled around her neck.

Her fingers brushed against the icy cold handle. She twisted it and opened the door.

It was dark inside.

She left the door wide open and entered the space. Her hand searched for a switch. Encountering one, she flicked it.

Bright light flooded the room. It was blazing enough for her to squint and moan.

"What the hell?" Nick cursed behind her.

It looked nothing like its exterior. If outside it was rickety and shady, then inside it was modern and clean. The walls had been freshly painted. The floor tiles were gray stones.

A makeshift operating table in the middle—somewhere between an actual table and an inclined armchair. Mobile surgical lights. A glass cabinet with sterilization equipment. A shelf with disposables and consumables like gloves and biohazard bags. Surgical tools and accessories—like in Bella's pictures. Mirrors mounted on walls.

In Bella's pictures, the lights weren't turned on. It was a dimmed view and didn't reveal the level of sophistication.

"It smells like burning hair." Nick scrunched his nose.

"Because there isn't enough ventilation."

"What case is this?" John whistled. "Dr. Frankenstein?"

Nick pressed a handkerchief over his nose.

Mackenzie looked around for anything out of place. But this entire clinic was out of place. "No personal belongings."

"Bella probably wasn't kept here," Nick said. "No bed. No restroom."

"The killer could have gotten rid of anything of hers."

"I'll call the CSI, if that's okay? Figure you guys are looking for prints and DNA," John offered.

"Yes, please. Thanks, John."

Mackenzie was mesmerized by the room. She located the shelf containing vials and bottles. Some she recognized as prescription painkillers and antibiotics. Others she had never heard of before.

"Some of these instruments look older just by visual inspection." Nick picked up scissors.

"That's strange," she said. "Some of the stuff is new, so they clearly had access to it. Why work with old instruments?"

Nick sighed. "Maybe it's expensive? I doubt we'll find usable prints. This place looks scrubbed clean."

Mackenzie bit her lip. There was a little trash can next to the stool by the instrument tray. She opened it, expecting to find towels and gloves. There was some bubble wrap and one piece of paper, half-burned.

Nick smiled. "Let's pick this place apart. Hopefully we'll catch a break and get this bastard's DNA."

# CHAPTER FIFTY-FOUR

The air in the conference room was brittle. The cappuccino machine made a grating sound as Nick poured himself a cup, wearing a thoughtful expression. Mackenzie sat back on her chair, clicking her pen, staring at the pictures of the shed. There were plates with piles of muffins and donuts. Sully's greedy eyes kept flitting toward them, the tip of his tongue reaching out to lick his lips. But seeing Lieutenant Rivera read the case files with utmost seriousness, he turned his attention to his copy and tried to concentrate. Justin slurped his coffee and pulled a face. It was too watery—a common complaint for the last few days.

"Is Jenna going to be joining us?" Rivera asked.

"She's on a case with Dennis, but we have everyone's reports." Nick took his seat next to Mackenzie.

Rivera put on her reading glasses. "Let's get started then."

"The tattoo on Bella's body led us to this shed, where we believe that her cosmetic procedures were performed," Mackenzie said. "She took photographs and left a trail to them on her body, in case something went wrong."

"Rightfully so," Sully said, stuffing his face with a muffin. "It was creepy enough in the first place."

"Any security footage from the bank?" Rivera asked.

"She was picked up at the bank but the car was out of view." Nick pursed his lips in disappointment. "On the one hand, she was collecting evidence and, on the other, she was able to get around town pretty freely."

"And she waved at whoever came to pick her up," Mackenzie added. "Casts doubt on her innocence."

Rivera flicked through copies of Bella's pictures. "We should ask Dr. Preston. He knows to expect your call around this time, right?"

"Yeah, we warned him earlier today," Mackenzie nodded and dialed him, putting him on speaker. "Dr. Preston? Can you hear me?"

"Hello, Detective Price. How are you doing?" Preston's voice sounded tinny through the phone.

"Good." Her cheeks warmed. "Thank you for your help. I'm sending you an email with photos of a makeshift cabin."

"No problem. I'm glad to be able to help. Okay, got it. Yes, I see face-lift scissors and retractors. The labels on the medicines aren't very clear, so I can't help you there. The laser machine looks old, but that cauterizing instrument kit is new. As is the procedure chair and floor lamp with rolling base. I have the same ones in my practice, actually."

"Are these instruments consistent with the work done on Bella's face?" she asked.

Preston made an agreeing sound. "Definitely."

"Thanks. Really appreciate it."

"Anytime, Detective Price."

"We're looking at someone with knowledge and access," Nick concluded after she'd hung up.

Rivera tapped her finger on the pictures. "This is in Woodburn too, right? I thought there was a team looking through the woods. How come they missed this?"

Mackenzie unrolled a map of Woodburn Park—the dense woods with the Westley River flowing through the middle. She took a Sharpie and made a circle. "The woods in Woodburn are notoriously difficult to access. This is where Katy and Bella's bodies were recovered by the fishermen in Crescent Lake. Bella and Alison were asked to meet at Woodburn, in different locations though." She marked the spots. "Both locations are more than five hundred meters from where the bodies were found. But it still leaves a large area and not enough data points to narrow it down."

"And the weather has slowed the search right down, too," Nick pointed out. "The shed is out of the way from the trail, hidden in the thickets."

"Robbie Elfman." Rivera pursed her lips in distaste at his mugshot. "What's his status?"

"He's still in lockup. His arraignment date is coming up. No way he's making bail with the trafficking charge and his history," Nick said.

"Katy was in Woodburn to collect money from Derek Lee to give to Kim." Sully burped and pushed the empty plate away. "Where is his cabin?"

Mackenzie checked her phone and marked the map. "Over here. South of the shed, around two hundred meters."

"That's close."

"Yeah, we estimate that Katy entered the park through the trail up north." Nick trailed his finger on the map. "Because that's the side she'd encounter from home. Almost all the cabins are situated along the trail, including Derek's."

Mackenzie's eyes caught the post-mortem photographs peeking out from the files. Her mind buzzed with a thought. She flipped through them to find the pictures of the bottom of their feet. Bella's feet had a lot more abrasions than Katy's. "Becky identified the abrasions at the bottom of the feet to be antemortem. There are some postmortem as a result of being carried by the river. The antemortem abrasions are reddish-brown in color rather than yellow, have raised scab, and inflammatory cells."

Mackenzie assessed the photos. Bella's feet had plenty of reddish-brown abrasions, her milky soles barely visible, whereas Katy's feet had only three yellowing injuries. "Look at the difference between the bottom of their feet. Katy doesn't have any antemortem injuries, but Bella has several."

Nick stroked his chin. "She was running in the woods and cut her feet."

"Or maybe she was being chased," Mackenzie said. "Maybe he or she caught her snooping."

She imagined how it played out. The chilly Saturday morning with a storm right around the corner. A terrified Bella, running away from the shed, bumping into Katy, who was heading in the same direction to meet with Derek. The killer caught up with them and had no choice but to kill them both. A remarkable coincidence, with tragic consequences.

"Let's talk about the ads," Rivera said. "All the 'subjects' are local community heroes, always female. Much like Katy, Carrie was a well-known face back then, but after the suicide, she kept a low profile. She was a schoolteacher and spent all her time volunteering."

"The woman in the latest ad, the one who looks like Alison, provides free legal services," Mackenzie added. "The other three women in Seattle are all successful women in their thirties."

"All respectable professions too," Nick chimed in. "Nurse. Firefighter. Head of an institute to help children with special needs. He isn't targeting them based on salary or ethnicity or age."

Rivera brooded. "This man takes vulnerable women addicted to drugs and gives them the faces of inspirational women. *Ideal* women."

Her observation made Mackenzie's blood freeze.

"He thinks of himself as a savior," Rivera continued, her words sending shivers down Mackenzie's spine. "It explains why none of them demonstrates any signs of abuse. He doesn't want to hurt them. He thinks he's making them *better*."

"Anything new on the women from Seattle?" Sully asked.

Nick directed them to the page with the copies of the ads. "Detective Ethan Spitz from Seattle PD confirmed that there is an African American woman missing who looks like the woman referred to in the third advertisement. Her sister reported her missing."

"Steven Brennan, formerly Steven Boyle, has dementia. It's definitely not him," Mackenzie emphasized. "But maybe someone connected to him? His research on perfection and ugliness is accessible to anyone, really. We're looking at links between him and the clinic, but we haven't found any yet."

"Where is he keeping them?" Sully voiced the heavy question.

"The crime scene investigators are going through the shed?" asked Rivera.

"Yes. We hope to find some DNA or prints, but it will take at least a week. Maybe more." Mackenzie noticed Nick brooding at the file. His thick eyebrows drew together and his eyes tapered. "Nick? What do you have?"

He presented a close-up picture of the half-burned piece of paper. "It's a customer copy of a receipt, found in the trash can."

Mackenzie analyzed it. "Looks like they sell makeup?"

"Yeah, it shows a partial list of products purchased."

"Foundation, concealer, bronzer, lip balm… and then it cuts off. Someone tried to destroy evidence but did a sloppy job of it."

"Bella had been to the shed," Justin pointed out. "It's possible that this belongs to her. She was moving around freely enough to go to the bank. Could have gone shopping."

"Check out the date, though." Nick stood up and placed his hands on his waist.

"November twenty-third," Mackenzie whispered, then looked at Nick. "A few days after Bella's body was found—and nearly a week after she was murdered."

"And more than three weeks after Alison was last heard from."

They had been monitoring Alison's bank account. Her credit card hadn't been used, nor had any money been deposited or withdrawn from her account. She could have used cash, but why would she go shopping but not contact her mother and child? She had promised in her letter to get in touch in around two weeks. The date on the receipt was way past that.

Justin scratched his jaw.

Sully bit his nails.

Wind slammed into the window, rattling it against the hinges.

"What does this mean?" Sully asked. "Bella didn't buy it, and it's highly unlikely Alison did, which means it's the doctor working out of this shed, right?"

"There was also no sexual assault, which is uncommon when you have someone *collecting* women. I'd say it's likely that we're looking for a woman," Rivera announced.

# CHAPTER FIFTY-FIVE

Mackenzie tossed the stress ball in the air and caught it. A few hours after the meeting, she was still in the office, salvaging facts about Elisa James. The nurse had just rocketed up their list of suspects, but whatever scraps of her life Mackenzie could find didn't reveal any link to Steven Boyle.

"She has a couple of parking tickets to her name," she said to Nick. "She had a DUI and paid a fine. Barring that, her record's OK. Not nearly as messed up as Robbie's."

Nick's head was tilted back with a wet cloth covering his face. "We should check her employment history again."

Mackenzie was on it, typing away on her computer. "Like we already know, she worked for a facial cosmetic surgeon from 2009 to 2011. Her focus was on anti-aging fillers and injectables. Then from 2011 to 2013, she worked at an outpatient surgery clinic for a plastic surgeon specializing in liposuction, face-lifts, and body contouring. Another short stint at a private practice before her current job at the laser hair-removal clinic. She's a certified aesthetic nurse specialist, which is offered through the Plastic Surgical Nursing Certification Board."

"What's the difference between cosmetic and plastic nurses?" The cloth fluttered above his mouth.

"Cosmetic treatments are more in-office, as opposed to plastics, which are the more invasive and surgical aspect of things. Plastics isn't purely cosmetic—it covers reconstructive surgery as well.

But Elisa's jobs have been on the cosmetic side. Nurses assist in procedures and are mainly responsible for post- and pre-op care."

Nick removed the cloth from his face and blinked rapidly. "But Elisa could have picked up the skills needed to do this."

"And she has access to medicines and equipment."

"Hmm. And her link to Steven?"

"His area of research is only a Google search away." Mackenzie tapped a pen against the edge of her desk to a random rhythm, her mind connecting the dots. "Maybe that's why she moved to Lakemore? She was emulating Steven's career?"

"Yeah, Lakemore isn't the kind of place you move to," Nick snorted. When Mackenzie gave him the stink eye, he shrugged. "Hard truth, Mack."

"Why would she idolize Steven in the first place?"

Mackenzie had read Steven's articles in her free time—his take on "beauty" and "perfection" could imply a man with a God complex. Someone who might want to "fix" his wife by turning her into Carrie Breslow—an accomplished, confident, and bright woman. His *ideal* woman. Though there was no hard evidence.

Could Elisa James have continued what he started? Might they have encountered each other professionally?

"She must be as crazy as he was," Nick said, sounding disgusted. "Like some sick fan. That's why she's using his name on the dark web. I'm going to have Jenna tail her." He took out his phone and started thumbing a message. "We still don't have enough for a warrant to go through her electronics and financials."

Mackenzie clicked her tongue in disappointment and inspected the picture of the receipt closely. The words "customer copy" were printed at the bottom. The total price came to one hundred and sixty dollars—a significant amount of money to spend. The partial list of products was clear but the others were lost from the paper, being partially burned. The top part was concealed by soot sticking to the paper and a brownish stain. She fished out a magnifying glass. But she could only make out random letters: "H," "D," "T."

"Can we get the name of the store?" Mackenzie asked. "If we can link this to Elisa…"

"I asked Anthony to look at it personally."

With the discovery of the shed, they were able to optimize their search pattern in Woodburn Park. Patrol was due to be dispatched tomorrow, once the weather had cleared. But there was no evidence that Alison and the others were being held elsewhere in the park.

Mackenzie's phone rang. She picked up in a heartbeat when she saw it was Michelle Gable.

"Detective Price, any news?"

"We're getting there." She heard Oliver coo in the background.

"But it's been weeks."

"I know." Mackenzie's eyes found Alison's picture pinned to her desk. "Did Alison spend a lot of money on makeup?" She was almost certain that the receipt wasn't Alison's, considering the date stamp, but it was worth confirming.

"Makeup?"

"Yes, we found a receipt. We don't know who it belongs to. I was wondering, considering Alison's job, did she invest in makeup? And was there a particular store she liked?"

"No. She wasn't into it at all," Michelle sighed. "She used Lila's clothes and makeup. Every penny she made went into taking care of Oliver."

"I see. Thank you, Michelle. I'll keep you updated."

"Please do. And about that TV interview… I only went there to spread the word about Alison. I know Debbie's kind of obnoxious, but a lot of people watch her show."

"I know. And I appreciate your faith in us. I promise finding Alison is our priority."

When Mackenzie hung up, she felt a heavy weight on her chest.

"Nothing?" Nick asked from behind her.

She shook her head. "Alison doesn't buy makeup. And based on the date, it couldn't have belonged to Bella."

The office was empty. This time of year, if people weren't taking vacation days then they were at least making sure that they went home early. Holiday season was a dampened concept among those in law enforcement—much like doctors and nurses. Mackenzie's first Christmas after getting married was spent right there, in the chair she was sitting in. She had been determined to have a tradition once she had a family—a husband—but crime didn't care about Santa. She'd had to deal with a mountain of paperwork, going over incident reports and transcripts. Sterling must have been disappointed, but it didn't show. Instead, he'd spent Christmas Eve decorating the office Christmas tree, while Mackenzie slogged away at her desk. And he was a gentleman about it, letting Mackenzie take all the credit in front of her co-workers.

"You never told me what Shelly's boyfriend's like."

Nick grunted. "He's good."

"*But...*" she baited him.

"I don't know. I think Luna's too young, you know? What if things don't work out between them? I don't want her to get confused."

"Is Shelly in a rush to get married?"

"I haven't asked."

"Why not?"

"Detectives?" An officer poked his head inside. "There's someone wanting to talk to you."

In the lounge, a man stood watching the game on the television. His hair was white as snow under a baseball cap. He turned around. It was Frank Harris—Katy and Kim's father.

"Mr. Harris!" Mackenzie blinked in surprise but recovered quickly. "Sorry, I wasn't expecting you. Is everything okay?"

Frank Harris wasn't an easy read. Behind the horn-rimmed glasses were ghostly eyes that seemed disenchanted with the world around him. He was passive, while his wife, Charlotte, did the talking. At least that had been Mackenzie's initial impression. Today, she didn't miss the fidgeting of his fists in his pockets.

"I-I wanted to know how the investigation is going." His voice was curt, but his eyelids flickered.

"I'm very sorry about what happened to Katy in that encounter." Mackenzie gulped and glanced at Nick. The fact that she still couldn't disclose that the twins had switched places made her feel sick with guilt, and she could tell Nick wasn't happy about it either. But Rivera was proving unmovable on that point.

Protocol dictated they wait for DNA confirmation as next of kin identification wasn't reliable. With the FBI sniffing around and Lakemore PD gaining a reputation in town, the brass was being extreme about following the rules. And it was going to take a few more days for the test results to get back.

"Thank you." His voice broke. "Can you tell me anything about Kim?"

Mackenzie spotted the tears shining in his eyes, despite the light reflecting in his glasses. Her tongue was tied in a knot. She could almost feel Kim's fingers on her arm, her erratic breathing tickling her ears.

"We've been looking into her past. It sounds like she grew up to be a good woman." The half-truth seemed to placate Frank.

"Did she try looking for us?"

"I don't know, I'm sorry."

"You know, I've never met Ben Harlan in my life," Frank sniffled. "Didn't even know he existed. And yet it seems he killed both my children."

Mackenzie felt a burst of grief. "We're still investigating, and we don't think Ben was involved in the murders. I know we don't have all the answers now, but we will soon."

"You'll be our first call, Frank," Nick promised.

He turned to leave, but stopped. "I have a request. Please don't tell Charlotte I was here."

"Oh?"

"It's just easier that way. My wife doesn't care about Kim." Frank nodded feebly. "Katy was her world, and she's devastated."

Mackenzie and Nick watched Frank walk away with his head hung low. Mackenzie rubbed her chest, realizing how much Frank still cared about the little girl he had left in the treatment center. Maybe the guilt of sending her away was weighing heavy on his shoulders. She opened her phone to the messages Charles had sent her.

*I'm really sorry, Micky. Can we please talk?*
*Maybe we moved too fast. Can we start again?*
*If you need time, then I understand. I'm not leaving this time. I'll wait as long as it takes, Micky.*

No time in the world was enough for Mackenzie to accept the lies she'd been told. But she swore that Frank, Charlotte, and Michelle would get the closure Mackenzie had been denied.

"How do we get to Elisa?" Nick muttered. "Crime lab might take weeks processing the results."

Mackenzie looked at him. "Robbie."

# CHAPTER FIFTY-SIX

*December 12*

Robbie Elfman was being detained at the Thurston County Corrections Facility in Olympia. As Mackenzie walked the dingy hallway, a cold caress spread across her skin. The cameras were following them.

It was a new building—better fluorescent lighting and yellow walls that hadn't become grimy yet. But some things about prison were always consistent regardless of the infrastructure: the hard-edged faces of the deputies and the stale air.

The deputy led them to round tables with chairs. A steel staircase ran up the corner to a floor with closed doors. Mackenzie shifted uncomfortably at the hollowness of her surroundings.

"Relax, Mack. They'll protect us if we're attacked." Nick gestured to the armed prison guard.

She rolled her eyes. "I'm not scared."

"Then what?"

"I don't like prison. Reminds me of a cemetery. Except everyone's alive."

Nick looked around. "It could use some color, I guess."

A clang. A squeak.

Robbie appeared at the top of the staircase in an orange jumpsuit. His hands were cuffed in front of him. A deputy nudged him down the stairs. Mackenzie followed Robbie's heavy tread. His head was shaven clean, and his round belly looked smaller.

"Sit down, Robbie," Mackenzie said.

Robbie eyed them with suspicion. "What do you want now?"

"Heard your bail got rejected."

He growled under his breath. "I did nothing wrong. I didn't lie to Bella or lure her into a trap."

"We're actually here to talk about your ex-girlfriend, Elisa James."

Robbie blushed. His eyes twinkled, like hearing that name flipped a switch. "How is she? Is she worried about me?"

Mackenzie glanced at Nick. It was obvious Robbie still harbored feelings for her. "Still holding a candle?"

"N-no. I... She's special."

"When was the last time you talked to her?" Nick asked.

"I don't recall. A long time ago."

"Five years, by her estimate."

"So you talked to her?" Robbie leaned forward. "Does she know where I am?"

"No." Mackenzie frowned. "Do you want her to know?"

He didn't answer. Instead he looked around, frustrated, rubbing his hands together.

Nick showed him Alison's picture on his phone. "Recognize her?"

Robbie looked reluctantly and shook his head. "Am I supposed to?"

"I'll be straight with you, Robbie," Mackenzie said firmly. "It will be in your best interests to help us. You have a serious charge leveled against you. If you cooperate with us, we can put in a good word for you at the DA's office. Maybe even get you a deal. Because otherwise you're going away for a very long time."

The first ad they could find on the website went back to 2014, a year after Elisa ended her relationship with Robbie. Her decision to date Robbie was nothing short of strange. Robbie was an unstable man with a history of harassment who couldn't even hold down a job, the polar opposite to the outgoing and driven Elisa. But perhaps that had been the point.

Mackenzie imagined how her mind might have worked. How she might have identified Robbie as someone she could easily exploit. She established an emotional bond, then recruited him in her mission. In her words, he was a sheep—a follower.

"I don't know this woman," Robbie repeated. "What do you want from me?"

"We want to know more about Elisa." Nick's voice was gentle. Mackenzie knew he was playing the good cop, adopting a different approach. "She's important to you."

"Yes." Robbie's eyebrows dipped. "Is she in trouble?"

"Do you think she did something that could get her in trouble?"

"No… She was…" He sighed. "Elisa's great. She had a rough upbringing. In and out of foster homes. I'm sure whatever it is, it's a misunderstanding. She wouldn't hurt anyone. She just wants to help people. Like my Katy."

"Help people? How?" Mackenzie pressed, running out of patience.

"She's a nurse."

"Robbie, did Elisa ask you to find women for her? Like Bella?"

"No, she didn't," he scowled. "I told you. I just responded to an ad."

"If you're lying—"

"Why would I?"

"Because you're protecting her. You still have feelings for her," Nick said. "I get it. But you're in deep water, man. You have to look out for yourself. Now, tell us. Did she get in touch with you to find someone who looked like Katy?"

"*No.* I haven't spoken to her in years."

"We can help you if you cooperate—"

"Want me to lie?"

Mackenzie released a frustrated breath. Nick spent a few more minutes trying to tempt Robbie into a confession, but he didn't budge from his story. When the deputy took him away, they were on their way out.

"Think Elisa is actually innocent?" Nick asked. "Why wouldn't he cut a deal?"

"He isn't what you'd call mentally stable. I don't expect him to do the sensible thing. Remember how he said *my* Katy?"

"Yeah… I guess he could just be protecting Elisa. But isn't he 'in love' with Katy now?"

Mackenzie brushed his comment aside. "He's in love with all of them. If he can't help us, then the only thing to do now is wait for the crime lab."

Impatience punched her in the gut. She felt like they were only an inch away from catching the culprit.

"Anthony has that makeup receipt. If we have the store information…" She unlocked her car and climbed inside. "By the way, why do you always get to play good cop?"

Nick shot her a look of disbelief. "Have you met yourself?"

"Shut up."

Hours merged together. After a fruitless early visit to Robbie, Nick spent some time going over the evidence logs and forensic reports and collecting all the information a prosecutor would need if they ever made an arrest. Mackenzie was spending the last of the morning sifting through Alison's belongings, hoping that she had left some clue as to who she was meeting and where. But all she found was evidence of a woman who loved her family and wanted a better life.

A Post-it reminding her to buy Oliver an activity table. She wanted him to gain more dexterity.

A pamphlet giving information on finance courses at the community college.

A relief cream she intended to give Michelle for arthritis.

But Alison had been hounded by her poor choices. Lila had admitted that they'd had some rough clients and their dealer was a dangerous man, with even more dangerous friends.

It was understandable that Alison would want a fresh start for her child. If only she had known what horrors that would entail.

"You look more like you." Nick's voice distracted her.

Mackenzie caught her reflection in the computer screen. She was mildly surprised—her skin glowed almost translucent, but her cheeks were a rosy color. If she didn't know what was going on inside her brain, she'd believe that the woman staring back at her was calm and content.

"Trust me, I'm less composed on the inside. Maybe we should talk to Anthony again?" She bobbed her knee up and down impatiently.

Nick shot her a look, half amused, half incredulous. "Curb that enthusiasm. I'm sure Anthony's on it."

She tossed a pen across her desk and clenched her jaw. "What about Elisa?"

"Jenna has been keeping an eye on her, but nothing yet." Nick rubbed the back of his neck.

His phone rang. He showed her the screen. It was the crime lab. Mackenzie's body stilled in anticipation. Nick put the phone on speaker.

"Hey, Anthony. You got something?"

"You owe me big time, Nick," Anthony droned. "Despite my backlog, I got a chance to look at that receipt."

"Any prints?" Mackenzie jumped in.

"Now, now, Mad Mack. Don't get greedy. The Latent Print Unit will take time, but I was able to clear up that receipt using the basic vinegar method, since it was a water-based stain. The store's name is *Aphrodite*."

"Aphrodite?" Nick repeated.

"Yes. The Greek goddess of beauty."

"I know who she is. I've never heard of this store before."

Mackenzie was already on her computer. "Found it. It's an old store, been around since the 1950s. Looks like we're going to find our link."

# CHAPTER FIFTY-SEVEN

The car went over another bump. The radio was turned on. Spokane's Jefferson Frogs were the new favorites to win the Olympic Championship. The Riverview Ravens had also advanced to the next round. The entire dynamic had been altered, making the results unpredictable for the first time in years. All the towns but Lakemore were giddy about it.

Nick turned off the radio with a long sigh and chewed on a cigarette to relieve his stress.

Mackenzie stared at the arching motion of the wiper blades. They made a squealing sound against the glass and briefly gave her a clear glimpse of the empty road ahead.

Nick picked up his coffee cup. Realizing it was empty, he spat his cigarette into it and tossed it in the backseat. "I'll clean it later. Don't judge."

"I wasn't," she lied smoothly.

"Speaking of Sterling—"

"We actually weren't speaking of Sterling at all."

"Heard something interesting from a friend in the courthouse. He's subletting his apartment to Sterling."

Mackenzie braced herself. "Yes, we're getting a divorce."

The car swerved sharply. "*What*?"

"Are you surprised?"

"No. But I thought you'd say something."

"I was embarrassed."

"Half of America is divorced, Mack. Nothing to be embarrassed about."

"I'm embarrassed it took me so long. I kept wondering if I could get over it," she whispered, almost horrified with herself. She never imagined she'd be one of *those* women. The ones who took their cheating husbands back. The ones who forgave infidelity. "Trust me, I know how pathetic it sounds."

"It's different when you're the one it happens to, Mack. Easy to judge from the outside."

"Is it?" Her voice raised an octave, frustration bubbling out. "I just kept thinking, what if I regret leaving him? What if this is something I can live with? There are people who properly start fresh. It's rare, but it happens."

"It's not a switch. Like someone cheats and you can just turn it off. It never really goes away. That's why it sucks. And you don't have to explain to me. I get where you're coming from."

Mackenzie struggled for the right words, as the car came to a halt at a traffic light. "Here's a scenario for you. If you were in a situation where you knew you were going to die, and you could call one person, who would you call?"

"I'd call Luna." He didn't hesitate.

"I… I don't know who I would call." Saying it aloud gutted her—that she had no one except for Sterling. And now she didn't have that either.

She had friends, but family was family.

"You should call me. I was literally there the day you were born."

She cracked a smile. "And made a fuss because you didn't get to hold me?"

"Let's pretend that never happened."

After enduring the rain for a few more minutes, the clouds decided to give Lakemore some reprieve. By the time Mackenzie and Nick reached their destination, the rain had died off, and the sun was shining bright.

Aphrodite was a small store located closer to Tacoma. It looked like an extension of an old house, covered in vines and creepers.

There was a wooden sign outside with the store's name carved into it.

A cacophony of scents flooded their senses as they entered, from eucalyptus and lavender to sweet orange and honeydew. The store was quaint, if a little over the top. Mackenzie picked up a tube out of curiosity. It was a primer.

"Can I help you? I'm Xavier," a young man with wild hair asked them cheerfully. When Mackenzie and Nick showed their identification, he didn't falter. "Oops. I hope I'm not in trouble."

"Do you just work here or do you own this place?" Nick asked.

"It's a family business. We're only one store and have been operational since 1953. This is one of the less-known historic sites in Lakemore. Only history buffs know about us."

Mackenzie showed him a picture of the receipt. "We're looking for the woman who purchased this. Do you have surveillance?"

"No, we don't." He grinned and took the phone from her. "We're old school that way. Oh, I recognize this transaction, though. Just the one customer who buys that full line all at once."

A thrill surged through Mackenzie. "What line?"

"All these, the concealer, foundation, etcetera, are men's products."

"This is makeup for men?" Nick asked.

"Oh, come on. No age to be narrow-minded," Xavier teased good-naturedly.

"I didn't mean it like that. It's just not as common. And you remember the customer?"

Xavier handed back the phone. "Yeah, he's one of our regulars. Rees Preston. A very handsome man."

# CHAPTER FIFTY-EIGHT

Back at the station, Mackenzie recalled their first meeting with Dr. Rees Preston. He had exuded charm and had been nothing but cooperative throughout the whole investigation. But he'd had them all fooled.

Preston certainly had the expertise—enough for Becky to recommend him. She thought of his symmetrical, unblemished face. He valued beauty and perfection above all things. And they had been stupid enough to go to him for his help. They'd helped *him* keep tabs on their investigation.

But they had finally caught a break. Too bad for Preston his receipt hadn't burned all the way through.

"He would have been the expert witness at the trial if we had charged someone else," Mackenzie said to Nick, appalled at the possibility. She had sat across from him, interacted with him, and asked him his opinion on *his* work.

"Becky recommended him. We had no reason to doubt him really." Nick took out a cigarette and twisted it. "He's a highly respected cosmetic surgeon with a flourishing practice. Hell, his practice provides free services to burn victims. There's nothing in his history that connects him to this."

"Okay. What about Steven Boyle? Preston must be connected to him, if he's the one behind the ads. The username was *Steven*, and there's the pen..." She leaned against the edge of her desk.

"Let's go get him."

*

Preston's house was slick and modern, with floors of glistening marble and gold-trimmed window frames. As the housekeeper led Mackenzie and Nick in, Mackenzie couldn't help but find the spacious house odd. Even for her, it lacked the basic clutter that was natural to any home. The artwork wasn't warm. No portraits or sceneries or colors, just pictures of objects or shapes—precise geometrical shapes. A triangular piece merged with an octagon mounted on the wall. A picture of concentric circles. One spiky object blending into another.

"Makes me feel nothing," Nick whispered next to her.

"It's not art. It's architecture," she noted.

Then there was another wall covered in pictures of Preston horseback riding—snapshots clicked from different angles and poses; in some the horse was suspended mid-jump, in another Preston stood next to the horse, patting its nose, and in others he held trophies after winning competitions.

Mackenzie remembered the gift that had been sent to Steven. The tool used to engrave it had been in a horse stable at one point.

"Self-obsessed much?" Nick scoffed.

She sniffed the air. The clean and sterile atmosphere was infused with the smell of disinfectant. Everything in this house screamed detachment.

The housekeeper led them through to the kitchen, where Mackenzie heard faint music rippling through the air. Mahler. The kitchen opened onto the backyard, which had a small gazebo with a dining table. In the twinkling evening, the gazebo was lit by warm light bulbs. Preston sat at the table, eating innocently.

Groomed and polished, his golden hair was arched in an elegant wave over his head, a napkin tucked neatly into his shirt. His movements were sharp and confident as he cut into his food. The movements of a surgeon; someone who knew his way around a knife.

Preston's eyes shot up for a second. "I hope you don't mind if I finish this, detectives. Please take a seat."

His chilling serenity made Mackenzie's breath hitch in her chest. They had walked into the home of a psychopath. Her hand went to her gun. Just to make sure it was still there.

Preston continued to eat, aloof. Like he was expecting company. He sat back and picked up his glass of red wine. "I don't understand the fascination with guns." He had observed Mackenzie's passing gesture. "They're so barbaric." He took a sip and rinsed his mouth. The sound tickled against the melody of Mahler's symphony. He closed his eyes and twirled his hand to the beat, savoring the sound.

"Dr. Preston, you need to come with us." Nick stepped forward.

He opened his eyes, mildly irritated at the interruption. "I'd like to finish my dinner first."

"It would be—"

"If you haven't noticed," he raised his voice, his jaw set in a hard line, "I'm not making any attempts to flee. And if you had an arrest warrant, I would have been in handcuffs already."

Mackenzie pulled out a chair and made herself comfortable. She crossed her arms and curled her toes inside her boots. Frostiness bit into her skin. His gaze was predatory. "Such a striking face, Detective Price. You know what I like the most about it?"

"My Roman nose?"

He smiled and went back to cutting his meat. "Your face is a contradiction. A thin chin but an upward curving mouth. Pronounced cheekbones but lower inner eyebrows. You're hard and soft at the same time. A savior and killer all at once."

Mackenzie stared at his handsome face, which she could now tell was enhanced by makeup. She glanced at Nick, walking around twitchy and impatient, but assessing Preston.

"What was so striking about Katy's face?" Mackenzie asked.

"Your attempts couldn't be more transparent, Detective. I will cooperate, but not without my lawyer." He wiped his mouth with the napkin and picked up the wine. He sipped it at leisure.

When the verse came to an end, so did the wine. He made a mollified sound in the back of his throat. An easy smile stretched across his lips. "Ready to go?"

# CHAPTER FIFTY-NINE

It was ten in the evening, and Dr. Rees Preston was patiently seated in the interrogation room. His posture was upright and stiff, but he looked almost comfortable in the toasty room. He watched the mirror with an amused glint in his eye. Like he knew exactly who was on the other side.

"That's Becky's friend?" Sully asked, his shirt buttoned incorrectly, probably in his haste to get to work after being called late in the night.

"Yeah." Mackenzie narrowed her eyes.

"I'm glad she didn't join his book club."

"Me too. He's unusually calm, isn't he?"

Nick was perched against the wall, drinking steaming coffee. "He must have a damn good lawyer. Or an ace up his sleeve."

"What could that be?"

He shrugged.

Mackenzie pressed her hands against the wall, leaning forward, and hung her head low. Her mind was buzzing with energy, but her body had been drained. She had removed her jacket, rolled up her sleeves, and unbuttoned the top of her shirt. It was the least "uptight" she had looked in years, but on the inside she was incredibly tense.

"Ah! Thank you for joining us. Sorry about the last-minute notice," Sully said.

Nick looked over his shoulder and stiffened.

"Mack. Nick," Sterling nodded. Looking immaculate in a custom-made suit, he was clean-shaven, and his soft curls were the perfect length. He regarded Mackenzie with his frosty blue eyes.

"What are you doing here?" Mackenzie's voice came out shrill.

"I'm the prosecutor assigned to the case." He remained unaffected. *Lawyer.* "You're going to make an arrest, right?"

She was still aghast. Their paths had crossed and merged and collided so many times. This is how they'd met and fallen in love. But she had forgotten how much their lives were woven together. She hadn't even thought about having to work with him now that they had separated.

It was too soon.

"Yes," said Nick.

"Did you request to be put on my case?"

Sterling's eyes widened. Nick swiftly turned away, engaging Sully in some conversation. Mackenzie wasn't known to slip at work like this. She was Mad Mack. She didn't get personal.

"I didn't," Sterling said, an edge to his voice. "I'm here to do my job. There's pressure to make sure we're making arrests and getting convictions after what came to light with your previous case. What do you have for me, Sergeant?"

Sully updated him on the recent events leading them to Preston.

"What's his motive?" Sterling asked.

"He enjoys it. Playing savior," Nick replied, his words sending a shiver down Mackenzie's spine. "He values beauty, ambition, confidence. Drug addicts and prostitutes repulse him. He thinks he's improving them, making them 'better.'"

"He's a narcissist with delusions of grandeur," Mackenzie added scornfully.

Sterling stifled a yawn. Was he not sleeping enough? Mackenzie tucked the question away. It wasn't her business anymore.

Heels clacked at the end of the hallway.

"Guess that's the lawyer." Sully poked his head out of the room. "Ah, Ms. Cummings. We've met before—Sergeant Jeff Sully of the Detectives Unit."

Mackenzie saw a hand creep out and shake Sully's. The long fingers were covered in rings of various shapes and sizes.

"Of course. Always a pleasure."

"Nice to see you."

Mackenzie nodded in greeting. Natalie Cummings was a tall woman, with hair just reaching her shoulders. She had thin lips and beady eyes, and an infectious laugh. Her fingers were always covered in colorful rings. She wore at least three necklaces. Always dressed in something bohemian, she was easy to underestimate and had a knack of getting on nerves—especially Nick's.

"I'm representing Dr. Preston. Excuse me, I'll need a few minutes to consult with my client." She walked past them and looked over her shoulder with a mischievous smile. "Make sure we're not getting recorded."

Cummings marched inside the interrogation room. Through the glass, Mackenzie watched Preston speak with her calmly, the lawyer nodding, with a somber look on her face. Preston's tranquility was disturbing. His composed face didn't show any stress or trepidation.

"What do you think our strategy should be?" Mackenzie asked.

"Hold back," Sterling suggested, taking off his tie. He never tied it right, always too puffy. "They're expecting you to go in full throttle."

"How will that help?"

"It won't, but it'll save you energy. He has something, and it looks like he's fully willing to cooperate."

Mackenzie and Nick exchanged an uneasy glance. What could Preston possibly have for them but a confession?

"What can we charge him with?" Nick asked.

"Manslaughter or murder, illegal medical practice, trafficking... You should file a warrant to go through his computer and link him to those advertisements," Sterling said.

"Jenna's already on it."

"We're ready!" Natalie beamed and raised her hand to get their attention.

Mackenzie cracked her neck and followed Nick into the room. Preston tracked her movement through the glass even though he wouldn't have been able to see them.

"What evidence made my client a person of interest?"

The contrast between Preston and Natalie was glaring. Preston was about minimalism and austerity. His white shirt was devoid of any crinkles. Next to him, Natalie was flashing like a disco ball. Her bright rings and irregularly shaped necklaces blended with the floral print on her dress. There was so much going on that Mackenzie had an irrational urge to wipe her clean.

"Recognize this?" Nick slipped a picture of the shed toward Preston.

Preston barely even looked. "Yes."

"We found a half-burned receipt in there from a cosmetics store called Aphrodite."

"That place is a hidden gem. What did you think of it?" Preston asked.

Mackenzie curled her fingers into a fist in her lap. Her eyes searched the man she had sought for weeks. He spoke in a measured voice, like words were too valuable to just be spilled. He took care of things; he valued beauty and manners. Killing seemed almost too rudimentary for him, especially a stabbing. What had triggered him?

"Do you know Bella Fox, also known as Isabella Fabio?"

"Yes."

"Did you perform medical procedures on her face?"

A coy smile made his cheeks protrude under his eyes. "Yes. She expressed a strong desire to improve herself."

"Was it her idea?"

"Of course it was," Cummings interjected, appalled. "Isabella Fabio was a consenting adult of sound mind. Dr. Preston merely provided her a service."

"Then why do it in a shed deep in the woods?" Nick challenged with flared nostrils.

"Two reasons. First, Bella couldn't pay me, and I have my partners to answer to at the practice. Second, she wanted to be discreet."

"Your little clinic in the woods violates a lot of codes of practice."

"Well, we should probably wait for an investigation before jumping to conclusions, Detective Blackwood. Neither of us are experts here." Cummings raised her eyebrows playfully.

"She was terrified of you," Mackenzie blurted, watching Preston's eyes grow darker. "Did you know that? She tattooed the backs of her knees, leaving us clues."

"I didn't." He sat back, confusion written on his face. "I don't know why she'd feel that way. I was her guide. Like a shepherd. She was astray. I got her off drugs, inculcated healthy habits in her, and gave her a new face—of someone she should aspire to be like. Everything she needed for a fresh start, a new life. I gave her freedom. When she wanted to open a bank account, I didn't protest. I believed she shared my desire for perfection."

"Is that what you did with these other four women?" Nick placed a printout of the other advertisements on the table. "You were *guiding* them."

"Yes. The women I helped were given a second chance at life. When they came to me, they were weak and pliant. They had wasted years on drugs and bad choices. The evidence was written all over their bodies. They wanted to move forward, but it's not easy in today's world, when we leave our digital footprints to live forever on the internet, when there's a record of our faces with every government agency. I gave them a new identity. I molded them from the inside *and* the outside. Now, when they walk the streets, they are quite literally different people. No risk of someone toxic from their past luring them back, no unpleasant reminder when they look in the mirror."

"That's why you chose these faces," Mackenzie said, meeting Preston's gaze evenly. "These women. They're role models."

"It's flattery, really. I'd like to think of us as artists. Changing faces. Improving them. If eyes are the windows to the soul, then the face is the door. It's how everyone judges you, no matter what people say about inner beauty. It's your introduction to the world."

"What we're saying here," Cummings straightened and motioned for Preston to stop talking, "is that what my client did might be very unusual and even unfathomable to many. But not illegal."

"He killed two women," Nick said flatly.

"Who else knew about your activities?" Mackenzie asked.

"Nobody. I'm a recluse."

Underneath his facade of cooperation, he was holding back. He was taunting her, seeing if she could ask the right questions, like he wanted to tell her the truth but wasn't sure if she deserved it. She controlled a sneer from contorting her face. That was the power the most twisted minds wielded. They could make a police officer feel like they had something to prove to them.

"Why did you perform such… crude operations on Bella?" Mackenzie asked. "You didn't approve of them when we came to you."

"I still don't. It's not my best work. But I also believe in continuity and not compromising the sanctity of the process. I was merely continuing Dr. Boyle's work."

"And how exactly do you know Steven?" Nick asked.

Preston raised an eyebrow almost pompously. "I thought you'd know."

"Enlighten us," Nick replied with a tight smile.

"He was my mentor. He came to give a talk at UW, my alma mater. I wasn't supposed to attend but caught it by chance. He talked about beauty—what it means socially, physically, and psychologically. More importantly, what it means to those working in cosmetics. I went up to him after, and the rest is history. Everything I learned, I learned from him. He made me realize the power we wield. How we're more than just Botox and breast enhancements. How we impact self-esteem and self-worth and can mold destinies. My father was a rudimentary man. He didn't take care of things, of himself. I never liked looking at him. But Steven showed me how to fix ugliness in people. He taught me that we were artists beyond just shaping faces; the external was incomplete without the internal. He showed me how true perfection can be achieved."

"That suicide..." Mackenzie pressed. At last they were getting answers; the thread that connected Steven to the advertisements and the procedures and finally, Mackenzie hoped, to the murders.

"Yes, that was his wife, Sofia. He told me all about her. She was a fragile soul. But he failed. Making someone look different isn't enough. Creating someone better means helping their minds, curbing their insecurities and shame, *disciplining* them. He couldn't. Depression killed her. He disappeared, embarrassed by his own failure and hounded by the small minds in Lakemore. It took me two years to locate his shed in Woodburn Park."

"Have you been in touch with Steven?" Mackenzie asked.

"I heard he was in a retirement home in Olympia. I didn't visit him, but saw him from afar a few years ago." Preston looked horrified at the memory. "What a pity. The man I looked up to, who taught me everything I knew, reduced to a pile of ugly bones and flaccid skin. I couldn't even look at him without gagging. If he were healthy, he would understand. I left him a little token."

"The pen," Mackenzie said.

Preston grinned. "So you've seen it? Excellent piece, isn't it?"

"And what is your definition of *disciplining* them?" Nick cut in before they could get sidetracked.

"Oh, come on, Detective Blackwood. It was just an expression," Cummings groaned.

"You preyed on weak women," Mackenzie voiced her thoughts. "They're extremely vulnerable. Drug addicts."

"They were adults—" Cummings insisted.

"He manipulated them. Your client had no right to *correct* these women," Nick said.

"He offered a service, and they responded. He didn't force himself on them. It is odd; I'll give you that. But not illegal. You want to claim emotional abuse? Show us the evidence."

"He offered someone money to bring him a woman."

Cummings remained silent.

"Where are the other four women?" Mackenzie asked. "Where is Alison Gable?"

Preston shrugged. "Out in the world somewhere."

"You're lying. You'd really let them get away? They're precious to you. I think you like having them around, so you can admire your handiwork."

"Speculating once again, Detective," Cummings said in a singsong voice.

Mackenzie kept her scorching gaze on Preston. "Alison Gable has a child. She would never disappear on her son like that."

"She was looking for a fresh start and my client gave her one. If she abandoned her child in the process, it's not my client's fault."

Preston's lips twitched in amusement. He studied Mackenzie closely with his gray eyes, like he was analyzing every inch of her face. It made Mackenzie feel naked.

The circumstantial evidence against Preston was overwhelming. He was behind the cosmetic procedures, behind the ads, and the shed was in Woodburn Park, where the bodies were found. But, as yet, there was no physical evidence or eyewitness account that tied him to the murders, nor anything to suggest he had kept the other women captive. Alison's mother was certain she wouldn't have run away—and Mackenzie believed her. But it wouldn't hold up in court.

Mackenzie looked over her shoulder at Sterling. She knew how he worked; he needed hard evidence. Natalie Cummings was right.

"What charges is my client potentially facing?" she said.

"Apart from murder, obviously," Nick said sarcastically, "he paid a man to have a woman delivered to him. He has surplus amounts of prescription medicine in that shed. And we'll be going through his computer—"

"Accessing the dark web isn't illegal."

"No, but some websites on it are, including the one he was using."

Cummings gave him a tight smile. "I know an ASA is standing there, watching us. Everyone knows the environment now. There's pressure to prosecute and convict."

"What are you getting at?" Nick narrowed his eyes.

She shrugged innocently.

"If Dr. Preston knows anything then he has an obligation to share it with us. Otherwise, we will charge him with obstruction of justice," Mackenzie reminded them.

Preston looked at Cummings, who gave him a curt nod. "I'll cooperate fully, detectives. But I'm afraid my memory isn't very sharp at the moment."

Mackenzie was exasperated. She eyed Nick, whose Adam's apple dipped incessantly. *Ask the right questions.* They had him cornered. But this could either be over in a few seconds or stretch for a few hours. "Why didn't you come clean when we first came to you?"

"Two women had been murdered. I wanted to distance myself from it. Naturally."

"Because you killed them?" Nick asked. "It appears that Katy ran into Bella when she was in Woodburn Park on the trail, presumably running away from *you.* In the mayhem, you caught up with her and killed them both. That's what I think."

"When was the last time you saw Bella?" Mackenzie asked.

"November seventeenth, I believe. Saturday morning. In that shed. I'd gone to restock some supplies and wasn't expecting to find her there. She panicked and ran away from me, giving me some incoherent answer. I tried going after her, but I got paged for work. I assumed that she'd had a relapse, even though she had been doing so well. You never know with women in this line of work."

Preston looked bored. But there was a slight tremble in his lower lip. It was so fleeting that Mackenzie would have missed it if she'd blinked. "Do you regret that Bella died?"

"Of course I do," he said with a wistful longing. "She was my creation. So much potential. She was my favorite. She understood what I was doing, why I was doing it. At least that's what I thought."

"You wouldn't kill what you create."

"No."

"Then I'm sure you want to help us catch her killer, then."

Nick stirred in his seat. Preston appraised Mackenzie before looking at Cummings. She nodded.

"I do," Preston said coolly. "I believe I have the murder weapon."

# CHAPTER SIXTY

"You have been concealing the murder weapon this entire time?" Nick was quick to respond. The veins in his neck jutted out. "Didn't your talented lawyer explain to you what obstruction of justice means?"

Cummings laughed. "Thanks for that backhanded compliment, Detective. But my client said he *believes* he has the murder weapon. Since he wasn't a witness to the crime or the perpetrator, he has no way of *knowing* if the object is in fact the murder weapon."

Nick and Natalie stared at each other, frustrated and bitter.

"And why are you coming forward with this now?" Mackenzie asked, placing her hands on the table.

"I found it very close to my property in Woodburn—"

"Your mentor's illegal construction."

His lips pressed in a hard line. He didn't like being interrupted. But Mackenzie enjoyed ruffling his feathers. "As I was saying, I didn't turn it in before because I didn't want to risk exposing my property. And I didn't want any unnecessary hassle. I found it when I returned to the shed, hoping to find Bella there after she didn't return home. She was staying with me, you see. I retraced her steps in the direction she had run in, and found this knife on the trail not too far from my cabin."

"And what made you believe that what you found was a murder weapon?"

A sickening smile curled up his face. He was savoring this moment. "It was a gut hook knife. And it had blood on it."

*

Mackenzie and Nick were in Sully's office with Sterling. It was close to midnight, but the room was charged with tension and full of movement. Preston had volunteered to submit his fingerprints, rendering the emergency warrant pointless. Sully's hands moved frantically, searching for something to do. But he had made the mistake of taking his latest hobby home. Nick was buzzing, leaning against the wall. His knee bobbed to a random rhythm. The high from the coffee finally peaking. He wasn't sleeping tonight. Mackenzie and Sterling sat on the chairs across from Sully.

Her empty stomach turned, threatening to release a rumble when she spoke over the sound. "Are you going to charge him?"

Sterling interlaced his fingers in front of him. "I think it's best to wait for the crime lab to analyze the murder weapon first."

"Why? You saw him in there. He's playing a sick game with us."

He licked his lips. "I get that. But Natalie has a point. We need more proof."

"He's holding Alison and the others captive." Mackenzie's voice was hard and loud. "You heard how obsessed he is. Do you think he'll just let them walk away?"

Sterling stared at her with flared nostrils and pursed lips. Her breaths were sharp, grazing through her windpipe painfully. She knew her boss and partner were watching them. The air between them was palpably strained. She didn't like the idea of her relationship being sliced open for Sully to see.

"At the very least, he'll almost certainly lose his medical license. I don't see that the American Medical Association will have a choice," Sterling said.

"His *license*?" Mack exploded. "I don't give a damn about his license—the man deserves to be locked away in a cell for the rest of his life."

"Mack, I know. We all want to charge someone with murder here. But we need to wait for the crime lab. Our office will work closely with the board of ethics to see what charges we can bring against Preston in the meantime."

"Yeah, and a doctor engaging in illegal practice isn't a good enough conviction for your résumé," she sniped, and crossed her arms.

"Okay." Sully smacked his palms on the desk to divert attention. "While the crime lab looks into that knife, I'll call the police in Seattle and inform them of developments."

Sully dismissed them after going over plans of action. By the time Mackenzie left his office and packed her bag, her bones were too tired to carry the weight of her muscles. Her feet dragged on the floor, and her eyes struggled to stay open. But her mind was going at full speed. She could only hope that the murder weapon would have some physical evidence pointing them to Preston. If they could get him on that, maybe he would tell them where Alison was. Where all the girls were.

"I can hear you grinding your teeth," Nick commented from behind her.

She huffed. "He was right in front of our eyes the whole time. I can't believe I didn't see it. And I *know* he's lying about Alison."

"He put on a good act, playing the willing adviser, correctly pointing us toward Alison. And this connection to Steven wasn't on paper. Steven wasn't an alumnus of his university nor did they ever cross paths at any hospital or clinic."

"Some nerve, he's got. Doesn't it make you angry?" It almost sounded like an accusation.

"It does."

"He's a self-described artist. He wouldn't let his *work* get away. He keeps them. Like trophies in a display case. At least that's my assessment."

Nick brooded. "I think you're right. But he handed us the murder weapon. Do you think he would be that careless if he had killed Bella and Katy?"

"He could have easily misled us about Alison when we consulted him, but he pointed us toward her. He's that confident that he'll get away."

"Okay, but for argument's sake. What if he didn't kill them?" Nick rubbed the back of his neck. "Those are his creations, his trophies."

Mackenzie fell on her chair, tired after a long day. "If not him, then who?"

"Are you staying?" Nick asked, packing his own bag. "You look beat."

"Yeah… I don't feel like going home yet."

He nodded and squeezed her shoulder before leaving the office.

Mackenzie rang Ethan Spitz. Even though Sully was going to contact Spitz's sergeant, she trusted Ethan's speed and efficiency. He picked up after a single ring, and she updated him on their arrest and discovery.

"Alright. I'll look into any properties owned by this doctor in Seattle. Nothing in his house there?"

"No. We've turned it inside out," she confirmed. After they'd apprehended Preston, a team had checked his house for the captive women.

"If he's been picking up women from down there and from Seattle, he could be holding them somewhere in the middle."

An idea came to her. "You keep looking. I have a lead I'll follow up on. Will let you know if it pans out."

"Sure thing. And Mack, we'll get them."

*

Over an hour later, Mackenzie was still in the office. The lamp made her desk glow in the otherwise pitch-black darkness. Her eyes throbbed from exhaustion, but her brain was still firing on all cylinders.

Preston might appear to be cooperating, admitting to his part in the surgeries, handing them the murder weapon, but Mackenzie didn't buy it. He was keeping Alison and the other women somewhere. The Alison she had got to know in the little pieces she'd left behind wouldn't have abandoned her child under any circumstances.

Mackenzie looked at the picture of the pen Preston had dropped off for Steven Boyle at the retirement home in Olympia. An elegant gift for his former mentor—a man he couldn't even bear to look at anymore, now that he didn't fit Preston's warped definition of beauty. But he still respected him, continued his work, and left a little token for the shell of a man Boyle had become.

She also had the crime lab report open. She had gone over the mass spectrometry reports before. The engraved markings on the pen meant some particles had lodged themselves inside the crevices, and those particles suggested the pen had been in a stable at one point, or the tool used on it had been. Before, that hadn't really helped them. But now that they knew Preston was behind this, maybe it was the key to finding Alison.

Mackenzie looked up Preston's address on Google Maps. There was no stable in the vicinity. Lakemore had one country club with a horse stable, but it was public—he couldn't have kept Alison there. She clicked her tongue and slumped down in her chair.

Preston's house had pictures of him on horses, participating in competitions. He was a passionate equestrian and surely wealthy enough to have his own horses. Was he wealthy enough to have his own land to keep them on? Probably.

She accessed the local records. Preston had three properties in the county. One was his home in Lakemore, and another an apartment in downtown Olympia. There was another address—farmland on the edge of Lakemore and Riverview. Mackenzie looked up the street view. Set back from the nearest road, she could make out what looked like a barn.

"Gotcha."

# CHAPTER SIXTY-ONE

*December 13*

Gray clouds swirled in the sky. Mackenzie stepped in a puddle. She closed the car door behind her and looked at the black SUV turning around the corner. There was a vast stretch of land ahead of them, behind a black fence with barbed wire atop. A red structure sat nearby.

"It's a good spot to hold someone captive." Nick looked around.

Secluded and chilling.

The woods surrounding the field would swallow any screams. It was disturbingly quiet. Not even the wind blew. The closest house was miles away. The roar of an engine sliced through the silence. The black SUV floundered over the dirt road and parked behind the squad car also on site.

Detective Ethan Spitz greeted them. "Thanks for the call. Think this is it?"

"It's the best lead we've got," Mackenzie confirmed. "County records show it's Preston's. He's paying property tax on it."

Ethan nodded. "Could be it. It's a stable with a loft. Enough space."

Mackenzie turned to the three uniformed cops that were assisting them. She instructed them to circle around the property and be ready to call for backup. If they did find Alison and the others in there, they would most likely need an ambulance.

Together they ventured toward the stable, walking across a field left sodden due to the wet weather, their footsteps making squelching sounds. A flock of birds tapered swiftly across the sky. As they got closer, Mackenzie's senses went into overdrive.

"Do we have a warrant?" Ethan checked.

Nick showed him the piece of paper. "Went through an hour ago. Peterson, open it."

One of the cops swung a hammer into the lock, breaking it, and slid the double doors open. A cocktail of scents assaulted Mackenzie's nose. Hay, pine shavings, and manure. The roof panels provided sufficient lighting. Nick motioned for the uniformed officers to walk down the central walkway, checking the stalls on either side.

On their right, the wall was laden with feeding and watering equipment.

On the left was a wooden door.

Ethan turned the knob. "It's locked or stuck. Can't tell."

Mackenzie backed a few feet away then ran into it with her shoulder. The door crashed open, sending a sharp pain up her injured arm.

They flicked a switch, and the room lit up. It was an office. Mirrored panels covered the entire wall opposite them. A simple table sat in the middle, along with a chair and a shelf.

"What's this for?" Nick wondered. "He already has an office."

Ethan picked up some of the papers, assessing them. "Looks like inventory for the stable, paperwork for renovations, that kind of stuff."

Mackenzie peered at the mirror, her reflection staring back at her. She wasn't too surprised. Preston was shallow and obsessed with perfection, especially when it came to faces. He must like to admire his reflection—that's why the chair faced the mirror.

"Can't believe this was a bust," Nick sighed. "Maybe we'll find something on the property. An underground bunker even? Can't put anything past him."

"We should check out neighboring counties," Ethan replied. "He could be hiding them somewhere else."

Mackenzie continued staring at the mirror. The property had looked bigger from the outside. She had been expecting bigger rooms. The office was well lit, almost too bright. She looked up. All lights were pointed at the mirror, illuminating the room even more.

"That's a neat trick." She sounded unsure, even to herself.

"What is?" Nick came to her side.

She peered intently at the hairline seam between two of the panels. "That's a hinge."

Mackenzie hooked her finger into the gap where the mirror met the side wall and swung it back. It was covering a glass wall looking into darkness. They could only see their own reflection. Again.

"What the hell is this about?" Mackenzie said.

"There's a switch here." Ethan flipped it.

Light flooded the other side of the glass.

Mackenzie staggered backward, gasping.

Four women chained to the wall. Their eyes were large and teary. Their bodies writhed and twisted wildly against their constraints. Their lips were parted as screams escaped their throats, but no sound came. It was deadly silent on this side of the glass.

"Oh my God," Mackenzie whispered, a chill running down her spine. The room on the other side was smaller than the office, and the walls were dark, giving it the appearance of a box. The only source of light and fresh air was a clerestory window.

"There must be a door!" Ethan cried.

"Not here," Nick said.

The women's arms and necks were covered in blood and bruises. Some fresh and others healed. But their faces were perfect—unblemished if not for the palpable fear and streaming tears.

She recognized Alison Gable on the far left. Her hair was cut and dyed differently to the picture they had of her. Her face had some scarring, transformed slightly into someone else's. Then there was an African American woman next to her, matching the description of the woman from Seattle. The other two women resembled the women from the other ads.

One woman didn't move. She stayed put, watching Mackenzie with dull eyes.

"Sir, there's a door outside." Peterson walked in, his face changing. "I'll call an ambulance."

Mackenzie pressed her badge against the glass. "I'm Detective Mackenzie Price with the Lakemore PD." She mouthed the words slowly, unsure if they could even hear her. "Stay put. We have arrested Preston. You're safe now. It's over."

# CHAPTER SIXTY-TWO

*December 14*

The sky burst into a flaming blue, dragging Mackenzie into the morning. A spear of lightning slashed the sky open, releasing raindrops that danced before her. The vivid blue blurred into a metallic gray. Dewdrops adorned the forest in front of her—glistening and radiant. The scenery was striking. The sound of sparrows singing drowned by the pitter-patter of sprinkling rain.

Mackenzie's arms and legs were covered, but the cold made her bones rattle. She stood at the edge of the woods by Hidden Lake. She swallowed hard and ventured in. She had only come here three times before. But today marked the first voluntary expedition undertaken with a sound mind.

Her legs felt woolly. Her eyes struggled to stay open under the scattered light from the rain and bopping leaves.

*You have to help me bury him.*

*Charles.*

*The man with you is not Robert Price.*

The memories made her chest feel like it was filled with needles. Her muscles twitched in different places. Her skin became oversensitive to the wind and rain.

Mackenzie came to a halt at the edge of Hidden Lake. It was oddly shaped—like an ink-splat. Rain drummed the surface, causing ripples that merged and clashed. She removed her earphones and listened to the sounds of the rain and the wind in the trees.

Lakemore's beauty was underrated.

Raindrops ran down her face, plastering her hair to her skin. Her throat closed, remembering the fleeting memories she had of Robert Price that she was trying to hold on to.

Her only sense of relief came from the fact that they had been able to rescue Alison and the other women. They were immediately taken to the hospital to be treated for their injuries and undergo psych evaluation. Preston had been charged with unlawful imprisonment, trafficking, simple assault, and assault causing bodily harm. Other charges related to performing unsafe medical procedures and stealing prescription pills from his practice were right around the corner.

Preston was adamant that he hadn't committed any murders. But he had looked Mackenzie in the eye and asserted that he didn't know the whereabouts of Alison and the other women. He was a smooth liar, and Mackenzie was positive this was just another trick of his to avoid a murder charge.

Her phone rang. "Detective Price."

"Mack, I got Anthony on the call," Nick said. "Are you outside? It's raining cats and dogs."

"Yeah, no kidding. Hey, Anthony. What do you have?"

"Becky confirmed that the knife Preston gave us is the murder weapon. His prints were on the blade, not on the handle, consistent with him picking it up and not using it."

"Well, he could have cleaned the handle to mislead us," Mackenzie replied.

"True, but there's some good news too. The knife is mostly covered in the blood of the victims. But there were *three* distinct DNA sets."

"The killer must have nicked themselves during the attack," Nick said, excited. "Did you find any hits?"

"No..."

"Then what's the good news?"

"First set is Katy Becker's. Second set belongs to Isabella Fabio. But the third one is a fifty percent match to Katy's."

Mackenzie's breath hitched. "Her parents?"

"The DNA is female."

Charlotte Harris.

# CHAPTER SIXTY-THREE

Mackenzie and Nick huddled together under his umbrella after climbing out of the car. Nick had picked her up on the way and given her an earful about going out for a run during a thunderstorm. She had rolled her eyes but now she was shaking with cold.

"Katy's mother, really?" Nick took off his scarf and handed it to Mackenzie. "It doesn't make sense. Maybe there's been some mistake."

He had normal parents. His father had always been busy and had high expectations. His mother had died when he was just a teenager. But they had loved and protected him. He was always reluctant to believe a parent could harm a child. Mackenzie didn't blame him. It was a blessing he wasn't jaded that way.

She rang the bell with a heavy arm. The wind made raindrops fly into their eyes. After a few seconds, the door opened. Frank Harris was wearing his pajamas and a look of bleary confusion. It was still early in the morning. "Detectives?"

"Can we come in? Sorry to bother you so early," Nick said.

"Sure." He frowned.

Inside, Mackenzie relaxed when warmth kissed her skin. They took off their soiled shoes and followed Frank into the living room.

"Did you find anything?" Frank asked.

Mackenzie wondered if he knew she was involved. She didn't believe he did. Behind him, Charlotte came out of the kitchen with a towel in her hands.

The pressure in the air nosedived, making Mackenzie lightheaded. As Charlotte got closer she momentarily morphed into

Melody, before changing shape again. "Can I get you anything? Coffee? Tea?"

Nick cleared his throat. "Just water, please. We need to talk."

Charlotte slightly staggered back and eyed them cautiously, with lips parted. If Mackenzie hadn't been paying close attention to her, she wouldn't have noticed. Charlotte retreated into the kitchen. Frank gestured for them to sit, then fidgeted. The rain was beginning to die off, making the silence in the house seem eerie.

Mackenzie spotted a picture of Katy at her graduation, flanked by her parents. Frank had his arm around her. Charlotte was half hugging her.

Charlotte returned with a tray. She set it on the table, trembling. When she sat next to Frank, her face was pale.

"Do either of you hunt?" Nick picked up a glass of water and guzzled it.

"Both of us. Why?" Frank asked.

"How long have you been hunting for?"

"Years. Charlotte got me into it. She used to go hunting with her father when she was younger. Why are you asking all this?"

It gave Charlotte enough expertise to use a gut hook knife effectively.

"I'll explain. Can you bring any knives you keep for hunting?"

"Sure," Frank said, nodding. "We keep them together in a case." He left the room.

Mackenzie glared at Charlotte. Tears collected in the corners of her eyes. She knew. Everyone in the room did. Mackenzie observed the wrinkled fingers gripping the cuffs of her sleeves. She had noted earlier that Charlotte was a strapping woman. Strong and sturdy. Today, she looked puny.

Frank returned with his case and placed it on the table. "Here you go."

"Is anything missing?" Mackenzie asked.

He rummaged around for a bit and then grimaced. "Yes. A gut hook knife. We only hunt in summer, so I don't know where I left it. Charlotte, have you seen it?"

She looked down at her lap. Her chest rose and fell.

"Charlotte?" he asked again.

"We found the murder weapon," Mackenzie said. "It had the DNA of the murderer."

Charlotte closed her eyes and took a deep breath.

"What's going on?" Frank was baffled.

Time had stilled. A revolting and utterly devastating insinuation hung in the air. Suddenly, a hot flash flooded Mackenzie's senses. Her ears felt hot. She stared at Charlotte, waiting for her to break down and divulge what had happened in the early hours of that fated Saturday.

"What happened, Charlotte?" Mackenzie asked.

"What?!" Frank's jaw hung open. "I don't understand."

"I knew Kim was back," Charlotte said through gritted teeth. "I saw her on Friday at the market. For a second I thought it was Katy, but then I realized something was very off about her. Wearing a ratty old T-shirt with holes in it and hair pinned up in a messy bun. Katy wouldn't dress like that in public. She walked with a hunched back and smacked gum. Little things that Katy would never do. She just looked so *different*..." Charlotte's eyes twitched. "I immediately called Katy, and she answered the phone. She said she was leaving for the weekend and to call later. She sounded busy. But the woman in front of me wasn't busy, and she hadn't received a call. And I knew... knew that it was Kim shopping for jewelry, right in front of my eyes."

Katy had invited Kim to stay with her that weekend while Cole was away. Mackenzie recalled Kim telling her about their conversation. Kim wasn't ready to meet their parents, so Katy had made sure that they stayed away that weekend. She'd told them she wasn't there.

"Then what happened?" Nick urged her to continue.

"I was stunned. I froze. It was like I was back in the past again. By the time I absorbed the reality that Kim was in town, she had wandered away. I lost sight of her and drove back home."

Charlotte's face was hard as stone. It was clear she didn't share any of her husband's regrets about Kim. All her compassion was reserved for just one daughter. "I spent the entire night wondering what Kim could possibly want. Why was she here? What was she planning? I couldn't tell Frank. My husband has a soft spot for Kim. Not that she deserves it. I realized she must be back to hurt Katy, maybe even to kill her. It couldn't have been a coincidence for her to end up here. I had to protect my child. I couldn't let Kim harm Katy. You don't know how violent she was, even at four years old. She was a monster even then, imagine what she would have been capable of now."

"You hate her so much," Mackenzie blurted out, her chest feeling tight as she thought of another mother who had rejected her daughter.

"She killed my child!" Charlotte cried. Her eyes were bloodshot, like the tip of her nose. Her hand flew to her stomach. "When she pushed me down those stairs, he was inside me. I was eight months pregnant. I felt him every day. He danced to songs by Prince. He loved tamarind. He hated cheese. Whenever I lay on my right side, his elbow would jut out."

"Honey, Kim was only four. It was an accident—"

"No, it wasn't. You went to work, Frank. I stayed home those four years and dealt with that *psychopath*. Do you know how much she used to hit Katy? One time she almost needed stitches. Kim pushed me down the stairs after I scolded her for breaking Katy's toy. It wasn't an accident. I remember looking at her standing at the top of the stairs with a blank look on her face. No tears, no shock. She *wanted* to hurt me. Every single day, I looked at her and searched for my child. But every day she proved that there was nothing good inside her."

Mackenzie looked at Nick uncomfortably. She couldn't fathom what it meant to be a mother. But even as she stared at a bitter Charlotte, she couldn't deny her pain. Years later, she still grieved the life that was inside her, the life that was taken away so unfairly. She imagined how much Charlotte must have struggled to understand and love Kim. But eventually Kim's mental illness wore down her mother's determination.

"You loved Katy," Mackenzie said.

"The most." Charlotte sniffed. "She was all I had after my one child killed the other. She was a good daughter. But Kim took her away from me. That boyfriend who had followed her here mistook Katy for Kim and snatched her. If Kim hadn't come to Lakemore, my daughter would still be alive. I told you, Frank. Everywhere she goes, trouble follows. She came back into our lives and our daughter died at the hands of *Kim's* crazy ex-boyfriend."

Charlotte still didn't know that Katy and Kim had switched places.

"What happened that morning?" Nick asked.

"I went over to Katy and Cole's to make sure that Kim wasn't sniffing around. But then I saw her coming out of the house, wearing Katy's clothes, looking exactly like her, wearing that necklace I saw her buy at the market. It *disgusted* me. But it was her. Katy had told me she would be away all weekend. And here Kim was, trying to look like Katy. Like she was trying to steal Katy's life. She was going to hurt her and take away what was hers. I had to stop her. She was on foot, so I got out of my car and followed her into Woodburn Park."

And Mackenzie could see how it went down. A mother with a tattered soul and no closure following an unsuspecting Katy into the woods, mistaking her for Kim.

"I lost track of her for a bit. She was hurrying along the trail. When I eventually caught up to her, I saw her with that girl."

Bella—running away after she unexpectedly encountered Preston.

"That girl looked so much like Katy. Not exactly like her, but close enough that I expect even Frank would confuse them if he weren't wearing his glasses. She was kneeling on the ground, panting, like she had tripped, and Kim was standing over her. I didn't understand what Kim was planning, but it horrified me. It was so sick. So wrong." She looked Mackenzie firmly in the eye. "I decided to protect my daughter. They were a threat. I was carrying a knife in case anything went wrong. I confronted them, and there was so much commotion."

Mackenzie saw it in her head. Katy's confusion over seeing Bella, who in turn would have been terrified. Then Charlotte emerged, wielding a knife with blind fury and a single-point agenda. Katy must have been stunned. Bella would have panicked.

Arguments. Accusations. Miscommunication.

"The lake was the closest, so I dropped them there. Almost sprained my wrist in the process. It was such a surreal moment." Charlotte's eyes misted with tears, as she massaged her joint. "I hated myself, but it was necessary. It was justice for my son. Katy was starting a family. I couldn't let Kim destroy that. I ran out of there and only later did I realize I had dropped the knife at some point."

Frank's head hung loosely, like it had become detached. The strength had been sucked out of him. He had blanched at her words, but now he looked empty.

Mackenzie didn't have the heart to tell Charlotte that she had killed the daughter she loved. Not that she condoned the idea of Charlotte killing Kim. But the woman sitting across from her was no unfeeling villain. She was a deeply disturbed mother, whose trauma years before had warped her maternal instincts into something terrible.

Nick sighed and stood up, taking out the handcuffs. "Charlotte Harris, you're under arrest for the murders of Isabella Fabio and Katy Becker. You have the—"

"*What*?" Charlotte protested as Nick gently pulled her up. "What do you mean by Katy?"

"Katy knew about Kim and was helping her," Mackenzie croaked. "She lied to you about being away, because Kim didn't want to see you. It was Katy who left the house that morning, wearing the necklace Kim had given her. We got DNA confirmation last night."

Nick resumed reciting Charlotte her Miranda rights. But his voice was drowned by the sounds of the bone-crushing grief that escaped Charlotte.

# EPILOGUE

*December 15*

Mackenzie plugged her nose and popped open her ears. She stretched back her shoulders and a crack rippled up her spine. In the conference room, Sully and Rivera went over the final details with her and Nick. Still reeling from the discovery yesterday, she was exhausted. All she could think of was Dr. Rees Preston. A dangerous but refined man. A self-declared savior. His calculating eyes and amused smile, like he knew everyone's secret. He worshipped his mentor and continued his work.

"Good save, you two," Sully praised Mackenzie and Nick. "The women you and Spitz rescued from Preston's barn are in the hospital recovering. Did you talk to any of them?"

"Yeah, Alison and Tamara." Mackenzie winced at the memory. Seeing those women had rattled her bones. They were dressed impeccably, but their haggard faces conveyed their fear and torment. As did the bruised and swollen skin on their wrists and ankles and everywhere below the neck. "They confirmed what we know. He made them believe he'd make them look more beautiful, give them a fresh start, help them get off drugs, etcetera. And then he threw them in that box of a room after gaining their trust. There was no sexual assault. Only physical torture."

"Bella was given more freedom because she was able to manipulate Preston into thinking that she was on his side. That's also why she had no signs of physical assault, unlike the other women. She made him believe that she would help him find new faces and girls," Nick said.

"It was Bella who helped Preston take Alison," Mackenzie added. "To prove her loyalty to Preston, so that he would allow her more freedom."

Nick nodded. "They all thought that Bella was his partner. But we think she did all this so that she could collect evidence against Preston before she went to the police."

Then the whole situation with Kim and Charlotte became entangled, and lives were lost. Mackenzie shook her head. They all felt the disappointment in the air. The mayhem that ensued from the confusion caused by the twins. Kim showing up in Lakemore had triggered a cascade of events that no one could ever have imagined.

Sully twirled the ends of his mustache. "Well, the good news is that we nailed the bastard. We have plenty of evidence, and three out of four women have agreed to testify."

One of the women had shown no relief on being rescued. She'd just followed Mackenzie's lead with dead eyes. It had chilled Mackenzie. Later, they found out that she had been living in that room for four years.

"Natalie Cummings dropped him as a client. She doesn't like being lied to. He's going to spend a very long time in prison." Nick smiled, but his eyes spelled fury.

"And Charlotte Harris is going to plead guilty to all charges," Rivera declared, haughtily. "Congratulations, detectives. It was a bumpy ride, but I'm glad that we wrapped this one up."

"What a waste." Nick clicked his tongue. He'd had his hair cropped shorter on the sides, revealing dots of gray. "She ended up killing the person she thought she was protecting."

"So Ben Harlan had nothing to do with Preston's operation?" Sully asked.

"Nope. He was a blip in the case. An abusive ex-boyfriend who followed Kim."

"He did a lot of damage for a blip," Sully snorted. "Anyway, the tradition is we go for drinks, but I'm swamped. So, tomorrow! I'm looking at you, Mack. Don't flake out. Have fun once in a while. You always look like you're about to write an exam."

They all chuckled. As they began to disperse out of the room, Rivera called her over to one side. Mackenzie braced herself. The new lieutenant paid close attention and had high expectations. She had also maintained a distance from Mackenzie since the incident involving Kim and Ben.

"How're you doing, Detective Price?"

"Good. Good."

"I realized I didn't check in with you after what happened. I should have."

"It's okay. It wasn't one of my best decisions."

"Take some time off if you want," Rivera hitched her shoulder up. "Spend time with your father and husband."

Mackenzie faltered, but nodded.

"Is everything okay?"

"Yes." She turned before Rivera's prying could pull out any revelations from her. She walked back to her desk, gnashing her teeth and chewing the insides of her cheeks. Now that the case was solved, her past was screaming like a banshee inside her head.

Her desk was cluttered. Pens and papers lay haphazardly. Her keyboard had crumbs of bread lodged in the crevices. There was a ring of fading brown liquid—no doubt from Nick placing his coffee there at some point.

Dark tendrils spread across her skin, coaxing her to clean. But she wanted to resist until she was alone.

"How about *I* buy you a drink? Prepare for Sully tomorrow night," Nick asked.

"Sure. Give me ten minutes."

Nick cast his eyes over her desk and the emptying office knowingly, and nodded.

Mackenzie threw her head back and laughed. She hadn't heard herself laugh uncontrollably in a long time. She almost didn't recognize the baritone of her voice.

"You haven't even finished a drink," Nick gasped from her side.

They were seated at the bar in the Oaktree—the go-to bar for Lakemore PD, being the closest one to the station. It was like a furnace inside compared to the biting cold outside. The place was packed, much to Mackenzie's surprise, since the television wasn't even turned on. But people huddled around the pool table and the karaoke machine. A new foosball table had been added to expand the entertainment. It was the holiday season. But once the festivities died down, Lakemore would return to being angry.

"I'm laughing at the song."

"Stand by Your Man" by Tammy Wynette played on the speakers. When Nick realized, he looked uncomfortable. "I never liked that song."

"God. I have to find a divorce lawyer. How do you even go about that?"

"How're you doing with everything?"

She sipped on her red wine and contemplated. "I feel porous."

"Porous?"

"Yes." That was the most accurate description she could conjure up. Everything had punched holes inside of her, leaving her light but weak. Like she could bruise too easily.

"I don't understand."

"You don't have to." She gulped the remaining wine and ordered another one. "I'm just so sick of myself these days. I'm trying to let loose."

He arched an eyebrow. "Is that why you waited for everyone to leave before you cleaned your desk?"

She narrowed her eyes. "Baby steps."

"Explains why the top two buttons of your shirt are undone and your sleeves are rolled up."

Mackenzie shuddered. She didn't like it one bit. It made her feel like she was inside someone else's skin. But she was so determined to change that she told herself this was an adjustment period.

"Quit it." Nick nursed his precious beer.

"What?"

"You just have to let go a little from here." He tapped her temple with his finger. "It has nothing to do with anything else. It's kind of your thing, you know. Looking like a warden and scrubbing water rings clean at bars."

She grinned and deftly buttoned her shirt back up and rolled down her sleeves, breathing a sigh of relief. Nick chuckled into his beer.

Another glass was placed in front of her, and she took two more large sips. "I… I've been stuck for a very long time. I didn't want to move forward because I didn't think I could or that I deserved to."

"I have no idea what you're saying."

Her shoulders slumped. "I'm moving on. Actively."

Nick stroked his chin. "From Sterling?"

"Yes. And my father." *And my mother.*

"I thought your father was just away for a few days?"

She didn't answer. There was one unopened voicemail from him on her phone that she hadn't deleted. Fortunately, Nick's father, Alan, hadn't told his son anything about Charles. She had called him asking to keep it between them, and she was touched by his respect for her privacy.

"Do you think it'd be better if Charlotte didn't know the truth? If she never found out that she killed Katy?" Mackenzie said.

The corner of Nick's eyes creased. "Yes. Sometimes it's better not to know the truth if it doesn't help. Tough case, wasn't it?"

"They all are. It doesn't get easier."

The bar blared with chatter and music. Drinking together and cracking mundane jokes. Mackenzie made a proactive effort to actually listen and tether herself to the present. It wasn't easy. Every time Nick talked about Luna, her mind wandered to her own lack of attachment in life. When Nick told her about Dennis's cigar collection, she felt left out and reprimanded herself for not knowing her co-workers that well.

She gripped the stem of the wine glass tighter and swallowed hard. There was time to change. She might never be able to obliterate her past, but she could yank herself out of it.

Nick's phone rang. "I'm going to take this outside. Too loud in here."

"Sure."

She gazed at her wedding band. She hadn't taken it off. The wine made her head swim and gave her the strength. Quickly, she took it off and shoved it in her pocket. A daring move for her that left her hand feel lacking and foreign. She caught her reflection in the mirror behind the bar.

She saw a rigid woman with a shimmer of optimism. There were still unanswered questions. Where had Melody moved Robert's body? What lies did Melody tell the authorities? And the biggest one: how much did Charles *really* know? He had lied before. He could have lied again.

But like Nick had said—sometimes it was better not to know the truth if knowing didn't help. She took out the necklace Bruce had gotten her from Kenya. She looked at the colorful beads and felt her heart soar.

*Determination.*

It was something she was good at. And this necklace, crafted on the other side of the world by a strong and determined woman she'd never met, served as a reminder.

Nick returned, clutching his phone.

"Do you want to order a pitcher? If you're fine with getting a hangover tomorrow."

"Mack… I'm so sorry. You have to come with me."

His face was white as bone. Her knees knocked into each other. Her fingers tightened around the necklace.

"Your father's been murdered."

Glass crashed somewhere in the bar.

A cloth wiped a surface with a whoosh.

A pool cue struck a ball.

Nick's words stirred a kind of fear that made her insides turn to liquid. Truth didn't care about helping. Truth only cared about coming out. And Mackenzie had been naive enough to believe that what happened twenty years ago would remain hidden.

This wasn't over.

# A LETTER FROM RUHI

Dear Readers,

Thank you so much for choosing to read *Their Frozen Graves*. If you enjoyed it, and want to keep up to date with all my latest releases, just sign up here. Your email address will never be shared, and you can unsubscribe at any time.

*www.bookouture.com/ruhi-choudhary*

It has been a joy to revisit the fictional town of Lakemore and Mack Price. I hope you had fun on Mack's latest adventure. I'm so grateful to you for reading and hope you stick around for the next one—packed with more surprises and answers! If you liked this story, then please consider leaving a review and spread the word to your friends and family. I'd appreciate your support very much. You can also connect with me on Twitter.

Many thanks,
Ruhi

# ACKNOWLEDGMENTS

Writing is a lonely job, but publishing is all about teamwork. I'm extremely grateful to the following people.

My editor Lucy Dauman for her brilliant editing skills and keen insights, for her commitment and diligence, and for being supportive and overall lovely throughout this journey.

Big thanks to editors Alexandra Holmes, Fraser Crichton, and Abby Parsons, the cover designer Chris Shamwana and my publicist, Noelle Holten, for their hard work and passion. The entire team at Bookouture is dedicated and excellent.

My sister and dear friend, Dhriti, for always watching over her loved ones.

My best friend, Akanksha Nair, for helping me become a better writer.

Thanks to all my friends, especially Rachel Drisdelle, Dafni Giannari, Scott Proulx, Kaushik Raj, Danyal Rehman, and Sheida Stephens for their excitement.

Most of all, I am grateful to the readers. Thank you so much for taking the time! I appreciate each and every one of you, and would love to hear what you thought of the book.

Printed in Great Britain
by Amazon

41761373R00205